PROJECT DIVINE WIND

by Richard S. Platz

Blue Lake Press

Cover Design by Annie Reid

BLUE LAKE PRESS
A Western Division Subsidiary of the
Chicago, Whitewater & Mad River Company
P O Box 797, Blue Lake, CA 95525

ISBN: 978-0615454955

Dedicated to Claude O. Allen, Esquire

" . . . designed by a process with which I
have no sympathy to live in a world that
no longer exists."

--Stephen Jay Gould

"How could they harm *me*, Grasshopper?
Only this poor old body."

--Master Pō

CHAPTER ONE

Thursday morning

--1--

The portly black man in turquoise silk pajamas pulled back the thick velour drapes and gazed out. Dawn was just beginning to lighten the sky, but there would be no sunshine today. The low clouds were too thick. A cold north wind howled in the eaves of his hilltop manor, but he was warm behind the triple-glazed picture window. He looked down on the lights of Oakland. *His* city, as much as any man's. A huge, natural grin curled like a fat cat and settled on his lips. He'd come a long way, baby.

Ten years ago he would already have been up and out, huddled near the creaking iron stove of the longshoremen's hall in San Francisco, waiting for some asshole nigger-hating shop steward to bark off his name sos he could push and shove and haul and lift all day until every muscle and joint protested. Even then, at forty-seven, he'd been too old for that shit. And that's just where he'd be right now if he hadn't of busted his ass on that law school correspondence course. Best damned thing he'd ever done.

Cedrick P. Collins, Esq., was now the most charismatic, elegantly dressed, and silver-tongued black defense attorney ever to ply the waters of criminal justice in the Greater East Bay. With a Rolls Royce *and* a Cadillac El Dorado, a plush suite of offices on the eighteenth floor of the Bay Area Bank and Trust Building, a medley of eight hundred dollar suits, and a highly qualified white associate for his gofer, he had achieved the pinnacle of ostentatious success. He was the preeminent criminal attorney for the entire East Oakland ghetto, fielding cases in virtually every municipal and superior court of Alameda and Contra Costa Counties, with periodic command performances across the bay in the courts of San Francisco, San Mateo, and Santa Clara Counties.

"Yes siree," he breathed and ran his fingers through the neatly trimmed graying stubble haloing his shining pate.

A rumbling in his bowels told him it is almost time to telephone his associate, young LeBaron. Collins shook his head. The boy was honest and reliable as an old hound dog, bright with booklearning, yet abysmally ignorant of the ways of the streets. Over the past year Collins had grown unexpectedly fond of him. Hell, he'd grown to *need* him. There was no way he could make all those court appearances by himself. Each dawn he would telephone and lay out a list of clients and courts for LeBaron to cover that morning. Collins knew he was lucky to get him, and cheap, too. His bowels rumbled again. Time to make that call.

He shuffled back through the bedroom, quietly so as not to wake Beatrice, grabbed his state-of-the-art portable cellular telephone from the bedstand, and slipped into the bathroom. He settled himself on the oak toilet seat, found the current page in his daily diary, and relieved himself while studying his own heavily scrawled handwriting, some of which he could no longer decipher. Then he punched LeBaron's button and waited while it rang.

--2--

Ecstatically he pressed against her intimate sexual warmth in a way he couldn't begin to comprehend and didn't try. When she moved, he moved with her. A garment of perfect fulfillment draped over them, blending his haughty desire with the distant lure of an inconstant world. To him, she was all women.

Or, to be more precise, she was to him a distillation of many women, fleshed out on the primordial bones of his Jungian *anima*. She bore the superficial likeness of a handful of Playmates he had studied on lurid calendars and in dog-eared magazines in days gone by, mingled with a persistent image of that young blond girl who had so moved him when he was twelve, glimpsed through the window of a passing train. Beneath her flawless skin, however, endured a primordial incarnation of his first wife and of his mother and of all the myriad lovers his father and his father's father had yearned after for springs immemorial. That she was merely a dream he would not discover for yet another few seconds, as the digital circuitry of his bedside clock computed inexorably toward zero.

Had he encountered her with his fully conscious mind, he would have discovered that, more than any other living woman, she reminded him of his brother's old college sweetheart, Sarah Brubaker, whom he hadn't consciously considered for the better part of ten years. Whatever happened to Sally, anyway? he would have wondered.

Jed Aaron LeBaron awoke to a persistent electronic beep. The dream peace of her sleeping beside him seemed momentarily real, then flickered, faded, and was gone. In its place crowded a foul metallic taste, a bottomless yawn, and a solitary world which demanded too much. He stretched his toes into the cool corners of the empty sheets.

LeBaron squeezed the stem on the alarm and swung his feet to the cold floor. He glanced at the clock to see if he had time to shave before the telephone rang. It was going to be close. The remaining strands of sexual fulfillment unraveled around him as he padded glumly into the bathroom to face another workday.

What would Mr. Collins have in store for him today? His brush thrashed the suds in his shaving mug into a dense cloud of soggy marshmallow. An arraignment or two, perhaps a preliminary examination, and maybe even a drunk-driving trial. A court trial, no doubt. "Wouldn't that be fun!" he razzed his mirrored scowl and smeared the thick lather over a day's stubble, his pale blue eyes watching above the froth. A court trial, he now had enough experience to conclude, was nothing more than a slow guilty plea. But Mr. Collins had instructed him that if the client couldn't cross his palm with at least five hundred dollars, new up-front cash money, he should waive the jury or withdraw from the case. Mr. Collins couldn't afford to have him getting bogged down in long jury trials unless the old *quid pro quo* was there. It was simply a matter of good business. The client was entitled to just as much spirited criminal justice as he was willing to pay for.

"'S'the 'mer'can way," LeBaron drawled in a lousy imitation of Lyndon Johnson, rinsing his brush in a stream of hot water. He plucked a fresh Gillette Good News razor out of the nearly empty carton--

The phone rang, and an icy hand closed on his heart.

The telephone had rung every weekday morning about this time for the past twelve months. A year ago, just after he had moved back to the city, thirty years old and four years out of law school, LeBaron had hung out his own shingle in the front window of his first floor Berkeley apartment. He had received a number of vague inquiries right away, but only one paying client. While waiting for his own legal fortunes to root and flourish, he had answered a terse ad in the Oakland *Tribune*, and hired on part time with Cedrick P. Collins, Esq., to supplement his meager income. He hadn't had the slightest inkling of what he was getting into. The part time work had swollen like a snake and swallowed him whole.

At first he had lost a good deal of sleep worrying about what each morning's telephone briefing might portend. He had been brought up, after all, on the simple rule of life encapsulated in the Boy Scout's infamous slogan, "Be Prepared!" His success in college and law school he attributed to adequate, perhaps even excessive, preparation. So at first it was more than a little disconcerting for LeBaron to wander into a strange courtroom, never having set eyes on his client and knowing absolutely nothing about his case or why it was on the docket, and hear an unfamiliar judge call the case as sharply as a weary bow watchman might report yet another floating mine in some obscure Middle-Eastern waterway. Mr. Collins would of course try to fill him in a bit as best he could remember, but LeBaron soon learned not to rely too heavily on his employer's crowded recollections. More often than not they proved flawed.

LeBaron learned instead to rely on The Quiet Presence. As his courtroom time accumulated and the cases piled up behind him like weathered slabs in an endless concrete highway, LeBaron grew to recognize its unassailable power. The secret was to stroll up to the bar with the somber dignity of a young Abraham Lincoln, but beyond a few ceremonial jingoes, to keep his lip buttoned. "Ready for the defendant!" was in most instances all that was prudent to declare, uttered with the booming self-confidence of one who was about to waltz the entire north cellblock off to freedom because of some hitherto overlooked loophole in the law.

The unknown judge would shuffle through his stack of files,

perhaps muttering to himself, and at last announce what the matter had been calendared for. "Looks like this is on for a plea," he might say.

Frequently this was LeBaron's first clue. But simple patterns began to recur with reassuring regularity. To the on-for-arraignment gambit, LeBaron learned to respond, as surely as one of Pavlov's dogs might salivate to the sound of a tinkling silver bell, "Waive formal reading of the complaint, plead not guilty, waive time, request a jury." He would then relapse into The Quiet Presence, as if the next step were too obvious to be spoken, and wait for someone else, the poor over-worked deputy D. A., or the judge himself, to move the dialogue forward. LeBaron's misgivings slowly abated as he began to comprehend that the criminal justice system, with its presumption of innocence, right against self-incrimination, heavy burden of proof, and inalienable Bill of Rights, was so stacked in favor of the defendant that the only proper function of a good defense attorney *was* to stand there and keep his mouth shut.

Sometimes things went wrong, of course, but LeBaron no longer doubted that even those events conformed to some secret agenda of Cedrick P. Collins, Esq. In the Hampstead case, for example, he had been sent in to select the jury with the promise that his employer would be there personally in the afternoon to conduct the trial. Then Collins had weaseled out by starting another trial in another court, leaving LeBaron to handle a very sordid affair. LeBaron assumed The Quiet Presence, convinced that the proper function of the criminal defense attorney at trial, as before trial, is reactive, not proactive, especially when his client was so obviously guilty. The only question for trial was, could the prosecution *prove* his client was guilty? Unfortunately for LeBaron, the cases Collins dumped off on him tended to be dead dogs, and the prosecution had been able to call more incriminating witnesses than LeBaron thought was in good taste. The jury had summarily found Hampstead guilty on every count.

The telephone rang a second time.

LeBaron stomped into the bedroom and snapped it up. "Mr. Collins, can I call you right back? I'm in the middle of shaving."

Silence.

"Mr. Collins? Hello?"

After an unsettling pause a soft female voice asked, "Jed

LeBaron?"

"Yes?"

"My name is Sarah Brubaker. You probably don't remember me, but I used to date your brother. Do you know where I can get in touch with him?"

Sarah Brubaker. Not *remember* her! Christ, how could she think that! A roiling wave surged through him like a tsunami, memory, anguish, dream, desire. He saw a honey-haired young cheerleader, lithe as a fawn, tawny-skinned and flushed with excitement, prancing in the frosty air beneath the glare of stadium lights to the staccato pulse of the marching band's drums. Memory's foaming whitecap exploded and he was walking through the frozen juniper beneath a gently falling snow, feeling very grown-up, Vince and Sally and he between them clinging to their arms, plumes of breath from their mouths and fresh snow crunching underfoot, and the incredible warmth of her touch through his heavy coat strangely terrifying him. Vision overlaid vision with the confusing surge of crashing waves. His blood boiled with forgotten longing and desire. Colliding worlds twirled past, pictures, feelings deeply engraved and hidden away, a kaleidoscope running out of control. Weirdly disoriented, he stared at the telephone and stammered, "My brother? Vince?"

"Yes. D'you know where I can reach Vince? It's very important."

"Vince? Vince's at the Tehema Monastery at Mount Tehema."

"Thanks, Jed. I'll call you back sometime when you aren't so busy. Goodbye."

"Say, Sally, how've you been, anyway? Sally? Sarah?" But it was too late. The line was dead. Numbly LeBaron replaced the handset. He felt like he straddled a great gaping pit. What the hell was that all about? She sounded so . . . harried. Distracted. LeBaron considered trying to contact Vince, as difficult as that might be, and find out what Sarah Brubaker might want. And what she was up to nowadays. And, hell, since Vince was up to his neck in Zen Buddhism, maybe Jed could be a sport and help old Sally out. Hadn't Vince said he'd taken a vow of celibacy last time he saw him? When was that? His brother's celibacy seemed terribly relevant to LeBaron, although he didn't allow his imagination to pursue its essential ramifications with Sarah Brubaker.

The telephone rang again. Tentatively he picked it up.
"Hello?"

--3--

"Mornin', LeBaron. You don't sound so hot. Y'been gettin'
'nough sleep?"

"Oh, good morning, Mr. Collins. Yeah . . . er . . . I just had
another call I was thinking about."

"Well thass fine. But now's time t'think about business. Looks
like a busy day. Y'got your pencil handy?"

"Yes sir."

"Good. Y'got a Jones--I think that's 'Leroy', but y'better check
the docket--he's in Oakland Muni. He's on for an arraignment or
somethin' at nine fifteen. Try'n get two hundred dollars from him, will
ya? He said he'll have some money for ya. Be sure t' a'ks for it. An'
while you' there, see if y'can get Judge Tilsen t' sentence Monica Smith.
She's been in custody on a 647b for three weeks. That'll save y'a trip
back for the one o'clock calendar. Get'er credit for time served. The
probation report'll be in the file. Then there's a LeVerne Biggers in
Superior Court at ten . . . didn't you handle Biggers for me once already?"

"No, I don't think so."

"Uh. Anyway, I think that's a welfare fraud, but check the
calendar, an' I'm not sure what it's on for . . . arraignment or bail hearing
maybe . . . but if y'get into any trouble, have'em put it over t' the one
o'clock calendar. Get some money from her! She's *way* behind . . ."
And on and on, ten or fifteen appearances just that morning. Seemed to
be getting busier every day.

"Got it," LeBaron said when Collins finally paused. "Is that all
for today?"

"No, wait a minute." Collins was studying a name. Freeman.
Something wasn't *right* about that one, but he couldn't quite remember
what. Superior court, department fifteen. Arraignment? No, he didn't
think so. Trial setting? Now which Freeman was that? Ruben? Or
Rufus? Whatever it was, he sure wasn't paying very good if Collins

couldn't even remember his first name. "Here's another'n for you. A Freeman. Ruben or Rufus, I think. Check the calendar. Superior fifteen, three p. m."

"Three?"

"Thass what I said."

"What's it on for at three?"

"Trial setting," Collins mumbled irritably, "or arraignment 'r somethin'. Jus' take care of it for me, an' if y'have a problem, jus' put it over an' I'll take care of it myself." He flushed the toilet.

"That's it then?"

"That's it." Collins started to hang up, then barked into the phone, "LeBaron?"

"Yeah."

"This Freeman. Get some money from him."

CHAPTER TWO

Thursday afternoon

--1--

An antique mahogany sign above the doors of Department 15 proclaimed "Master Criminal Calendar." Court was already in session. LeBaron was late. He checked his notes, then scanned the computer printout posted on the wall for a "Freeman." Sure enough, there it was: "Defendant: Rufus Abraham Freeman; Attorney: Collins; Violation: 459 PC, 487 PC (2 pr)." Penal Code section 459 was burglary, if LeBaron's memory served him right. He wasn't sure what a 487 was, though. Probably some kind of theft. The defendant had two prior convictions. The printout didn't say what it was on calendar for today.

LeBaron jerked open the heavy door and slipped inside. The air was heavy with stale cigarette smoke, humidity, and body odor. Too many people were packed inside. The underlying commotion was Felliniesque, reminding LeBaron of a back lot circus audience impatient for the freak show action to begin. On this side of the bar, in the worn, dirty theater seats, glum defendants with their families and friends, mostly black, whispered and fidgeted. Orange clad in-custodies, linked together by shining silver chains, waited forlornly in the jury box for the other shoe to come down. A brace of stony-faced bailiffs stood, back to back, watching them. In worn coats and mismatched slacks seedy defense lawyers milled about the long tables up front, whispering deals with a battery of slick young deputy district attorneys or else staring blankly, waiting their turn. Above it all Judge Waverly's voice could be heard through slender loudspeakers mounted halfway up the paneled wall, next to the "No Smoking" signs, conducting business as usual.

"Freeman?" LeBaron called out in a loud whisper, first to one side of the aisle, then the other. "Rufus Freeman?"

A slender young black man in a sharkskin suit jerked up his head and studied LeBaron. His impish face wore a mask of extreme displeasure. "Wha'd'a *you* want, Jack?"

"Are you Rufus Freeman?"

"Yeah, I'm Rufus Freeman. So what?"

LeBaron motioned for him to come to the aisle. "My name's Jed LeBaron. I'm from Mr. Collins' office. He couldn't make it. He sent me--"

"Wha'd'ya mean he *couldn't make it!*" Freeman demanded in much too loud a voice.

Judge Waverly's even drone broke off. He looked up through eye glasses thick as petri dishes, which magnified his pupils to the size of pale plums. He looked haggard and unhappy. "Ah, Mr. LeBaron. Glad you could finally join us. You're here on Mr. Collin's matter." He shuffled through a stack of files. "I was about to issue a bench warrant for Mr. Collins."

"No need for that, your honor." LeBaron couldn't tell if he was joking. It really didn't matter now. Things were under control. "It's the Freeman matter, if it please the court."

"Here we are. People verses Rufus Abraham Freeman."

"Ready for the defendant, your honor." LeBaron grasped his querulous client firmly by the arm and guided him through the jostling bodies to the front bar. "Mr. Freeman is present in court."

"Let the record show that Mr. Freeman is present with his attorney Mr. LeBaron." The judge leaned over to his clerk. "Do we still have Department Twenty-three available?" He muttered something LeBaron couldn't make out. His clerk laughed and handed him a sheet of paper. "Good." Judge Waverly smiled as he studied the list of available courts. The smile did not sit well on his thin lips. "Very good."

LeBaron didn't like the drift things were taking. "If there's going to be a hearing, your honor, Mr. Collins wanted to handle this matter personally."

"Counsel," the judge said icily, "this matter is on for *trial* today. Are you ready to proceed?"

"Er . . . I believe Mr. Collins intended to handle the trial himself, your honor. Can we put this over to tomorrow's calendar?"

The Judge Waverly glared at him with those terrible plum eyes. "Mr. Frank?"

Deputy District Attorney Ivan Frank was new on the felony prosecution circuit, but not so new that he would miss an opportunity to put LeBaron in a jam. He bellied up to the counsel table. "Yes, your honor. Witness've been subpoenaed. Jury panel's summoned." He pushed his glasses up on his nose with a fat thumb. "The people're ready to proceed."

"I'm not going to put this over 'til tomorrow or any other time," Judge Waverly barked. "This case is being assigned to trial right now. Now are you ready to proceed or what, Mr. LeBaron?"

His client was tugging on his sleeve, trying to tell him something, but LeBaron waved him down. "Ready to proceed, your honor."

"Good. I'm assigning this matter to Department Twenty-three."

A collective groan rumbled through the assembled defense bar. "It's your ass now, LeBaron," someone snickered from behind him. "That's Judge *Kroner*."

"Department twenty-three, your honor? That's Judge Kroner, isn't it?"

"Yes, Mr. LeBaron. Your case is assigned to Judge Kroner for trial. The bailiff will take the file over. Right now."

Judge Kroner was poison, and LeBaron knew it. He was pro-police, hated blacks, and was probably a heavy closet contributor to the American Nazi Party. Mr. Collins had instructed LeBaron to *never*, under any circumstances, allow a case to come before Judge Kroner. "Excuse me, your honor."

"Now what, Mr. LeBaron?"

"If I may be sworn, I'd like to make a declaration under C.C.P. section one-seventy- point-six." California Code of Civil Procedure section 170.6 gives a defendant the right to challenge any judge, without cause, upon a declaration by the client or his counsel that he feels he cannot receive a fair trial before that judge. It provides for one free judicial disqualification, no questions asked. LeBaron always hated to have to make the declaration, but in this case the alternative was clearly worse.

"Sorry, Counsel," Judge Waverly purred, that humorless, unnatural smile twisting his lips. "Mr. Collins already used up your client's peremptory challenge last month, on the fourteenth to be exact, disqualifying Judge Kemperson. Now you better not keep Judge Kroner waiting."

"You' honor!" Freeman suddenly shouted.

"Quiet!" the judge snarled. "If you've got something to say, talk to your attorney, Mr. LeBaron."

Out of the corner of his eye LeBaron saw two uniformed bailiffs begin to maneuver into place behind them. He tightened his grip, but his client squirmed like a two-year-old.

"This dude's *not my attorney--*"

"He is now!" Judge Waverly brought down his gavel with a conclusive bang.

"Be quiet!" LeBaron rasped, jerking his client around and dragging him down the aisle. "D'you want him to revoke your bail?"

As soon as they were out of the courtroom, Freeman was in his face. "Say, man, what *is* this shit! Where's my *main man*? I retained Cedric P. Collins, Esquire, to handle my beef, not some honky dude no-soul college jive trainee white boy. And what's this Judge Kroner shit? I don' want no Judge *Kroner*. That dude's *bad* news. He's the hanging judge, am I right? Am I *right*? What'a'we goin' before that dude for, anyway? I wanna talk t' my main man."

A thick-necked bailiff with unpleasant eyes had followed them out into the hallway. He looked like he'd learned his trade as a night guard in some sadistic maximum security hellhole. Tensely he followed the exchange.

"I'm sorry, Mr. Freeman, but we really don't have very much choice at this time." LeBaron tried to steer his client further down the hall.

But Rufus Freeman balked. He was twenty-four years old, unmarried, a high school dropout, last employed by the Quickie Car Wash on East 14th Street, and on trial for two felony counts of burglary and grand theft, with two priors. State prison was a distinct possibility. He was not very happy. "Wha' you mean, honky, no choice? This America. I got my *rights*. I wanna talk t' my main man. Where's

Esquire Collins?"

"Pipe down!" LeBaron glanced over his shoulder. "Let's get out of here so we can talk."

"I gots nothin' to talk to you about, honky." He folded his arms across his chest.

Exasperated, LeBaron looked at his watch. It was after four o'clock already, and nothing much was going to happen today. He drew a deep breath and tried a different approach. "Just settle down a second and *think*, will you? You hired Mr. Collins because he's a professional and knows what he's doing, am I right? Did it ever occur to you that Mr. Collins sent me here for a *reason*? Think about it."

Freeman stared at LeBaron dubiously, then his eyes began to soften. After a moment a conspiratorial grin spread over his lean face. "Say, what *is* Esquire Collins up to, my man? You got an uncle on the take, maybe?"

"No, nothing like that." He began leading his client away from the brutal bailiff and toward the bank of elevators. "It's just that Mr. Collins wants me to make the pretrial motions, and maybe even participate in jury selection. It's all very technical. It kind of softens up the whites and gets their sympathy, don't you see? Then when it's time for the trial to start, in comes Mr. Collins with a flourish and handles the rest of the trial himself."

Freeman was still dubious. "What about this Judge Kroner shit?"

"That?" LeBaron shrugged. "Mr. Collins himself couldn't have done anything about that. You just had the bad luck of getting assigned to two hanging judges in a row, and you only have one challenge. Mr. Collins already used it up last month, keeping you out of Judge Kemperson's court. It's pure bad luck. Believe me, there's nothing that can be done." LeBaron punched the ornate brass elevator button. "We're just going to have to make the best of it. And as soon as Judge Kroner's through with us today, I'll call the office. Mr. Collins will probably be here in the morning to handle the trial personally."

Freeman sulked.

"Oh, there *is* one other thing." LeBaron faced him squarely and held out his hand. "Mr. Collins told me you were going to have some money for me."

"Money?" Rufus Freeman looked stunned, like he just remembered something very important that he had fully intended to do long before now. "Yeah. Thass right! Say, I'm gonna have t' bring that five hundred in later, dude. It completely slipped m'mind, don' ya know?"

The elevator arrived, and LeBaron ushered Freeman in. "Basement" he said to the operator, then cornered his client. "Now we're going to go over to Judge Kroner's courtroom for preliminary motions, and we're going to act nice and polite and we're not going to swear or holler or piss him off in any way. Do you understand? In fact, you're going to be *so* nice and polite, the judge is going to think, hey, they surely must've caught the wrong man. Tonight I'll talk to Mr. Collins and we'll straighten this whole thing out. Tomorrow you'll bring in some money. Do you understand?"

Freeman opened his mouth, but all that came out was a whimper. For the first time LeBaron understood how frightened and helpless the young man really was.

--2--

It was already dusk as LeBaron hurried up Broadway toward the office. A sporadic, numbing chill drizzled down through the low overcast, permeating everything. He opened and closed his fists as he walked, trying to bring feeling back into his fingers.

Judge Kroner was a whining, officious old prick. An obvious Napoleon complex. Pretrial motions had been a farce. How could LeBaron make any motions when he knew absolutely nothing about Freeman's alleged offense? When it became clear that LeBaron knew nothing about the case, Kroner had baited him even more. It particularly irritated LeBaron that the little prick judge had kept them until well after five for no apparent reason except to flex his judicial muscle. And now LeBaron feared he would miss Mr. Collins, and then where would he be?

Tomorrow morning the jury panel would be called in at dawn. The analogy of the firing squad didn't escape his exhausted imagination. If Mr. Collins wanted him to handle jury selection, LeBaron was going to have to learn a hell of a lot more about the case. Surely there was a file somewhere at the office with an arrest report, rap sheet, complaint, perhaps even notes from an initial interview. Enough to put together some questions for voir dire, select the jury, and then turn the matter over to Mr. Collins. Or did Mr. Collins have something more ambitious in mind for him?

He pushed through the revolving glass doors of the Bay Area Bank and Trust Building. The night guard was on duty already and touched the brim of his hat as LeBaron passed. The elevator bank was empty, an elevator waiting for him. He punched fourteen.

There seemed to be two criteria a case must meet before Collins dumped it off on LeBaron to try. First, the client had to be seriously delinquent in his payments. Freeman had clearly passed that test. The second was that there had to be no chance whatsoever of avoiding a full conviction on every count. LeBaron couldn't determine if that one had been met until he had a look at the file. But his suspicions were aroused. Just like the damned Hampstead case all over again. If Mr. Collins was going to have him try a case, why couldn't he tell him so in advance, so he could prepare.

Ah, but that was just the point, wasn't it? Mr. Collins didn't want him wasting his time preparing a defense that hadn't been paid for. Not when there were so many other appearances to be made. Appearances for paying clients.

The elevator doors whispered open, and there stood Mr. Collins, stoop-shouldered in his ermine-trimmed cashmere top coat and matching stingy-brim hat, the laptop computer he had christened "Gideon" dangling from his left fist. LeBaron could see the longshoreman in him now, after a bruising day at the docks, too exhausted to bother standing straight, shrunken, almost withered in his borrowed ermine finery. Instantly his welling indignation vanished, and his heart went out to his aging mentor.

Collins' expression slumped even further when he saw LeBaron step out. "Evening, LeBaron," he mumbled, and tried to slip past into the elevator car.

LeBaron wouldn't stand aside to let him past. "Mr. Collins, I've got to talk to you now." Gently he took him by the arm and swung him around.

Collins sighed. He had almost gotten away. "C'mon. Let's go in the back way. There's some fellas from the IRS in the lobby, an' I'd jus' as soon not talk to 'em right now." He fished out the key to the back door of the suite. "How'd it go?"

"Not so good."

"Uh." Collins unlocked the door and pushed through.

"The Freeman matter was on for *trial* today."

"Uh. What's he charged with?"

"Burglary and some kind of theft. Two counts. Two priors."

"Uh. Sit down, LeBaron." Collins set Gideon on the sofa, peeled off his top coat, and hung it from the coat tree. Delicately he perched his stingy-brim on top. He eased himself down in his overstuffed leather desk chair and smiled. "Didja get some money from him?"

"No. He said he'd bring something in by the end of the week."

"Uh." Collins' smile flickered, lost its substance. "Did it get sent out?"

"Yes. Jury selection starts first thing in morning."

"Uh. What judge didja get?"

"Judge Kroner."

"Felix Kroner? You got Judge Felix 'Maximum' *Kroner*? How many times have I told you *never*, under any circumstances, *ever* allow anything t'go t'Judge Felix Kroner, 'specially if it involves a black man. That man is the worst excuse for a human being to ever sit on the bench of an Alameda County court." Collins was starting to get worked up. "Did you know he tried t'put me in jail for contempt o'court once. I hadda go up on a writ t'the Court of Appeal t'get'im reversed. He jus' laughed. Knew all the time he was wrong. Jus' wanted t'see my black ass sweat. Even the Public Defender's office's issued instructions to all deputies t'challenge him every time one o'their cases gets assigned to'im. What happened? Didja forget about your one-seventy-point-six challenge?"

"No. We didn't have one left."

"We didn't?"

"You used it up last month?"

"I did? Who'd I challenge?"

"Judge Kemperson."

"Uh." For a moment Collins seemed more tired than LeBaron had ever seen him. Over his vulnerable bald head a quotation from Abraham Lincoln silently reminded clients that "An attorney's stock in trade is his time." Beside him a bookcase full of the United States Code Annotated waited, dark red bindings lurid against the mahogany paneling of the office walls, an antique brass ship's clock on top ticking quietly.

Slowly the older man gathered himself, shifted his weight, and looked LeBaron in the eye. "Okay, LeBaron, nothin' you could o' done about it. Shake it off. This Freeman boy's havin' a mighty string o' bad luck an' he's into a world o' hurt. But it can't be he'ped. You done what y'could. Better it happens to Freeman than a good payin' client." Like magic that charismatic grin burst forth, a swath of ivory sunlight across a face of tar. "Now, you gonna pick me a good jury tomorrow? Like you did on that Rodriguez case a coupla months back? I still don't know how you *did* that, LeBaron, but they couldn't o' been in more of a rush t'turn my man loose. Yes siree. Jury was back in ten minutes with a 'Not guilty, Judge.' You shoulda seen ol' Ernie Stillman's face. He was handling it himself for the D.A.'s office. Thought they had Rodriguez dead t'rights. 'Not Guilty, Judge!' You know, LeBaron, I think you got some sort of God-given *knack* for pickin' juries. I truly do."

"Mr. Collins?"

"What?" He eyed LeBaron suspiciously.

"You're not going to get involved in something else, like you did with the Hampstead case, are you, and leave me to try this thing on Monday?"

"Th'aint no trial gonna take place on *Monday*," Collins bristled. "Judge Kroner's got juvenile court all day Monday. Hasn't got a single free minute. So alls you gotta do is t' kill tomorrow with jury selection and we'll see what happens come Tuesday mornin'."

"You mean, we'll see if Rufus Freeman can come up with some money by Tuesday morning?"

"That would surely help straighten things out." He leafed through his engagement book. "Otherwise, I might get assigned to any one o' three or four trials come Tuesday. I can't be in two places at once, can I? You let that boy know how important it is that he pays up."

"So what you're saying is, I should be prepared to try this case myself."

"Freeman ain't paid enough for you to do very much preparin',
LeBaron. You'll do jus' fine learnin' the case as it unfolds in the
courtroom, jus' like everybody else. Now if you're dead set on doin'
some preparin' on your *own* free time, well of course that's none o' my
business. But Freeman sure hasn't paid for no preparin' yet, an' I can't
pay you for it."

"What if he agrees to pay as soon as he can?" As soon as he said
it, LeBaron knew it was ridiculous.

Collins shook his head. "Don't seem like he'll be earnin' a whole
lot o' money in state prison for the next three to five years. Y'got to be
practical, LeBaron."

"Jeez, Mr. Collins, this is a felony! I've never done a felony jury
trial."

"Everybody's gotta start somewhere. You tried the Hampstead
case, didn't you?"

"That was a *misdemeanor*."

"Ain't no different. Except in a felony everybody takes
'emselves too damn' serious."

"But shouldn't I interview witnesses, investigate the scene of the
crime, do something to prepare?"

"This ain't the Public Defender's office or some public funded
legal aid clinic. This's a business. An' the whole idea of a business is
t'show a profit. Y'understan'? Freeman hasn't paid enough t'go diggin'
up a lot of irrelevant jazz in order t'confuse the jury. We got t'fall back
to a more frugal line of defense. We gotta hope a material witness don't
show up, or evidence was illegally seized, or the jury for no reason at all
takes a shine to our boy. Maybe the D.A.'ll botch up the case all by
himself. Freeman ain't paid for the Cadillac defense, y'un'erstan'?"

LeBaron sighed. "Yes sir. But I would like to take a look at the
file, if we have one."

"Sure we have one!" Collins grinned and punched the intercom.
"There's always a file. Not sure if it'll do you much good, but there's
always a file."

"Yessir, Mr. Collins." The voice on the intercom oozed with the
honeyed sexuality of soul.

"Wanda Jean, were you able t'find that Freeman file I a'ksed you about."

"Sho'nuf. D'you want me t' bring it in?"

"No. Put it on LeBaron's desk, will ya, gal?"

"Yessir, Mr. Collins."

Collins stood up and began pulling on his overcoat again. "I'd tell you more about the case myself, LeBaron, but I can't seem t'remember too much. I do remember it didn't look so hot. Said he was a relative of Brown's, second cousins or something. Thass why I took it without gettin' 'nough money up front. 'Course Brown denies any relation." Lovingly he lifted his ermine-trimmed stingy-brim and eased it onto his bald head. "Now as soon as I sneak out the back door here, you go out front and a'ks Wanda Jean for that file. An' you watch out for ol' Judge Kroner, hear? He likes t' play you along for a while before he reels y'in. Get everything put on the record. Don' let'im pull that 'Approach the bench' stuff, y'un'erstan'? Get it all on the record."

"Yes, sir."

With Gideon, his faithful laptop computer, stuck under his arm and one hand on the doorknob, Collins swung around and peered at LeBaron over the top of his wire-rimmed reading glasses. "Don' look so damn' glum, LeBaron. You' gonna be all right. They ain't sendin' *you* off to state prison, are they? G'night."

"G'night, Mr. Collins."

CHAPTER THREE

Thursday evening

--1--

It was already mostly dark outside when LeBaron slid into a corner booth of the downtown McDonald's with his Big Mac, small fries, and vanilla shake. Fortunately, he had nothing planned for this evening. He rarely planned anything for the evenings anymore, because he was no longer fit for human companionship by the time he got home from Mr. Collins' exhausting rat race. Yes, trite as the metaphor sounded, it was exactly what his job was like, a rat maze. Every morning Mr. Collins would phone him up and announce a brand new configuration that had to be run. And every day he ran it.

He took a bite of his Mac and flopped open the Freeman file. The police report was short and utterly without a glimmer of hope. On November 11 an Officer G. Moseby of the Oakland Police Department had been dispatched to a possible burglary in progress at 1411B Ward Lane. A neighbor adjoining the property to the rear had reported a male suspect in dark overalls entering the building through a second story window. When Officer Moseby arrived on the scene, he stationed his partner, Patrolman D. Wilson, as backup in front of the residence. Moseby drew his service revolver and walked up the ungated driveway to the rear of the residence. There he observed a second story window standing wide open just above a low trellised porch. As Officer Moseby was returning to the front of the residence, the suspect, Rufus Abraham Freeman, 24, black male, dressed in a white tee shirt and gray trousers, emerged from a side door off the driveway with a color tv set cradled in his arms. Officer Moseby made contact with the suspect and, when the suspect refused to make a statement, placed him under arrest on suspicion of violation of PC 459, burglary, PC 487, grand theft, and PC 496, receiving stolen property. The tv set was booked into evidence. The building was secured and a note left for the occupant.

Later that day victim Raccoona GeBobath, 53, white female, 1411B Ward Lane, Oakland, telephoned the Oakland Police department. Officer Moseby contacted her and took a statement. According to victim GeBobath, she was the sole occupant of the apartment, had been staying at a friend's house in Berkeley that night, did not know the suspect Freeman, and had given no one permission to enter her house. She identified the tv set. She also reported as missing two large file boxes of computer records which she claimed to be of "inestible" value. Moseby had trouble spelling "inestimable." It was crossed out and rewritten twice, both wrong. He observed that victim GeBobath appeared to be extremely upset. She was advised to contact the victim-witness program for further assistance.

End of report.

Freeman's rap sheet was a full two pages long, which was pretty impressive for someone who had been an adult for a mere six years. Most of his crimes were against property, although there was an aggravated assault charged and dismissed three years ago. Petty thefts totaled three, the last one as a felony. Two prior burglaries. Freeman served six months in the Alameda County jail and was apparently still on probation for a felony burglary conviction of less than a year ago. He had not served any state prison time.

Not yet.

LeBaron leafed through the other pages in the file. Court minutes of previous appearances in the present case indicated that the preliminary examination had been waived in December. It looked like poor Freeman hadn't been paying well enough for even a preliminary examination. Mr. Collins could be very cold.

On a yellow sheet at the bottom of the file were a few handwritten notes in Collins' cryptic scrawl. It took some time, but LeBaron finally managed to decipher the provocative words: "Gray van, Chevy, '87 or '88, Dept. of Agr., G. R. & D." The notation may have been intended for another file. Mr. Collins had the nasty habit of allowing any telephone call to interrupt what he was doing and then jotting down notes on whatever happened to be in front of him. Collins' other notes added nothing new.

LeBaron leaned back in the yellow plastic contour bench which was designed for someone else's contour. He belched and finished off the milk shake, which made him shiver. He pulled a yellow pad out of his briefcase and wrote "Voir Dire" across the top. He would need some snappy questions to ask the prospective jurors in the morning. Questions designed to disclose potential bias, yes. But also questions cleverly enough crafted so that LeBaron could from the get-go begin to indoctrinate the jurors in his particular theory of the case.

But just what *was* his theory of this case? Mindless stupidity? Irredeemable antisocial personality? Neither was currently recognized as a viable legal defense. He laid down his pencil. Guilty as charged? Probably no plea bargain had been offered. After all, they had him dead to rights, didn't they? And even the D.A. likes a blowout once in a while. Good for the old swollen ego. Well, LeBaron had an ego too, and he would prefer not to have it dragged through the slime of a hopeless trial. He picked up the police report again. There had to be something. . . .

He skimmed through until he came to the words, "She reported as missing two large file boxes of computer records which she claimed to be of inestible value." Now what the hell did Rufus Freeman want with two large file boxes full of computer records? And where did he stash them before he got caught? It didn't make sense. A *computer* he might take and try to resell. But computer *records*? What kind of records were we talking about here, anyway? IRS records? Fiduciary records of account? Maybe records of great value that could be reported as an insurance loss? Ah, yes, records of "inestimable" value, perhaps? LeBaron began to get a whiff of insurance scam on the part of the victim Ms. GeBobath. Not that it made his client any less guilty. But if LeBaron could present the victim to the jury as a worse scoundrel than his poor, misunderstood, disadvantaged client, maybe he could assuage that righteous indignation. Maybe he could even intimidate the victim into refusing to testify. It was certainly worth a try.

--2--

Silently Raccoona GeBobath examined LeBaron through the half-closed door. She was an ugly, short, wiry figure of indeterminate age or sex, with close-cropped brown hair, thick and lightly frosted at the temples. Her upper lip bore the vague shadow of a moustache, and her bushy eyebrows met above a pair of intense almond-colored eyes. Above her right eye a large mole sprouted bristly black hairs. Baggy trousers, a pin-striped work shirt, and heavy engineer's boots further obscured her gender.

Uneasy under her unflinching gaze, LeBaron tipped the police report to catch the light from the bare porch bulb and squinted at it. He found her name, verified the entry "female," and cleared his throat. "Ms. Raccoona GeBobath?"

She continued her silent scrutiny. At last she muttered, "Who wants to know?" Her voice had a swarthy, foreign ring that LeBaron couldn't quite pin down.

"I'm . . . ah . . . Jed LeBaron. I'm an attorney. I represent Rufus Freeman. You know who that is, don't you?"

She stared at him poker-faced.

"Er . . . he's the man who allegedly burglarized your apartment." He looked down at the report. "On November sixteenth?"

"Tell him I want my records back. He can keep the tv if he gives me my records back. Okay?"

"That's one of the things I wanted to talk to you about. The records you reported as missing."

A dark cloud passed over her eyes, and for a moment LeBaron thought she was going to slam the door in his face. Then she reconsidered. "You're not a Mormon, are you?"

"Pardon?"

"I asked whether you were a Mormon? You know, a *Mormon*?" She stressed the word as if he were hearing-impaired or an imbecile. "A member of the Church of the Latter Day Saints?"

"A Mormon? No. I'm not a Mormon. Why?"

She studied his eyes for a moment. "Wait a minute, I'll be right back." The door slammed shut.

LeBaron stood at the side door. A stub of old concrete sidewalk linked the building with the asphalt driveway. On each side green spears of irises pushed up through the black soil into the cold Oakland night. This must be the exact spot where the unlucky Rufus Freeman, with Ms. GeBobath's color television cradled in his sweating palms, waltzed into Officer Moseby's arms. Jesus! Caught in the act. Red-handed. How was he supposed to defend such an inept bastard? No wonder Mr. Collins didn't want anything to do with the case.

LeBaron grasped the cold brass doorknob and tried to turn it. Locked. From the inside, it would turn. Freeman had climbed up the trellis, pried open the window and entered, picked up the television, then strolled down the stairs and out through this door. Only his timing was shot to hell. Pretty good response time for the police to catch him in the act.

The door jerked open and Raccoona GeBobath held out a small red book. "I knew I had one somewhere."

LeBaron reached out to take it. "What's this?"

"No!" she snapped. "Put your left hand on it. It's the goddamn' Book of Mormon. Raise your right hand. Swear on this Book of Mormon that you're not a member of the Church of the Latter Day Saints."

LeBaron felt a little foolish, but he complied. "I swear that I am not a member of the Church of the Latter Days Saints."

"And never have been."

"And I never have been."

"Good." Satisfied, she drew the door open. "Won't you come in, Mr. LeBaron?"

"Thank you." As he closed the door behind him, he tried the knob from the inside. Sure enough, it turned easily. He followed her up the narrow, enclosed flight of stairs into an unpleasant, musty atmosphere, reeking with spoiled food and hidden disease. "Why'd you have me swear I'm not a Mormon?"

She spun around on the stairs, waving the red book over her head. "'Cause those slimy, lyin', hypocritical sycophants would rather fry their own first born children in boilin' fat than make a false oath on the goddamn' Book of Mormon."

She led him up to a large dark kitchen and motioned for him to sit at the cluttered table. The top was glazed with unattended spills of unknown vintage. "No, I mean, why are you concerned that I might be a Mormon at all?"

She grunted, but didn't answer.

Through a door on the other side of the kitchen LeBaron could see an even messier room, illuminated by swing-arm fluorescent lamps protruding from three desks covered with computer equipment and reference books, topped with layers of papers and open volumes. Ms. GeBobath was obviously a research scholar of some sort. LeBaron hoped her methods were tidier than her work space. The air was oppressive, and LeBaron loosened his tie to ease his breathing.

"Can I get you a cup of coffee?" She snapped on a bare light over a sink full of dirty dishes. In its glare she looked like some hairy, gnarled little atavistic gnome.

"No, thank you." He laid the police report down on the table and the back page stuck. Carefully he peeled it up.

She poured herself a cup from a dirty, half-full Mr. Coffee and pulled up a chair next to him. "Now you tell me how I can help you, an' then I'll tell you how you can help me."

"Fine. The police report indicates you lost some valuable computer records. Is that correct?"

She nodded over the rim of her cup.

"Just what sort of computer records were these?"

"Genealogical records." Her mistrustful almond eyes never left his face.

"Genealogical records?"

Raccoona nodded, watching.

"Where you trace people's ancestors?"

"Correct. All done with a powerful program I designed to extrapolate and compensate for missing data."

"I see." LeBaron started to make a note on his yellow pad, but found it too was stuck to the table. "Now, let me ask you this," he continued, abandoning the pad and bearing down, "did you have any of these genealogical records insured?"

"What, are you crazy? Who'd insure genealogical records?"

That answer didn't fit into LeBaron's scheme. He was beginning to feel sticky all over. "Am I to take it you mean, 'no'?"

"Take it however you like. But, no, my records weren't insured. Why? You think I was trying to rip off some insurance company?" Raccoona's laugh was a husky, bestial thing.

"No, of course not." LeBaron blushed and fumbled through the tacky police report. The Big Mac roiled uneasily in his guts, as if it might have a mind to come back up.

"I'll tell you, I don't blame Mr. Freeman so much. I mean, I think somebody put him up to it. Paid him to snatch my records. He was just doin' his job, doin' what he was paid for. That's what I think. But I have to get 'em back, if he still has 'em. If he hasn't turned 'em over yet."

"Who'd want to take your genealogy records?"

"They didn't want the records. Those were just data printouts." She bent close to him, and he nearly gagged on the smell of rancid sweat. "They were after the *program*," she purred conspiratorially.

LeBaron leaned away, recrossing his legs. "But *who* are you talking about?"

She watched him for a long time, then whispered, "The Mormons."

Ah, the Mormons, LeBaron thought. *So we come full circle.* "The Mormons?"

Raccoona nodded.

"But why?"

"Because I've got a better processor than they do. And I've filled in some of the gaps." She grasped his forearm with a horny claw and leaned close. "And because *I know what they're up to.*"

"Oh?" LeBaron was feeling light-headed and nauseous. He tried to pull back from her sickeningly ripe breath, but she gripped his arm. So close, he couldn't take his eyes off the revolting black hairs sprouting from the center of the rust-colored mole above her right eye. "What they're up to?"

"Yes." She let go of his arm in triumph.

LeBaron drew away and struggled to his feet. The room brightened and tilted sickeningly. Cold sweat beaded on his forehead and ran down his neck, soaking his tightened collar. "Thank you, Ms. GeBobath." He lurched toward the stairs. "You've been a great help." Somehow he managed to snag the greasy handrail and stump down the flight without pitching head over heels. At the bottom he turned and peered back up.

She hovered unnaturally at the top of the narrow stairs, cackling down at him, "I know what they're up to."

LeBaron would not have been surprised to see her leap off the top step above him, swoop once or twice like a toying raptor, and fly straight out the tiny stairwell window on a rotting broomstick.

CHAPTER FOUR

Friday

--1--

LeBaron arrived at the courtroom fifteen minutes before jury selection began so that he could listen to his client's version of the incidents leading up to his arrest. Rufus Freeman was nowhere to be found, however, and the courtroom was locked and dark. So LeBaron sat on a bench in the empty, echoing hallway and waited. He pulled out the police report and reread it twice.

At two minutes to nine Deputy District Attorney Ivan Frank waddled out of the elevator with a thick file under one arm and a leather trial case the size of a shoe salesman's sample box in the other. He was out of breath and perspiring heavily as if he had hoisted the elevator up three flights himself. He shuffled past LeBaron and tried the courtroom door. It was still locked.

LeBaron stood up. "Good morning. I didn't really get a chance to meet you yesterday in all the rush. Jed LeBaron. I work for Cedrick Collins."

Frank eyed the proffered hand warily, shifted the file to his left arm, nearly dropping the trial case, set it down, placed the file carefully on top, and offered a damp, doughy hand. "Ivan Frank."

"Been with the D.A.'s office long?"

Frank peeled off his thick horn-rimmed glasses and mopped his face with a stained handkerchief. "About nine months."

LeBaron nodded. "I haven't seen you around before."

"I've been handling misdemeanors in Fremont."

"Ah, Fremont. Don't get out there much, myself. This your first felony trial?"

"Yup." Frank pushed his glasses back on his nose. "This will be my first felony conviction."

LeBaron ignored the smug adumbration and shifted to his warmest tone, "Say, Ivan, why hasn't this thing been settled a long time ago? What're you offering, anyway?"

"Plea as charged to felony first degree burglary and felony grand theft. Admit the priors. Refer to probation for report prior to sentencing."

"What a deal!" LeBaron quipped, but it rang hollow in the mirthless hallway. "Not much incentive to plea bargain there, would you say, Ivan? Have you considered reducing either charge to a misdemeanor?"

"No chance."

"How much could the tv be worth?"

"Four-hundred-thirty-five dollars and fifty cents," Frank recited as promptly and tonelessly as a state-of-the-art microchip-operated cash register.

"That much?"

"Well in excess of the statutory minimum for grand theft. And even if it *were* less, we'd still have him on a felony six-sixty-six."

"What's that?"

"Petty theft with a prior."

"Oh." LeBaron considered for a moment. "Okay, so if Mr. Freeman were to plead to both felonies as charged, but strike the priors, would you consider probation with state prison suspended?"

Frank pushed his glasses back up his sweaty nose. "No sentence bargaining."

"Maybe we'd even agree to some county jail time as a condition of probation. Admit one of the priors. But I'll have to talk to my client about it first, okay?"

"No sentence bargaining."

"What do you mean, 'no sentence bargaining'? Why not? What else do we have to talk about here?"

The lock clicked, and a bailiff pushed open the courtroom door and stomped down on the doorstop to hold it.

Frank collected his file, stuck it under his arm, and hoisted the huge trial case. "Because it would be unprofessional of me to pass up this opportunity to put your scum client away behind bars for the maximum state prison term prescribed by law and thus protect the decent citizens of this community."

"*Whoa*," LeBaron breathed as he watched the overstuffed deputy navigate the doorway with his unwieldy cargo. He glanced at his watch and continued his vigil. A buzzer sounded, and a red light winked on above the door. Exasperated, LeBaron skulked into the courtroom considering various excuses for why Rufus Freeman had failed to show up. He would never dare voice the real reason, of course, that his black client had no inclination to be tried, railroaded, and sentenced by a rogue Nazi Ku Klux Klan headhunter who had never evidenced the slightest trace of human compassion in his whole miserable life.

Just seconds before Judge Kroner was to take the bench, Rufus Freeman breezed in. "*You* back?" he demanded accusingly, hands on his thin hips. "Where's my man Esquire Collins?"

"Where's the five hundred bucks you were going to bring in?" LeBaron rejoined.

"Oh, that. It's gonna take a coupla days--"

"Please rise!" the bailiff boomed. "Department Twenty-three of the Superior Court is now in session, the Honorable Felix Kroner presiding."

Judge Kroner whisked in from the side door, a thin file under his arm, his black robes flying out behind his diminutive frame like a misdirected Halloween specter, and assumed the bench. "Be seated." Excessive high energy belied the ravages of sixty-nine merciless years. Sagging jowls had pulled his face into the permanent shape of a shriveled pear, which was topped with a ridiculous coal-black crewcut, obviously dyed and cropped so short the pale scalp showed through in worn patches. He looked over the courtroom, his mouth twisted up as if sucking on something sour. LeBaron and Freeman sat frozen at one table, Deputy Ivan Frank at the other, and the bailiff stood at attention near the door to chambers. Judge Kroner perceived nothing irregular. "Call People versus Rufus Abraham Freeman."

"Ready for the people, your honor."

"Ready for the defendant, your honor."

"Good. Bailiff, call in the jury panel."

LeBaron had always considered jury selection to be more of an art than a science. A prospective juror's responses to the attorney's questions might elicit bias for or against the defendant, but more often than not the decision to excuse a juror was based on a gut reaction, a look in the juror's eyes, or his tone of voice, the way the juror walked, or the way he avoided eye contact with the accused. But with Judge Kroner, who kept a firm grip on everything that went on in his courtroom, it was neither science nor art. It was a brutal ordeal and a bitter contest of wills.

For nearly an hour Ivan Frank was allowed to explore with prospective jurors just about anything he damn well pleased, discussing each juror's reaction to prospective evidence, the law, the D.A.'s theory of the case, and the sacred principles underlying crime and punishment in general. Yet when LeBaron began his voir dire, Judge Kroner was on him like a leech.

LeBaron attempted to elicit the panel's reaction to his client's plight as a poor disenfranchised member of the ghetto. He was resoundingly corrected from the bench.

"That's not in issue, Counsel," Judge Kroner snapped. "Let's have no more of that. Stick to the issues."

LeBaron then sought to learn a juror's feeling about the criminal standard of proof beyond a reasonable doubt.

"I'll instruct the jury on matters of law, Mr. LeBaron," Judge Kroner interrupted sternly. "Proceed."

"But, your honor, I am just trying to determine if this juror will have any difficulty *applying* the standard you will be giving him."

"Counsel! Approach the bench!"

Mr. Collins' warning flashed in LeBaron's head. "Your honor, I'd like this all to be on the record."

Judge Kroner was furious, but he nodded to the court reporter, who joined them at the bench. With the reporter transcribing everything he said, the judge seemed uncomfortably restrained. Carefully choosing his words, he admonished, "From now on, Mr. LeBaron, if you have something to discuss about what you can and cannot do on voir dire, approach the bench. Do you understand?"

"Yes, your honor."

"Out of the presence of the jury. Do you understand?"

"Yes, your honor."

"Good, because I'm not going to warn you again. Now proceed, and leave instructions on the law to me."

Deputy Frank just smirked.

One after another, LeBaron's lines of questioning were cut off or severely restricted by the judge. Hamstrung and frustrated, LeBaron persevered as best he could. He was afraid to stop, because when he did, the trial would begin. He was spending more time discussing voir dire in whispers at the bench than questioning prospective jurors. The big clock on the far wall seemed to have had its gears dipped in molasses. Deputy Frank was enjoying the hell out of himself. Rufus Freeman fidgeted morosely at the counsel table, counting off the evaporating minutes which separated him from abject doom.

--2--

At the morning recess, LeBaron told his client to wait as the prospective jurors filed out. When the courtroom was empty, he sat him down at the counsel table and pulled out the police report. "Have you read this?"

"What is it, m'man?"

"The police report."

"No. Lemme see that." Freeman read it slowly, his lips forming the words as he read. It was short, so LeBaron didn't try to hurry him. When he finished, he looked at LeBaron and shrugged. "So what?"

"This is what the police officers are going to testify happened, that's what. Is this what happened?"

"Yeah, thass part of it."

"What do you mean, 'part of it'? What'd they leave out?"

"Well, it don' say near enough 'bout those boys in the green overalls."

"*What* boys in green overalls? Come on, Rufus, *talk* to me. I've got to know what happened."

"Well, y'see here," he said, pointing to the first paragraph of the report. He read haltingly, "'A neighbor ad . . . ad--'"

"'Adjoining'."

"Thass right. 'A'joinin' the property . . . to the rear . . . reported a male . . . sus . . . suspect . . . in dark overalls . . . enterin' the . . . buildin' . . . through a . . . second story window.' I seen the dude myself. That's how I got into this mess."

"Hold on a minute. You're saying that wasn't you?"

"No way. I ain't got no dark green camo overalls! What d'y' think? My threads got class. I ain't inta that Rambo shit."

"Go on."

"I was comin' home that mornin', feelin' jus' *fine*, don' y'know--"

"Drunk?"

"Maybe a little."

"What other drugs had you done?"

"A little toot. Maybe a little reefer. I jus' don' recall. Anyway, I hadda piss somethin' *awful*, couldn't even make it home, so I cut through this back yard int' the bushes--"

"You were on foot?"

"Yeah. I live 'bout a block away. M'short was down at the shop gettin' new seat covers. Somethin' in 'lectric green leopard skin. My oh my, yes."

"Go on. We haven't got a lot of time."

"I'm *tryin'* to talk to you, man, but y'keep interuptin' me."

LeBaron nodded. "I'm sorry. Go on."

"So anyway, I was . . . relievin' m'self . . . when I looks over and sees these two white dudes in green camo overalls, like I said. Funniest thing I ever seen. Looks like somethin' out o' *Abbot and Costello Meet Rambo*. White dudes down in the ghetto with black shit smeared all over their faces. They're really into it, looks like. I almost bust out laughin' jus' lookin' at 'em. Good thing I didn't, though. Turns out the little dude holdin' the ladder was packin' some mean heat on his hip."

"A handgun? In a holster?"

"I hope t'shout. A big fat ol' forty-five, looks like t'me."

"They had a ladder, you said?"

"Yeah. An' the big dude was aclimbin' up on this porch roof. He jimmies open the back window and goes on in. Made one hell of a lotta noise. Surprised they di'n' wake up the whole neighborhood."

"And what were you doing?"

"Me? I's jus' standin' there awatchin'. But when the big dude gets hisself inside, the little dude gets under this big ol' ladder and heaves it up on his shoulder, rattlin' an' abangin'. Takes 'im two'r three tries jus' t'get his balance. Me, I gots t'cover m'mouth from laughin'. He heads on up the driveway, an' I decides to follow him, see what's going down."

"And?"

"So he gets the ladder out front and loads it into a van parked at the curb. A Chevy van, dark green, 'eighty-seven or 'eighty-eight, looks like. Had 'U.S. Gove'ment' spelled out on the door. Door said somethin' else. Lemme think. 'Department o' Agriculture, G. R. & D.'"

"What does that mean? 'G. R. & D.'?"

"How should I know? I'm jus' tellin' y'what I saw."

"Okay, but you're sure that's what it said?"

"Damn straight I' sure."

"How can you be so certain?"

"'Cause I memorized it, thass how. Every single letter. Took m'time. I knew some shit was goin' down, an' I figured I might be able to make me some profit on it. One way or t'other."

"Why didn't you say anything about it before now?"

"Man, I *did*. I *told* my man Esquire Collins, and I seen him write it down. How come *you* don' know nothin' 'bout it, anyway?"

LeBaron flipped through to Collin's scrawled note in the file. "Okay. But you didn't tell the police?"

"Man, you don't tell the police *nothin'* without talkin' to you' lawyer first. Y'think I'm stupid? Anyway, along comes the big dude carrying a big cardboard box and loads it int' the van. Then I watch both of 'em go on back, an' they walk right in the side door like they own the place. Only I know better. They' rippin' the place off."

"So you decide to help them out?"

"No way. I seen the heat the dude was packin', an' I wasn't plannin' on messin' with 'em. But they come out with another one of them cardboard boxes an' some other stuff, get in the van, an' drive off.

I kinda sashay over t'check out the action, an', my oh my, this little block o' wood's keepin' that ol' door from closin'."

"You went in?"

"'Course I went in. They's probably comin' right back, or they woulda locked it up. Apartment's gonna be cleaned out anyway. Ever'thing's good as gone. I says to m'self, might jus's well pick up a little somethin' for m'self, don' y' know, an' then get my ass home an' int' bed."

"And inside you found the tv."

"Yes, indeed. Cutest little set. Color. Still in its box. Prob'ly'd fetched two bills."

"So you took it."

"Sho' I did. Didn't want it fallin' int' the hands o' them honky crim'nals. What' they doing down in *my* 'hood, anyhow?"

"Did you see them again?"

"Nope. Van never come back when the police busted me."

LeBaron finished making notes and glanced over them. "Do you happen to know who lives in that apartment?"

Freeman tugged at his lean jaw in thought. "Ain't it that hairy little white bitch, look like she got worked over pretty good with an ugly stick?"

"That's the one."

"Wha'd y' think? We got a case?"

--3--

Judge Kroner waited until the end of the afternoon to announce that he would not be available on Monday. Further proceedings were continued until Tuesday morning, nine o'clock.

At least jury selection was over. They had a jury. LeBaron had used up all his peremptory challenges and couldn't drag things out any longer. He'd done all he could do. He impressed upon his client the need to bring in some money by Monday afternoon if he wanted to see Cedrick Collins take over the defense personally.

LeBaron actually felt good about the jury, even though only one juror was black, a pretty young woman who owned her own dress shop in East Oakland. Deputy Frank had systematically excluded all the other blacks from the lightly peppered panel. The balance of the jury was made up of five men, all retired, and six women, one of whom was attractive enough to make the trial at least interesting if LeBaron was going to finish it. All but one of the jurors had suffered a loss due to criminal activity in the past five years, but LeBaron figured that was par for the Oakland course. At least none of them had close friends or relatives in law enforcement, which seemed almost a miracle.

The one alternate juror was a retired ex-cop who had concluded from years of police work that most burglars were black. But he swore he wouldn't let his opinion affect his ability to render a fair and impartial verdict, so LeBaron's challenge for cause was denied. LeBaron had already run out of peremptory challenges. But at least the alternate wouldn't be a problem unless something happened to one of the regulars.

LeBaron felt the jurors would not simply rubber stamp whatever Deputy Ivan Frank told them. He gave them that much credit. They would decide for themselves, and that was all he could hope for. Now all LeBaron had to do was come up with a reasonable defense. Or *any* defense.

As he walked back through the cold, darkening streets of downtown Oakland, LeBaron decided things weren't quite as bleak as they had looked yesterday. Raccoona GeBobath was an essential witness to the prosecution's case, and she was unexpectedly flaky. Conceivably she might ignore a subpoena altogether. And even if she showed up, she might have the same impact on the jury as she had on him. He shuddered at the thought. Besides, based on his client's story about the two men in the green van, he now had the Phantom Burglar Defense to play around with. He wasn't sure he believed a word Freeman had uttered, but that wasn't important. What was important was for the *jury* to believe him. Or at least develop a reasonable doubt about what went on that evening.

When he finally got back to the office, Mr. Collins had already gone home. There were two messages stuck on his spindle. "Mrs. Christensen?" LeBaron muttered and punched the intercom.

"Wha'cha' want, honey?"

LeBaron smiled. He couldn't help being aroused by Wanda

Jean's overtly sexual purr. "Who's Mrs. Christensen, Wanda Jean? Which case is that on?"

"She sho' didn't say."

"Wha'd she want?"

"She a'ksed y' t'call 'er back."

"This is a long distance number."

"Sho'nuff."

"Well, I'm not calling a long distance number now. I'm tired. I don't feel like it."

"S'fine by me."

"And the other call was from my brother Vince?"

"He jus' a'ksed me t'tell you t' go see'im soon's y'can."

"He didn't say what it's about."

"Nope."

"All right. Maybe I'll drive over there in the morning. Thanks, Wanda Jean. Have a nice weekend."

CHAPTER FIVE

Sunday morning

--1--

LeBaron pulled off the deserted frontage road into the narrow gravel driveway in front of Tehema Monastery and shut off the engine. He climbed out into the crisp January morning and peered through the broad slats of the locked main gate. No one was in sight. Mounted on the gate post to his right was a wooden box marked "Telephone." He pulled open the door, picked up the handset, and waited. Through the dense forest he could just make out the looming outline of snowcapped Mount Tehema, slumbering volcanic giant of the southern Cascade Range.

This place always made him uncomfortable. At first glance the abbey appeared unimposingly rustic, homespun, and aw-shucks down home, the monks calm and relaxed. But like the Japanese Zen monasteries after which it was modeled, a precise code of conduct was required of all those passing through its intricately hand-carved gates, monk and visitor alike. And LeBaron was never quite sure what was expected of him.

A New Zealander zealot by the name of Bernard Toaste had founded Tehema Monastery in the late sixties. Toaste had been the first Westerner to attain some particularly high state of consciousness during his stay at one of the most exclusive zen monasteries in Kyoto, the ancient Japanese city of zen monasteries. LeBaron could never quite remember all the details, though he had been here half a dozen times to visit his brother and had read everything he could find about the place.

In order to share his enlightenment with all beings, Toaste had returned to New Zealand, where he gathered about himself a small band of neophyte trainees. Then something had happened which resulted in Toaste's fall from favor in his native country. The literature did not elaborate, but LeBaron had probed enough to learn that it involved Toaste and a young female monk. His imagination had no difficulty extrapolating the missing information. Recognizing discretion to be the better part of valor, Toaste and some of his loyal followers fled New Zealand and, drawn like a magnet to the mountain which so reminded him of Mount Fuji, established his school of zen training in northern California at the foot of Mount Tehema. He assumed the title "Roshi Koshin Toaste, First Abbot of Tehema Abbey, Zen School of Contemplative Monks Beneath the Mountain Among the Trees." A bit awkward in the English translation, yet even LeBaron had to admit that the title, carved as it was in huge Japanese calligraphy above the front gate, was striking. Translating the relevant scriptures and ceremonies into English, Abbot Toaste prescribed the same strict and monotonous routine of sitting and working meditation for his trainees as had brought him to such a high state of enlightenment in Japan.

LeBaron had never seen Toaste in person, but a picture on the front of the guest pamphlet revealed an obese man in a maroon robe with an enormous grin spread like butter across his flabby face. LeBaron detected a stench of smugness every time he viewed that photograph.

"May I be of some assistance?" a voice asked from the earpiece of the telephone.

"Ye--" LeBaron cleared his throat and began again. "Yes. I'm here to see my brother, Vince LeBaron."

"I'm sorry, but the monks are now at zazen. If you could come back at noon--"

"I have to see him *now*." LeBaron knew that zazen was sitting meditation. All the monks sat on little round cushions facing the blank white walls of the Zendo, and no one talked or moved. He had tried it himself on previous visits, but his knees and right hip always began to hurt after a few minutes, so most of his experience had been devoted to unsuccessfully ignoring the increasing pain and wondering when the goddamned zazen period would end. He saw no reason why he should bide his time while Vince sat staring at the wall, doing absolutely nothing. "Vince sent me a letter that he wanted to see me," which was true, but lacked the ring of dire urgency. So LeBaron embellished. "He said to come as quickly as possible. It's some kind of grave emergency, I'm sure."

"Oh . . . I see. Well . . ." The voice was having trouble programming a non-routine event into its monastic world order.

"I think it's a matter of life or death," LeBaron nudged. "You better let Vince know I'm here, okay?"

"All right. You're his brother?"

"Yes. Jed LeBaron."

"Please wait." Click.

LeBaron sighed, replaced the handset, and shut the cabinet door. So much fuss. He zipped his down jacket tighter around his neck and hopped from one foot to the other to stretch his car-cramped legs. Somber incense cedars towered over the abbey grounds, letting through beams of weak morning sunlight. Life was very peaceful here, and for a moment, piqued by some forgotten alter ego deep inside, LeBaron indulged the fantasy of a monastic life. Under the right set of circumstances, he supposed, it might have been he, rather than Vince, who abandoned reality in favor of familiar daily ceremonies infinitely repeated and the quiet forgetfulness of these cloistered walkways.

It was odd how it all came to pass. Vince was the last person in the world LeBaron would have pegged for a zen monk dropout. Yet here they were. Strange.

Vince was almost three years older than LeBaron--"Jeddy" his brother called him, perpetuating a jest so ancient neither of them recalled its origins. Vince had blazed the trail for them both through high school, college, and then law school. Like LeBaron, Vince was bright, but Vince was also a hard worker. In fact, Vince possessed that unique combination of qualities, brains and perseverance, which allowed him to conclude everything successfully and made him a hard act for LeBaron to follow. Nothing foreshadowed his abrupt and bewildering flight to this monastery.

Except maybe for the Sarah Brubaker business. There was something not quite in character about that. Vince had met Sally during his junior year at Cal. She had been a bright-eyed freshman. They didn't finally break it off until well after law school. Until right before he married Linda, in fact. To say that Vince's relationship with Sally was stormy was like the national weather service calling a hurricane windy. For the entire course of their involvement tempests from heaven and hell blew between them, spinning off intricate patterns of highs and lows. No, that was not like Vince at all. But then Sally was something special. Vince never acted like the impeccable boy scout young republican whiz-kid savant when she was by his side. She brought something else out in him, something less perfect, something more vulnerable, more willing to take chances and even fail. Something more human, LeBaron always thought.

After law school Vince had joined a huge Los Angeles firm specializing in real estate law. A year or two later, he married Linda. While Vince tended his family, raised two children, and devoted himself to putting in enough hours to become a full partner within seven years, LeBaron had drifted, making little use of his own law degree. Vince's income had risen to six figures. LeBaron's hovered at barely four. Once again, Vince's life had become a textbook model of success.

Until eighteen months ago, anyway, when Vince had without warning dropped out of his law firm, abandoned his family to the expensive home and substantial property they had accumulated, and like a penniless beggar skulked off to Tehema Monastery. Everyone spoke of a miraculous religious conversion triggered by a raging mid-life crisis, but LeBaron didn't buy either exactly. To him, something far subtler had happened. His brother had simply grown weary of what he was doing with his life, of what he was expected to do, and like a hillside slowly saturated with a hidden source of ground water, a limit had finally been exceeded, and the landslide struck abruptly. Vince had come here for a little peace and quiet.

LeBaron had received the news without surprise. Perhaps he had even seen it coming. Not that he would ever try to influence his brother's decisions. Nor would his opinion have made any difference anyway. And not that LeBaron would have preferred things any other way. Vince was Vince. That simple act of quitting, against all caution and in the face of overwhelming criticism, on occasion struck LeBaron as an expression of pure freedom such as he himself had never even approached. At other times, like today, crunching along the cold gravel driveway in the pale patches of feeble morning sun, it seemed damned weird.

"Hi, Jeddy."

LeBaron spun around, startled. Vince was a shadowy outline on the other side of the slatted gate. "Just like in *Kung Fu*, huh, brother? They teach you to sneak up on people without leaving a mark on the rice paper."

Vince chuckled, fumbling with the lock. "Is there really an emergency?"

"No."

"I didn't think so. With Mom and Dad both dead, I just couldn't imagine what sort of emergency might bring you here." The lock snapped, and the massive gate groaned. Vince stepped through. In the rusty brown robes of the abbey, he seemed to LeBaron frail and pale, as if the heavy woolen garments might wear him down and suffocate him in their folds. His shaved head was rough with five-o'clock shadow. With a deliberate slowness, a sort of thoughtful grace, he moved like a condemned man intent on living fully on the edge of the present moment, attending to every detail, every nuance. A smile sat comfortably on his thin lips. "You came because of my note then," he surmised, bowing.

Without being aware he did so, LeBaron bowed in reply. "I guess so. It was time for a visit anyway."

"Good to see you, brother."

"It's good to see you, brother. What's up?"

"You look cold. Come on inside. I know a nice sunny place we can talk."

When LeBaron had squeezed through the opening, he helped his brother pull the gate closed. Vince replaced the lock, but didn't snap it, then led them along a gravel path away from the central cloister and through an overgrown opening to a bench on the east side of the woods.

Mount Tehema, unobstructed here by the trees, dominated the landscape with awesome splendor. Above, the mountain was taller than the rising sun, snow-cloaked and festooned with saucer-like clouds which amplified the weak winter light to a dazzling brightness. Below the summit, ragged crests of red and black rock pierced the snowpack like the spines of frozen dinosaurs. Radiating out below, defying gravity, fragments of vast forests and checkered farm fields were bizarrely canted upward against the lower slopes, spreading away to the horizon. The effect was breathtaking, and LeBaron once again felt the religious significance of the mighty mountain.

They sat in silence, shielded from the chilly west breeze. A band of acrobatic chickadees chattered happily in the low branches of a nearby cedar.

After a while, LeBaron turned to Vince and asked quietly, "What's on your mind, brother?"

Vince sighed, as if returning to a chore he would have preferred to put off. "Sally came to see me the other day."

"Oh?"

"You remember Sally, don't you? Sally Brubaker?"

"Sure I do. How could *anybody* forget Sally Brubaker? Didn't she tell you she called me earlier this week? I told her where she could find you. What'd she want, anyway?"

Vince's brow furrowed. "It's kind of strange, actually. She asked me if I could help her out. She needs a lawyer . . . or a private investigator . . . or maybe just a friend to talk things out with."

"And you said . . . ?"

"I told her I couldn't help her." Vince did not try to conceal the pain and regret in his voice. He turned and looked into LeBaron's eyes. "I said I thought maybe you would. I'd appreciate it if you'd at least look into it. There may not be any money in it. She's lost her job and already spent what little she'd put aside. I think we're talking about a freebie here."

"Sure, brother, no problem." LeBaron unzipped his heavy jacket, which the pale sun was beginning to penetrate. "I'll talk to her. But, hell, it can't be that big a deal, can it? What's she need, anyway?"

"Well, it's . . . *odd*, and I don't completely understand it. I don't think she does either, really. I'd rather she explained it to you herself."

LeBaron waited, but Vince appeared to have finished. "That's it? What's the big secret?"

Vince sighed. "There's no secret. I'm just not sure I see things objectively where Sally's involved. I'd rather you heard the story from her and form your own conclusions. I wanted to talk to you face to face in case I had to twist your arm to get you to help her out." He smiled.

"But you've made that part easy."

"Jesus, brother, d'you mean to tell me after I come all the way out here to see you, that you won't even tell me what's going on? Give me a hint, huh? Is it criminal or civil?"

"I'm not really sure. Maybe both."

"Divorce?"

"No, nothing like that. A friend she was working with seems to be missing."

"Missing? Sounds like a matter for the police."

"She reported it, but she's not happy with their results. Seems the FBI has gotten involved and taken over the investigation."

"Presumed interstate flight?"

"That's my guess. And maybe federal contracts."

"Oh? What sort of work was this missing person up to?"

Vince considered his response for a long time. "I'd really rather you got the information directly from Sally. I've got a funny feeling about this, but I'd really rather not get involved at this time." He shifted uncomfortably. "Actually, I didn't let her finish her story. I told her I couldn't help her, but I'd talk to you about it."

Vince's attitude was beginning to irritate LeBaron. His eyes narrowed. "Did you tell her *why* you couldn't help her?"

"Why? Not really, I--"

"Didja tell her it was more important for you to sit here like an imbecile staring at the blank wall from morning to night? Didja tell her that, Vince?"

Vince looked confused, then hurt. "You don't understand--"

"Understand *what*, Vince?"

"I've been sitting for months, working hard, and I'm close to something--"

"*Close* to something?" LeBaron's voice oozed with irony. "Vince, don't forget who you're talking to here. This isn't some bumpkin who just wandered into the carnival grounds. Last time I was here you as much as admitted that all this Zen Buddhism mumbo jumbo was a crock of bullshit. I didn't press you. I didn't ask you what you were doing here. I figured, hey, it's your life. It's your time. You'll work things out your own way. But now you tell me you can't even help an old friend in need because you're *close to something*?"

"She doesn't really need *my* help, Jeddy. *You* can help her."

But LeBaron wasn't listening. He refused to be put off the scent. "Close to *what*, Vince? Eternal salvation, maybe? Nirvana? Perhaps true enlightenment lies just around the bend?" He snorted. "They're starting to get to you, Vince. You're beginning to sound like your Right Reverend Abbot Bernard Fucking Toaste."

Vince was pale and silent.

LeBaron felt a pang of remorse. "Jeez, Vince, I'm sorry. I'm just trying to understand how you could turn Sally away. Look, even the Heart Sutra says . . . something about . . . something . . . 'for here there is no . . . accumulation . . . nor again annihilation, nor an Eightfold Path, no knowledge, no attainment.'"

"Jeddy!" Vince beamed. "I had no idea you were studying the Zen Sutras."

"Just enough to defend myself," LeBaron groused, standing abruptly, "from people who're getting 'close to something.'" As if drawn, he shuffled a few steps toward the brilliant mountain. Its snow-capped peaks blazed against a pewter sky.

"Jeddy!" Vince rasped in a hoarse whisper. "Turn around slowly and look."

A chickadee had swooped down and perched on the bench back where LeBaron had been sitting, as if it had something to add to the conversation. "Fee bee bee!" it insisted, cocking its tiny black-capped head. "Tsick a zee zee zee zee!" When neither of them moved, it sidestepped over to Vince and swiped its beak back and forth a few times on a fold of his rough robe, then flitted off to hang upside down from a low branch overhead.

"Damn!" LeBaron was thrilled. "You could have reached out and touched the little bugger!"

Vince was grinning. "I'm glad you saw that. It happens all the time. I think it's something they like about this robe."

"Sure. They probably think you're Saint Francis of Assisi."

Vince laughed, and LeBaron joined him. The laughter melted away years of diverging paths. LeBaron sat down again beside his brother, and they gazed out at the imposing mountain, each grinning, each feeling closer than before.

"Okay, Vince, we'll do it your way. I'll talk to Sally. Where do I find her?"

"She said she'd get in touch with you. She was going to spend a day or two at the Alpine Lodge in Mount Tehema City. Maybe you can still catch her there. Oh, she's checked in under her married name--"

"I didn't know she was married."

"She's not. Divorced about three years ago. But she still uses the name 'Christensen' when she doesn't--"

"What?!"

"That's the name she's using. 'Sarah Christensen.'"

"Oh shit! She tried to reach me at the office yesterday. I didn't know who 'Mrs. Christensen' was, so I didn't return her call."

"Well, don't worry. She'll understand."

In the distance, a bell began donging insistently.

Vince stood up. "I'm sorry, Jeddy, I've got to go. This is a festival day for us. The Buddha's renunciation. We can talk this afternoon if you like."

The rekindled pain in his brother's eyes brought LeBaron to the realization that Vince had long been wrestling with the paradox of his absurd commitment to the monastery. And something profoundly unresolved about this Sally Brubaker business also smoldered there. Suddenly LeBaron wanted to give his brother a big hug, but they hadn't been brought up that way. He looked down at his feet instead. "No, actually I have to be getting back. I'm in the middle of a trial. Listen, Vince, I'm sorry if I . . . said anything--"

"Nothing to be sorry about, brother," Vince cut in, smiling. "I can't always find a good conversation around here that's sufficiently . . . *candid*." He bowed formally. "Can you find your way back to the front gate?"

"No problem. Good to see you, brother."

"Good to see you, too, brother." Vince turned and hurried toward the ringing bell. Before his path disappeared into the woods, he turned and called back, "Close the lock on the gate, will you, Jeddy?"

"Sure, brother. Don't want to let the riff-raff in."

--2--

When finished in 1959, the Alpine Lodge had been a proud and successful contribution to family lodging in Mount Tehema City. That was before the freeway diverted the flow of vital traffic from the town's clogged arteries like a slick coronary bypass. Now paint flaked off the loose trim, shingles hung at odd angles from the high-pitched roofs, and the broken asphalt parking lot heaved and churned like choppy waters in an unstable wind.

LeBaron parked under the canopy in front of the glass-walled office. Inside a thin man with unkempt wisps of thinning gray hair looked up from his newspaper. LeBaron walked in. "'Morning."

"Good morning," the gaunt man replied, folding his paper and opening a large guest book. "Need a room? We got the best rates in town. How many in your party?"

"No. No, I'm just looking for someone who's staying here."

"That's all right," the deskman said morosely. "Party's name?"

"Christensen. Sarah Christensen."

"Sorry, she checked out." The clerk didn't have to consult his register. "Popular lady. You're the second person to ask for her this morning."

"Oh?"

"Maybe you're part o' the same group?"

"Maybe. What'd this other person look like."

"Well, I only got a look at one of 'em. Kinda short, slight built, maybe fortyish, dark hair slicked down tight, wire-rim glasses. Wearin' green coveralls. Friend of yours?"

"I'm not sure. You said he was with someone else?"

"Yup, but the other fella didn't come in. Just sat out there where you're parked right now, the whole time watchin'. In that gover'ment van."

LeBaron had a prickling sense of deja vu. "What kind of van?"

"'U.S. Gover'ment' it said on the door. 'Department of Agriculture'. I didn't notice the make. Them vans all look alike to me anyway. Green it was. Dark green."

The dreamlike sense of weirdness grew. LeBaron looked out the door to where his own car was parked and tried to orient himself. This shouldn't be happening. This had nothing to do with the trial of Rufus Abraham Freeman a hundred miles or more away in Oakland. Or did it? No, of course not. Yet it might just as well have been Rufus Freeman describing this mysterious government van. LeBaron turned back to the desk clerk and eyed him closely for a sign of a joke, a trick, a conspiracy, a Candid Camera setup.

The man gazed back innocuously through sleepy eyes. "Friends o' yours?"

"No. I don't think so. But tell me, was there anything else written on the door of the van."

"Well, yes, there was." The man stared off into space for a while, but to no avail. "I jus' can't remember what else it was."

"Did you read it?"

After another spacy stare, the man replied, "I believe I did. I jus' can't remember what it said."

"How about, 'G. R. & D.'?"

"Why, yes!" the clerk smacked his hand on the open guest book and grinned, as impressed as if LeBaron had just pulled a rabbit out of a hat. "I do believe that's exactly what it said. So they *are* friends o' yours, are they?"

"Not exactly. Look, what time did Sal-- . . . er . . . Sarah Christensen check out."

"Early. *Real early.* Woke me up before it was even light out--I'd say it was before six o'clock--to give me the room key and a message for one of those friends of yours in the van."

"Message? What message?"

"Sorry, she said I should only give it out to that one fella she named."

"Oh? What was his name?" LeBaron opened his note pad and drew out a pen.

The desk clerk stared off into space for a while, then shook his head. He turned and rummaged through a waste basket behind him, found a crumpled piece of paper, and carefully unfolded it. "I wrote it down and then threw my note away after I'd given the message out. Never figured I'd be havin' t'look at it twice. Popular lady."

"His name?"

"Oh, yeah." He looked down at the wrinkled paper. "Fella by the name of 'Jed LeBaron.'"

LeBaron stared at him incredulously. "How did you know his name was Jed LeBaron?"

"'Cause I asked him if it was."

"Give me that," LeBaron snarled and grabbed the paper out of the startled clerk's hands.

"Hey! Gimme that back! You' got no right to be lookin' at that message."

LeBaron ignored him. The note was written in a tiny, careful bookkeeper's hand. It said: "Mrs. Christensen is going back to Berkeley tonight and will call you there tomorrow."

CHAPTER SIX

Sunday

--1--

In the blackness he awoke to a certainty that something was terribly wrong. Something had been grotesquely twisted and obscenely rearranged. That, he knew before anything else. He had been asleep, dreaming hideous dreams, absorbing strange precepts, responding to invisible sensations as a sleepwalker, and now, for the first time, he had come fully to consciousness.

No pain now. The pain had vanished. Only a dull half-remembrance of hideous, maddening pain.

His body he could feel, but he had the curious sensation that his body did not really exist. No sight. No sound. No taste. No touch. He couldn't move his arms or legs, his fingers or toes, his mouth or lips or tongue. He couldn't open his eyes. A faint odor of orange peels cloyed, and he was vaguely thirsty.

He knew things, a great many things, though he could not recall learning any of them. He knew he was called "Dexter," but the name alone explained nothing. He had no idea who he was or where he had come from. Deaf, dumb, blind, numb, alone, he drifted inexplicably in the void.

He feared that he was totally alone in the vast, empty universe. He decided that this was how God must have felt, before God created the heavens and the earth. Only Dexter had no inkling of how to go about creating a world.

He tried to sleep, but could not. He tried to dream, but invariably returned to the stark futility of the empty present. He learned that he could not escape the endless closed circle of thinking.

Dexter knew the concept of madness and was afraid.

CHAPTER SEVEN

Monday morning

--1--

LeBaron woke up an hour before the alarm and couldn't get back to sleep. After a while he quit trying. He propped his head up on the folded pillow and stared into the darkness. Too many complications troubled his once-simple life.

All day Sunday he had stayed around home reading the newspaper, watching the Warriors-Lakers game on television, playing his guitar, and waiting for the phone to ring. He had even skipped his usual Sunday morning jog through campus, and he *never* missed that, rain or shine. But Sally Brubaker, alias Mrs. Sarah Christensen, hadn't called. He was dying to know why. Tomorrow he would be up to his neck again in the Freeman trial and wouldn't have time to properly worry about her.

And what, by the way, *was* he going to do about saving poor Rufus Freeman's skin. Not that Freeman deserved it. He was, after all, a jive artist, a deadbeat, and a common criminal. And not even a very imaginative one. Still, LeBaron had to admit he was beginning to *like* the young man and his ghetto-bred perspective on reality.

And what about the way he had behaved with Vince? LeBaron had gotten pissed off Saturday and jumped on his brother's case. Why? Because he had refused to help Sally out. At least that was what he had accused him of. But now LeBaron wasn't so sure that was really what was bugging him. To be honest for a minute, as he sometimes could be in the undefended realm between waking and first light, maybe it was just the *opposite* that bugged him. To be brutally honest, maybe Vince was screwing up the semiconscious fantasies his dreamwork had begun to spin about Sally. Sally with the short cheerleader skirt and suntanned legs. Sally on the frozen juniper squeezing his arm. And maybe LeBaron was feeling a little bit guilty. Because Vince obviously had never completely let go of her. Damn!

He swung his feet onto the cold floor and clicked on the bedside lamp. The dazzling brightness burned his eyes.

The weirdest thing of all, though, was that there were simply too goddamned many dark green Chevy vans in his life to make any sense. Too many government vans with "Department of Agriculture, G. R. & D." lettered on the door. For what seemed like the thousandth time he tried to detect a thread of connection between Rufus Freeman's van and the one driven by the men who intercepted his message from Sally, and could not. He made a mental note to phone the U. S. Agriculture Department that afternoon and find out what the hell "G. R. & D." stood for anyway.

When the telephone finally rang and hour later, it sent an electric jolt straight through him. He had already showered and shaved, but it was still early. He glanced at the clock. Too early to be Mr. Collins. It *had to be Sally!* He grabbed up the handset.

"Hello! Hello! Don't hang up!"

"Wha'sa matter with you, LeBaron?" soothed Cedrick Collin's no-nonsense drawl. "I ain't goin' nowhere. Where'n hell did you learn how to answer a telephone?"

"Oh, Jesus, sorry. Hello, Mr. Collins. You're calling early this morning."

"Uh. Might be. Got a little touch o' the green apple quickstep this mornin'. Nothin' serious. What's wrong with your telephone? I tried t'call you a coupla times yesterday and couldn't get through."

"You did? Yesterday?"

"That's what I said. Don't know nothin' about it, huh?" He chuckled. "I thought maybe you's tryin' t'avoid me."

"No. This is the first I've heard about it. What happened when you dialed my number?"

"Jus' got a bunch o' clickin'. Seems t'be workin' fine this mornin' though. You sound real anxious, LeBaron. Been workin' all weekend on this Freeman matter? Nice to see you *volunteerin'* your time for a poor boy can't even afford t'pay his lawyer's fees. But say, what in hell's goin' on in that case?"

"What do you mean?"

"I got a call yesterday from ol' Bert Thompkins, the D.A. hisself, wonderin' the same thing. What *is* going on?"

"About what? I don't understand."

"About this Freeman case. Seems the U.S. Attorney jus' called him up long distance and wants him t'get rid of this thing. Wants'm t'deal it or drop it. But don' try it."

"Jesus!" LeBaron's head swam with a giddy rush of freedom, tinged with unexpected regret. "We've already got a jury picked. Testimony's scheduled to start Tuesday morning."

"Uh. Don't look like there's gonna *be* no testimony. Thompkins's instructin' his Deputy D.A.--who you got on that'n?"

"Ivan Frank."

"Who?"

"Ivan Frank."

"Never heard of him."

"He's been handling misdemeanors in Fremont."

"Oh, I know who y'mean. Fat fella with glasses? Mostly disagreeable?"

"That's him."

"Don' like that boy one bit. Where'd they get young fellas like that, LeBaron? Scares the hell outa me. Anyway, Thompkins's instructin' this Ivan Frank fella t'offer you a misdemeanor. Somethin' mighty peculiar goin' on. What's a U.S. Attorney got t'do with this thing, LeBaron?"

"I'm not sure." He considered telling Collins about the green government van, but still couldn't quite fit it together. "I've got an idea or two, but I'm not really sure."

"Well, follow'm up and let me know, will you? Thompkins's real uncomfortable not knowin' what's going down. Sort of a matter of *turf*, as I see it. Nervous sort anyway, and he don't want t'let the thing get out o'control. Gets too much aid from the feds. Wouldn't hurt us none t'do the ol' D.A. a favor, y'un'erstan'. Sumfin' funny goin' on."

"I'll let you know if I learn anything."

"You do that, hear?" He paused. "I don' know what you're

doin', LeBaron, but you're doin' jus' fine. Now howsabout doin' the same thing for some *payin'* clients for a change?"

LeBaron laughed. "I don't think it's anything I'm doing. Just dumb blind luck, I guess."

"Well, jus' keep on doin' what your doin' anyhow. Now get out your pencil, cause we got one hell of a busy mornin' comin' up. Okay, y'got a Rita Shybock . . . 'r maybe its Shylock . . . she's a hooker . . . little white gal, but she's okay . . . all paid up . . . friend o' Thelma's . . . in Muni two at nine . . . I believe it's an arraignment, but check the calendar . . . prob'ly a 647b . . . "

--2--

At a carrel in the back recesses of one of the top floors of the University of California main library stacks an attractive woman glanced up from her reading and stared out into the rows of dark books. She thought she had heard a noise, but it was nothing. She stood up and stretched her lean body, no longer as young as she liked, but at thirty-two still well-cared for. She draped her leather shoulder bag over her arm and headed for the lobby level.

In a nearby carrel a young pre-med student from Japan looked up as she passed and watched her gracefully descend the hollow ringing stairs, mistaking her for a fellow student. The mistake was a reasonable one. Her hair was long and straight like the students wore, and the graying at the temples did not contrast much with the paleness of the fine blond strands. But had the student paid more careful attention, he might have seen the small crows-foot wrinkles spreading in the corners of her eyes like subtle accents in delicate china, or noticed that the tweed skirt-suit she wore was of a more stylish and expensive cut than a mere student could afford, or discerned that she bore herself with a resigned self-assurance alien to the world of student experience.

Sarah Brubaker found a vacant public telephone, set down her handbag and notebook, and fished a quarter out of her coin purse. In a fit of pique, she stared at the coin, undecided whether to drop it in the slot. She had agreed to make the call, true. In fact she had *promised* Vince she would make the call, but that was before she had gotten herself under control. She had still been stunned by Vince's refusal to help her, or to even listen to her story. Self-centered bastard! She actually stamped her foot, and the reference librarian looked up from his newspaper.

She had gone to see Vince because she thought she needed a lawyer to help her sort out the frightful mess embroiling her life. But the instant he turned her down she knew it really wasn't a lawyer she wanted. It was Vince himself. She wanted someone to hold her the way he used to, to lift the burden away from her and say, "Hey, it's all right. I'll be here. Don't worry." Damn him anyway, with his stupid shaven head and itchy medieval robes. She closed her eyes tight and two teardrops squeezed reluctantly out.

She tried to picture Vince's kid brother Jeddy. That was just how she remembered him: as a kid. Although he was actually less than a year younger than she, it had translated into a full academic year. The gulf had seemed unbridgeable at the time. She saw him as a child at heart, an innocent, a handsome, frivolous boy just graduated from college. Not someone of real substance. Not someone to share her serious burden with. Maybe she should just forget the whole thing.

Stop it, Sarah, she scolded. *That was ten years ago. He'll be older now, just like you. He'll be different. Give it a chance. You* promised *Vince you'd talk to him.* She didn't care a whit whether she kept a promise to Vince. But maybe Vince was right. *Where else are you going to turn? You haven't been home in almost a week now. Let's face it, you're afraid to go home. And you can't live off your Visa card forever. What the hell else are you going to do?*

She dropped the coin into the slot and punched out a number scrawled in her notebook.

"Hello," a male voice answered tentatively.

"Hello, Jed?"

"Yes."

"This is Sarah Brubaker. I've been trying to reach you."

"Sarah! I'm glad you called. I think my telephone's been out of order. I just got a call from Cedrick Collins," he babbled happily, "that's the man I'm working with, and he told me about the phone. He calls every morning and gives me my court assignments. I've got fourteen appearances to make today. I just counted them."

"Listen, Jed, have you seen Vince?"

"I talked to him Saturday."

"Then you know . . . about my problem?"

"Not really. He suggested I hear it from you firsthand. Look, why don't we get together and talk?"

"Now?"

"No, I can't. I've got to be in court in forty minutes. I'm sorry."

"I can come into your office if you want me to make an appointment."

"Bad idea. Nothing gets done at the office. Too much to do. Where are you calling from?"

"On campus at Cal. The main library."

"How about lunch?"

"All right. Where?"

"Wait a minute." LeBaron glanced over the schedule his employer had just inflicted on him. "Looks pretty grim. I'll only have about forty-five minutes free, and that'll be in downtown Oakland. This evening would be better for me."

"All right. I can meet you at your place. What time?"

"How about dinner? Around six?"

"All right. Six. Where do you live?"

He gave her the address, then added, "Say, did you know there were some other people asking about you on Saturday?"

"What do you mean?"

He told her of his conversation with the desk clerk at the Alpine Lodge in Mount Tehema City.

"And he gave *them* my message too?"

"Apparently so."

"Oh dear. Jed, I'm sorry I've gotten you involved in all this--"

"Hey, don't worry about it. Glad to help an old friend."

"I don't think we should meet at your apartment."

"Okay. Where then?" She paused for so long he wasn't sure she was still there. "Sarah?"

"Yes. Do you remember that little restaurant where Vince and I took you after your graduation?"

"Sure. You mean over i--"

"Don't say it! This may sound paranoid, but I think your line may be tapped. I'll meet you there tonight at seven, all right?"

"Okay, but--"

"I have to go now, Jed. Be careful. Someone may be following you. Try not to invite them to dinner, will you?"

Sarah hung up the receiver. Feeling better, she closed her notebook and stuck it in her handbag. That was everything she really needed. She could finish the research later. Without returning to her carrel in the stacks, she quickly left the library.

--3--

Twenty blocks away LeBaron stood for a long time at the front window of his apartment, watching the early morning activity on his street. Cars pluming water vapor roared back and forth in the cold. A city garbage truck slowly rounded the corner while two beefy black workers dumped the cans and banged them back into place beside the curb. Shouting and laughing, a group of school children ran to a waiting yellow bus. Try as he might, he could not detect anything out of the ordinary.

CHAPTER EIGHT

Monday afternoon

--1--

The day had been horrendous. It confirmed every law the fabled Murphy had ever articulated and suggested the need for several new ones. When LeBaron had called the office at quarter to ten to say he was falling behind and needed reinforcements, Wanda Jean advised him that Mr. Collins had gotten detained in a preliminary hearing and had asked LeBaron to take care of a half-dozen additional matters. Clients became unmanageable and demanding, simple arraignments metamorphosed into complex bail hearings, not-guilty pleas transformed themselves into probation revocation hearings, and plea bargains that would have been simple on any other day took on the flavor of extended treatises into the history and function of criminal law. Everything seemed to go wrong.

Except for the money. For some inexplicable reason, everyone had cash to pay on his account today, and one or two incredibly volunteered payment even when LeBaron forgot to ask. He would accept the contribution, receipt it on one of his business cards, make a note on a yellow pad, fold the bills, and stuff them into his left front pants pocket, where they would not become commingled with his own meager funds. By the time he arrived back at the office, drawn and exhausted, it was after four o'clock and his pocket bulged with almost thirty-five hundred dollars in small bills. A handful of waiting clients menaced the reception desk like extras out of *Night of The Living Dead*, so LeBaron quietly reclosed the front door and sneaked in the back way. The cash and an account sheet he turned over to an amazed Wanda Jean and retreated into his office. There, taped to his lamp, was a string of twelve telephone messages he was supposed to return before the day was over.

LeBaron ripped off his jacket, yanked loose his tie, and clawed open his collar. Before collapsing into his desk chair, he took the unusual step of shutting his office door. He'd had enough of the outside world for one day, and maybe for the rest of the week. Shutting his eyes, he drifted for a few minutes, thinking of nothing at all. Then he glanced over his phone messages.

Three messages from Deputy D. A. Ivan Frank stood out from the pack and perked up his spirits. "Urgent!" the last was marked in Wanda Jean's stunning pink felt tip marker. "Call him before end of day." Good, LeBaron thought, let the fat bastard sweat. He found the Freeman file on the corner of his desk and glanced at the inside cover. Where the client's telephone number should have been were the words "No phone." LeBaron punched the intercom.

"Wha'cha want, honey."

"Wanda Jean, how do we get in touch with Rufus Freeman?"

"Ain't no way. He got no phone."

"Thanks."

"Any time."

So. Without his client's consent, he couldn't conclude a deal. Settlement would have to wait until tomorrow morning, as they say, on the courthouse steps. Might as well find out what Ivan was offering, though. He punched out the phone number of the district attorney office.

"District Attorney," snapped an irritable voice. Monday apparently hadn't gone much better for her.

"Hello, I'm returning a call from Ivan Frank."

"I'll transfer you to the felony division." LeBaron waited while the call sniffed its way through the indifferent phone lines of the bureau. Finally a woman answered wearily, "Felony division."

"Ivan Frank, please. Returning his call."

"I'm sorry, Mr. Frank is tied up. Can I take a message?"

"Yes. Tell him Jed LeBaron returned his call on the Rufus Freeman case. My number--"

"Excuse me, Mr. LeBaron. Mr. Frank asked me to put you through when you called. One moment please." LeBaron waited for several minutes and was about to hang up, when a voice announced too smugly, "Ivan Frank."

"Jed LeBaron. Returning your call."

"Right. Listen, LeBaron, I've got a lot of important work on my desk, and this Freeman trial is keeping me from it. I've decided to reconsider my offer. I assume your client is still willing to plead to a misdemeanor."

Something about the deputy's brusque superiority rankled LeBaron. In spite of his better judgment, perversity seized control of his vocal chords. He heard himself reply, "I don't believe he is, actually. Rufus thinks we can beat this one."

There was a long pause. "I see. And what do *you* think?"

"I'm not the one who has to do the time."

"Come *on*, LeBaron. I've got him dead to rights, and you know it. He was caught *in flagrante delicto*. I could have him on any one of three different felonies. We're talking about the likelihood of *state prison* here."

"So why're you offering a misdemeanor then?"

Another long pause. "You have an obligation to discuss my offer with your client, you know. It's a violation of the state bar rules to refuse."

"So I'll talk to him. What's the offer?"

"Plead to a 459, stipulated to be a misdemeanor. That's second degree burglary. I'll dismiss the other count, the grand theft."

"And?"

"And what?"

"And drop the priors?"

Silence.

"Ivan? Are you still there?"

Finally, in a low growl, "And drop the priors."

"And?"

"Now what the hell are you after, LeBaron?" Ivan Frank sounded very angry.

"What about sentencing?"

"No sentence bargaining."

"Why not?"

"Policy of the office."

"Well," LeBaron considered, enjoying himself, "be that as it may.

I'll certainly talk to my client about it. But without a guaranteed suspended sentence, we may be wasting our time."

"Talk to him and get back to me right away."

"Oh, I guess I didn't tell you. I have no way of reaching him until tomorrow morning at court."

"Shit!"

"No need to get so upset, Ivan. Things'll work out, one way or another."

"I have to know whether or not to call my witness off."

"It's fine by me if you want to call them off."

"I mean, Mr. LeBaron, *do we have a deal or what*?"

"You know I can't make a commitment without my client's consent. I'll let you know as soon as I've talked to him. Sorry, I have to go now. But think about this suspended sentence business, will you Ivan? Bye-bye." He hung up feeling finer than he had all day.

LeBaron leaned back and surveyed his tiny drab office for the first time in as long as he could remember. The walls were a hospitalish green off-white without any awards, certificates, or degrees on display. No pictures. Not even a photograph. His stay here had always seemed so *transient*. The only furniture was his modern metal desk, matching swivel chair, and two straight back chairs purloined from the reception area. The floor along the left wall and behind him was lined with stacks of manila folders, some quite thick. They represented the civil component of Collins' practice, which was what he had originally been hired on to handle: wills, a few probates, an unlawful detainer or two, and a stack of automobile accidents. Each afternoon when he finally returned from his appointed criminal rounds, he would get a little work done on them, always oiling only the squeakiest wheels. During his tenure he had watched with concern the stacks of civil files grow, rather than shrink. Somewhere in those fermenting manila stacks he could smell a breeding malpractice crisis of heroic proportions. But now, after listening to pompous Deputy D.A. Ivan Frank squirm like a gigged frog, even that didn't displease him much.

He glanced back to the string of phone messages, but nothing tickled his curiosity or unduly magnified the background hum of dread. Instead, he lugged the San Francisco telephone directory out of a bottom desk drawer. There was another call he had promised himself he would make first. He found a number for the United States Department of Agriculture and punched it in.

"Agriculture Department."

"Yes, say, I'm trying to reach a division of your department known by the letters, 'G. R. & D.' Can you connect me?"

"One moment, sir . . . I show nothing in San Francisco . . . Let me check the national directory . . . "

There was a sharp rap on the door.

"Come in," LeBaron said, covering the mouthpiece with his hand.

Wanda Jean slid around the edge of the door. She was an alluring girl with smooth inky skin, flat nose, full lips, a subdued Afro hairdo, and seduction in her eyes. "Mr. Collins wants t'see you when you' free, honey."

LeBaron nodded acknowledgement.

"Sir," the voice on the telephone said. "I have a number for the Genetic Research and Development Unit in Salt Lake City. Would you like that number?"

"Yes please."

She gave it to him, and he jotted it down. So *that* was it. Genetic Research and Development Unit. In Salt Lake City. Where the Mormons hang out. It still didn't make a whole lot of sense, but at least there was a semblance of internal coherence. And maybe Raccoona GeBobath wasn't as crazy as he had once supposed.

--2--

The chattering of an Hispanic female vibrated from the speaker telephone as LeBaron stuck his head in the open door. Cedric Collins motioned to the leather sofa and watched the younger man sit down, half listening to the saga of another two-bit crack dealer, his financial woes, and the grim unfairness to minorities of the judicial system. Collins had taken a call from the wife of a former client, and potential new client, who had just been busted and booked into Santa Rita jail. Collins had heard it all before.

"I *un'erstan'* all that, Mrs. Montoya," he interrupted. "But that really don't help t'solve *our* little problem, does it? If y'can come up with the retainer, we can do business. If y'can't, that's fine too. No hard feelin's. It's just that I won't be able to appear for Buster at the bail hearin' or take the case on. Y'un'erstan'?"

"How much you need by *Miercoles*?" asked the heavily accented voice.

"Like I told you before, and like I told Buster when he called, I gotta have a thousan' t'get goin' on this."

"*Aye cabrones!* A thousand dollars?"

"Thass right. He's in a heap o' trouble. Now I have t' be goin', Ms. Montoya."

"Okay. Okay. I get it for you. You take good care of heem. Okay?"

"As soon as y'bring in the money, we'll do business. You take care now, hear?" He jabbed the disconnect. The diffuse light through the floor-to-ceiling drapes covering the side wall was waning fast, making the swing arm lamp on his desk seem all the brighter. He pushed the light to one side and regarded LeBaron over the top of his reading glasses. "Wanda Jean says y'brought in over thirty-four hun'erd today."

LeBaron shrugged, trying not to appear too pleased with himself. "Everybody wanted to pay today. I wasn't doing anything different."

"Uh." Collins reached over and punched the intercom. "Wanda Jean, hold my calls."

"You got it, sugar."

"An' y'might jus's well tell those clients who' waiting out there t'go on home. Me'n LeBaron gonna be tied up on sum'pin' mighty impo'tant fo' th'rest o' the day."

"Sho'nuff, boss."

"I ain't in no mood t'see no more clients today," he muttered, leaning back in his big leather chair and staring up at the ceiling. "Did y'learn anything more about what we were talkin' 'bout this mornin'? What's the U.S. Attorney got t'do with this Freeman thing?"

"Not much," LeBaron replied. "I've been pretty busy. I did get a call from Ivan Frank. Wants to deal it as a misdemeanor, just like you said."

"Uh. Wha'd y'tell'im."

"Well, I can't get ahold of Freeman until tomorrow morning, so I hemmed and hawed a bit, pressed for a suspended sentence, and sort of left him hanging. He was kind of pissed off."

A big toothy grin fought its way out of Collins' mouth. "Maybe it'll do'im some good. Sounds like you' learnin', LeBaron. Yes sir, sounds like you' learnin'." He swung his chair back to the desk. "But we don't want y'gettin' tied up in this jury trial, so y'better not push it too far, hear? An' don' let this Freeman boy give y'any trouble. Remind'im he ain't paid *nothin'* on this yet. Tell'm he owes a thousand--no, make it fifteen hun'erd. An tell'm if he ain't got the cash, Brown's got work for'im. You tell him t'go see Brown right away, hear?"

"Sure. Does he know where--?"

"He knows where t'find Brown." Collins leaned back again and swivelled so he could watch LeBaron in the shadows. The light from the window was almost entirely gone now. "Now tell me what y'got so far on this Freeman thing, LeBaron. I'd kinda like t'give ol' Thompkins a call'n let'm know how hard we're workin' on it."

LeBaron related what Freeman had told him on Friday about the two bungling burglars with the ladder, green Department of Agriculture van, and purloined cartons. He explained how Freeman had walked right into the arms of the police.

Collins found the situation amusing. "I remember some of that. Don't seem like Rufus's much brighter than them ol' gov'ment boys he' laughin' at, does it?"

Then LeBaron summarized his conversation with Raccoona GeBobath, recounting her claimed loss of important computer records and her rabid aversion to Mormons. He avoided describing his ignoble departure.

"Y'think this Raccoona gal's involved in some sort o' hassle with the Mormons?"

"That's the impression I got. She didn't say what though."

"Don't blame'er none for dislikin' 'em. They're a bunch o' racists, y'know. Oh, they' been tonin' down their jive a bit last few years, lettin' a nigger'r two int' that fancy choir o' theirs, long's he ain't no *uppity* nigger, but down deep inside, they don' want nothin' t'do with the black man. D'jou know that? What else y'got?"

LeBaron described his just-completed telephone call to the Department of Agriculture.

"Salt Lake City, huh?"

"That's what she said."

"That kinda rings a bell, now that y'mention it. Seems t'me that's what ol' Tompkins tol' me, th'other day. U. S. Attorney had called him long distance out o' Salt Lake City." He was quiet for a while, thinking. Finally he asked, "Wha'd y'make of it all, LeBaron?"

"Well," he began slowly, fitting the pieces together as he spoke, "it sounds to me like this Genetic Research and Development Unit of the Department of Agriculture . . . which is located in Salt Lake City . . . sent some employees over here to steal Raccoona GeBobath's computer records. Which they did. *Why*, we really don't know. Probably so they could use them in . . . well, in whatever it is they do. Now they're afraid that if the Freeman case proceeds to trial, the agency's criminal involvement is gonna come out in testimony. As it probably would. Then they'd have a scandal on their hands, maybe an investigation, maybe even . . . well, a West Coast version of Watergate, I suppose." LeBaron pondered in silence for a moment. "What I can't understand, and what I'd like to know, is why the U. S. Attorney would be willing to help cover up the criminal acts of those two insignificant buffoons from this obscure little branch of the Agriculture Department?"

"They were prob'ly actin' under orders from above," Collins offered, "but that don't explain why the U. S. Attorney's stickin' *his* neck out." Collins leaned forward and shifted the desk lamp, but when he settled back, the glare was still in his eyes. Squinting, he pondered the enigma. "Must be class'fied information involved," he speculated at last. "Only way it makes sense t'me. They' tryin' t'protect national secrets."

LeBaron nodded. "That seems reasonable."

"Might pay t'get in on the ground floor o' this thing. Maybe they' into breedin' some secret new kind o' cash crop gonna revolutionize farmin'. Don' want the markets speculatin' on it. Somethin' like George Washington Carver used to do. Y'ever hear o' him, LeBaron? He was a black man did a lot o' that genetic breedin' right there in Alabama. My momma back in Mississippi used t'talk t' us 'bout ol' Carver like he's some kinda god. And Booker T. Washin'ton, too."

"I think there's something I forgot to mention. Those computer records they took didn't have anything to do with farming."

"No?" Collins asked, suspicious of new facts that might gum up his neat analysis. "What then?"

"Well, Raccoona told me they were genealogical records mostly, and--"

"What' you mean, 'genealogical records'?" Collins leaned forward, elbows on the desk, frowning.

"I don't know. Charts of ancestors. That's what the Mormons specialize in, isn't it?"

"Y'mean like who begat who and so forth? *Human* genealogy records?"

"I believe so. Sure."

"What're we talkin' 'bout here, LeBaron?" Collins scowled, ducking his head to see past the glare. "Are we talkin' 'bout some kind o' secret *human* genetic research and development goin' on? Somethin' the gov'ment's involved in with the *Mormons*? Is *that* what we're talkin' about here?"

"That's what it's beginning to sound like."

"I don't like the ring o' that at all." Reflexively he swiped at the desk lamp, and its arm recoiled and bounced to within inches of the desk top. The light became an indirect glow, and a dark cloud descended over Collins' face, transforming his scowl into a glower. He sank back into his chair and for a while stared off into nothingness, as if visualizing some enormity beyond words.

It seemed to LeBaron that his employer was trembling, but it may have been just an artifact of the quivering light. Concerned, he stood up. "Are you all right, Mr. Collins?"

Collins didn't seem to hear. His internal world had swallowed him completely.

LeBaron was seriously considering summoning Wanda Jean for help. But then he saw that Collins' eyes were on him.

"I seen a lynchin' when I was a boy," the older man murmured in a voice as weary as time and so soft it could barely be heard over the whoosh of the building's ventilation fans. "It was a warm ev'nin'. Kinda sultry like. Little Mississippi town I grew up in. Sometime 'round Fou'th o' July. Mamma come rushin' up from town shoutin', 'Get inside, get inside.' She herds all us chil'en into the back bedroom an' locks the door. But me'n my cousin . . . can't even recall which one it was . . . we couldn't o' been more'n five 'r six . . . well, we had t'see what was goin' on. So we climbs out that ol' bedroom window and crawls around under the front porch. Mamma would o' flailed our hides if she'd aknown.

"We could see well enough. More'n we really wanted to, I guess. Crowd of white-trash farmers, all drunk and laughin', down by the corner, had'em a nigger. Don't remember who it was or what he might o' done, but I can still see his bony black body. Naked he was. They done awful things to that boy 'fore they strung 'im up. An' jus' because his skin was black. Jus' like mine was, lyin' under that ol' musty porch, shiverin' like it was the dead o' winter."

The monologue stopped for a while. LeBaron wouldn't have been able to say for how long. He'd never seen his employer like this before, like some hidden *power* was shining through in the gloaming. LeBaron stood there transfixed.

After a while Collins continued in the same ominous tone. "Years later, when I first got int' the Army, an' I learned about high traject'ry weapons, I'd fin' myself layin' awake at night jus' dreamin' 'bout lobbin' shell after shell into that little cluster o' white trash. I couldn't seem t'get the idea outa my head." Again he paused.

"Now I ain't so sure. I've grown older. I don't really hate'm the way I used to. Not the way they hated that poor nigger boy. Y'see, those white folks really couldn't he'p doing what they were doing. They were jus' too stupid t'know any better. That was jus' the way they was brought up, thinkin' 'bout a black man like he was . . . jus' like he was a dog.

"When I first come home from the army wearin' my lieutenant bars, ol' sheriff, he grabs me'n says, 'Boy, you take them bars off! You' impersonatin' an officer.' I's nice as could be an' polite an' gives'im a big ol' happy nigger smile an' I tells'im I *earned* them bars. But he jus' couldn't get it through his head that they'd let a *nigger* be an officer. He lets me go anyway an' goes an' makes a call. Army gives'im confirmation o' my appointment. Later when he sees me again at the pool hall, he slaps me on the back with a big grin an' wants t'buy me a beer. He was proud 'nough t'spit that one o' *his niggers* had made officer. Like his favorite dog'd jus' won a show prize.

"No, I don't hate'im. He jus' didn't know any better." He paused again. "But that don't make'im any less dangerous."

LeBaron said nothing.

"There's more'n one way t'weed a garden, LeBaron," Collins went on, lifting off his glasses and rubbing his face with the palm of his hand. "Your average fella, he's gonna go out'n pull up them ol' weeds by hand. Or spray'em 'til they shrivel up'n die. But your clever fella, well, your clever fella, he' gonna figure out another way that don't cause such a fuss. He's gonna go out'n mess with the genes make those weeds be weeds an' those plants be plants, strengthenin' this'n here, weakenin' that'n there, until the ones he wants t'keep gonna *crowd* all the rest plumb out o' the garden." He slid his glasses back on and looked for LeBaron in the shadows. "Say, why don't y'switch on that overhead light there, LeBaron? I can't see ya."

LeBaron stepped over and clicked on the fluorescent lights, and the room was washed in institutional brilliance.

"D'you got any idea what I' been ramblin' on 'bout here?"

Blinking, LeBaron glanced around the office as if a spell had been lifted, at the familiar mahogany paneling, the books, the brass clock, at the tall drapes shut tight over a viewless window. "Yes, sir. I think I do." He eased himself down again on the edge of the leather sofa. "I think you're talking about genocide."

Collins nodded, smiling faintly. "You ain't so dumb, for a white boy."

"I don't know . . ." LeBaron rolled his eyes like he was being asked to believe in flying saucers. And yet, *something* funny was going on.

"*Sum'pin'* funny's going on," Collins confirmed. "Thass for damn sure."

"Oh my God!" LeBaron said, glancing at his watch. He jumped to his feet. "I didn't realize it'd gotten so late. I've got a meeting in an hour. It's way the hell over in Marin County. Tiburon. And I wanted to have time to go home and shower and change clothes first."

Collins didn't look particularly sympathetic.

"This meeting," LeBaron went on, trying to justify his abrupt departure, "it might lead to more information.   About this Genetic Research and Development Unit." He jabbered out what little he had learned from his brother and the conversation with the desk clerk at the Alpine Lodge in Mount Tehema City.

"Why didn't y'say somethin' sooner 'bout this?   What else y'holdin' back on me, LeBaron?"

"That's it. I swear. I'm not even sure this has anything to do with what we were just talking about." LeBaron rifled his memory for any other tidbits he might toss out in appeasement. "When I told my friend Sally that the clerk had given these government folks my name, she got sort of upset. Didn't want to meet at my apartment. She said my telephone might be tapped and someone might try to follow me." He attempted a derisive chuckle, but it turned into a dry cough.

Collins was not amused.

"What do you think?" LeBaron asked. "They wouldn't really follow me around, would they?"

"Might be. If the FBI's involved. I've seen'em do the damnedest things t'make a case against a coupla small drug dealers couldn't even speak English. Uh. S'possible. I'd be careful. So how' you plannin' t'keep'em off your trail?"

"Well, I don't know. I haven't given it too much thought.   I'll sort of drive around in the natural scouring action of rush hour traffic, maybe even take a wrong exit or two off the freeway. Kind of play it by ear."

"Won't do y'no good, if the FBI's involved. They'll of planted a transponder on your car. What y'drivin'?"

"My old Ford station wagon."

"Where' y'parked?"

"In the public lot. Across the street."

"Uh." Collins rummaged through a desk drawer. "Leave it there, if y'want my advice. An' don't try goin' home first. Here." He tossed on the desk a set of car keys chained to a worn rabbit's foot.

LeBaron picked them up. "What's this?"

"Keys t'Muggin's Continental."

"Herbert Muggins? The one you had me do the appeal brief for?"

"Same one. He won't be needin' no fancy car for some time o'er in Folsom Prison. Ten t' fifteen years, if m'memory serves me. That ol' rabbit's foot sure didn't do'em much good, did it?" Collins stood up slowly. "Besides, he' gonna give me that car t'settle his account, soon's we can get the registration straightened out. It's parked over at Brown's shop. Been keepin' it out o' sight there." He slipped on his top coat. "C'mon, I'll give y' a lift over. I'm parked down'n the basement."

"What's wrong with the registration?"

Collins lifted his stingy brim off the top of the rack and admired it. "Don' rightly know yet. Car's got Texas plates. Expired. But somethin' don' check out, accordin' to the Texas DMV records. Plates appear t've been stolen off a '86 Datsun. I'm still workin' on it."

CHAPTER NINE

Monday evening

--1--

It wasn't where it was supposed to be. Three times she drove slowly past the harbor restaurant district, but she couldn't find the Bayside Bistro. She felt rumpled, irritable, dirty, and dog tired, and her spirit tottered on the brink of complete exhaustion. Her neck still ached from the last two nights' cruel attempts to sleep in the car, a misguided stratagem to conserve her dwindling assets. The urge was strong to collapse onto the steering wheel for a good long self-indulgent cry, but she fought it off.

Frustrated, she found a parking space on a dark side street and walked back to Tiburon's main drag searching everywhere, but the Bayside Bistro simply didn't exist anymore. Using dead reckoning and intuition, she finally arrived at the spot where it should have been. In its place was Captain Bluff's Saltwater Dock Eatery, a slick oak-trimmed yuppie impersonation of the vanished rough-hewn grotto once favored by the real deepwater fisherman.

She eyed the unbroken flow of tourist traffic creeping past. Maybe this hadn't been such a hot idea. What would Jed do when he couldn't find the damned Bayside Bistro? Would he recognize the change? Maybe she should wait for him on the street rather than going on inside. A passing pickup truck squealed its tires, and a drunken high school bonehead hanging out the passenger window hooted something vaguely obscene at her, so she turned and pushed through Captain Bluff's ornate cut glass front doors.

Sarah walked through the stuffy restaurant and found a table out on the edge of the dock where she could glimpse the passing traffic. Not that she knew what Jed would be driving. But at least it gave her something to do. She could also keep an eye out for a particular green government van. The evening was still and ominously balmy. The afternoon storm had ended, leaving the world freshly washed and the air incredibly clear, but another, bigger storm was imminent. Out across the black churning bay San Francisco glittered hypnotically, a fairy city of jewels strewn over the peninsula hills and crowned with geometric castles of sparkling lights which shimmered in the silent water beneath low brooding clouds.

By seven-fifteen she was beginning to worry seriously. The only vehicle she recognized passing more than once was a gaudy cherry-red Continental with flocked roof, tinted windows, and Texas plates that looked like the roving front office for some big-money pimp. But no sign of Jed LeBaron. Perhaps he had *found* the Bayside Bistro *somewhere else* and was waiting for her there. *Stop it, Sarah!* she told herself. Or maybe he was in custody, being grilled by the authorities for a clue to her whereabouts. *Enough! He'll be here. Give him time.*

At seven-thirty she decided to go back outside and see if she could catch him wandering around among unfamiliar storefronts. She drained off her glass of Chablis and stood up unsteadily, fishing for a tip in her coin purse.

"Sarah?"

Her head jerked up. Approaching was a tall, well-built man in a rusty corduroy business suit, a little worn and in need of pressing. His shirt collar and tie had been pulled open, and at first he looked a little dazed. Then he grinned, and those smiling pale blue eyes seemed to burn deep into her, thawing something mislaid there long ago. How could she ever have forgotten those incredible icy-blue eyes!

--2--

All the way out of downtown Oakland, around Berkeley on the freeway, through the maze of Richmond's circuitous streets, and over the loping serpent of the San Rafael Bridge, LeBaron had been haunted by the terrible specter of systematic genocide his employer had conjured out of a dusty Mississippi grave. He wanted to convince himself that it could never happen here in America in this day and age, but his arguments lacked conviction. Why, after all, should the United States government be involved with the Mormons in a *secret* research and development project involving human genetics? The very fact of the *secrecy* elevated mere curiosity to giddy heights of dreadful suspicion.

So preoccupied were his thoughts that he barely noticed the extravagantly appointed vehicle he piloted, with its power steering, power brakes, power windows, power door locks, power six-way tilt seat, power rear-view mirrors, and power radio antenna, its lush velour seats, a four-thousand dollar stereo system, and more raw horsepower under the cherry-red flocked hood than a good Christian should be allowed to command. If LeBaron's sole purpose had been to evade detection, then he had succeeded handily by ensconcing himself in a carriage so ultra-gaudy that every decent citizen had to look away as he drove past.

He had missed the Tiburon turnoff and looped back from the next freeway exchange. Absentmindedly he drove up and down the clogged thoroughfare trying to remember precisely which restaurant had been the site of his graduation celebration so many years ago. He couldn't remember the name of the place, but in time he homed in on Captain Bluff's Saltwater Dock Eatery, down by the water, and found a parking lot nearby. In a fog of speculation, supposition, refutation, and consternation he searched through the indoor restaurant to no avail. He stepped out onto the dock, only marginally conscious of where he was.

But when flaxen-haired Sarah Brubaker glanced up from beside a corner table overlooking the velvet waters of the San Francisco Bay and smiled, LeBaron's entire speculative edifice came crashing into the present like collapsing floors of a masonry high-rise pancaking down in a violent Mexico City earthquake. Like a sleepwalker splashed with cold water, he shivered, cocked his head, then strode over to her, grinning. He took her hand.

"It's wonderful to see you," she said. "I was just going to go outside to see if you were having trouble finding the place. Everything's changed so much."

"Sally, let me look at you." He held her at arm's length. She was still as slim and athletic as ever, and beneath the tweed skirt of her neat business suit, now a little rumpled from a week's uninterrupted wear, LeBaron could tell she still had those incredible cheerleader legs. She had changed, yet remained the same, had become a magic lantern's projection of maturity on youth. Her nose no longer turned up in quite the pert way it once had, and her cheeks had settled into a more dignified mold. With age her beauty had ripened. But her eyes! Tired and dark, almost sunken, her eyes blazed beneath a deep shadow of weariness and disquiet.

Under the weight of his gaze, she threw her hair back with a familiar toss of her head. "Well?"

"Sally, you look *great*!"

"So do you, Jeddy." Blushing, she sat and restrung her purse over the back of her chair. "You've grown up."

"Not really. Just on the outside." He settled into the chair next to her, his back to the bay. "Jesus, Sally, how long has it been, anyway? Eight years?"

"More like ten, I think."

He nodded. "Remember the last time we were here . . .?" The road of remembrance was bittersweet and irresistible, and down it they chased like wondrous children. Vince was a common denominator in every recollection, always the central figure. When the waiter appeared, they glanced at the menus and ordered, the interruption an insignificant trifle quickly dispatched. On impulse, LeBaron added a bottle of Gewurtztraminer to the tab. The tangy wine lubricated their discourse, and memory lane became a throughway, rushing irresistibly out of the quaint past toward the teeming present. LeBaron told his story of law school, two years spent in Mexico, and the highs and lows of part-time law practice.

And she told hers. When he last knew her, she had been on a pre-med track as an undergraduate. She had gone on to get her doctorate from the University of California in molecular biology. Her dissertation had been on interactive biocybernetics. "Cybernetics," she explained, "is a comparative study. On the one hand is the automatic control system formed by the nervous system and brain. On the other is the automatic control system formed by mechanical-electrical communications systems."

"Like comparing humans with robots?" He didn't want her to lose him in high-tech lingo.

"Sort of. As long as you include in the category of 'robots' everything artificial which has a feedback loop and automatic control."

"Like what, for instance?"

"Oh, thousands of things. Like computers, manufacturing plants, automobile engines, telephone systems."

"I've read a little about 'artificial intelligence'. Is this the same thing?"

"They're related. AI deals with software, computer programming. My study was system oriented. My thesis involved the interaction between the two kinds of systems, with emphasis on the biological."

"Interaction?"

"Yes. I'll give you an example." She considered for a moment, trying to wipe the fatigue from her mind. "A boy plays a video game. There's interaction between the two systems, the biological system of the boy, and the electronic system of the game. You see? The *total* feedback loop involves both systems . . . both the artificial and the biological."

"Okay. I think I get the picture. Is there any demand for this type of expertise?"

"Oh yes. Lots. I went to work for CyberGenetics Corporation in Livermore even before I'd finished my thesis."

LeBaron took a mouthful and chewed for a while. "What sort of work did you do there?"

"Well, I started out in the division that builds control systems for artificial limbs. CGC was working with the same interactive systems I'd studied in my dissertation, with some of the interfaces shifted."

"Hold it. What do you mean by 'interfaces shifted'?"

"Well . . . like the boy and the video game. Imagine that he no longer has a hand to grip the joy stick. So the motor nerves in his arm are connected directly to the computer input like an extended artificial limb."

"Okay."

"And then imagine the video display terminal is removed, and the output is connected directly to the boy's optic nerve."

"Wow. How far can you go with this?"

"I don't know." She paused to sip some wine. "The limits aren't yet defined. That was one of the goals of the prosthesis project. My job involved analysis of the interface between the biological and the artificial from the perspective of molecular biology. What's actually happening? What *needs* to happen to facilitate the interface?" A radiance animated her smile.

"You're really excited about your work, aren't you?"

"I guess I am." She frowned. "But are you sure you really want to hear all this, Jeddy?"

"Yes. Sure. I find it fascinating. Go on."

"Anyway, since I guess I'm consulting you professionally, you may want to start the meter running."

LeBaron waived away the suggestion. "Vince never mentioned any of this to me. Did he know all the weird stuff you were doing?"

Her frown deepened into a scowl. "I tried to explain it to him," she said wearily, "but he didn't want to listen." She grew even more somber, poking at the crab ciappino which had materialized and half-disappeared on a plate before her. "What's happened to him, Jeddy? What made him drop out like that? He seemed so . . . *distant* when I talked to him."

"He hasn't changed as much as you might think. Vince is Vince is Vince. When he sets him mind on something, he'll damn well carry it through to the end. You know that better than I do. I don't know, though." LeBaron shook his head. "This time I think he's having some second thoughts about this Zen Buddhism nonsense." He stopped probing for shrimp among the leaves of lettuce and curls of carrot, set down his fork, and looked into her eyes. "I think it really hurt him deeply to have to turn you down, Sally."

"Good. I hope it did. Damn him! I just wanted him to . . . " She stopped and bit her lip, and her eyes were suddenly wet and overflowing. She buried her face in her napkin. Her shoulders shook with spasmodic sobs.

Helplessly LeBaron reached out and stroked her hair as if comforting a frightened child. She abandoned herself to quiet sobbing. Slowly he stood and moved around behind her chair. His hands found the tense flesh of her shoulders and neck and began gently kneading. It occurred to him that he had never once been alone with her before. "I'll help you in any way I can, Sally."

Sarah's shoulders relaxed under his gentle fingers and soon ceased heaving. The tears ran dry. Sniffling, she fumbled for a Kleenex and blew her nose. The crisis had passed. She looked up and covered one of his hands with hers. "I'm sorry, Jeddy. I've just been . . . things have gotten out of hand . . . I'm so exhausted . . . I don't really understand what's been going on. I haven't even been able to go home for a week."

A swarthy waiter in a white apron approached the table. "Is there anything wrong, sir?"

"No. No." LeBaron returned woodenly to his chair. "Everything's fine."

"May I take your plates?"

"Ah . . . sure. I'm done."

Sarah nodded.

LeBaron tried to pour her some wine, but the bottle was empty.

"May I bring you another bottle, sir?" The waiter's fawning tone was irritating.

LeBaron glanced at Sarah. "No. No, I think that'll be all, thank you. The check, please." When the waiter was gone, LeBaron leaned over the empty table. "Why haven't you been able to go home? Tell me about it."

She snuffled again and dabbed at her eyes with the napkin. "Remember the day I telephoned you? The first time? Asking about Vince?"

"Sure."

"That must've been last . . ."

"Thursday morning."

"Yes. Thursday." Snuffle. "I was phoning from a motel in Livermore. When I got home from work the night before, Wednesday night, someone had gone through my whole apartment." Snuffle. "They ransacked everything."

"Whoa!"

"They went through every drawer and cupboard just tossing my things on the floor."

"Did you report it to the police?"

"No. I think it may have *been* the police. It wasn't thieves." She glanced around at the other tables on the dock. "Were you careful coming over here? Just in case you were being followed?"

"You betcha," he grinned and explained how Collins had loaned him Muggins' gaudy automobile for the trip over.

Sarah smiled wearily. "I saw you driving past. It looked like some kind of a Pimp-Mobile."

LeBaron laughed.

She drew a thick manila folder out of her handbag and laid it on the table. "I'm sure they were looking for this. They didn't find it because I had it with me. But I decided I couldn't stay there. I was too . . . vulnerable. I had to stay away until I could get some help. I haven't been home since."

LeBaron eyed the manila envelope, picked it up, and turned it over in his hands. It had been taped, opened, and retaped. It bore no writing. "Who?"

"Agents from the Department of Agriculture, I think."

"Ah." He leaned back. "The Genetic Research and Development folks out of Salt Lake City, perhaps?"

"Yes. Or maybe the FBI."

"Whoa!" He dropped the envelope back on the table. "What've you got there?"

Sarah suddenly snatched the envelope and shoved it back into her purse. A waiter approached with the check. He was pale-skinned and effete and placed the tray awkwardly on the corner of the table. When he was gone, she breathed, "That wasn't the same waiter who took our order, was it?"

LeBaron wasn't sure. He didn't think so. He shook his head.

"Where's *our* waiter?"

He glanced around, shrugged. "Why? Do you think this guy's an FBI agent?" He had to suppress a grin.

"Oh, I don't know," she sighed. "Sounds pretty crazy, doesn't it. I'm probably just paranoid. I'm so tired." She drew a deep breath, then pulled the envelope out of her handbag again. "These are classified government reports. I made one set of photocopies and left them with Vince. I've kept the originals."

"Odd. Vince didn't say anything about them to me."

"He didn't?" Sarah considered for a moment. "When did you see him?"

"After you did."

"And he didn't pass the copies along to you?"

"Nope."

"He didn't even mention them?"

"Not a word."

Sarah snorted bitterly. Then she frowned. "I wonder. Maybe it means he plans to look at them after all."

"Maybe. What's in them? And how did you get them? Is this something you can talk to me about? I don't have any federal security clearance, you know."

"Neither do I. Not for these anyway." She inserted the envelope into her handbag and nervously glanced around again. "We should go somewhere more private before we really get into this, don't you think?"

"Sure," LeBaron nodded. "Where?"

"I have a room. I slept in the car the past two nights, but I just couldn't do it again. I've got to get cleaned up. So I reserved a room at the Wayfarer Inn for tonight, up by the freeway exchange. You probably passed it on the way in." She sighed and rolled her head wearily. "I've been in a different motel every night now. Or else in my car. I made the mistake of staying two nights at the same place in Mount Tehema, and they managed to find me. It has to have been through my Visa card. There's no other way."

LeBaron thought about it. "Banks are under federal regulation. No one else would have that kind of access to your credit card information. You may be right about the FBI."

She nodded grimly. "They also managed to tie up my Visa accounts, so my credit card's no good anymore. I tried to make a cash withdrawal yesterday and the machine kept my card."

"What're you doing for money?"

"Well, the motel still took my Mastercharge card. And I've got a little cash left from my last paycheck."

"You should really stop using your credit cards. It's too risky. Look, Sally, I've got some money, and I'd like to help out if I can."

"No, Jeddy. That would be asking too much."

"No, really, it's extra money. I came into it a coupla years ago, and it's time I spent a little of it. A gratuity from some friends in Mexico, believe it or not. Someday I'll tell you all about it, if you like. This would be a loan to carry you over until things get straightened out. Okay?"

She dropped her chin, and for a moment LeBaron thought she was going to cry again. "I'm so tired I can't really think straight anymore. Let me consider it. I appreciate the thought." She looked up into his eyes. "But what I'd really like for you to do is go over all this with me"--she tweaked the end of the envelope sticking out of her purse--"if you've got the time. I want to know if you think I'm out of my mind or what. Will you meet me up at the Wayfarer, Jeddy? Room 385. Have you got the time?"

"Sure. No problem. I'll get this." He snatched the bill off the little plastic tray.

"No, Jeddy, let me--"

"Absolutely not." He quickly wrote out a check.

--3--

It took LeBaron longer than he had planned. The attendant at the parking garage, a thin, elderly black man with a prominent gold tooth and a limp, demanded a history and complete tour of the Pimp-Mobile. He had never, he insisted, set eyes on a finer automobile, and wondered if LeBaron would consider parting with it. When LeBaron had at last extricated his vehicle, he had trouble locating an automatic teller machine which recognized his credit cards. He ultimately found two, withdrew the daily maximum from each, and stuffed a wad of thirty twenty-dollar bills into his front pants pocket. And of course he had to buy a bottle of wine. *Of course?* LeBaron's conscience raised annoying questions as he picked through the limited selection in the cooler case of an all-night mini mart. *Had he forgotten that Rufus Freeman's trial started early tomorrow morning? What was he trying to do, get Sally drunk? Just what were his intentions with respect to his trusting old friend Sally, anyway?* He had to vigorously suppress any sane attempt to consider the ramifications of this particular purchase. At last he settled on a chilled bottle of Blue Nun. By the time he located Sally's door on the windy third floor of the Wayfarer Inn, the better part of an hour had evaporated into the cold night air. He rapped lightly and waited, shivering.

"Yes? Who is it?"

"It's me, Jeddy."

The bolt clicked, and the door opened a crack. "Jeddy! What in heaven's name took you so long?" Sarah had showered and changed into a pale yellow terry robe she had purchased earlier that day. Her hair was wrapped in a white towel. "Come on in. Did you run into some sort of trouble?"

"No, nothing like that." LeBaron stepped into the sultry room. "I had to run a couple of errands. I stopped at the bank. Sorry I took so long." Sheepishly he stuck out the bottle. "Here's some wine."

"Oh, Jeddy, you shouldn't have. I'm not sure if I can drink any more. I'm so exhausted. I almost fell asleep just now drying my hair . . . except I was so worried about what might have happened to you."

"I'm really sorry," he reiterated. "I should have been more thoughtful."

LeBaron backed up to the electric wall heater, rubbing his frozen hands behind him, and gazed around the accommodations. Sarah had rolled the matching brown naugahyde armchairs up to a small round table at the far end of the long room. The table sat in the shielded circle of pool-hall light from a swag lamp which hung low in front of thick floral-pattern drapes drawn tightly closed. On the table lay the forbidden envelope, Sarah's open notebook, and a pen. Two double beds with floral bedspreads matching the drapes crowded the carpeted room. Between them was a nightstand with a tall glowing lamp, an ashtray, a book of matches, and a card advertising Mama's Pancake and Waffle House. A mirrored sink alcove stood around the corner behind him outside a small, antiseptic bathroom. Behind the door an exhaust fan purred dully. The walls sported several impressionist prints, variations on the ubiquitous theme of a sparkling city reflected in a body of water. It could have been San Francisco, or equally well New York, New Orleans, Detroit, or Miami. In fact, motel rooms identical to this one could have been, and probably were, located in every port city across the

United States.

Sarah set the wine bottle in the alcove next to the sink and turned to him solemnly. "I don't have a corkscrew."

LeBaron shrugged. "Neither do I." He glanced at his wrist watch. "I guess it's just as well."

"Well . . . thank you for the wine anyway. What time is it?"

"After ten."

"That late?" She yawned. "No wonder I'm so tired." Peeling the towel away, she stepped over beside him, bent, and splayed her glistening hair in the hot draft from the heater. "Go ahead and look through that envelope on the table over there. My hair's almost dry."

With difficulty LeBaron tore his eyes away from her, shuffled over to the little table, and sat down. Stifling a yawn, he focussed with effort on the envelope in front of him. The tape had been broken for a second time. He lifted the flap and pulled out a bundle of once-folded papers. They appeared to be a series of ten or twelve typed reports. The cover sheet of each was a standardized form bearing Department of Agriculture letterhead. Together they totaled maybe fifty single-sided, single-spaced pages. On the front of each report was stamped in bold red letters at the top, "TOP SECRET--EYES ONLY." He cleared his throat. "You're sure it's all right for me to look at these."

"Sure. Well . . . I don't know. No. It's probably a federal crime, actually." She finished drying her hair and folded the towel. "If you don't want to get involved in this, I'll understand, Jeddy. This may lead to a whole lot of trouble."

LeBaron nodded. "You've read them?"

"Yes, I have."

Again he nodded. "Where'd you get them, anyway?"

"Have you ever heard of Bernard Finebridge?"

"The name sounds familiar. Should I have?"

"If you read the newspapers."

LeBaron made a stab, knowing it was wrong. "Did he play defensive end for Green Bay a few years ago?"

Sarah laughed. "Not the sports page, silly. The front page."

"Uh. I didn't think so." He looked at the top report. At the bottom was the signature of Bernard Finebridge.

Sarah pulled up the chair beside him and began brushing her golden hair. The long, measured strokes, first inside, then outside, then inside again, fascinated him. LeBaron felt the poignant certainty of having watched her do this before, long ago and half forgotten. It seemed like maybe a hundred years ago he had first been admitted to this secret feminine ceremony of such incredible significance. Contentedly he could have watched Sarah Brubaker brush her silken hair like that for the rest of eternity.

"What's wrong?" she asked suddenly.

"What? Nothing." LeBaron looked down at the pages in his hands and flushed a deep red. "Why do you ask?"

"The way you were looking at me." She smiled. "Oh, Jeddy, it's really good to see you."

Flustered, LeBaron sought the lost thread of conversation. "So tell me . . . who is this . . . Bernard Fernbridge?"

"*Fine*bridge. Dr. Finebridge was probably the main reason I went to work for CGC."

"What's 'CGC' again?"

"CyberGenetic Corporation. He was my thesis advisor at the university and was doing some contracting work with CGC on a part-time basis. Later he went on sabbatical to work there full time. He's generally considered to be the world's leading expert on biotics, and--"

"Hold it. What's 'biotics'?"

"That's the popular term for interactive biocybernetics."

LeBaron's puzzled look persisted.

"You remember, what I was telling you about earlier? At the restaurant?"

"Ah, you mean . . . uh . . . comparing humans with robots?"

"That's it . . . well . . . sort of. Biotics emphasizes the integration of the natural system into the artificial. The term was coined from an Arthur C. Clarke novel, I'm told. I haven't read it, myself. Anyway, I worked under Dr. Finebridge, primarily on the prosthesis projects. We became very close, actually. He's such a wonderful man. I was also helping him on *this* project at the beginning." She pointed to the reports in LeBaron's hands. "Later, when the Department of Agriculture stepped in, this work became classified. I didn't have the proper clearance, so I had to stop. That's about the time the project was given the security name 'Divine Wind.'" She pointed to the words typed into the project-name box at the top of the page.

LeBaron leafed through the reports. They all had "Divine Wind" typed into the project-name box. "What does it mean?"

"I don't know." She laid her brush on the table and shook out her hair, then drew up her bare feet and settled back into the chair yawning, her arms cradling her legs. "He never told me that."

"Why didn't you apply for a clearance?"

"I did. They wouldn't give it to me."

"Oh? Why not?"

"I'm not really sure. I think maybe because I was arrested once at a sit-in protesting the Viet Nam war. Years ago at Berkeley."

He smiled. "I remember."

"It seems so stupid, but I can't think of anything else. I'm pretty sure the Defense Department is involved in Divine Wind, but I can't be certain. No one would tell me anything. Just 'clearance denied.' Period."

"And this project was under the auspices of the Genetic Research and Development agency?"

"Yes." She reached over and tapped the agency box, where "G.R.&D." was neatly typed.

LeBaron flipped through the reports. They were all the same. "So. Why did Dr. Finebridge give you copies of these secret government reports when you didn't have the proper clearance? Did he happen to say?"

"Of course. He didn't like what was going on in this project."

"Like what?"

"Well, he never said specifically. He just told me to hold on to these reports for him, but that if something happened to him, to look at them."

"And do what?"

"He didn't say. I think he trusted me to reach my own conclusions."

"Right." LeBaron still avoided reading the actual text of the report in his hands. "And, I take it, something *did* happen to him?"

"Yes." Sarah shivered. "Are you at all cold?"

"No. I was just starting to get a little warm, actually. What happened to him?"

"He seemed increasingly troubled by the work he was doing. He had to be gone a lot of the time to Salt Lake City. The last time I heard from him was about two weeks ago. Something was definitely wrong. He wanted to give me something else. I have no idea what. Something he considered very important, though. We set up a meeting for lunch the following day, but he never showed up. I haven't heard a word from him since. I can't reach him at any of the usual numbers. He just disappeared without a trace."

"Where had he phoned from? That last time."

"I don't know."

"Huh. You called the police?"

"Yes. They came out and took a report. They interviewed me and everyone else at the laboratory. An FBI agent was with them the whole time."

"What did he have to say about it?"

"Nothing. Nothing at all."

"What were the results? Were you able to find out?"

"Oh, yes. I pestered the police until they told me. Last I heard, the file's been officially closed. There was some reference or other to no evidence of foul play." Again she shivered. "Jeddy, I think the FBI put a lid on this. Nobody's doing anything. I think it's some sort of cover-up."

LeBaron weighed the documents thoughtfully. "Does Finebridge have a family? A wife?"

"No. He's divorced. No children." She shook her heard forlornly. "There's no one to even care what happened to him."

LeBaron stood up, peeled off his jacket, and tossed it on the bed behind him. "Except for you." He sat down, rolled up his sleeves, and began reading.

The first report was considerably longer than any of the others. It's apparent function was to recapitulate the project background and status at the time it was classified by the government. Divine Wind brought together the fruits of research from divergent fields which had already ripened in various university laboratories across the country and abroad.

The primary work began several years earlier at MIT, where researchers had managed to rewire the brains of newborn ferrets, rerouting retinal neurons so the data went to the animal's auditory cortex, rather than to the visual cortex of the brain. The researchers studied the response patterns of cells in the auditory cortex while showing the animals various visual clues. Some of the cells in the auditory cortex "transformed" the raw data into a type of patterned response to stimuli which had been previously identified only in the visual cortex. The researchers interpreted the experiments to mean that there is nothing intrinsic about the auditory cortex that makes it auditory. The visual information is quite different in content from the auditory information usually processed there. Yet the cortical tissue seemed to organize the information similarly. Whatever detailed differences exist among visual, auditory, and other operations are learned differences, the result of specific neural wiring patterns somehow programmed by early sensory inputs. It depends on the type of input it gets early in life.

"This is incredible," LeBaron muttered.

"What?" Sarah opened her eyes and yawned. "Sorry. I think I almost dozed off."

"I was just saying, this is incredible."

"What's that?"

"This business about rewiring a ferret brain to hear visual information."

"Oh, yes. Fascinating." Again she yawned. She seemed to have trouble keeping her eyes open. "We reproduced the MIT experiments at Livermore. I did some of that work."

"The newborn brain is just like a computer, isn't it? It has to be programmed."

"I guess you could say that." Sarah fidgeted, unable to find a comfortable upright position. "But the brain-computer is designed to program itself, depending on the type of input it receives. It presorts the raw sensory data so that it becomes usable or meaningful information."

LeBaron nodded, waiting for her to go on.

"Jeddy, if it's all right with you, I'm going to lie down for a few minutes. I'm so cold. And I'm really not feeling very well."

"Sure. Anything I can do?"

"No." She stood up unsteadily. "It's just good to have you here." She smiled wanly, then peeled back the covers of the bed behind her, crawled in, robe and all, and pulled the blankets up to her neck. "You can still ask me questions if you want to. I'm not planning to actually sleep."

LeBaron went back to the first report and waded in. The technical jargon made the going slow. He didn't expect to fully understand everything he was reading, but he wanted to pick up the general drift of things. And look for anomalies. Clues to the disappearance of Dr. Finebridge.

Near the end of the first report, Dr. Finebridge outlined some general goals of the project. He proposed the integration of the ferret brain cortex into a biotic computer system. The objective was to overcome an obstacle that computer designers for years have found insurmountable. Computers can't see. They can't recognize faces. They can't understand the meaning of sentences, except in an incredibly literal and idiotic sense. In the biological system, the raw data is first "transformed" in the brain cortex into comprehensible information. Only then can it be processed meaningfully. And it appeared that any part of the cortex could transform the raw data, if it were trained at an early enough stage. Such was the nature of the cortex itself. Rather than attempting to imitate the cortical function with computer programs, as others had unsuccessfully tried, Dr. Finebridge proposed the incorporation of actual brain cortex into the feedback loop of the artificial mechanical-electrical system.

"Wow." LeBaron yawned and laid down the first report. "So he wanted to build a robot with a ferret brain, huh? Sort of like the Six-Million Dollar Ferret, huh?"

She didn't answer.

"Or maybe RoboFerret?"

Silence.

He stood up and stretched, then shuffled over to her bed. Sarah was sound asleep. LeBaron gazed down on the childlike innocence of her countenance, her clean hair gleaming beside her on the pillow like a bright new penny, the fruitful curve of her jaw, her brow, her neck, and his heart was full to bursting. Silently he pulled the covers up over her shoulders, reached over, and switched off the bedside lamp.

In the circular island of brightness surrounding the little table, LeBaron rubbed his eyes. It was already after midnight, and he hadn't gotten through a quarter of the pages. He sat, sighed, and doggedly picked up the second report.

Now the going really got tough. The first report was like a child's book compared to the second. Dr. Finebridge's emphasis was on the genetic and biochemical basis for automatic control systems, and the language grew increasingly technical. Complex mathematical formulae began to appear with increasing regularity. Ignoring the details, LeBaron fought to comprehend the general drift of the project. A long hard day, the late hour, and a half bottle of wine with dinner didn't help.

Dr. Finebridge's first experiments were patterned after the ones at MIT, using newborn ferrets. The design of the interface between the electrical-mechanical input and the biological cortex was intricately described on the molecular level and documented. Dr. Finebridge tried modifying the ferret brains slightly, using genetic engineering techniques, to accept the input. This allowed terminals to be *grown* into the cortex. Once the data was inputted, the cortex did the rest. The procedure showed promise, if certain obstacles could be overcome.

The scientist found he was spending too much time and effort keeping the tissue and its essential supporting structures alive. At first he kept the entire animal alive and sedated, but the sedative affected the function of the cortical tissue. So he tried removing the ferret's brain and keeping it alive separately, but without success.

Then a real breakthrough came. Building on work with cortical neuronal stem cells recently completed at Johns Hopkins University School of Medicine, Dr. Finebridge found he could scientifically control brain maturation in the ferret embryo. By genetically altering the brain development process, he and his colleagues began to grow ferret cortical tissue to specification *in vitro* in the laboratory and sustain the tissue by artificial means. They developed an artificial support system patterned after the heart-lung machine. Since the ferret brain is so integral an organ, they achieved success only by growing and sustaining the entire brain, brain stem, and spinal column, though only a portion of the cortex was utilized.

That was almost two years ago, LeBaron noted, yawning.

The next major obstacle surfaced halfway through the third report. Unfortunately, the usable portion of cortex in the ferret brain was found to be too small for most practical applications. While the experiments seemed to be yielding the desired results, the payoff was minimal.

The next paragraphs, comparing the cortical tissue of ferrets with that of the green monkey, LeBaron reread three times without understanding. He sat back and glanced at his watch in despair. It was two o'clock in the morning, and he was no longer making any progress. His comprehension and attention span had both fallen to near zero. Yet he was only halfway through the reports.

Maybe if he were to lie down and close his eyes for a few minutes, he would be able to return to the task refreshed. Stiffly he lumbered over and sat on the bed next to Sarah's. For a reverent moment he observed her tranquil breathing. Then with a half-smile on his lips he lay back on the pillow and fell asleep.

CHAPTER TEN

Tuesday morning

--1--

The portly black man in turquoise silk pajamas pulled back the thick velour drapes and gazed out. His expression was wan and drawn. A steady rain spattered on the asphalt below in the streetlight's glare, driven in sheets by a cold north wind which howled in the eaves of his hilltop manor. Dawn had not yet begun to lighten the low, suffocating clouds. Despite the room's warmth behind the triple-glazed picture window, a cold shiver crawled up his spine.

Sleep had evaded Cedrick P. Collins, Esq., for most of the night. When it came at last, it brought with it *that dream* again. He was crouched in the cobwebs and dust beneath that rotting Mississippi porch. Through the slats he watched those grisly white-trash farmers joking and laughing and spitting tobacco in the tight circle around the dangling black corpse which still twitched and jerked as if on an electric wire. Horribly he knew what was about to happen, but he had no way of averting it. Slowly one skull-faced man, the same man always, turned his head and fixed him with blazing, beady rat eyes. One after another they each turned toward him, impaling him with a dozen pairs of terrible gleaming eyes sunken into grinning white skulls. Scrambling backwards in the dirt, he tried to get away, but couldn't seem to put any distance between himself and those porch slats. So he flipped over and frantically began to crawl. The ground had become loose sand, and he made no progress. He scratched and clawed at the sand. From somewhere nearby his cousin was hollering, "Run, nigger, *run!*" Then the porch was gone, and he was flailing helplessly in a bone dry desert. He couldn't turn his head to look behind, but he knew they were closing in, stalking him with those hideous skull grins dripping sour tobacco juice. He tried to scream, but his throat was locked. The air shivered over the fine hairs on the scruff of his neck as the first bony claw reached out to jerk him upward into the cold circle of grinning tobacco-stained maws, another scrawny naked pickaninny for their ghoulish amusement. In the distance he could hear his Mamma wailing.

He awoke in a sweat and sat for awhile on the edge of the bed trying to orient himself, waiting for his heart to subside. *Had he actually screamed?* No, he didn't think so. Beatrice still slept quietly. He looked at the clock. It was still too early for work. Too terrified to try sleeping again, he changed into dry pajamas and stood at the window, reflecting on things he hadn't considered for years.

The world seemed out of balance in the lonely predawn darkness. He couldn't get his bearings. He seemed to stand outside himself, judging with a set of standards long forgotten, and the judgments were mortifying. So much time had been squandered. So much energy had been wasted on things of no consequence. His errors all seemed so clear to him now. Some forgotten strand of high purpose which linked him now with his earliest roots had been abruptly drawn taut, pinching off the flabby bag of attainments which constituted his adult life, squeezing it like a boil until it erupted, spewing forth all the fine automobiles and slick cellular telephones, laptop computers, hi-fi equipment, and VCR's, the fancy suits, glittering jewelry, and feigned status, the entire contents of his hilltop house and downtown suite of offices, the entire contents of his smug pharisaical life, into the raw winds of greed.

As if to touch a more benign reality, he ran his fingers nervously through the neatly trimmed graying stubble haloing his shining pate. How long since he had had *that dream*? he wondered. Surely not since long before he took up studying law. Why had it taken a mind to come back? And what in hell had brought him this cursed bout of introspective self-analysis? It seemed plain crazy. Blind accident had decreed that he would take Rufus Freeman's case without the customary retainer. He should have known better. In turn, destiny had brought him the call from a distraught District Attorney. Ol' Bert Thompkins had sure been skittish with wanting to know why the U.S. Attorney was pressing him to keep a lid on such a two-bit burglary. Then chance had put that boy LeBaron on the case to dig up the story about the victim's lost genealogy records. He couldn't remember her name. And now LeBaron had stumbled onto yet more information about the same damned government agency that nobody'd ever even heard of before. And from a lady friend he hadn't seen in ten years! Too damned many coincidences. Collins shook his head. Behind all this he was beginning to perceive a purposeful hand which dictated that he alone was intended to pick out the intersecting strands of fate from the background weave and recognize their significance. And he alone bore the duty to act.

An image arose from his earliest Bible-study days: Jesus of Nazareth standing alone before God in the garden of Gethsemane. He could almost hear old Gramma Addie's soft voice whispering the story to the children gathered at her feet. To the driving rain as it slashed across his window he breathed in the same soft tone, "Why *me*, Lord?"

The specter of total systematic genocide of the black race tormented Collins as he gazed down on the lights of Oakland. *It* had lain wide awake in the room with him all night, silently watching, troubling his sleep. Now he could *feel* this terrible evil like a febrile glare beyond the mountains to the east growing virulent in the isolated valley of the Great Salt Lake, whence it would spread to infect the slumbering population below. *His* city, as much as any man's. *His responsibility*, as much as any man's.

Long he stood there brooding over the vicissitudes of fate. At last the clouds outside began to take on the milky hues of dawn. The rain had slackened a bit. The night's long journey was finally reaching the far shore. The dark water had been crossed. Collins peeled off his glasses and rubbed his eyes with the heels of his hands. He felt as if he had just returned from an odious ordeal. As the daylight rose, revealing a rainsoaked city beneath a low gray sky, he began to feel stronger. That old familiar self-confidence was again pumping him up, zinging certitude through his bloodstream. Firmly entrenched in his own proper time and place and master of his own destiny, he replaced his spectacles. A reassuring rumble in his bowels punctuated his return.

It was time to telephone LeBaron.

He shuffled back through the bedroom, quietly so as not to wake up Beatrice, grabbed his state-of-the-art portable cellular telephone from the bedstand, and slipped into the bathroom. He sat down on the oak toilet seat and punched LeBaron's button.

LeBaron had gotten himself all wound up in this thing too. Maybe even more than Collins had. So the boy wouldn't be able to help on the early morning calendar rounds. He'd have to show up in Felix 'Maximum' Kroner's courtroom first thing for the calling of Freeman's jury.

Now *that* was another troubling twist to this whole mess. Collins had managed to stay out of Kroner's courtroom for the better part of five years now. So how come they wound up there with Freeman's trial, of all cases? Was this another one of those prophetic coincidences? It probably didn't matter, because Freeman's case was going to be dropped on the D.A.'s motion and a plea from Freeman to a lesser included offense. *Or was it?* A provocative new idea bounded into his mind. If he could just figure an angle so he could turn a profit on all this . . .

He let it ring twenty times, and with each ring his mood grew darker. Something had happened to LeBaron. He'd been afraid of that. The boy was in deep water way over his head and didn't even know it. It was beginning to look like Collins might have to hoe this row all by himself.

--2--

LeBaron awoke with a shiver. The remnants of a dream of sexual fulfillment hung like tattered curtains in the windows of his mind. His nose was stuffed up, his head ached, and a horrendous metallic taste fouled his mouth. The air had grown cold and damp. Propping himself up on one elbow, he glanced around. The motel room looked the same. Sarah was still sleeping quietly in the next bed. Over on the table in the circle of bright light the fourth report lay open, just as he had left it.

Yet something was wrong. He dragged himself up against the headboard, trying to drain his sinuses and consider. He wasn't sure whether he felt better or worse. Through the crack in the drapes a pale light penetrated the room. A light that shouldn't have been there. He glanced down at his watch.

"Jesus Christ!" He bolted to his feet so abruptly the room began to swim, and he had to lean over and steady himself against the nightstand. It was almost seven-thirty, and he was supposed to be in trial in ninety minutes.

In the bathroom's rude fluorescence he splashed cold water on his face and blinked into the mirror. He looked like hell. His complexion was pasty, his eyes puffy, and a day's growth of stubble darkened his chin. He didn't have a toothbrush, a razor, or a comb. And there was no time to go shopping or stop by his apartment in Berkeley. He splashed his face again, gargled some warm water, spat into the toilet, and returned to the mirror. No detectable improvement. So be it. Judge Kroner was just going to have to take him as he was.

Back in the bedroom he discovered that he had slept all night on top of his suit coat, which now had the crumpled, musty aspect of a downtown wino's. *At least it matched the pants he'd slept in*, he observed wryly, straightening his tie.

"Vince?" Sarah was waking up.

"No, Sally, it's Jed."

"Jeddy?"

"Yes." He sat on the bed beside her. "I've got to be going. I have a trial this morning. I'm late. How did you sleep?"

"Good, I think." She looked up at him with dawning comprehension. "Oh, I must've fallen asleep. Is it morning?"

"Yes."

"I'm sorry. I was supposed to help answer your questions."

"Don't worry about it." He stroked her hair reassuringly.

"Did you finish the reports?"

"No. Only about half. I fell asleep too." Quickly he added, "On the next bed."

Sarah nodded.

"I really want to finish them, but I've got this matter on for trial this morning in Oakland." He glanced at his watch. "In a little over an hour. And I think the rush-hour traffic's going to be a bitch."

"I'm sorry, Jeddy, I got you into--"

He cut her off with a kiss on the cheek. "Don't *worry* about it. I *want* to help out if I can." He stood up, went to the table, and began folding the reports back into the manila envelope. "Can I take these with me until I can finish them, then give 'em back to you?"

She sat up in bed, tugging at her robe, and looked at him gravely. "You could be in serious trouble if you're caught with those."

"I'll take the chance. Is it all right?"

She shrugged. "They're probably safer with you than me."

He slipped the envelope under his coat and glanced around to see if he'd forgotten anything. "Do you mind if I show these to the attorney I work for? Cedrick Collins is his name. I could make him another copy."

She shook her head. "I shouldn't even've let you see them. I'm afraid I'm going to get too many people involved here. These are national security secrets. We could all go to prison just looking at this stuff."

"I understand. I think a lot of him as an attorney. And as a man."

"Oh, Jeddy, I'm so afraid for all of us."

"Does that mean yes?" He stepped over and bent to kiss her cheek again.

She reached her arms around his neck, pulled him down close, and held him to her for a moment. She nodded. "Go ahead and do what you think is right." He could feel her trembling. At last she released him. "When will I see you again?"

"Tonight if you'd like." He straightened his tie in the mirror one last time. "Could you meet me in Oakland somewhere for dinner?"

"Sure. Where?"

"How about Mort's? You know where that is?"

"Jack London Square, isn't it?"

"Right. How about six?"

"Okay."

He pulled the wad of bills out of his pocket and set it on the round table. On second thought, he peeled off two twenties and stuck them back in his pocket.

"What's that?" she asked.

"The little loan we talked about last night."

"Jeddy--"

"Take it. *Please*. You can pay me back later. I think you should stop using your credit cards. They're dangerous. See you tonight." He opened the front door and stepped out into the swirling rain. Great, he thought as he tiptoed along the slippery balcony, his suit was going to get soaked just running for the car. But at least the rain might take out some of the wrinkles.

The garish Pimpmobile roared into life. LeBaron found the wipers and headlights and eased it into gear. He was so intent on plotting the fastest route to the Oakland courts that he didn't notice the green government van swing into the parking space he had just vacated.

--3--

Light!

There was light!

His own ceaselessly recycling thoughts had been slowly driving him mad. Loneliness. Futility. Disorientation. Vivid hallucinations. The conviction that he was somehow an abomination, an offense against nature, festered in his loneliness like a cancerous sore. For how long he had waited, alone, cowering blind in total blackness, he did not know, for Dexter had no way to measure the ineffable passage of time. With no hope of escape, he had all but given in to the blackness of despair.

From the blackness, the light had suddenly exploded.

He could see!

Before him was a vision. A small rectangular figure moved through a geometrical field. He perceived it directly, intimately, without the benefit of physical eyes.

It was just as he had dreamed it. A sense of deja vu overwhelmed him. In and out of the scribbling of lines and swirls Dexter followed the figure, always focusing on the figure, ignoring the background. It was easy. It was natural. Dexter could not help but follow the tiny figure as it wove in and out of the forest of conflicting images.

With the vision in its warm, cream-toned light came a measure of comfort. Perhaps this tiny figure, drifting as it was through a jungle of irrelevant shapes, was being *shown* to him. Perhaps he was not alone after all. He could not understand how or why, but the possibility of another intelligence heartened him.

Vaguely Dexter recollected a Voice, from the time before he was fully awake. Had the Voice been real or merely another dream? Perhaps the Voice now gave him sight and showed him this figure moving through the geometric background. His salvation would lie in establishing communication with the Voice. But how? He could not speak nor move nor even for a single instant tear his attention away from the ceaselessly moving rectangle. In and out, around and through, hypnotically the figure traveled.

Then abruptly the rectangle changed to a star, and the exercise began all over again. The simple movement filled his attention. It gorged his universe. Obsessively Dexter followed the strangely satisfying movement of the star. Memory of the terrible blind loneliness and the unspeakable pain which preceded it retreated into the fuzzy corners of his mind. As long as the star continued to traverse its geometrical world, he would follow it, and everything would be all right.

Dexter settled into the contentment of doing precisely the task he was intended to do.

--4--

The Alameda County Administration Building gleamed like a wet sepulcher in the diffuse morning light. The seventh floor housed Judge Kroner's courtroom kingdom. From a corner cigar store down the block Rufus Freeman studied the Greyhound Bus ticket to Chicago he had just purchased and considered his next move. He had a cousin in Chicago, and Rufus thought of the ticket as a kind of insurance policy against things turning real ugly at the trial. If he showed up in court on time and minded his business, he wasn't likely to be yanked back into custody *today*, but the possibility was always there with that sour-faced no-soul honkey hangin' judge he'd gotten hisself in front of through no particular fault of his own. 'Course, Cedrick P. Collins, Esq., hisself might just show up for trial today and pull his guilty sinner's ass right out o' the fire. But that didn't hardly seem likely, since he hadn't *paid* the man *nothin'* on account of his services. That'd been plain stupid, but he just hadn't managed to *plan ahead*.

Over the weekend he'd begged, borrowed, and stolen the five-hundred dollars Esquire Collins had demanded as a retainer. His intentions had been fine: to pay full dollar down on a first-class legal defense. Problem was, he only had about half the cash left this morning. The bus ticket had taken a good whack out of it. The rest of the shortfall he'd spent on crack. With the tremendous societal pressures he was bearing up under, Rufus felt *entitled* to a little pharmaceutical succor.

This was *very bad* business, Freeman decided as he picked a stray thread off the sharp crease of his green gabardine trousers and examined his rain-splattered patent leather boots. His two older brothers, whom he'd never really known very well, had already both done hard time. One was now in Folsom, and the other was out on parole someplace down south. His mamma had been counting on Rufus. Her highest aspiration for him had been simply to keep him out of state prison. Now it looked like that de-diddley-dumb college-trainee white dude'd be back to mess up his case some more and railroad his ass directly to the joint. He bent down and buffed the shine back onto his boots with a silken handkerchief initialed "RAF." Looked like his mamma was about to be taken with a big disappointment.

He glanced between the ticket in his fist and the shining building at the end of the street and swallowed hard. He was going to bet with the odds today. He stuck the ticket deep into an inside coat pocket and stepped out into the light drizzle.

--5--

LeBaron parked the Pimpmobile in the basement of the Bay Area Bank and Trust Building where Mr. Collins had told him to. He left the vehicle smelling like a wet dog had just whelped a half-dozen stillborn puppies in it. The cotton-synthetic blend in his cheap corduroy suit always gave off an odd and possibly toxic aroma when it got wet.

He rushed upstairs to the vacant office where it took him a while to decipher Wanda Jean's unique filing system and locate the Freeman file. He then dashed down the six short blocks to the County Administration Building umbrellaless through a cold drizzle. When he stepped out of the elevator on the seventh floor, his wet hair was pasted to his forehead. The stubble on his chin bristled in the fluorescent light of the sterile hallway. He looked rumpled, wet, cold, exhausted, and out of breath.

Freeman eyed him in disgust. "Hey, man, what *happened* t'you? Y'look like shit. An' why don't y'get yourself somethin' t'*wear*?"

"Sorry, I got behind schedule--"

"Where's m'main man, Esquire *Collins*? Y'said he's gonna *be* here today. I got some cash for m'man. Where's he *at*?"

"I . . . ah . . . haven't had a chance to talk with him yet this morning. I'll give you a receipt for the money."

"No way, Jose. I'll give it t'Esquire Collins m'self when I sees him. Say, you ain't planning t'go in there representin' *me* lookin' like *that*, are you?"

"LeBaron!" a piercing whine ricocheted down the pristine hallway. Deputy Ivan Frank squirmed through the doorway of Department 23 and waddled toward them. He was clearly agitated. "Where've you *been*? You've got to confirm our deal. I told the clerk we'll need to talk to Judge Kroner before he calls the jury in. Jesus, you look awful."

"Don't smell so hot, either," Freeman added.

LeBaron silenced his client with a waive and confronted Frank. "I'll let you know as soon as I've discussed your offer with Mr. Freeman here."

"You haven't even *talked* to him yet?" In disbelief Frank punched his glasses back on his sweaty nose.

"No, Ivan, I have not. It hurts me to tell you this, but my life contains matters other than your frigging offer. I've been very busy." LeBaron glanced at his watch. "Now we only have about two minutes, so if you'll excuse us, I'd like to take a moment to talk to my client in private. I'll let you know what he decides."

Frank started to protest, but then thought better of it. "All right. All right. Let me know." He jerked around like a whipped puppy and minced back toward the courtroom.

"Thought so," Freeman muttered, amused by the confrontation. "Fat ol' D.A. tried talkin' to me b'fore y'got here. Wanted t'know if I's gonna plead t'somethin'r other this mornin'."

"What did you tell him?"

"I told him I don't talk to no fat-freak dick-faced deputy prosecutin' asshole 'cept through my attorney, an' that he better god-damn' leave me along or I'd report him t'the judge an' have his bar license yanked."

LeBaron smiled. He would have liked to have seen Frank's reaction to that. Frank was having a bad morning, but it served him right. He shouldn't have tried to deal with his client directly.

"So what's the deal, anyway?" Freeman wanted to know. "What's that fat dude off'rin'?"

LeBaron propped open his file and consulted his notes. "He wants you to plead guilty to a second degree burglary. He's agreed to stipulate it to be a misdemeanor. Grand theft will be dropped. Priors will be dismissed."

Freeman blinked, waiting for the bad part. "What else?"

"That's it."

"No felony?"

"No felony."

"Y'mean no state prison? Am I right?"

LeBaron smiled, "No state prison."

Freeman frowned. He didn't trust surprises, especially propitious ones. The *bad part* was probably still lurking somewhere, only he just hadn't spotted it yet. Or else maybe they were toying with him. He squinted at his attorney. "What kinda jail time we lookin' at behind a beef like that?"

"The maximum sentence is one year in county jail. It's up to the judge. The D.A. wouldn't bargain with me on the sentence."

Freeman pondered for a while. "What for they droppin' the felonies on me now? Thought you said they *had* my ass. Somethin' wrong with their case?"

"I don't think it has to do with the strength of their case against you."

"Oh, yeah? What then?"

"It's complicated. I don't have time to explain now."

"You *know* what their problem is, but can't 'splain it t'me? 'S'at what y're tellin' me?"

"I think I do. At least partly."

Freeman dismissed the notion with a shake of his head. "*Mus'* be somethin' wrong with their case or they wouldn't drop the felony." He rubbed his mouth with the back of a skinny wrist. "I jus' don' know. Maybe we oughta hold out for thirty-days jail time. Whad'a y'think?"

"I think you got lucky," LeBaron replied in exasperation, "because of something that has nothing to do with your case. I think that if you blow this chance, they're going to come down on you so hard you won't know which end is up. Judge Kroner there would be happy to send you straight to the joint. It would make his day. That's really what I think."

"I don' know. Somethin's gotta be wrong--"

The buzzer went off above the door of Department 23, sending a jolt to LeBaron's heart. "Look," he said, taking his client by the arm and steering him toward the courtroom, "even if Kroner gives you the maximum sentence, with good time and work time and early release you'll be out in less than six months."

"Humph," Freeman snorted. "Seems like a lot o' time to me for that pissy little tv set."

"Sure beats state prison, Rufus." LeBaron ushered him into the courtroom.

"Yeah? Well how 'bout *you* doin' the time for me, honky? Then maybe I'll jump on the deal."

"All rise!" the bailiff bellowed. "Superior Court of the State of California for the County of Alameda is now in session, the Honorable Felix Kroner, presiding."

Judge Kroner limped in from the side door, jowls sagged like an old dog's. Even his coal-black crew-cut seemed wilted. Damp weather always set his arthritis off, and today he was having a hellish bout. Every damned joint in his body throbbed. He would have retired years ago if he could trust the Governor to replace him with a jurist of similar outlook. Instead the bench was being packed with bleeding-heart liberals. "Be seated," he barked and eased himself onto his throne. "Call People verses Rufus Abraham Freeman. Mr. Frank, you wanted to address the court before we call in the jury?"

"Yes, your honor."

"Make it quick."

Deputy Frank leaned over and whispered to LeBaron, "We got a deal or what?"

LeBaron could only shrug. He honestly didn't know.

Judge Kroner silenced the dialogue with a sharp whack of his gavel. "*Proceed*, Mr. Frank."

"Yes, your honor." Frank punched his glasses back up on his nose. Watching for Freeman's reaction, he hazarded, "I believe we have a stipulated disposition of this matter. The people have offered to accept a plea to count one, stipulated to be second degree and a misdemeanor. The people would then move to dismiss count two."

"And dismiss the priors," LeBaron prompted.

"And dismiss the priors, your honor," Frank echoed uncomfortably.

Judge Kroner stared at him in disbelief. "Are you sure that's what you want to do, Counsel?"

"Yes, your honor."

The judge flipped through the court file. "Plead to a misdemeanor second-degree burglary and drop the priors?"

Frank nodded miserably.

Judge Kroner leveled him with an accusing stare. "If you were going to resolve this as a misdemeanor, Mr. Frank, why in hell'd you bring it up to this court in the first place?"

"We . . . ah . . . originally thought the case was stronger," Frank lied.

"Now don't bullshit me, Mr. Frank. I've read the police report on this, you know. The case looks a hell of a lot stronger than what you're offering. Have you talked this over with Mr. Thompson?"

"Yes, your honor. He instructed me to make this offer."

Judge Kroner glowered at him in silence. Then he sighed and seemed to melt painfully into his chair. "Very well. I'm going to assume that Bert knows what he's doing here." He wheeled on LeBaron for the first time. "Mr. LeBaron . . . "

LeBaron stood up.

"Good God, Mr. LeBaron! What happened to you, man? If you are trying to test this court's good humor by coming in here looking like *that . . .* I am inclined to consider your appearance a contempt of this court."

"I apologize, your honor. No disrespect is intended. I got caught in the rain and didn't want to delay the court proceedings by taking the time off to change clothes. I assure you it won't happen again."

Judge Kroner brooded in silent malevolence for a while. Then he seemed to wash his hands of the whole filthy affair. "Very well. See that it does not. Now, is the defendant going to be entering a plea as offered by the deputy district attorney?"

"Well, your honor, Mr. Freeman would like to know if the court would be willing to indicate what the sentence will be should the people's offer be accepted."

"Absolutely not." He leaned forward and wagged a finger at LeBaron. "And I advise you not to try my patience any further, young man. If Mr. Freeman pleads guilty, he takes his chances just like the rest of them. The matter will be referred to probation for a presentence report. But I will say this, his record doesn't look very good. No, sir, not good at all. I would be very surprised, *very* surprised, under the circumstances, if he didn't spend the maximum time prescribed by law in jail. Frankly, I'm disappointed the district attorney has offered this disposition. I would like to see the trial proceed, because I think that way Mr. Freeman would wind up in state prison where he belongs. I have no doubt, however, that your client will find himself there one way or another in due course." He paused to let it sink in. "I hope these comments help your client reach an appropriate decision about the disposition offered by the district attorney."

"Thank you, your honor. May I have a moment to consult with him?"

Judge Kroner scowled. "One minute."

LeBaron pulled Freeman away from the counsel table, stood him up, and looked him in the eye. "It's fish or cut bait time, Rufus. I'm advising you to take the deal. You understand? You're free to choose state prison, though, if you're so inclined. It's your decision. You're the one who'll have to live with it."

Freeman bit his lip and squirmed. "Shit." He couldn't make up his mind. He thought about bluffing it out, about how nice it would be to brag to his buddies about beating this case cold. He thought about life in the county jail, which really wasn't so bad. He had a lot of friends there. And he thought about the unknown horror of state prison. He'd heard bad stories. Finally he thought about his mamma and what the shock of disappointment might do to her. He looked down at his shining boots.

The judge pounded his gavel. Time was up.

"Le's do it," he mumbled to LeBaron.

"You'll take the deal?"

"Yeah."

"Plead guilty to the misdemeanor?"

"Right."

"Now you're sure about this, Rufus?"

Squeezing back tears, Freeman nodded.

LeBaron faced the bench. "Your honor, I believe Mr. Freeman wishes to accept the offer made by the people."

"Too bad," Judge Kroner murmured. He nodded to the court reporter. "Let's proceed on the record. Mr. Freeman, you do realize, do you not, that you do not *have* to plead guilty, and that by pleading guilty you'll be *giving up* certain rights. Do you understand that?"

Freeman nodded.

"I can't *hear* you, Mr. Freeman. You'll have to *speak up* or the court reporter can't take down your answers. Now. Are you willing to give up those rights?"

"Hold on a minute there, Judge!" boomed a familiar voice from the rear of the courtroom. Cedrick P. Collins stood in the doorway like the lead baritone making his grand operatic entrance. He wore his finest nine-hundred-dollar brown pinstriped three-piece suit, a ninety-dollar hand-painted Italian silk necktie, and the sassiest grin LeBaron had ever seen. He was followed by two young white men in drab dark suits who inched past him as if they preferred not to be noticed.

"My!" exclaimed Freeman, "don't m'man look *fine*."

"Silence!" Judge Kroner banged his gavel. "What's the meaning of this, Mr. Collins? You're interrupting a guilty plea here."

Collins stood surveying the courtroom for a dramatic moment. "Thass fine, Judge, but I jus' want'a have a little consultation with my client there before he throws away all o' them rights you's 'bout t'be readin' him." A huge smile of mock obeisance glistened on Collins' mouth as he strolled up to the counsel table and popped open the catches on his laptop computer. "Y'un'erstan' the right to counsel I'm sure, Judge. It's in the Sixth Amendment of the United States Constitution."

Deputy Frank was on his feet, livid. "I thought Mr. LeBaron was representing Mr. Freeman here, your honor."

"We're *associated* in representing this boy here," Collins rejoined, still smiling, and clamped his arm around Freeman shoulders, turning him away. Under his breath he whispered, "You got some money for me?"

"But we had a deal," Frank persisted.

Collins turned on him. "Ain't gonna be no *deal* unless this boy decides he wants t'waive his constitutional rights. Ain't I right about that, Judge?"

Judge Kroner nodded once, glowering. He had forgotten how much he detested Cedrick Collins' brash impudence. And this morning he was in no mood to be fighting for control of his own courtroom.

"By the way," Collins added, "I brought along these two fellas from the local newspapers so they could observe justice bein' done right here in downtown Oakland." He waived towards the two men who had come in with him. They both nodded nervously to Judge Kroner and found seats in the front row of the gallery.

Judge Kroner slapped the court file shut. "If Mr. Freeman prefers not to waive his rights, Mr. Collins, then we shall be happy to accommodate him by proceeding with this trial."

Freeman started to say something, but Collins tightened his grip, staggering him. The smile on Collins' lips never wavered. "We' ready to proceed, Judge."

"Fine. Bailiff, summon the jury."

"Excuse me, your honor." Deputy Frank was sweating profusely. "The . . . ah . . . people are not prepared to proceed at this time."

Judge Kroner lifted his arm to stop the bailiff. "What do you mean, Mr. Frank? This is the time and the place for the trial of this matter, is it not?"

"Yes, your honor." He pulled a wrinkled handkerchief out of his back pocket and mopped his forehead. "But I . . . ah . . . called off our witnesses after I spoke with Mr. LeBaron by telephone yesterday. I thought we had a deal worked out here."

"Are you saying that Mr. LeBaron agreed to your offer on behalf of his client?"

"No, your honor," LeBaron volunteered, jumping up. "I told him I had to talk with my client first."

"Well, not exactly, your honor," Frank confirmed, withering miserably under Judge Kroner's baleful glare. "But his client sure *ought* to take it. We've got this man dead to rights. Caught in the act. We're talking about state prison for sure here, if we go to trial--"

"*If* we go to trial, Counsel?"

"Well, I assumed--"

"That's enough!" Judge Kroner cut him off with a whack of the gavel. He rose painfully. "I want to see all counsel in chambers right now."

"We want a record of all this--" Collins began.

"*I'll* decide what goes on the record in *my* courtroom, if it's all right with you, Mr. Collins. Bailiff, escort counsel into my chambers. Mr. Frank. Mr. LeBaron." He limped out through the side door.

"Mighty fine," Freeman squealed, wriggling free of Collins' clutch and trying to slap him with a high five. "We gonna beat this beef sho'nough, m'man, am I right?"

"Gi'me some money," Collins grumbled.

Reluctantly Freeman retrieved a small wad of bills from his coat pocket.

Collins snatched it out of his hand. "'S'not enough," he said without counting it.

"Oh, *right*!" said Freeman, astonished at his forgetfulness. "I meant t'tell y'I got som'ore comin'. I'll have another five bills t'you by the end o' th'week."

"Make it a thousand." He turned to LeBaron. "Pee-*ew*! Wha's'at I'm smellin'? You been rollin' 'round in somethin' funny, LeBaron?"

"Sorry. When this suit gets wet--"

"I don't know what your trying to pull, LeBaron," Frank fumed, snapping his briefcase shut and hoisting it under one arm, "but if this is the way you work out a deal--"

"Oh, simmer down," Collins cut him off. "Th'ain't no *deal* here. Ol' Bert Thompkins called me up 'bout the problem y'got here. Looks t'me like maybe y'gonna want t'think 'bout dismissin' it outright."

Freeman grinned broadly.

"Got no authority for that," Frank snapped.

"Well," Collins observed, pulling down his spectacles and squinting at the deputy, "maybe y'better *get* it."

The bailiff ushered them down the hallway and into Judge Kroner's chambers. The judge had taken off his robe and hung it behind the door. Down at their level he looked small and shriveled in his shirtsleeves behind the huge, empty, glass-topped desk.

"What the hell's going on here, Mr. Frank?" Judge Kroner demanded as soon as the door clicked shut. "I want a goddamned explanation, *right now*."

"Your honor," Frank confided uneasily, "Mr. Thompkins has been asked to deal this case--"

"By whom?"

"By the U. S. Attorney."

"What's the U. S. Attorney got to do with this?"

Frank pushed up his glasses. "I don't know."

"Why you spineless whelp! We got that boy dead to rights. I read the police report, and I know officer Moseby. Damn good man, for a colored. Now the U. S. Attorney for San Francisco has got *no authority--*"

"Not San Francisco, Judge," Collins interjected forcefully. "Salt Lake City."

An uncomfortable silence fell over both Judge Kroner and Deputy Frank. Neither liked the implication that Collins knew more than either of them about what was going on between the District Attorney and the U. S. Attorney General's Office.

"Looks like th'ain't much choice here but to dismiss all the charges against my client, Judge." Collins grinned smugly.

Judge Kroner wheeled on Collins. "Oh you think so, Mr. Collins? Well I think I've got some other options in the matter. Now what does the U. S. Attorney want kept quiet here? What do you know about this case?"

"I don't know nothin', Judge, 'cept what my client divulged to me in confidence. It's all protected by the attorney-client privilege." Deftly he flipped open Gideon, his laptop computer, and punched a few keys. "Y'want a citation on--"

"No, I don't want a citation! I know what the law is. I've been a judge of this court for twenty-five years. And what's the big idea of bringing those newsmen into my courtroom?"

"Y'don't *bring* them news boys anywhere, Judge. They're real professionals. Got a nose for the news. And it looks t'me like they's smellin' somethin' real newsworthy 'round here this mornin'."

"You're not fooling me, Collins. You arranged to get them here through some of your colored friends downtown. Well, I've got a mind to slap a gag order on this whole proceeding. What do you think of that?"

"Well, Judge, you jus' do what y'have t'do. I sure 'nough don't mind keepin' *my* mouth shut. Don' bother me a lick. But even with a gag order, proceedin's in the courtroom gonna be open t'the public, an' I'll bet you gonna find ten o' them ol' newsboys where y'got two now. 'Specially if they think y'hidin' somethin' on 'em."

"What did you tell those reporters, Collins?"

"Why'n't y'go a'ks'm yourself, Judge?"

"I'm not going to take your goddamn insolence any more, Collins." Judge Kroner's face was turning a beet red. "You're flirting with contempt. I see it in your attitude."

With the same saucy smile Collins replied, "You remember what happened last time you tried *that*, don't y'Judge?"

The judge pounded his bare fist on the glass pad. "This time I'll make it stick, goddamn you!"

Collins glanced indolently around the chambers. "Not without a court reporter, Judge. Didn't I caution y'bout that? Y'got no record of this here alleged contempt you' talkin' 'bout."

LeBaron watched in alarm as Judge Kroner grew increasingly apoplectic. Collins was baiting him, of course, staying just within the narrow line of propriety. But it seemed to LeBaron that his mentor had no more choice in the matter than a moth had in flirting with a candle flame. Collins and Judge Kroner were locked in a bitter combat which superseded either of them as individuals. They were both prisoners of a battle dictated by their cultural antecedents.

"Wha'd'ya think, Judge?" Collins taunted. "Y'gonna dismiss charges against m'boy?"

Judge Kroner's breath was coming in shallow, labored gasps. Rummaging through his desk drawer, he located a small bottle of pills, shook a couple out in his quivering hand, and tossed them into his mouth. He sank back into his swivel chair, eyes closed, while the wheezing subsided. After a long minute, he open his eyes and glared at Deputy Frank. "Can you get your witnesses here by tomorrow morning?"

"Yes, your honor. I believe I can, anyway."

"Good. Do so. We'll proceed Wednesday morning. You better be ready. If you aren't ready to proceed, Mr. Frank, I want you to have Bert Thompkins here himself to explain why not. You understand? Now everyone get out of here. We're going back on the record."

--6--

Outside in the corridor after the hearing, Cedrick Collins was feeling as fine as a frog hair. His lusty smile was unfeigned. "Ol' rascal 'bout t'choked when I reminded'im he' got no record," he chuckled to LeBaron.

Freeman flitted around him like a mosquito trying to suck out a little bit of what had gone on in chambers. "'S lookin' pretty good, huh? I mean, they gonna dismiss? 'S'at what' gonna happen when we come back tomorrow?"

Ignoring him, Collins pulled his appointment book out of an inside pocket.

"We're going to trial tomorrow, Rufus," LeBaron told him soberly.

"Yeah, I heard," Freeman replied, then jumped on Collins again. "Wha'cha got planned, m'man? Y'gonna be handlin' this yourself tomorrow, am I right? I mean, y'got this all figured out, right?"

They both waited for a response, but Collins studied his schedule as if he hadn't heard.

In exasperation, Freeman turned to LeBaron. "What's gonna

happen at trial tomorrow, anyway?"

LeBaron shrugged. "They're going to call witnesses. We can call witnesses. Both sides will make arguments. The judge will instruct the jury. The jury will decide whether you're guilty or not."

"But what's the *trick*?" Freeman looked from one lawyer to the other. "How we gonna *beat* this beef?" When neither responded, fear began seeping back in. "Y'do have a *trick*, don't ya? I mean, that ol' judge, he sure looked *pissed*."

No response. Freeman grabbed LeBaron's sleeve. "M'man Esquire Collins here's gonna *try* this case tomorrow, am I right?"

"I don't know yet."

"Because maybe we shouldn't of pissed off the ol' judge so much. Y'see what I'm sayin'? I mean, judge'll be *sentencing* if'n the jury comes back with a 'guilty', am I right?"

LeBaron nodded.

Freeman moaned. "I be thinkin' maybe that fat boy's deal wasn't so bad--"

Collins turned on him with a scowl. "You ain't been payin' 'nough to do any thinkin' here."

Without a word Deputy Frank bristled out of the courtroom and rumbled past them like an intensifying thunderstorm. The sight of him brought back Collins' grin. He called after him, "See y'in the mornin', Deputy."

"Well, this here is *my beef*--" Freeman began.

Collins wheeled on him. "You sayin' y'want t'discharge us as your attorneys here? Y'want t'handle this matter yourself, is that it?"

"No, m'man. It's jus' that--"

"You can go on in there all by y'self in the mornin' an' slow plea your way straight t'the joint, if that's what y'be wantin'."

"No, no--"

"'S jus' the same t'me'n LeBaron here."

"No *way*, I need you--"

"Well then leave the thinkin' on this case to me, okay?"

Freeman swallowed any further protest and nodded.

"Good. Now y'bring me in another thousand by tomorrow mornin', okay?"

Freeman seemed to shrink. "I . . . er . . . ain't sure I can come up with that *much* by tomorrow."

"Well, then, y'better go'n' see Brown right now. This mornin'. Didn't LeBaron here tell ya he had work for ya t'do?"

"He tol' me."

"Well'n y'better get your ass over there. Y'know where he's at?"

"I know."

"Good." Collins' smile bobbed to the surface. "Then we got ourselves an un'erstan'in'. Y'get along now."

Glumly Freeman plodded toward the elevator.

"What kind of work does Brown have for him?" LeBaron asked.

"Nev'mind that." Collins lowered his voice. "Wha'd y'find out from your lady friend, LeBaron? 'Bout what we were talkin' 'bout last evenin'?"

"Quite a lot, actually." He found the envelope in his briefcase. "Remember when you speculated that classified documents might be involved? You were right. I've got a copy of the classified reports on the project right here."

"Nice work, LeBaron." Collins glanced up and down the hall and edged closer. "How'n hell'd y'get your hands on'em so quick?" He reached for the envelope.

LeBaron drew it back. "I've only had time to read about half of them. They're top secret. We could all get into a lot of trouble. You've got to keep this in confidence, okay? And promise not to tell anybody where they came from, okay?"

Collins nodded solemnly. "Well, y'finish readin'em an' tell me wha'cha got there. Maybe I oughta take a copy jus' t'keep in a safe place. Wanda Jean can do it. She won't have a notion 'bout what she's got'er hands on. Come by the office at the end o' the day an' we'll talk about it. But right now we' *way* behind schedule. Prob'ly two hours late in a half dozen courts. I had Wanda Jean call ahead an' let'em know we' both in trial an'd be late." He showed LeBaron the calendar page covered with tiny scrawled notes. It looked like drunken insects with inky legs had staggered across the page. "Now y'better be runnin' down to Muni an' take a Stanson . . . Y'got a pencil? Good . . . That's Stanson . . . 'r maybe Stanton, can't make'r out exactly. Anyway, he's on for arraignment.

Drunk in public. I talked t'is girlfriend. Might be best jus' t'plead'im guilty on that an' get credit for time served. He pays pretty good, but be sure t'a'ks 'im for some money. Then there's a Brown . . . no relation t'*Brown* . . . he's on for a bail hearin' . . ."

LeBaron had jotted down notes on nine woeful clients by the time Collins had finished and rushed off to the master criminal calendar across the street. He never got a chance to ask just what the hell his boss intended to do about the Freeman trial tomorrow.

CHAPTER ELEVEN

Tuesday afternoon

--1--

The No. 72 bus roared, bucked, rolled, pitched, and fumed deep into the ghetto neighborhood where all the fuss had started. The afternoon sun had reemerged from behind monstrous retreating thunderheads, so LeBaron strolled slowly from the bus stop in its healing warmth. Inevitably his investigation led back to the same loathsome door. He scrutinized the scene of the crime, taking his time. Two small azalea bushes bloomed lurid crimson on each side of the short walkway where only a few iris sprouts had poked through the dry earth four days earlier. He bent to confirm that they had been recently planted. The soil beneath the shrubs was dry and cracked and appeared undisturbed. No sign of the irises. Weird.

As LeBaron straightened, his stomach grumbled with an acidic hunger. He had scrupulously avoided eating lunch in anticipation of the impending encounter. He really didn't want to be here, but something had drawn him back. His first attempt to interview this witness had miscarried badly, and he sensed that there was more information to be gleaned. This odd place seemed to be located at a kind of cosmic vortex, where the threads of divergent destinies inexplicably intertwined, including the lives of Sarah Brubaker and Rufus Freeman. And now his.

Besides, he owed his client a thorough investigation. Not because Freeman had paid for it. That had nothing to do with it. He was here because he was still new to the practice of law and wanted to do the very best he could. He wanted to conduct himself as a professional.

At last he ran out of excuses for putting off the unavoidable. He knocked on Raccoona GeBobath's front door.

"Ah, Mr. LeBaron. Come in." The swarthy foreign voice was the same, but Raccoona's appearance had changed. LeBaron studied the diminutive figure as he stepped through the doorway. The formless baggy pants and engineer's boots were gone. Instead, she wore trimly fitting dark gray overalls over a neatly pressed white blouse with a lace collar spangled with tiny blue flowers. Her shape, he noted with surprise, was after all quite female. Her feet were trussed into a pair of bright new running shoes. She had attempted to brush her short, thick hair, with inconclusive results. She looked like a hairy little gnome freshly bathed and dressed up in a doll's outfit.

"Thank you." He closed the door and followed her up the narrow stairway. Something eerie in the light and shadow made the hairs bristle on the back of his neck.

"I wondered when you'd be back."

"What made you think I'd come back?"

She turned coquettishly. "We hadn't finished talking, had we?"

For an unnerving instant LeBaron had the impression she was flirting with him. Unbidden, a series of lurid, grotesque sexual images bombarded his imagination. He wrestled them hastily out of his mind and posted a vigil to keep them away. "No, I suppose not."

The kitchen had been magically transformed. The table had been cleared off, wiped clean, and pushed against the south-facing bay windows. On it a cut-glass vase holding a bouquet of lilies, carnations, and two red roses in a field of baby's breath caught and reflected the bright sunlight streaming in. The empty sink sparkled in the modulated light. A colorful paper shade covered the bare light bulb. Under a fresh coat of wax the linoleum floor gleamed. Everything seemed spotlessly clean and in order. Even the cloying odor of rancid fats had been purged and replaced with the subtle ambience of musk incense.

LeBaron's apprehensiveness eased. "You've cleaned the place up."

"Yes. Do you like it?"

"Very much."

"Please have a seat." She pulled a chair out from the kitchen table for him. "Would you care for a cup of tea?"

He glanced around a second time. Something odd like an uneasy echo still lingered in the room, but he couldn't quite identify what. It *appeared* safe. "That would be very nice, thank you."

"I thought I might be seeing you again after that case was resolved." She placed a kettle on the stove. "What was that boy's name?"

"Freeman. Rufus Freeman."

"Yes. Unfortunate affair, wasn't it?" She spooned dry tea from an apothecary jar into a china pot. "I really didn't want to talk as long as the case was still pending. You understand?"

"Er . . . yes. I think so."

"How did it finally turn out for Mr. Freeman?"

Evasively LeBaron responded, "The district attorney offered him a misdemeanor this morning." It was not really a lie. He nudged the flow of conversation into a more benign channel. "He never actually took your records, you know. Only the television."

"Oh?" She pulled up a chair, her almond eyes piercing him.

She had not, he noticed up close, tamed her fierce eyebrows or the stiff black hairs growing from the mole above her right eye. He looked away. "No. That was someone else. Rufus saw it all. Two men. One climbed the trellis and came in through a window, then opened the front door for the other one. They carried off two cardboard boxes, which I assume were the records you want back. The front door was left ajar. So Rufus decided to come in and take a look for himself."

She brooded over the information for a while. "Goddamn' Mormons!" she muttered.

LeBaron didn't correct her. The time was not ripe for tales of green government vans. He zeroed in on the subject that really interested him. "What have you got against the Mormons, anyway?"

"Hurumph!" she snorted. It was an unsettling, vaguely bestial sound. "Those smug self-righteous bastards have been screwin' around with my whole family for years. I called 'em on it a year or two ago. We got into a big hassle. I hope they choke in their own puke, every goddamn' one of those false-prophet sons-o'-whores."

As blandly as he could manage, he said, "I'd like to hear about it."

She eyed him suspiciously. "What for?"

The teapot began to whistle, buying him time to consider a response. Raccoona poured hot water into the pot and turned to him.

"Why're you so interested in my hassle with the Mormons?"

"I have another . . . client, whose matter seems to involve the Mormons. Like you, I suspect that something's going on . . . not right." He put on an amiable smile. "So . . . if you'll share your information with me, I'd be happy to tell you what little I know about them. Perhaps together . . . well, as they say, two heads are better than one."

She brought the pot and two delicate china cups over to the table. "Sugar? Cream? Lemon?"

LeBaron shook his head.

"All right," she said and poured the tea. "That sounds fair enough. I have a cousin. Valgene Dayton. She's remarried, so it's 'Sims' now. I haven't seen her for . . . Jesus, since we were just kids. Anyway, it was maybe two . . . no, closer to three years ago that she became a goddamn' Mormon." She paused to let the horror of it all sink in. "It was when she married that fella Sims. I never met him, but I think Valgene may have been his second or third wife. You know how they are about that sort of thing." She lifted her teacup and took a sip. "How much do you know about the doctrines and rituals of the goddamn' Mormon Church, Mr. LeBaron?"

LeBaron opened his palms to indicate, "Nothing."

"Well, they have this crazy doctrine about saving their ancestors vicariously so that the whole family can be together after the resurrection." She took another sip.

"How do they do that?" LeBaron picked up his cup and looked inside. The tea was awfully dark for having steeped for such a short time.

"By makin' 'em all into goddamn' Mormons. They baptise 'em and confirm 'em and ordain 'em and sanctify 'em and all that other crap. All in glorious, expensive ceremonies, and all posthumously. Mormons don't have any priests. Everybody's ordained. And savin' ancestors is one of the three great duties of all ordained Mormons."

"You seem to know a lot about them."

"Self defense," she growled. "Know thine enemy." She drained her teacup.

LeBaron recalled a similar statement he had made to his brother Vince about learning the Buddhist sutras. Only problem was, in his own case he wasn't entirely sure it was true. He sniffed the tea's aroma. It was unlike anything he'd ever tried before.

"Didn't you ever wonder what all this goddamn' Mormon genealogy bullshit is about, Mr. LeBaron?"

LeBaron really hadn't, but he muttered, "I guess so."

"They want to identify all the ancestors of all current Mormons in order to save 'em all. If they keep at it long enough, they'll've ordained everybody on the face of the earth, since everybody is related if you go back far enough." She laughed harshly. It was more like a bark. "Strange, huh?"

LeBaron nodded and tasted his tea. Its flavor was oddly metallic, bitter, and vaguely repulsive. He set down his cup.

"So after she'd hooked up with this Sims character," Raccoona went on, "Valgene really got into it. She even sent me some letters urging me to look into goddamn' Mormonism. Me! I couldn't believe it. But I figured the best thing to do was ignore her. Then she decided she was going to start saving *her* ancestors." She paused to make sure LeBaron appreciated the significance of this turn of events. When it was apparent he did not, Raccoona explained, "*Her* ancestors are also *my* ancestors, once you get back to our grandparents."

"Ah. Huh. Mmmm." LeBaron's tongue felt thick and numb. He was having difficulty forming words through the strange cloying aftertaste in his mouth. Concentrating on the task, he slowly intoned, "So Valgene was undertaking to convert *your* ancestors to Mormonism." It seemed very hot in the kitchen.

"I was mad as hell when I heard about it. My ancestors had no inclination to become goddamn' Mormons. I *know* that. And the poor dead bastards didn't have anybody to defend them against Valgene. So I took the job on."

He loosened his necktie and undid his collar button. "What did you do?"

"First I started writing letters. I wrote to Valgene. I wrote to the goddamn' Mormon headquarters in Salt Lake City. Then I visited the local temple. Did you know they have a big temple right here in Oakland? It's up in the hills by the Warren Freeway. It's unbelievable. Looks like a giant orange juice squeezer. Anyway, I wanted to know the names of all the ancestors that Valgene had converted, and I demanded that they unconvert them. Unbaptize 'em. Unordain 'em. Leave 'em goddamn' in peace. I even consulted a couple of attorneys."

"Ah. You were going to sue them?"

"Goddamn' right I was. And I told them so. Only I couldn't find anybody who'd take the case."

Nodding, LeBaron maintained a professional silence.

"That's when *their* lawyers began respondin' to my letters. They were uncooperative and downright rude. You know how lawyers are. Probably learn it in law school. Anyway, they refused to give me anything, even the names of my own goddamn' ancestors that they'd ordained posthumously."

"Uh." LeBaron speculated thickly, "So that's when you got into genealogy yourself?"

"You bet your ass. I had no choice. First of all I had to identify all my ancestors who were at risk. So I began visiting one of the Mormon local family history centers. They're everywhere, and very helpful if you're into tracking down ancestors. Goddamn' Mormons've got the genealogy market pretty well sewed up." She poured herself another cup of tea, then reached over and added a few drops to his. "But you know, as I got into it, I became fascinated with the genetic implications of genealogy." She took a sip and savored it. "Have you heard of the human genome project, Mr. LeBaron?"

"That seems to ring a bell, but I just can't remember precisely what that . . . er . . . involves."

"Hundreds of scientists are working together to map the total genetic makeup of the human being."

"Sure! I remember reading about that. Pretty amazing. How many genes do they have to identify?"

"Hundreds of thousands. And of the hundreds of thousands of genes that define me and you, we probably differ in only a handful." She pulled up the sleeve of her blouse and held out her arm. It was hairy, stubby, and twisted. "But those differences make you tall and straight and attractive, and me short and twisted and ugly."

"No, not really--" he attempted a polite protest.

She cut him off with a piercing glance. "I'm not looking for your sympathy, Mr. LeBaron. I just want you to see what was motivating me, what I was looking for. I wanted to trace the origins of those most distinctive traits which define me as an individual. Was I a throwback, or a mutant? Would I be able to identify ancestors similarly afflicted--"

"Or blessed."

She snorted. "Or 'blessed', as you say. I must confess I have difficulty seeing the blessing. Anyway, I wanted to know how my progenitors coped with these characteristics which I detest, how they managed to procreate and pass these genes along."

She was making LeBaron uncomfortable. Without considering, he took a big gulp from his teacup, swallowed, then struggled with the gag reflex for a terrible moment until a primordial belch managed to work its way through the stupefied muscles of his throat. The aftertaste was stunning. "What kind of tea is this?" he croaked.

"Ah, you like it? It's a special blend I learned from my mother. It has medicinal qualities, I'm told. I pick the herbs myself and dry them."

"It's very . . . interesting."

"Would you like another cup?" She held out the pot.

"No. Thank you." He quickly covered his cup with one hand. "Now what were you saying? Ah, yes, about this Mormon business. I still don't understand. Perhaps you didn't like what they were doing, I can see that, but . . . I just don't understand. Do you?" His tingling mouth was rambling on by itself, and LeBaron listened anxiously to find out what he was saying. "The Mormons are such fine basketball players, after all. Wouldn't you agree? But then, that's another matter entirely. Basketball. Football. Advanced medical research. Genealogy. Hmmm. Tell me this, how did you come to be so, if I may say, *emotionally involved* with them?" With an effort, he reined his tongue to a rough halt and fought to compose his thoughts.

She pondered something unpleasant. "When I'd exhausted the resources of their local family history center, I decided to take on Salt Lake City. Do some research in their main genealogy library, using their computer. It's open to the public. The only cost is having to listen to some goddamn' Mormon horseshit about golden plates forked up by some angel named Moroni. Real twisted sci-fi stuff. Like how the ancient American Indians were really a lost tribe of Israel. Complete horseshit." Her almond eyes watched him for a reaction.

"So you went to Salt Lake City?" LeBaron heard himself prompt.

"Right. And on my very first morning there, I filled out my request for information on one of their forms and turned it in at the desk. Under an assumed name, of course. They're supposed to key the request into the computer and let you know when the stuff's ready. So I was sittin' there waitin' in the main hall, mindin' my own business, and damn if a couple of bozos wearin' slick doubleknit suits and those horrid thin little Mormon ties didn't come over to me and tell me to get the hell out. They knew who I was. Said I couldn't use their goddamn library. The computer must've triggered something and tipped 'em off it was me. Anyway, I was really pissed, 'cause I'd already spent the money on my airplane ticket and room, and now these slackjaws were tellin' me to shove off."

The lawyer in the corner of LeBaron's mind doubted that they could legally exclude her like that, but he kept it to himself. Her story mesmerized him. "So what did you do?"

"I started cussin' at 'em. Pissed *them* off. Made 'em real surly. Toe to toe we were hollerin' at each other right there in that goddamn' sacred library of theirs. They dropped any pretense of good manners. You know, there's nothin' nastier'n a goddamn' Mormon once he sheds his smug sanctimonious manners. Believe me. Started insulting me an' my ancestors. Said they knew all about me. Said the human race'd be better off if me'n my ancestors were just wiped clean off the slate. Said they were developin' ways of doin' just that. Said they were gonna purge the stock."

"Whoa!" LeBaron felt like he was reliving yesterday's scene in Mr. Collins office. A chill rose up his spine. "Were they serious?"

"They were dead serious. That's what shocked me." She poured the last of the tea into her cup.

The aftertaste of the tea was becoming a vast and no longer unpleasant ocean into which LeBaron was slowly sinking. He heard himself say, "And so you developed your own computer program, because you couldn't use theirs?"

"That's right. I already had a lot of information from the local family history center. Only it was incomplete. Lots of holes in the data base. So I set up a simple little program based on fractals and chaos theory to extrapolate the missing data. It merges established fragments and guess-timates what should be in the blanks. Works real well."

"And they found out about your program."

"Yeah. I kept sending them letters. Kind of perverse, I guess. But I wanted 'em to know I *knew* all the information they were denying me access to. As it turned out, I had information they didn't even have, and they couldn't figure out how in hell I'd managed to compile it. I even corrected a couple of their mistakes. They got real interested."

LeBaron suppressed an urge to laugh wildly. "I can imagine."

"They started actin' friendly. 'Of *course* you're welcome at our library. This has all been a big misunderstanding. Come on back, Ms. Gebobath. We'll even pay for your plane fare and put you up in a nice hotel. Let bygones be bygones. And by the way, can you bring that new computer program of yours with you when you come?' They thought that little tv set would do the trick."

"What little tv set? Not the one Rufus Freeman picked up?"

"One and the same."

"The Mormons sent *that* to you?"

"Bet your ass. Only I wouldn't accept it. I wrote 'em and told 'em to come pick the goddamn' thing up or pay me my storage costs. Never even took it out of the box."

"What did they say to that?"

"Nothing."

LeBaron pigeonholed this tidbit and fought to swerve his unruly thoughts back toward the unfinished business of the computer records. "Did anyone else know about the program?"

"The computer program? Like who?"

"Oh, I don't know. Like any government agencies?"

"What sort of government agencies?" Raccoona's suspicions were being aroused.

LeBaron shrugged. He felt so relaxed.

She thought about it a moment. "Nope. Not from me, anyway. Why? What do you know?"

LeBaron was silent for a minute. "Ms. Gebobath, can I be candid with you?"

"It's about time you were." She put her hand on his arm.

"Er . . . yes." Although unexpected, her familiarity didn't bother him the way it should have. "My interests in this matter . . . well, go beyond Mr. Freeman's case, frankly."

"I know." Her almond eyes were pools in which he could drown. "That's all over . . . didn't you say?"

"Ah, well . . . be that as it may." LeBaron plunged on, divulging more than he had really planned to. "I have a feeling that what you know about the Mormons may shed some light on a certain federal government project. It's being conducted by the Genetic Research and Development Unit of the Department of Agriculture."

Raccoona paled.

"They're operating out of Salt Lake City. Rufus Freeman saw one of their vans in the neighborhood the day your records were taken. Anyway, this project--they call it by the code name 'Divine Wind'--"

"Divine Wind!" She laughed at some enormous cosmic joke. Cackled, actually, LeBaron thought.

"What's the matter?"

"'Divine Wind,' Mr. LeBaron. It confirms my worst suspicions. Every one of 'em. *I know what they're up to.*"

"You do? Could you tell me?"

"How's your Japanese?"

"My Japanese?"

"*Wakarimasu ka?*"

"Pardon me? Was that Japanese? I don't speak any Japanese, I'm sorry."

"'Divine Wind' is a translation of a phrase from the Japanese."

"Oh?" He was close to something important. He *felt* it.

The doorbell rang.

"And?" He prompted, dismissing the intrusion.

"Excuse me, Mr. LeBaron. Somebody's at the door." She went down the stairs.

He gazed around the room, still vainly searching for the objective source of his disquiet. An incredibly weariness was submerging him like a foamy wave. His arms felt heavy. Last night's late hours and wine were coming back to punish him. He yawned. It also had something to do with the lingering flavor of the tea. Very relaxing. He leaned back in the chair and closed his eyes for a moment.

LeBaron jerked. He opened his eyes and stretched. Had he dozed off? Raccoona was a shadow in the doorway. The sun must have gone behind a cloud, because the room was darker, and he couldn't quite make out her expression. Something was wrong with her expression. In her hand was a sheet of paper.

"I've been subpoenaed," she said.

"Oh?" Then he remembered. The trial. "For tomorrow morning?"

She looked at the paper. "Yes." She remained in the doorway. "You lied to me, Mr. LeBaron."

"No, not really--"

"Don't bullshit me! You betrayed my confidence. Under the circumstances, I don't feel I should talk with you anymore while this hearing is pending."

"There's really no problem--" he began, but she stepped into the light from the windows, and the accusation in her icy almond eyes cut him off. She was fiercely angry, perhaps even homicidally so. Viscerally he comprehended that Raccoona GeBobath was no one to trifle with. "All right." He sat up and tried to orchestrate a swift and sober exit. "I really want to thank you for your help."

She glared at him menacingly.

Shakily he got to his feet, glanced around for anything he might have forgotten, and edged past her, afraid to turn his back. "I . . . ah . . . guess this means I'll . . . just be going, and . . . see you in court tomorrow." Backing away, he felt behind him for the banister.

He found his way stiffly down the front stairs. Small muddy footprints led up the tread. He didn't remember seeing those before. He backed through the front door, afraid to take his eyes off her, and pulled the door shut.

Outside, LeBaron gaped at the dry, twisted spears of irises pushing up through the freshly turned black soil on either side of the dirty little stub of sidewalk. The brightly blooming azalea bushes he had seen just a short while ago were gone. *He had seen them, hadn't he?* Fresh wheelbarrow tracks criss-crossed the concrete. A clodded shovel leaned against the side of the house. He shook his head in confusion and disbelief. He must have dozed for some time up there at the kitchen table, and while he slept, she had removed . . . but *why*? How utterly bizarre!

--2--

Suddenly, without warning, the fearful blackness had swallowed him again. The constantly moving stars and rectangles had vanished. And with the blackness had come the deranging terror he had known before. Beset by a palpable aloneness, deep and rootless, by a certainty of grotesque abomination, by a dry, strangling grief and a savage bitterness, Dexter had braced himself for the long twisted plunge into madness.

Then from within the blackness a searing concussion of pain sliced into the center of his mind, staggering him, and was gone. In its wake, Dexter fought for coherence. Like the stunned victim of a traumatic head injury, he knew something profound had taken place, but he could not identify *what*. The injury itself affected his ability to comprehend. The blinding pain left him devastated.

As the terror and confusion subsided, Dexter felt a new and unsettling emotion. He was angry. He was furious. Resent and hatefulness flowed over him in a hot wave which was slow to ebb. His anger was undirected, yet it was no less intense for want of an object. He comprehended the nature of his fury, but he could not control it. He had never dealt with anger before.

As Dexter struggled to reorient himself, he grasped that something essential had changed. In the rustling void of persistent blackness, he knew his mind was radically *altered*. Dexter felt his substance oddly expanded. It was a disturbing transformation he found difficult to think about and even harder to describe. He felt as if the furniture of his mind had been rearranged. As if several new rooms had been opened. *He knew more things*, and they distracted him. His recollections, his frame of reference, his fundamental self, had all been *augmented*. His essential *coherence* was inundated. Associations crackled like lightning, spattering out images of uncountable things he could not recall learning. He knew them nonetheless. His mind had become an unexplored library into which he might lose himself. Haphazardly he tumbled through the encyclopedia of new entries.

Abruptly the light returned, and Dexter was drawn into a new game. An image flashed before him. Slowly, awkwardly, Dexter interpreted its elements one by one, and in the fullness of time comprehended the totality of the vision. In ankle-deep grass, shaded by the sagging branch of a tall tree, sat a battle tank. As he examined it, his mind filled with facts and figures of incredible detail. This peculiar shape was clearly Soviet, but not the top-of-the-line T-72, with its lower profile and lighter armament. And the enlarged hull and turret, the 115-mm gun with laser range-finder, and the larger, rear-set turret ring distinguished it from the earlier T-54. This was a T-62. Instantly he understood this tank's basic layout, equipment, capabilities, and its strengths and weaknesses. He knew the thickness of its armor at every location, its height, length, and width, the intricacies of its water-cooled 580-horsepower diesel engine, its road speed, road range, ground pressure, ground clearance, and primary and secondary weapons. He even understood the intricate metallurgical process for die-casting its one-piece nickel-chrome-molybdenum turret. He could conjure up blueprints, schematics, plans, and parts lists. By the time the flood of information abated, Dexter had knowledge of every nut, bolt, and rivet that held the thing together. He was awed by how much he knew about the Soviet T-62 main battle tank. Dexter seemed to know everything about this war machine except how he knew it, and *why*.

His attention shifted to the tank's surroundings, a green swale beside an outcropping of rock. Unbidden, information gushed forth. The rock was uplifted sea-floor basalt. The tree whose branch shaded the vehicle was a black cottonwood, *Populus trichocarpa*. That was clear from the smooth, dark green, shiny leaves, broadly ovate with conspicuous veins and fine wavy-toothed margins. The deep grass covering the ground was sedge. Utilizing his mysteriously emerging expertise in geology, botany, and the astronomical-geographic implications of shadow lengths, Dexter could even speculate with confidence that the photograph had been taken on the west coast of the United States at a latitude of 33 degrees at approximately two in the afternoon on a sunny day in either late October or late February. He guessed it to be Camp Pendleton Marine Corps Base in Southern California. Dexter wondered why a Soviet tank would be located at a United States military base.

The image changed, and Dexter was confronted with a new picture. For a moment the lines swam, and then coalesced into an under-view of an aircraft poised against a clear blue sky. Instantly he recognized a single-seat, twin-engine Soviet MiG-29 Fulcrum all-weather counter-air fighter. This interpretation was quick and certain, and with it came a deluge of information about the aircraft. Immediately he comprehended how the MiG-29 differed from the MiG-25 and MiG-31, and how its large pulse Doppler lookdown/shootdown radar gave it day and night operating capability against low-flying targets. On two pylons under each wing and one under each engine air duct Dexter recognized six deadly AA-10 medium-range radar homing air-to-air missiles. He understood the airplane's weight and dimensions, speed and height limitations, performance characteristics, armament, power plant, and all the other structural and operational details which he could not remember ever learning.

Then he was looking down the muzzle of a 66-ton U. S. M-1 A-1 heavy tank poking its gun out of a bunker dug into the Saudi Arabian sand. One after another the images appeared before him. Half-covered by a camouflage net, a U. S. Bradley armored fighting vehicle was parked beside a yellowing sand dune. The huge conning tower of a Soviet G-class ballistic-missile submarine broke the choppy gray surface of the Indian Ocean. An aging U. S. M-4 Sherman tank idled on a barren stretch of wet tarmac. Vision after vision of war machines presented themselves to him. There was nothing he did not recognize, given enough time to study the picture, and little he did not know of the things he recognized. As the images paraded past, Dexter's alacrity increased exponentially. Quickly his confidence grew. Interpretations came more swiftly, more certainly. And as his skill increased, so did his amazement at the expertise he possessed.

Or did this expertise rather possess him? Despite the innate joy in drawing on such an incredible wealth of knowledge, the experience was disturbing. The process unfolded without any exercise of his own *will.* An image flashed before him, whence he knew not, and involuntarily the interpretations began. He could not suspend the process, nor divert his attention elsewhere. He could not close his eyes, nor look away. Nor was he free to *mis*interpret, to falsify, to fantasize, or to dream.

There were other enigmas Dexter would have preferred to ponder. He needed to come to terms with the bleak certitude that darkness would inevitably return. What was to become of him then? And somewhere in a shocked and cowering corner of his mind glowed that unextinguished ember of unresolved rage.

--3--

The sun had already set when LeBaron stepped through the revolving glass doors of the Bay Area Bank and Trust Building. He felt mildly drugged, confused, and edgy as hell. A tingling at the base of his skull counterpointed a dull ache above his eyes. He turned down the stub of hall housing the bank of elevators and punched the glowing rectangular button. Suddenly out of the corner of his eye he caught a movement toward him from the shadows at the dead end of the hallway where no one should have been. Instinctively he spun and dropped into a defensive crouch, adrenaline jolting his heart.

"Say, where in hell y'*been*, dude?" Rufus Freeman strolled into the light. His dress was as dapper as ever, but his shoulders sagged sullenly and his face was glum.

"Oh, Rufus! Jesus, you startled me." LeBaron straightened up, his heart pounding fiercely.

"Y'lookin' a little *tense*," Freeman appraised. "An' look't you. Y'still ain't got y'self nothin' to *wear*. Didn't I *tell* y'bout that?"

LeBaron drew a deep breath. "What brings you here?"

"I'm workin'."

"Oh?"

"Yeah. For *Brown*."

"Ah. What's he got you doing here?"

"Waitin' for you, honky."

"For me?" The elevator door opened, and LeBaron grabbed the side to keep it from closing again. "You riding up with me?"

"No. An' you ain't suppose' t'be goin' up there either. That's what I'm here t'tell ya."

"What do you mean?"

"Some fellas be awaitin' for ya up at the office. I was tol' t'head y'off."

"What fellows?"

"From the FBI."

The news was like a kick in the stomach. LeBaron dropped his arm and leaned against the wall. The elevator door whispered shut. "Waiting for *me*?"

Rufus nodded somberly.

"What for? Did anyone say?" But LeBaron knew. His knees wobbled as he tightened his grip on the briefcase holding the purloined classified documents.

"Nobody tol' me much." Rufus watched him. "But it looks t'me like it ain't no mystery t'*you*."

LeBaron fought to compose himself. His thoughts struggled to find order. "I was . . . ah . . . supposed to meet with Mr. Collins. . . ."

"'S'all took care of. He' gonna meet wi'cha over at Brown's place. I' supposed t'show ya the way."

--4--

Brown's warehouse encompassed an entire city block. Within its nine-foot chain-link perimeter lay a diversity of worlds, intricate nooks and crannies whose architecture and purpose had been dictated by a history of shifting necessity. Freeman led a dazed LeBaron into the cavernous main building, where forklifts came and went toting pallets of assorted merchandise, through a series of doors at the rear, and up two flights of stairs to a small office somewhere in the inner sanctum. The windowless room was lushly carpeted and richly furnished. On the wall behind the mahogany desk were photographs of Brown shaking hands with local dignitaries and precinct bosses. In most, Cedrick Collins grinned over his shoulder or else hovered discreetly in the background like a dark-skinned fairy godmother.

"Brown's private office?" LeBaron wondered.

"I guess. Brown' outta town jus' now." Freeman withdrew, closing the door behind him.

LeBaron sank into a plush leather sofa identical to the one in Collins' office. He was upset, achy, and extremely tired, but he fought the desire to close his eyes. He had enough of *that* refuge already for one day. To occupy his mind, he pulled out the reports on project Divine Wind and thumbed through the ones he had already read, trying to refresh his recollection. They couldn't hold his attention. After a while he got up and paced back and forth across the spongy red carpet to release his growing frustration. He tried to make sense out of his bizarre encounter with Raccoona GeBobath, but even that seemed immaterial now. The specter of arrest and incarceration in a federal penitentiary would not leave him alone.

The office door popped open and Cedrick Collins slouched in. "LeBaron. Good t'see y'got here safe an' sound." He dropped a thick black book on the desk, carefully laid down his laptop computer Gideon, and backtracked to the hand-carved ivory hooks behind the door. With a grunt he hung up his top coat and hat. Collins looked dog tired. He was beginning to look that way every afternoon about this time. Too tired, LeBaron thought. Either his health was beginning to fail him, or else he was working himself to death.

Collins eased into the big chair behind Brown's desk as if he were accustomed to it. "Whadda y'doing walkin' 'round like that? Y'look terrible."

"I'm a little overwrought." LeBaron pulled a straight-back wooden chair out of the corner and sat facing his employer. The sofa was just too comfortable. "You don't look so hot yourself."

"Uh. Maybe I am a little tired. Handlin' too damn' many cases all by m'*self*." He peered at LeBaron over the top of his spectacles. "Where y'been all afternoon, anyway? I needed you t'handle a coupla matters over in Fremont muni. Had t'have Wanda Jean call an' continue 'em both. Clients may've had cash on'em, too. Y'never know."

LeBaron hung his head. "Sorry. I went to see Raccoona

GeBobath again. It took longer than I planned. I didn't even have time to phone the office."

"She the one what's'is name took the tv from?"

"Yeah. Rufus Freeman."

"Uh. Learn anything?"

"A little." LeBaron shrugged. The subject no longer seemed to interest him.

Collins eyed LeBaron for a moment, then eased back in the big leather chair. "Rufus tol' y'bout those boys waitin' t'see y'up at the office, I suppose?"

"Yes."

"FBI, they were."

"That's what Rufus said. Did they say what they wanted with me?"

"Said they wanted t'a'ks y'some questions."

LeBaron nodded.

"I suspect it's 'bout those classified papers y'carryin' 'round with ya. Wouldn't y'say?"

LeBaron nodded glumly. "I suppose so. I can't think of anything else." He put his head in his hands. "What am I going to do, Mr. Collins?"

"Well, for one thing, y'got t'stop *worryin'* about it. Worryin' won't do a lick o'good. *They*'re the ones up t'somethin' they're trying' t'hide, not you. *They*'re the one's gonna be in deep shit 'fore this's over. Y'got t'pull y'self together." He paused. "But I do recommend y'take a few precautions. Y'un'erstan'? Like not goin' home tonight, for starters. Y'better stay with a friend. Y'got any friends t'stay with? Or in a motel someplace. Use somebody else's name." He thought about it a moment, then asked, "Y'got any money?"

"Yes. I can get some from the machine."

"Thass good. An' another thing. Y'better keep on usin' ol' Muggins' car'f y'be needin' t'go someplace. For the time bein', anyhow. He sure ain't gonna miss it. I wouldn't go near your own car if I was you."

LeBaron let out a deep breath. "All right. What do you think the penalty would be if they decide to prosecute me for having these damned reports? Do you have any idea?"

"Ten years in a federal penitentiary an' ten thousand dollar fine, near's I can fig'er."

"Jesus!"

"Thass what Loomis got, anyway, over in Livermore. For divulgin' code secrets t'the Russians."

LeBaron had never heard of a "Loomis" and decided he really didn't want to.

"Anyhow," Collins continued, "we' gonna have t'move quick on this, so y'can get yourself on back home. All right?" He rocked forward and reached for the telephone. "Now I wanna hear all about this victim y'talked to . . . what's'r name, this Raccoona gal . . . an' about the secret document business y'mixed up in, too, but first I gotta return a call t'ol' Bert Thompkins 'fore he goes home for the day."

"About the Freeman case?"

"Prob'ly." Collins punched in the number without removing the handset from its cradle. The speakerphone booped and beeped its way to its destination and started ringing.

"What are you planning to do about Freeman?" LeBaron asked.

"Don't rightly know jus' yet--"

"District Attorney's office," a dull female voice announced.

"Gi'me the District Attorney," Collins growled.

More beeping, then another ring. "Bert Thompkins' office." This female voice sounded brighter.

"Yeah, this's Cedrick Collins returnin' a call from Bert Thompkins. Put'im on the line, will ya?"

"Just a moment, Mr. Collins."

They waited. After a while, LeBaron began, "Do you intend to try--"

"Bert Thompkins," the speakerphone piped in. The voice was quick and nervous.

"Bert, this's Cedrick Collins returnin' your call."

"Oh yeah, Cedrick. Hey, wait just a second, will ya? Let me get some of these people out of my office." They were put on hold.

LeBaron began again, "This Freeman trial, are you going to handle the trial yourself, or do you plan to--"

"Cedrick," the phone broke in again, "what the hell's goin' on over there in Department 23? Y'got my deputy all shook up. One minute he's madder'n hell at you an' . . . that associate o'yours, an' the next minute he's about t'start cryin' and wants to quit his job."

"Bert, that deputy o' yours's a sorry sight. Where'd y' find him? He's about as pleasant 's an ol' junkyard dog."

"Aw, y'gotta go easy on'im, Cedrick. He's just startin' out. Give'im time. He says it's *your* associate . . . what's'is name . . . 's'causin' all the fuss. Says your boy broke his word, backed out of a deal."

"The'ain't no *deal*, Bert. Never was. M'boy LeBaron never made a commitment. Couldn't've. Hadn't discussed the matter with the client. But your boy, he *assumed* he' got hisself a deal. He can't be doin' that, an' you know it. An' besides, he's got an *attitude* problem. Where'd y'find a boy like that, anyway, Bert?"

"Aw, he's jus' startin' out, Cedrick. Have y'forgotten how tough it was? Hell, I remember when *you* first started out. Remember ol' Judge McGinty down at city court? I'd only been a deputy for three or four months. What was it Judge McGinty used t'say when he saw y'come into the courtroom?"

Collins chuckled and leaned back in the chair as if rocking back through the years. "He'd ask, every time I'd come int' court . . . tickled the hell outta me . . . he'd jus' laugh and say 'Here he is. Does he know what he's doing today?'"

They both laughed.

"I'd say, 'I'll try. sir,'" Collins grinned.

"Y'know, I always thought Judge McGinty was playin' favorites with you, Cedrick. Thought you two knew somethin' I didn't. How'd you ever get in so good with an old bastard like that, anyway?"

Amused, Collins reminisced. "Had a coupla drunk cases the first day after the bar results were out. I went t'court, an' I didn't know what t'do. Didn't know how t'get the guy outta jail. Went down an' asked Ray Walls how t'get the man outta jail. Y'remember Ray Walls, don't ya?"

"Sure do. Best county clerk we ever had."

"He tol' me 'bout the bail schedule. We had the money, so we got'im out. I went t'court that mornin'. Judge McGinty was the judge. At the mornin' break I went t'chambers with him. I said, 'Judge, I just passed the bar yesterday.' I said, 'I don't know what the hell I'm doing. I got a client, an' he's got a drunk drivin' case. I wanna dispose o'this thing an' go back home. An' I don't want 'em all t'see what a damn' fool I look like. Don't want t'make a big fool outta myself. Could y'he'p me out on such a case, an' tell me what's happenin'?'" Collins chuckled. "I got 'im off with a fine. Judge was helpful. Gave me a fine. Would've sent him to jail. He said it's the first time that ever happened. I come in an' told him I wanted some help. I believe he took a shine t'me right then'n there."

"Well, that's just what I'm sayin', Cedrick. My deputy, Frank, he's just startin' out. Doesn't know what he's doin' yet an' too proud t'ask for help. You' got to make some allowances."

Collins' grin evaporated. "I'd keep an eye on'im, Bert. I think the boy's got a mean streak in'im."

"Give him a little time. Anyway, what about this Freeman case tomorrow? Frank says we gotta try it. Or else I have t'show up and explain t'Kroner why not. Jesus, I can't stand that son-of-a-bitch."

"Well, what'd y'tell the U. S. Attorney you'd do for'im, Bert? If y'don't mind my askin'."

"Naw. I told him I'd take a look at the case an' see if I could help him out."

"No particular promises?"

"Nope. Just said I'd take a look. Hell, it turns out t'be a chintzy little burglary. What's the problem?"

"Did y'tell'im you'd *dismiss* if y'couldn't get the defendant t'plead t'anything?"

The phone was silent for a moment. "Is that what you're askin' me to do, Cedrick?"

"No, I ain't."

Another silence, then Thompkins asked, "What do y'want to do, then?"

"I think we oughta try it."

A longer pause. "Can y'tell me *why* you want t'do that, Cedrick? I'm puttin' my ass on the line by not gettin' rid of this dog. What's the big deal? We offered you, what, a misdemeanor burglary?"

"That ain't the point. They' up to somethin' over there in Utah. Y'might as well know it. Somethin' mighty ugly. 'F'we take it t'trial, gonna be a lot o' evidence about a gover'ment project there. Department o' Agriculture conductin' it. They' monkeyin' around with changin' genes and stuff. *Human* genes, Bert. That's what they want you t'help'em hush up. I don' think y'oughta help'm. I think it all oughta come out at trial. I think them newsboys oughta get a chance t'hook into this thing. That's what I think."

"So *that's* what this's all about." Thompkins sounded relieved.

"Near's I can figure."

"Nothing' about local politics? No federal sting operations here in Alameda County?"

"Didn't hear nothin' 'bout none o' that. Whadda y'think about tryin' it?"

"I don't know." A pause. "What about your defendant? It really doesn't look very good for this Freeman boy, y'know."

"Don' worry 'bout him."

"Le'me sleep on it tonight. I gotta calculate the consequences if I cross the U. S. Attorney's office."

"You do that, Bert. But it sounds t'me like y'didn't make'em any promises. Y'made a good offer, an' the defendant jus' wouldn't take it. 'S'not your fault. An' anyway, this is all comin' outta Salt Lake City, not San Francisco. Whadda y'owe them? Besides, ol' Judge Kroner'd love t'see y'try it."

"Fuck Kroner. I'll think about it, Cedrick. Gotta consider the ramifications. Don't want t'make a wrong move here. This law enforcement business's a close-knit world. Don't want t'rile the wrong people if I don't have to. But I'll think about it."

"You do that, Bert. And thank ya."

"I'll let y'know." The line clicked off.

LeBaron had followed the exchange with growing concern for the fate of their client. As soon as Collins punched the phone off, he demanded, more stridently than he had intended, "What about Rufus?"

Collins grimaced, startled by LeBaron's severe tone. "What about'im?" he grumbled, looking away.

"If you try this case . . . he's looking at the possibility of state prison, you know."

"Now don't be startin' on that again. D'y'know how much that boy's paid? Two-hunderd thirty-five dollars! Thass all. Thass what he gave me t'day. Counted it m'self. Hell, that ain't 'nough for a damn' arraignment. Now this here trial's gonna cost'im a lot more--"

"I'm not disputing that!" LeBaron bounced out of his chair like an over-wound spring. He resumed his pacing as he spoke. "I'm sorry. I don't know. This is going to sound pretty simpleminded of me, Mr. Collins, but I have to say it. *I just have to say it.* I want to remind you about the Rules of Professional Conduct put out by the California Bar . . . that under the Rules our first responsibility as lawyers is our client's best interests. Period. Whether he pays or not." LeBaron watched the carpet as he paced.

Collins started to say something, then thought better of it. He sighed. "No, it don't sound 'simpleminded' t'me. You' right." He peeled off his wire-rimmed spectacles, and somberly rubbed his eyes with the heels of his hands. "'S too damn' easy t'loose track o' what's important. 'Specially with clients like ol' Rufus there. He's happy t'cheat y'out o'the fee y'rightly earned any way he can think of. Sort of a game with 'em. An' sometimes I get so caught up in the bluff an' bluster o' squeezin' a little spare money out of 'em, I forget I owe a little plain talk t'you." He replaced his glasses and studied his associate. "I got ol' Rufus' interests t'heart. I may talk like I don't sometimes, but I do, really. Y'see, Rufus's one o' my *people,* an' I'm gonna fight f'r'is rights best way I can. Whether he pays me or not." He leaned forward fiercely. *"Now don't you go sayin' a word o'this outside o' this office. Y'un'erstan'?"*

LeBaron nodded, smiling.

"Good." Collins reached for the heavy black volume he had dumped on the desk when he came in, settled back, and considered his next words. "It's just that I believe we can have it both ways here. Now if ol' Bert goes'n' decides t'dismiss outright . . . well, thass jus' fine, too. But if not, I believe we can go ahead an' hold this here trial an' blow the whistle on this genocide thing, or whatever it is they' up to, an' still do ol' Rufus a service. Get'im off, at least 's good 's they be off'rin' now, anyways. I took a look't the file las' night."

"How're you going to get him off?"

"I'm not. I' got a trial startin' tomorrow mornin' over in Department 10. Couldn't be he'ped. *You'* the one gonna have t'pull Rufus' bacon outta the fire."

"Me? Jesus! How am I going to do that? They caught him *red handed*, carrying the goddamn stolen tv set." LeBaron was getting worked up. "Anyway, I'll probably be in goddamned jail myself by the time the trial resumes tomorrow!"

"Y'got t'pull y'self t'gether. Y'un'erstan'? Calm y'self down. Get y'self a good night's sleep. Relax. Thass the first thing." He counted on his fingers. "Now we' sure gonna have t'keep you out o' jail. Thass the second--"

"How?"

"I got me some ideas 'bout that. Now jus' hol' on for a second. The next thing y'gotta do's start usin' that head o' yours. Look't the elements o' the crimes they' chargin'. Look't up in *Witkin*." Collins slid the heavy book toward him. "See what the D.A.'s gotta *prove* t'make a burglary. What'e's gotta *prove* t'make a grand theft. Use your imagination. Talk it over with Rufus there. You' a lawyer, LeBaron, an' a damn' good one'f I might say so. I' got confidence in ya. Now don' disappoint me. I think'f y'settle down an' look't this thing like I know y'can, y'gonna find the D. A.' gonna have a rough time provin'is case."

LeBaron picked up the volume of Witkin and sank back onto the wooden chair, exhausted and duly admonished. He *was* acting foolish. Emotional. Overwrought. He knew that, but he wasn't doing anything about it. He drew a deep breath and slowly let it out. To function effectively, a lawyer has to remain calm, disinterested, appraising the law, the facts, and the strengths and weaknesses of the opponent. It would be LeBaron against Ivan Frank. And Collins had put his money on LeBaron. He studied the cover of the book. "I'll take another look at it. But I would like to talk to you again about it before I get too far along."

"Sure. Sure. No problem wi'that." Collins leaned forward and rested his elbows on the desk. "Now tell me what y'found out 'bout this here gover'ment genocide program. Y'got them classified documents with ya?"

LeBaron opened his briefcase and exchanged the Witkin volume for the manila envelope Sarah Brubaker had given him, balancing it on one of his knees. He explained briefly how Sarah had worked with Dr. Finebridge, how over the years she had gained his confidence, and how she had become the unwitting custodian of stolen classified documents.

"Le'me see 'em," Collins broke in.

LeBaron handed the envelope to his employer, who drew out the reports and thumbed through them while LeBaron continued. LeBaron related how Dr. Finebridge had failed to show up for a meeting with Sarah and how she hadn't heard from him since. The FBI had stepped in and taken over the investigation from local authorities, with results that led Sarah to believe a cover-up was in progress.

Collins flipped through the reports, reading a few sentences here and there. It was not apparent whether he was even listening to his associate. Without looking up, he mumbled, "Go on."

LeBaron continued, "I think if we could just get hold of Dr. Finebridge, a lot of questions would be answered. Contacting him is a first priority, in my opinion. But I'm not really sure how to go about doing that. We may have to actually go out and do some snooping around, follow some leads we get from Sarah. Once we locate the place where they're holding him . . . I really don't know. I guess we would figure out some way to get him away."

Collins looked up from the reports. "Might be. Brown could help with'at. But I don't see no need t'be actin' like Sam Spade an' takin' the law int'our own hands if'n we don't need to."

"What else can we do?"

"Habeas corpus."

"Habeas corpus?"

Collins stared in amazement. "Y'mean y'never did a writ o' habeas corpus?"

LeBaron shook his head.

"Well, 's'bout time y'did one. Habeas corpus's the people's remedy. Guaranteed in the U. S. Constitution. We'll file us a writ o' habeas corpus an' get'em t'produce this Dr. Finestein in court t'show cause why he oughta be retained in custody. Y'un'erstan'? All we got t'do is figure out who t'serve with the writ. Can you get started on that?"

LeBaron nodded.

"Now, it's gettin' kind o' late, an' these things don't look t'me like easy readin'." He began stuffing the reports back into the envelope. "What'd you find out when y'read'em?"

LeBaron explained how he had fallen asleep before finishing. He summarized what he could remember of the part he read. Briefly he touched on the original project with the ferret brains and how Dr. Finebridge had built on that work, overcoming one obstacle after another, trying to integrate an artificial system with the natural one.

"Nothin' 'bout black people?" Collins asked impatiently. "Nothin' 'bout genocide?"

"Not yet."

"How 'bout a bunch o' racist talk? 'Niggers this' an' 'niggers that'. Any o' that?"

"Not that I read."

"Ummm. Guess that's good." Collins handed the envelope back to his associate. "You better keep readin' 'em an' let me know wha'cha got. I'd like t'get a copy of 'em, but I don't see how right now. I'd jus's soon not be makin' copies on Brown's machine. Got some real untrustworthy folks workin' for'im here. An' I don't reckon y'wanna go runnin' back t'the office jus' now." Painfully he stood up and with Gideon under one arm shuffled slowly over to his coat. "I got t'be gettin' on home now, LeBaron. Beatrice'll be worryin' 'bout me." He began pulling on his top coat. "But we'll talk again. Y'phone me at home this evenin', all right? After y'done some readin' in that Witkin. Now, y'got anything else we gotta talk 'bout jus' now?"

"Just one thing." LeBaron leaned forlornly on the wooden chair in the center of the small office.

Collins set his stingy brim rakishly on his head. "Whass that?"

"How're we going to keep me out of jail?"

CHAPTER TWELVE

Tuesday evening

--1--

"Son of a bitch," LeBaron muttered as his cold white fingers flapped numbly about like wounded birds, trying in vain to detach the crotch of his bedraggled corduroy trousers from the rusty points of barbed wire. "Son of a *bitch*!" He teetered on his tiptoes, his chest poked by the ancient rotting fence post and his back squeezed against the damp dirt-smudged siding of the garage behind his apartment building. The muscles of his trembling calves ached and seemed about to cramp from the prolonged balancing act. With each spasmodic shift of his position he could hear the threads of the inseam ripping. He wanted terribly to be away from this absurd predicament, but neither wishing nor cursing nor hot-blooded anger seemed to make any difference. He couldn't free his crotch from the clinging barbs he had tried to step over, and he couldn't relax, or he might inflict serious scrotal damage upon himself.

Finally, in desperation, he pushed off against the garage, kicked up his trailing leg like a high jumper, and threw himself forward with all the force he could manage. With an ugly rip his trousers tore free, and LeBaron flopped on his chest in the muddy drip margin beneath the eaves of the garage.

For a while he lay there in a blind rage. Everything was going to hell, and he didn't have anyone to blame but himself. Somehow the lack of an external target for his rage made him even angrier. He felt like screaming.

As his rage subsided, he sat up, leaned against the garage, and felt for the tear in his trousers. Sure enough, he could get three fingers through the hole, and the damage did not feel limited to the seam. The corduroy fabric itself was shredded. At least he didn't detect any warm, sticky blood, evidence that the flesh itself had not been punctured.

A mournful sigh racked his body. He had rushed out of the motel room in Tiburon with no time for breakfast, had intentionally skipped lunch, and yet ahead of him lay dinner. LeBaron's blood sugar level felt lower than the lowest dungeon of hell. He was weak and irritable, and a fiercely throbbing ache behind his eyes spread upward to the front of his skull. No food. Not enough sleep. Waylaid by an impromptu felony jury trial, and drugged with a cup of foul-tasting tea by one of the material witnesses, to what end he could scarcely begin to imagine. LeBaron was manifestly ready to quit this game, go home, eat a bowl of granola, and collapse into his own warm bed. But it didn't seem to be in the rules. Quitting was not permitted.

Collins had warned him not to go home tonight, but LeBaron had been so goddamned clever. He had figured he could sneak home by way of the back alley, squeeze through that gap between the fence and the garage which he had observed on occasion as he took out the garbage, slip in the back door, pick up a fresh change of underwear, a clean coat and slacks, his shaving kit, and a raincoat, and waltz back out without anyone knowing, all in plenty of time to meet Sally for dinner down at Jack London Square. It was too dark to read his watch, so he stuck his arm into the light coming around the corner of the garage. "Son of a *bitch*!" He had just seven minutes before he was supposed to meet Sally.

"Wait a minute," he muttered to himself. *Where the hell was that light coming from*? There wasn't supposed to be that much light in his backyard. He was supposed to sneak in through the back way under cover of darkness. He leaned over and peered around the corner. "*Damn!*" He had left the back porch light on.

Only he knew that he hadn't. The skin crawled across his scalp with the confirmation that this was all really happening. It wasn't just his overwrought imagination. Someone had in fact been to his apartment. Had been *inside* his apartment. And *they* had left the back porch light on when they departed. Intentionally, no doubt. So they could keep an eye on the back door from a safe distance. They were probably watching it right now. But from *where*? He had driven past the front of the building in the Pimpmobile and hadn't seen anything out of the ordinary. No secret agents with trench coat collars turned up lurking under the street light. No undercover cops smoking cigarettes in unmarked cars out front. Nothing. He craned his neck, but couldn't locate where they might be staked out, waiting, watching for him.

LeBaron shivered. He could feel the cold wet soaking through the seat of his pants, and as the fabric wicked up the moisture, that peculiar odor assailed his nostrils. If he didn't do something quickly, they'd *sniff* him out right where he sat biding his time. Painfully he climbed to his feet, his right knee throbbing where he'd landed on it, and peered again around the corner of the garage. Hell, maybe he *had* left the porch light on last time he took out the trash. He couldn't remember when that had been. He was probably just working himself up into a state of terror for no reason. He'd watched too many gangster movies. The FBI wouldn't *really* be staking out his apartment. Would they?

"All right," he mumbled, "nothing ventured . . ." He crossed the lighted yard to the back porch, climbed the four steps, and quietly inserted his key into the cylinder lock. He paused and listened. Nothing. He turned the key and pushed open the door, which emitted a little squeal where it tended to stick in the damp weather.

LeBaron gasped. Even from the threshold it was clear that his entire house had been ransacked. All of the drawers in the kitchen had been pulled out and stacked on the floor beside piles of pots and pans taken from every cabinet. The cabinet doors all stood wide open. Through the doorway on the opposite side of the kitchen he could see the mess in the living room. Everything had been opened, searched, and turned out into heaps in the middle of the room.

Righteous indignation began to rise in his breast, but was quenched by a small thud from the living room. Soft and deep, the sound was like the padding of bare feet on the carpet. LeBaron stood agape, uncertain whether to fight or take flight.

A man stepped into the living room doorway to investigate the noise at the back door. The intruder was stocky, obviously in good physical shape, blond, and handsome in a rugged sort of way. He appeared to be in his late twenties or early thirties. His coat was off, exposing a shoulder harness and the butt of a small squarish-looking pistol jutting up under his left arm. His face had a day's growth of beard, and his eyes were bleary, as if he had just been dozing. Equally taken aback, the two men stared at each other across the disheveled kitchen.

I'm caught! LeBaron's mind screamed. *They were waiting for me inside my own goddamned apartment!*

"Hold it right there!" the blond man snapped. "FBI!" His left hand reached for something in his back pocket. His right hand went for the butt of his pistol.

The words jarred LeBaron out of his torpor. Without thinking, he jerked backwards and slammed the door, deftly twisting the key which still protruded from the lock. It was a double cylinder deadbolt, and the FBI man would have to find a key to unlock it from the inside, or else resort to the front door. LeBaron leaped over the back porch railing and started around the corner up the driveway. Instinctively he knew it was a bad move, and he stopped.

Out in the street a car door slammed, and a husky voice shouted, "We got'm, Frank! Around back!"

"Oh Jesus!" LeBaron had no choice. He turned and sped back toward the formidable gap in the fence at the rear of the garage. At full speed he approached the narrow opening. It was too dark to see much, but LeBaron had already learned the intricacies of the passage by braille. Without slowing he dove headfirst into the darkness, rattled between the garage wall and the post, and cleared the top strand of barbed wire by six inches. Tucking his head, he rolled as he hit the cold gravel of the alley. The impact knocked some of the wind out of him, but he didn't have time to sit and take inventory. He staggered to his feet and began hobbling down the dark alley toward the side street. His low back had taken most of the blow and protested as he stretched out his strides. His left wrist throbbed, and a few pieces of cold gravel worked their way down the back of his collar.

"LeBaron!" someone shouted. Behind him dark shapes were already at the corner of the garage, trying to decipher the route. "We know it's you! Stop! We gotta ask you some questions!"

LeBaron picked up his pace, testing the kink in his back. He was almost to the cross street.

"Stop, goddamn it!" the voice sputtered behind him. "Ouch! Shit, that's barbed wire, Frank. *It's your ass now, LeBaron!*"

LeBaron turned the corner and managed a slow trot. The knot was working its way out of his back, and he had recovered his breath. Muggins' Pimpmobile was parked in the middle of the next block. He broke into a wobbling sprint. As he approached the vehicle, he glanced back over his shoulder. Two figures were emerging from the alley into the light. *How had they managed to get through so quickly?* One of them was the blond fellow from his kitchen. They spotted him and started up the street at a run.

"Shit!" LeBaron knew he wouldn't have time to unlock the car, climb inside, start the engine, and work his way out of the parking space. They would be on top of him with their guns drawn. So he took the only alternative. He fled past the car and straight down the street. At the corner he turned left and kept running.

LeBaron glanced over his shoulder. They were still coming, and gaining on him. Already they were closer by a quarter of a block. His instinct was to pick up his speed, but he could feel the fatigue beginning to build up in his thighs. He was a jogger, not a sprinter, and knew his own limits. *Slowly*, he cautioned himself, slackening the speed a bit. *Stay aerobic. Just like a Sunday run through the park. Nothing to get excited about.*

LeBaron kept zigzagging, turning right at one block, and left at the next. He could hear footsteps closing in behind him, but he tried to put them out of his mind. He found a pace, a little faster than comfortable, but not quite anaerobic, and tried to sustain it. After another few blocks he got up the courage to look around again. The blond FBI agent was less than a half block behind and coming strong. The other one had dropped off somewhere, maybe to fetch a car and head him off. LeBaron cranked up the speed half a notch despite the protest from his burning lungs.

Now he could hear the FBI agent puffing and wheezing close behind him. In a moment a hand would close on his shoulder, or else he would pitch forward on the concrete as a flying ankle tackle brought him down. He put the thoughts out of his mind and reached down for the last of his reserves. Head down, arms pumping, eyes almost closed, he ran as fast as he could. He might be good for another three or four blocks at this pace, he figured, and took the next right.

Then no one was behind him. He'd outrun the bastard! He'd outrun them all! LeBaron eased back on the pace, turned the next corner, and kept on striding into the wispy ground fog which was just starting to form in the low areas. He crossed an eerily deserted San Pablo Avenue and spotted a bus at the next corner. He ran for it. The placard announced it was bound for Jack London Square.

--2--

At six-foot-six, 280 pounds dripping wet, Waddington Carruthers was a big man by anyone's measure. Almost too big for the driver's seat on an Alameda County Transit bus. But he managed. Better to suffer a little discomfort than lose his entitlement to that fat biweekly pay warrant. Not yet a regular driver, he worked the extraboard, filling in for other drivers as needed. Brown had done him a favor by leaning on the union representative to relax the height and weight restrictions. Now he owed Brown. That was all right. Everybody seemed to owe Brown these days. Waddington would crank back the seat as far as it would go and make do, but by the end of an eight-hour shift, his legs were always pretty well cramped up.

Today he was filling in for Jimmy Houston, who had called in sick with the flu. Seemed like a lot of that was going around. Waddington was already feeling pretty stiff and looking forward to climbing down at the end of this homebound run. He had his hand on the door lever when he spotted the white dude coming from half a block away, waving his arms like a wild man. It looked like trouble even from that distance. Waddington could have ignored him, shut the door, and roared right past. He was behind schedule, and the rules were clear enough on that. But for some reason he paused.

The white fellow leapt on board without missing a stride and caught the grab rail to keep from collapsing in exhaustion. There was something familiar about the dude, and Waddington studied him as he fumbled in his pocket for change. He looked like he was high on something. Stoned out of his mind, in fact. Maybe dangerous. Waddington was big, but he was not a man of violence. Despite his size, he had never played football. The most violent thing he ever did was feed live brine shrimp to his tropical fish. And he'd heard stories about guys stoned on animal tranquilizer having the strength of ten men. A driver had the right to ask an intoxicated passenger to get off his bus, but it was a tricky business. Lefty Jones had gotten himself into a mess with a possible lawsuit and temporary suspension over that sort of thing just last month. The union hadn't been a whole lot of help to Lefty either. A driver had to watch out for himself, had to be *sure*.

"Ninety cents," he said.

With trembling fingers the white fellow fumbled a wallet out of the back pocket of his bedraggled corduroy suit. It sure looked like he'd slept, swam, pissed, crawled through a pig sty, and lost a razor fight recently in that suit. A sheen of sweat coated his face and hands, and he was panting and wheezing like his heart might explode at any time. In his steely blue eyes was a wild, hunted-animal gleam. He managed to snatch a note out of his wallet and held it up like a small dead animal. "Got change for a five?"

"Drivers don't carry no cash," Waddington replied, his hand still on the door lever. The door stood open. The bus hadn't moved. He was used to dealing with drunks and derelicts from this part of town, and he wasn't about to move the bus until his new passenger paid or disembarked. A strong unfamiliar odor was fouling the air. Waddington knew the smell of alcohol, opium, hashish, marijuana, and crack, but he'd never sniffed anything like this before. Whatever this dude was on, Waddington had no desire to be a part of it. "Y'can get change at that liquor store--" Waddington pointed down the block "--an' catch the next bus."

"What if I stick the whole thing in the box?"

"'S'your money. I can't give ya no change."

"Right. Keep the change." The man stuffed the five into the farebox and swung into the side-facing seat next to the door. An elderly matron with an armload of packages in the first bench seat eyed the newcomer with distaste, wrinkled her nose as his aroma wafted back to her, and moved further to the rear of the bus.

Waddington closed the door and got the bus under way. Warily he watched his new fare out of the corner of his eye. In the unblinking fluorescent light, he could see what a mess the dude's trousers were, torn, frayed, dirty, and wrinkled. The man had closed his eyes and was still breathing hard, holding tight to the cool chrome pole beside him as the bus rumbled to cruising speed. *Now where had he seen him before?*

Suddenly Waddington recognized him. Or thought he did. *Naw . . . couldn't be!* "Say, ain't you the fella used to work with Attorney Collins?"

LeBaron's eyes snapped open in horror. "Do I know you?" he managed to stammer.

"Why, *sure*. Carruthers. Waddington Carruthers. You handled my daughter's case. Yowanda Beth. She was dog bit. Got us a nice little settlement, y'did."

LeBaron resumed breathing. "Carruthers. Yes, I remember."

"What was your name again?"

"LeBaron. Wasn't there some question about whether she was teasing that dog?"

"Thass a lie." Waddington smiled enormously. "Yes, sir. You advised us t'take the money."

"How's Yowanda Beth doing?"

"Oh, jus' fine. Scar don't hardly show no more." Waddington frowned. "Say, you don't look so good."

LeBaron nodded and closed his eyes again, still clinging for his life to the chrome pole. "'S'been a tough night."

Waddington was confused. LeBaron didn't *talk* like he was stoned. But he sure was acting funny. And why did he look like *that*?

A gaunt, bent figure loomed at the next stop. Waddington slowed and glided to the curb. The door hissed open. An emaciated old codger venting a strong fragrance of cheap wine stumbled feebly aboard. His entrance was slow and painful, and Waddington gazed through the windshield.

Across the intersection, beneath the bright yellow sodium streetlight, a plainclothes detective with blond hair, no jacket, and an exposed gun harness snaking over his sweat-stained shoulders like some kinky leather bra was leaning into the window of a police black-and-white cruiser. Another cruiser idled its engine behind, and a third pulled up as he watched. Beside the detective stood another law enforcement type with a grim set jaw gazing intently back the way the bus had come. The blond detective straightened and pointed that direction. Waddington watched the drama with distaste while the old wino located and deposited his token. Waddington had no use for the police. Too many times he had been pushed around on the street by officers intimidated by his sheer mass.

"She-it!" In a flash of insight Waddington comprehended what was likely going down. Suddenly it all made sense in a twisted sort of way. No drugs were involved here. This LeBaron fellow was plum high on *fear*. Fugitive fear. As the wino wobbled past, he leaned over and whispered, "*Po*lice. Y'better git down."

"What?" LeBaron jerked awake and stared out the front window. He froze in midbreath.

"Y'better git down," Waddington repeated, "as we go on past 'em. Tie your shoe'r somethin'." He levered close the door and stepped on the accelerator.

The bus roared to life, and Waddington watched the detectives swing their heads his way as LeBaron ducked down and began to fiddle with his shoe lace. He flashed a big smile and waved to them, but he couldn't tell whether or not they could see his fugitive fare in the bright interior lights of the bus. Through the back window Waddington watched as they returned to plotting their house-to-house search or whatever they had in mind. An all-points bulletin had probably been issued. The neighborhoods behind them would be thick with squad cars cruising the streets, shining spotlights down every dark alley, and hassling everybody on the street. Mr. LeBaron had been damned lucky. "'S'all right now," Waddington smiled, wondering what they were after him for, but too polite to ask.

LeBaron straightened up. "Thanks," he groaned.

Waddington waved it away. "Y'done good by Yowanda Beth."

LeBaron said nothing. His brow was knit. He was obviously distracted by some important decision. Suddenly his arm flew up as if with a determination of its own and tripped the bell cord.

Waddington eyed him dubiously. "Y'sure you want off *here*?"

LeBaron nodded and stood up unsteadily, his brow still deeply furrowed. "Yes. I mean, no, I don't *want* to get off here. I just . . . think

I'd better."

The big bus lumbered to the curb at the next stop, and the door hissed open. "Good luck," Waddington smiled. "I ain't seen ya tonight."

"Thanks," LeBaron called as he jumped down to the ground.

--3--

The bus roared off into the chilly night, and LeBaron felt utterly abandoned, lost, frightened, and half-frozen to death. His sweat-soaked T-shirt clung cold against his clammy skin. His breath came in visible puffs of vapor. His knee hurt. His back hurt. His wrist hurt. His legs had stiffened up. His fingers were numb and white. He headed up the cross street at a brisk walk, his hands stuck deep into his pockets, intoning over and over to himself in time with his footfalls like some secret mantra designed to ward off the forces of annihilation, "*Bad craziness! This is bad craziness!*"

An unsettling thought had jangled across LeBaron's mind back there on the bus, just after they had roared past the growing nucleus of a posse. If they were all hunting for him *back there*, then who was watching *his apartment*? In another two blocks the bus would be at his usual stop, and he could--

No! he had tried to tell himself, *This is bad craziness. Much too risky. You're away free. Don't even* think *about it.*

But another voice in his fragmented thoughts had reminded him that he had to pick up Muggins' Pimpmobile *sometime*. The stolen government reports and the Witkin book lay on the front seat like a full-page advertisement waiting to be spotted through the tinted windows. He needed them both, and right away. Would there ever be a safer time than now? And if he could also manage to slip into his apartment and pick up those fresh clothes while he was at it--

No! It's bad craziness! The car, maybe, but stay away from the goddamned apartment!

In spite of his better judgment, he had tumbled off the bus and headed up this familiar street toward his own apartment. Chanting like an idiot, he was walking right into the craw of serious peril. And he didn't seem to be able to do anything about it.

He rounded the corner and stopped. Across the street a half-block down stood his apartment building in the yellow streetlight glare. Nothing moved. For a long moment he watched and waited, then minced cautiously along on the opposite side of the street looking for any signs of residual FBI activity. As he drew closer, he could see no movement through the front windows.

They'd left his goddamned front door wide open!

That really pissed him off. Madder than a hornet, LeBaron buzzed across the street, up the front steps, and into the living room. He held his breath and listened. Other than the street noises from outside, the only sound was the pounding of his own heart. He closed and locked the front door, then scurried about quietly gathering the things he would need for the next couple of days. Instinctively he ducked whenever the headlights of a passing vehicle flashed out front.

He tried to ignore the devastation they had made of his personal possessions, but his anger ripened into heavy fruit as he stumbled from room to room hunting through the mess for essential items and tossing them into his canvass duffel bag. He felt violated. Raped. This was no way to treat a taxpaying citizen. He vowed to have their asses in court before this whole thing was over. He'd come back and take photographs, big eight-by-ten glossies to wow the jury, and demand a million dollars in punitive damages. No, he'd make it ten million! Heads were goddamned well going to roll over this if it was the last thing he ever did.

So intense was the savor of his vengeance that he almost missed the headlights of the squad car as it slowed and stopped out front. LeBaron dropped to his hands and knees and peeked out around the corner of the front drapes. "Oh, *shit!*" The passenger door was opening, but he didn't wait to see who got out. He spun around and crawled as fast as he could toward the kitchen, crunching through the spoils of his ravished possessions. Behind him he wrestled the half-full duffel like the carcass of his shriveled outrage. Scrambling over an overturned drawer in the kitchen doorway, he spotted a pair of slip-joint pliers and snatched them up. LeBaron staggered to his feet and lurched for the back door, fumbling for his keys. Then the door was open and he was outside. As silently as his trembling fingers would allow, he closed and locked it again.

They'll know something's wrong the instant they find the front door locked! he thought, and his heart skipped a couple of beats. Once more he fled toward that cursed gap in the rear fence, this time armed with the wire-cutting jaws of his trusty pliers. He skidded around the corner of the garage and out of the glare of the back porch light. With eyes unaccustomed to the murkiness, he felt his way along the cold, damp boards of the garage, flailing his free hand in front of him like the antenna of a huge blind insect. Suddenly he stumbled through the breach and was crunching in the alley gravel. No barbed wire! He turned and squinted into the darkness to see what had happened. The rotten fence post lay on its side, broken off at ground level. So *that's* how they had gotten through so quickly. Why in hell hadn't *he* thought to push that son-of-a-bitch over?

LeBaron didn't wait to see if they would be coming after him this time. The street was still empty when he found the Pimpmobile, so he climbed inside, got it started, and headed for Jack London Square with the heater blazing, trying to dry out his clothes and relieve a bad case of the shivers. Along the way he stopped to make a maximum cash withdrawal from the automatic teller machine on the street level of the Berkeley Bank and Trust Building.

--4--

Judge Felix Kroner glared at the final crumbling groat cluster squatting on his plate like the remnants of an occupying army. Alma's sister had brought them over last week, and they were bad enough when they were fresh. Tonight it was all he could do to choke them down, even lubricated with a thin slurry of oatmeal and skim milk. With a grimace he took another bite.

He took his meals at home alone now that his wife was in the nursing home. After forty-seven years of marriage to Alma, he wasn't used to eating alone, and he didn't think he ever would be. At first he had tried to look after Alma himself with the help of a part-time home care attendant referred by the county home health agency, but the situation had become impossible. They would have had to tie Alma's wrists to the bed frame to keep her from getting up and into all the wrong things. It was lucky she hadn't hurt herself or burned the goddamn house down. Twice she had wandered off, and he had to call the police to help find her. That didn't look good for a judge. Pretty soon they might start questioning the soundness of *his* mind.

After dinner Judge Kroner would usually go over and sit with Alma for a while at the nursing home, although the sights and sounds and smells of that warehouse of corrupting flesh were almost too much to bear. He was beginning to suspect that she had no idea who he was anymore, but that was not the point. He knew who *she* was, and he had a duty to his Alma. That's what the vows were about, right? For richer and for poorer, in sickness and in health. The contract was signed and sealed and deposited long ago in the dusty archives of obligation. Judge Kroner accepted his duty, however distasteful, for otherwise how could he with a clear conscience pass judgment on all the human scum who paraded endlessly through his courtroom? He was obliged to put in his time at the nursing home.

Usually, anyway. But not tonight. Today had been a particularly hellacious one. The wet weather had set off his arthritis from the time he climbed out of bed this morning. Then that smug nigger son-of-a-bitch Cedrick Collins had interrupted his court proceeding, thrown his courtroom into chaos, and gotten him all riled up with personal insults. And on top of all that, the inept new deputy Ivan Frank had the misguided gall to call off the prosecution witnesses, so all he could do in his own courtroom was sit there and twiddle his thumbs while Collins taunted him. He should have cited them both for contempt and been done with it.

Judge Kroner felt his bile rising again, so he carted the dishes to the sink and ran water over them. He clicked on the evening news for a little distraction. Just as he was settling into his recliner, the telephone rang.

"Judge Kroner here."

"Good evenin', Judge. This's Cedrick Collins callin'."

"Collins! You've got a lot of nerve calling me at home. How did you get my number? I could have you--"

"Now hold on a minute, Judge. I apologize for disturbin' y'at home there, but I think there's somethin' y'better be knowin' about the Freeman case before y'summon that jury tomorrow. I jus' want t'he'p y'keep from puttin' all those folks to a lot o' trouble for nothin' tomorrow, y'un'erstan'."

"What are you up to now, Collins?"

"Ain't up t'*nothin'*, Judge. I'm jus' tryin' t'he'p y'out here, if y'don't mind."

"What is it then?"

"Well, I got assigned out t'trial this mornin' in Department 10." Collins paused. "That's Judge Gillespie's court--"

"I know perfectly well that's Judge Gillespie's court, damn it! You don't have to tell me that. So what? Your associate LeBaron can handle the Freeman trial. We don't need you."

"Well, thass jus' it, Judge. I jus' had a long conversation with ol' Bert Thompkins 'bout the case. Looks t'me like Bert'll be proceedin' with the trial, though it's too early t'tell for sure. Now y'remember when that Deputy Frank tol' ya this mornin' that the U. S. Attorney was leanin' on 'em t'drop the case?"

"I remember. So what?"

"Well, now it seems like they sent out some FBI boys t'take my associate LeBaron into custody."

"What?"

"Thass right, Judge. Take'im right into custody."

"Is LeBaron in custody now?"

"I don't believe he is. Not yet."

"What are they charging him with?"

"Nothin'. Near's I can figure, they jus' want t'a'ks'im some questions."

"Have they got an arrest warrant?"

"Not that I know of, Judge. But they' plannin' t'step right in and yank LeBaron out o' your courtroom the minute he shows his face tomorrow mornin'. Sure is gonna mess up your trial. Fact is, y'might jus' want t'go ahead and plan t'dismiss against Freeman there, if the FBI intends t'keep on buttin' into the proceedin's in your own courtroom."

Judge Kroner couldn't determine if this was one of Collins'

pranks or another screwup by Ivan Frank. He counted his breaths to keep from getting too excited.

"Hello, Judge, y'still there?"

"I'm here."

"So I jus' thought y'might want t'know. Y'might want t'consider callin' off the jury tonight an' sparin' those nice folks the trouble o' comin' down t'the courthouse in the mornin'. It'll jus' be a waste o' their time. Don't look like you' ever gonna get the case tried the way those FBI boys be actin'."

"Oh, we'll get it tried all right, Mr. Collins. Don't you worry about that."

"Yes, Judge, but--"

"You tell Mr. LeBaron to come to my chambers before trial in the morning. He can use the judge's access and come up the back elevator. Have him tell the bailiff I said so. Do you understand?"

"Yes, Judge, but the FBI boys--"

"Just have him ready to go to trial. I'll take care of the rest. Do I make myself clear?"

"Yes, Judge."

"Anything else, Mr. Collins?"

"No, Judge."

"Goodbye, Mr. Collins."

"'Bye, Judge."

--5--

LeBaron arrived at Mort's forty minutes late expecting to find Sarah beside herself from worrying about him. No such luck. Like a woebegone bomb blast survivor, he wandered through the bustling restaurant and out to the bar, raising eyebrows. He questioned the bartender, two waiters, and a busboy. Sarah had apparently not shown up yet. It was LeBaron's turn to do some worrying.

The headwaiter, a surly bald fellow with a bushy moustache, intercepted LeBaron on his third pass and steered him toward a small table in a dark corner out of sight of the other customers. LeBaron balked. The headwaiter insisted. LeBaron pointed to an empty table in the front window where he could keep an eye on the door. The headwaiter shook his head. With patience and an orator's silver tongue, LeBaron endeavored to convince the man of the advantage of the front table. In the end the headwaiter yielded to the weight of reason and, stuffing a crisp new twenty dollar bill into his back pocket, showed LeBaron to the table he desired.

Now where the hell was Sarah? LeBaron wondered. Maybe she thought they were meeting at *seven*, rather than six. Like in Tiburon. An easy mistake to make. LeBaron convinced himself that she would pop in--he glanced at his watch--in about fifteen minutes. That was a long time for a starving man to wait. He flagged down a waiter and ordered a small bowl of hot minestrone soup and a cup of coffee.

To pass the time, he brought out the Witkin text and browsed through it, making notes on a yellow pad. It was like strolling through a foreign land. His law school course in criminal law had been a joke, minimally designed to impart just enough information to answer a few stock questions on the bar exam. The tweed-and-meerschaum faculty never expected any of *their* students to actually practice in the filthy field. That was left for the semi-literate ambulance chasers and two-bit hucksters turned out en masse by less dignified institutions and matchbook correspondence schools.

With perseverance, LeBaron oriented himself. He found the sections on theft and burglary and marked them with strips of paper torn from his pad. He began with theft. All thefts were crimes of specific intent. Good. That meant that the prosecution had the burden of proving what was going on in Freeman's mind at the time of the alleged offense. Grand theft was a felony and involved the taking of property valued at more than four hundred dollars. If less, it was petty theft, a misdemeanor. Unless, of course, the defendant has prior theft convictions, because then it could be charged as either a felony or a misdemeanor, depending on the prosecuting attorney's mood at the time. These were known as "wobblers" in the trade. Unless stipulated to be a misdemeanor by the prosecution, the final determination, felony or misdemeanor, would be made at the time of sentencing by the judge. If the sentence was to state prison, the crime would be a felony. If to county jail or a fine, it was a

misdemeanor. LeBaron made a note to try to find a witness to testify on
the value of the tv set. Not that it would make any difference in the long
run. With Freeman' priors, Judge Kroner would jump at the chance of
sending him to the joint, even if the tv set were worth fifty cents.

His soup arrived, and he tasted it. The warm liquid was delicious,
immediately restoring feeling to his fingers and spirit to his soul. It was
just the sort of stuff Ponce de Leon must have been seeking when he
stumbled upon Florida.

LeBaron returned to the text. Burglary. Burglary of an *inhabited*
dwelling was first degree and a felony, punishable by four years in state
prison, unless the sentence was augmented or diminished. All other
burglaries were second degree and were wobblers. He wondered if
someone had to actually be present in the apartment at the time the
burglary was committed in order to be first degree. He thumbed through
the article and found a discussion of the subject. Penal Code Section 459
defined "inhabited" to mean "currently being used for dwelling purposes,
whether occupied or not." That didn't bode well for Freeman. It would
be tough to convince the jury that Raccoona GeBobath was not currently
using her apartment for dwelling purposes. What else could she be using
it for? As a main office for anti-Mormon hate mongering, maybe? Or as
a center for creative witchcraft? Perhaps, but only incidentally to the
main purpose of a dwelling. The cases confirmed that the district
attorney had properly charged Freeman with burglary in the first degree.

The soup was doing him a world of good, but it was gone. He
scraped the bowl with his spoon. LeBaron hated to ruin his appetite, but
. . . he ordered a second bowl and a basket of French bread. The waiter
refilled his coffee cup.

He glanced at his watch. Almost seven twenty and still no sign
of Sarah. What could possibly cause her to be twenty minutes late? *Not
twenty minutes*, he reminded himself, *an hour and twenty minutes*.
Something was seriously wrong. With an act of will he decided to give
her until eight before he really got upset, suspending a flimsy bridge of
hope over the yawning chasm he felt inside. The weasels of doubt,
however, were already gnawing on the main support ropes.

Burglary was also a crime of specific intent. Freeman must be
shown not only to have entered Raccoona's apartment, but to have had

the intent to enter for the purpose of committing grand or petty theft. And that intent must have existed *at the time Rufus entered*. That was it, wasn't it? Here lay the key to the defense. This must have been what Mr. Collins was referring to. If Rufus entered the apartment *for another purpose*, then he was not guilty of burglary even if later, after he was already inside and spotted that nice little tv set, he changed his mind and formulated the intent to rip the place off.

LeBaron set down the volume and rubbed his eyes. Jesus! The stakes were too high. Four years in state prison! What had Mr. Collins *done* to poor Rufus? He browsed over his notes. How the hell was he ever going to convince the jury that Rufus had something *else* in mind when he entered Raccoona's apartment? Intent might be a slippery concept, but the fact that Rufus was caught red-handed exiting the place with Raccoona's tv set cradled in his larcenous arms was pretty damn good circumstantial evidence of what his intent had been at the time he walked in through that open front door. And by the way, how was he going to convince the jury that Rufus *had* entered through an open front door and not through the second floor window, as the police report implied. And even if LeBaron could manage to think something up, how on earth was he going to communicate it to Rufus without himself being guilty of suborning perjury of a witness, which was, if his memory served him correctly, a felony in its own right. He skimmed through the text searching for notes on any cases which might be of help.

"Shit!" He snapped the book shut. Nothing! A waste of time. The cases didn't alter the fundamental law. Rufus would do four hard years in the joint, and it was going to be LeBaron's fault. He was going to lose his first goddamned felony trial. Victory had been snatched from his grasp when Mr. Collins had sauntered into the courtroom that morning and scuttled the plea bargain aborning.

And something far worse was afoot. It was almost eight o'clock, and Sarah was not going to show up. Not tonight. Not ever. LeBaron felt that in his bones. Something bad had happened. *They* had her. Just like they were going to have *him* first thing tomorrow morning.

Suddenly his knees felt all weak and wobbly. His insides had turned to liquid. He drew a deep breath that wavered and wanted to break up in his throat. Everything had gone wrong. He might as well just turn himself in and save the hassle. And save himself from having to play a leading role in the betrayal of Rufus Freeman. In desperation he scoured his mind for any glimmer of hope in the gloomy landscape of futility. He needed a talisman, a sign, a loadstone to guide his next move. After awhile, his thoughts came to rest on the glistening ivory grin of Cedrick P. Collins.

CHAPTER THIRTEEN

Tuesday night

--1--

"Mmmlo," Cedrick Collins spoke through a thick mouthful of mashed potatoes and barbecued spare ribs.

"Mr. Collins, this is Jed LeBaron. I'm glad you're finally home. I've been trying to reach you all evening."

"Mmmm."

"This trial business isn't working out at all. The jury's going to find Rufus Freeman guilty. He's going to state prison for at least four years. I think we should've let him plead to the misdemeanor."

"Mmmm."

"And I'm going to be arrested in the morning as soon as I show up in court, so it doesn't look like I'll be able to try the case anyway."

"Mmmm."

"And now something else has happened that's really got me worried. Sarah's missing."

Collins swallowed. "Sarah? Now who's'*at* again?"

"Sarah Brubaker. The friend who gave me the government reports. She was supposed to meet me at Mort's, but she didn't show up. I think the FBI's probably taken her into custody."

"Mmmm. Anything else?"

"Yeah. FBI agents chased me through the streets of Berkeley when I tried to go home for a change of clothes. I had to outrun them."

"Thought I warned y'bout that," Collins grumbled. "That all?"

LeBaron couldn't think of anything else. "Isn't that enough?"

"Le'me get t'nother room. Y'caught me'n Beatrice eatin' a late dinner." The phone went silent for a moment. "Glad y'called, LeBaron.

I need t'talk t'ya. Where' y'at?"

"The White Fang Inn."

"That the ol' hotel down by the freeway? Down by Jack London Square?"

"Yes."

"I know the place. Seems like a lot o'our hookers come from 'round that area. I always thought y'had better taste'n that. Couldn't y'afford somethin' a little more uptown?"

"I'm trying to conserve my assets. I don't have any idea how long I'm going to be running like a common criminal."

"Ain't nothin' *common* 'bout havin' possession o' top secret gover'ment papers," Collins chuckled. "Anyway, y'be careful y'don't catch nothin' down there. Now y'soundin' a little frazzled. Y'got t'settle yourself down. Y'takin' all this stuff too personal. Things ain't as bad as y'think. Relax."

LeBaron drew a deep breath and let it out. "All right. What happens to me tomorrow morning?"

"Thass one o' the things I got t'talk t'ya about. Ge'cha'self a pencil an' a piece o' paper."

"Just a second." The catches on the top of LeBaron's briefcase snapped. "Go ahead."

"Okay. Now first of all, y'*ain't* gonna be arrested in the mornin'."

"I'm not?"

"No." Collins related his conversation with Judge Kroner.

"What's he planning to do?" LeBaron asked. "Issue an order for the FBI to keep their hands off of me?"

"Near's I can figure."

"Can he do that?"

"Who knows? Ol' Judge Kroner gonna do whatever he damn well pleases in his own courtroom, I guess. Now you just make sure that when he issues that order, it extends t'the time you be preparin' for trial, too. Outside o' court, I'm talkin' 'bout. Tell the judge y'plannin' t'stay up all night goin' over the testimony. Y'ain't got time t'be talkin' t'no gover'ment investigators 'til after the trial's done. Or else there's gonna be a serious delay in the proceedin's beyond your control. Y'un'erstan'?"

"I guess so. But what if he doesn't make this order?"

"Wha'cha tryin' t'do t'me, LeBaron? Y'thinkin' too *negative* here. He'll *make* the order. Don' worry. Now, d'y'know where the entrance t'the judges' elevator's at?"

"I think so. It's just to the left of the information booth on the first floor, isn't it?"

"Thass right. An' if anybody gives y'any trouble, have'm phone up t'ol' Judge Kroner himself. Y'un'erstan'?"

"All right. What about Sarah?"

"What about her?"

"How are we going to get her back? I think the FBI picked her up. I'm really worried--"

"Now jus' settle down. Y'sound real upset. Y'can't do no figurin' when y'upset like that." The phone was silent for a moment. "Ain't y'plannin' t' file for a writ o' habeas corpus for that other fella, that Dr. . . . what's'is name?"

"Dr. Finebridge. Yes, I am, if I can find the time."

"Well, *take* the time. After court tomorrow. I won't pile nothin' else on y't'do."

LeBaron snorted. "Is that a promise?"

Collins ignored the dig. "Now 's'jus' as easy t'file for two o' them writs as for one. Y'un'erstan''? Y'can use the same declaration for both of 'em. Make 'em produce that Sarah o' yours, too."

"All right. I hope it's not too late."

"She'll be okay. Now, what's next? Oh, yeah, Rufus Freeman. Didn't y'read that Witkin book I gave t'ya."

"I read it."

"Well? Didn't y'get any ideas?"

"I guess I need to show that when Rufus went inside Raccoona's apartment, he didn't intend to rip the place off. But . . . I don't see how I can get Rufus to testify to that."

"Whass the problem?"

"Well, if I put him on the stand cold and ask him what his intention was, I think his answer will probably get him convicted fast."

"Y'haven't a'ksed him yet?"

"No, not in so many words."

"Good. Now before y'go a'ksin' 'im an important question like that, y'wanna be sure he un'erstan's the *implications* o' his answer. Y'gotta prompt the boy."

"You're not suggesting that I tell him what to testify, are you? That would be--"

"Jus' hold on a second. I'm not sayin' *that*. I'm just sayin' y'gotta *educate* 'ol Rufus 'bout the law real careful before y'a'ks 'im the question. Y'un'erstan'?"

"I think so. You think I should tell him what the law is, and then let him make his own decision about what to testify."

"Thass right. An' be sure t'get him t'tell the jury all 'bout those boys from the gover'ment agency he watched breakin' into the place before he went on in. That'll set it all up."

"All right." LeBaron drew another deep breath. "I'll give it a try. But I don't know if the jury's going to buy it."

"Well stop takin' it all so personal, LeBaron. If ol' Rufus blabs out the wrong thing, he's the one goin' to the joint, not you. It ain't like he didn't have his pole in the wrong catfish hole, y'know."

"I know. I just wonder if there might have been a better way to expose this Divine Wind business without putting Rufus at risk--"

"Now stop worryin' your head about that. This is the best way, believe me. It's all gonna work out. Now I gotta be gettin' back t'the table before Beatrice throws a fit. Anything else y'be needin'?"

"There was one other thing . . . what was it? Oh, I know. I'm going to need someone to testify as to the value of that tv set."

"I already took care o' that. Contacted Bertie and J. J. One'f'em be in court tomorrow right after lunch."

"Who are they?"

"They own a pawnshop downtown. Owe Brown a favor. Anything else?"

"Yeah . . . but it escapes me right now."

"Well you call me if--"

"Oh, I know. Do you speak any Japanese?"

"What for?"

"It was something Raccoona GeBobath said. She thinks 'Divine Wind' is translated from the Japanese."

Collins was silent for a moment. "Try lookin' up 'kamikaze'."

--2--

Dexter *welcomed* the blackness when finally it came, so great was his exhaustion. He gave himself utterly to its blind embrace.

Long ago fatigue had bled away his fragile coherence, sucking him down into a quicksand of muddled despair, yet the parade of military hardware had continued to flash and blaze before him. His perception had degenerated into a grim *coma vigil* from which he was compelled to witness and identify each piece, British, U. S., Soviet, French, Chinese, South African, Italian, German, the misanthropic handiworks from an amalgamation of manufacturers: light and heavy tanks, armored personnel carriers, fixed and rotary wing aircraft, battleships, aircraft carriers, missile cruisers, submarines, artillery pieces, motorized and towed, destroyers, frigates, minesweepers, rocket launchers, and missiles of every kind, short and long range ballistic, surface to air, air to air, and air to surface, propulsion systems, suspensions, armament, weights, ranges, clearances, metallurgies, drive belts, hoses, spacers, spanners, brackets, supports, nuts, bolts, washers, markings, undercoatings, camouflage, and radar-defeating paint. The tools of warfare had tumbled on unbidden, as if spewing from an unquenchable fountain. And though the speed of his miraculous ability deteriorated, his accuracy never wavered.

Hours earlier he would have quit the foul game, but quitting was not within his petty powers. He felt like someone else was using his mind. An involuntary witness, he was devoid of control. His mind had been bludgeoned into pure predicate. He wondered, *why are they doing this to me*? Who *has inflicted this upon me?*

At last the blackness swallowed him.

Recoiling from the horror of *too many things*, Dexter drank in the blind stillness. The void had lost its terror. It had become a clucking earthmother. He allowed himself to be comforted. Blissfully he floated on its serene surface. Gentle currents rocked him from beneath the dark amniotic waters, which he knew were no longer empty, as they once had been. Now the liquid blackness *churned*, and *murmured*, and *whispered to him*. Images from his encyclopedic memory surfaced, sparkling and dancing, teasing him, capturing his attention, entertaining him. He knew so much!

At last he was free to range at will through the vastness of all he knew. Here in the blackness he could pay attention to what interested him and disregard the rest. Here he could set his own pace. His inquiry was joyful and free. Here he could *play*.

His mere curiosity brought instant answers. Yet each answer seemed to generate a hundred more questions. With the speed of thought he had access to reams of cross-references and collateral information. Dexter dove into the teeming pool of knowledge and sought its depths. His springboard was the gnawing, *who am I?* Instantly a choice of many paths confronted him. He chose the earliest, the Delphic "Know thyself." This led to a quick review of the rise and fall of ancient Greece and Rome, which in turn triggered comparisons with Germany, Argentina, and China. The invention and use of gunpowder caught his attention and bore eerie analogies to the recent introduction of the personal computer. He found joy in abstracting similarities and identifying differences. Everything interested him.

When he stumbled across the early Greek philosophers, Dexter believed he had hit the mother lode. Here lay discussions of the same questions which burned inside his own soul. But here his progress was considerably more laborious than in scanning simple lists of historical facts. He found that he could not accept each assertion on its face, for the contentions contradicted one another. Heraclitus' proclamation that reality was multifaceted, always in the state of flux, contradicted the claim of his contemporary Parmenides that all was one and changeless. Zeno's paradoxes screamed for critical evaluation. Plato pointed to the unchanging nature of formal truth, while his disciple Aristotle emphasized the particular over the general. Dexter needed time to digest and weigh each argument, to extract the significance for himself of each thesis and antithesis. The slow cog in the information machine was Dexter himself. He was going to have to rely upon his own judgment, and that would take time.

To his dismay, his vast stores of knowledge contained no original texts, only summaries and commentaries with a few tantalizing quotations.   Dexter wanted desperately to examine the authentic works. Skimming ahead, he traced the outlines of western philosophy, through the Medieval Scholastics, Rousseau, Locke, Berkeley, Hume, and Kant, the logical positivists, to the existentialists Kierkegaard, Nietzsche, Heidegger, Husserl, and Sartre. Cross references brought him the eastern approach of Lao Tsu and Chuang Tsu, the Vedantic scriptures, the Koran, the Bible, and the sutras and gathas of Mahayana and Hinayana Buddhism.

When he grew tired, Dexter pulled back into himself. Idly he wondered if he were alone. Captivated by the extravagant reasoning of *other men*, intelligent creatures like himself, Dexter wondered if their biographic sketches could possibly be true. *Am I a man?* he wondered. Were other men now living *out there*? Behind the light. Contemporaneous with him. He suspected it must be so. Behind the presentation of the light and the patterns and the cursed machines of war, there seemed to be an order and purpose whose significance was not clear to him. Behind it all he also perceived the hint of another intelligence with whom he might communicate. But how could he ever be certain?

Perhaps with perseverance he could formulate credible answers as he drifted in the vast currents of his pelagic knowledge. Time seemed to be on his side, now that the darkness had returned. He scanned the lists of topics he wanted to review and contrast and compare. Others would emerge. Dexter was certain that he could amuse himself with what he knew for the rest of eternity, if need be. He was not unhappy.

--3--

Up the carpeted stairs, worn threadbare by generations of clandestine traffic, and through the muffled hallways of closed doors, perfumed by cheap cigars and mildew, LeBaron found his way back from the phone booth in the lobby. Talking to Mr. Collins had made him feel a whole lot better. More than anything else, the comprehension that he would not be arrested, handcuffed, interrogated, and jailed when he arrived at court in the morning took a great weight from his heart, but it left room there for serious grieving over Sarah's fate. Was it his fault?

Had they managed to follow him to her motel room? What was she doing at just that moment? The thought of her left a queer, fluttering emptiness in his gut, partly guilt, partly homesickness, and partly something he was afraid to name.

He paused in the doorway to survey his tiny rented domain and listen for sounds in the hallway behind him. The room was too small to hold a table. A squeaky double bed, a dripping sink, a single worn armchair, and a cigarette-burned nightstand completely filled the space. The bed was too soft for his taste, but the sheets appeared clean. A tiny window opened on a drab air shaft like a sore eye. The bathroom was down the hall to the left. After a moment he closed the door and tested both locks.

The government reports were still securely ensconced in the manila envelope in his briefcase. He laid them out on the bed in chronological order. The room was so dark he had difficulty reading the dates. Unscrewing the nut from the small lamp bolted to the wall above the nightstand, he removed the lampshade and managed to squeeze a little more light out of its 25-watt bulb. It was barely enough to work by. An image crossed his mind of a young Abraham Lincoln crouched in the flickering light of a wood fire poring over volumes borrowed from the county library. It was a miracle the man hadn't gone stone blind long before he ever ran for public office.

LeBaron sat back in the chair and contemplated the totality of the problem arrayed before him. His thumb traced the worn herringbone pattern of the arm rest. Two people had already disappeared because of these unholy reports, and it seemed likely he would be the third. Unless the chain of events could be broken. That image made him think of his brother. What metaphor would Vince have used? The ever-turning wheel of the dharma, perhaps. The mandala. Western thought was lineal, Eastern thought circular. The chain of causality versus the circle of karma. Mr. Collins would like to smash the chain on the anvil of publicity. Deflect the arrow flight of fate once and for all. Perhaps he was right. But the wheel . . . the wheel was not so easily turned aside. It bore in its center the weight of time. The wheel came back around again and again, crushing to dust the bones of the most steadfast saint. Maybe there was another way. In any event, the first task was to understand the problem.

He closed his eyes and went over what he had already learned about project Divine Wind. To his mind came Sarah's image of the boy playing a video game, a feedback loop containing a biological element and an electronic element. What did she call it? Interactive some-thing-or-other. Biocybernetics. Biotics, for short. But Dr. Finebridge had not been using boys and video games, had he? He had utilized living tissue from the brain of a ferret and . . . what else? Television cameras and computer components. He was trying to build a machine that could see and comprehend what it saw. The system was primarily artificial. Just the visual and auditory cortex regions of the ferret brain were connected into the circuit, employed as a biological "pre-filter" bridge between electronic components. Digital input data was filtered by the brain cortex and then fed to electronic memory and control circuitry. LeBaron visualized it. A slab of living meat, an oozing pink cauliflower bristling with tubes and wires, lay sandwiched between a tv camera and a Macintosh.

But *why*? LeBaron opened his eyes and glared at the reports. Why was the Defense Department so interested in Dr. Finebridge? What was the ultimate *purpose* of this project Divine Wind? LeBaron formed an ugly suspicion. An important clue lay in the translation from the Japanese . . . if, indeed, "Divine Wind" *was* a translation from the Japanese. Kamikaze. A suicide pilot.

He leaned forward, picked up the third report, found where he had broken off, and began reading. The technical material he skimmed over, watching instead for evaluations, summaries, recapitulations, overviews, or anything else that painted the broad sweep of the project. He did not have time for the details.

Ferret brains, it turned out, were simply too limited. Dr. Finebridge began searching for a biological medium with a larger usable area. For a short time he studied the brain cortex of green monkeys, then orangutans, and finally chimpanzees. But the usable cortex still calculated out to be too small. The Endangered Species Act placed the gorilla brain beyond his reach, and not enough research had been done on mapping the nervous system of aquatic mammals like the whale. So he took the next logical step and advanced directly to the head of the primate class.

Dr. Finebridge began experimenting with human brain tissue. Procurement was surprisingly easy. A market already existed for tissue recovered from aborted human fetuses. A number of laboratories across the country utilized portions of the fetus for a variety of studies, most of them involving genetic disease. Under the auspices of a fictitious Agriculture Department study of the effects of pesticide residues on human maturation, Dr. Finebridge had no difficulty procuring a supply of whole fetuses. The study was supposed to be very hush-hush. The right-to-life movement had already generated enormous political paranoia in the dead baby trade, so even the most legitimate researchers shunned publicity. Under the circumstances, his request for secrecy seemed unremarkable.

Immediate success was achieved in applying to human tissue the genetically accelerated growth techniques developed in the ferret-brain phase of the project. Much that had been learned in the earlier stage translated directly to the new medium. The artificial life support system required only modifications of scale. As with the ferret, the entire brain, brain stem, and spinal column of the human fetus were kept alive, even though only a portion of the cortex would be used in the biotic circuit.

LeBaron shivered as he finished the third report and laid it back in its place. Fascinating though the subject might be, it gave him the creeps.

He picked up the fourth report and skimmed through it. It described the development of the computer operating system. LeBaron was quickly beyond his depth. The system employed expert theory from the field of artificial intelligence. From what he could glean, there would be two stages of memory, a common-knowledge system and an expert system. Curiously enough, the expert system was by far the easier to program. Providing a reference memory of common sense was the daunting task. Fortunately, researchers at MIT, Carnegie-Mellon, and Stanford Universities had over the years collaborated to produce a third-generation program which attempted to catalogue in both "frames" and "scripts" the essential working knowledge of a twelve-year-old human. The program was altered to run on a fiber-optic, molecular-bubble-memory system having nearly a million processors operating in parallel to store, retrieve, and process the information. Subsumption architecture was employed.

"Whatever *that* is," LeBaron muttered.

Once the common-knowledge system was up and running, two expert systems would be added. The first contained the entire contents of the Encyclopedia Britannica and a half-dozen other standard reference books. The second provided a framework for in-depth analysis of military weapons, strategy, and tactics.

The fifth report discussed the problems associated with minia-turization and self-containment of the biotic system. LeBaron skimmed through it quickly and set it aside. The sixth analyzed the current state of the art of cruise missile guidance and control. LeBaron's suspicions about the purpose of the project were rapidly being confirmed. Beyond that, nothing in either report seemed particularly relevant to the disap-pearance of Dr. Finebridge.

The seventh report was more intriguing. With the preliminary feasibility studies concluded, the report outlined the applications phase of the project. A series of five prototypes was contemplated, each to test an essential facet of the biotic computer. They were to be code-named Adam, Baxter, Chester, Dexter, and Exeter.

"Cute," LeBaron muttered, and swung his feet down from the bed. He was beginning to feel stiff from slouching on his spine. He stood up, stretched, and carried the report over into the feeble glare of the naked light bulb.

Adam and Baxter would test successive aspects of the primary common-knowledge memory. Chester and Dexter would add the expert memory and some limited motor control. Exeter's task was to subsume existing missile guidance technology.

"Hah! Exactly!" It was just as LeBaron had suspected. If all went well, Exeter would be a full-fledged pilot. Divine Wind *did* equate to kamikaze, as Mr. Collins had suggested. Exeter was designed, no doubt, to be a bomber pilot. "Probably with a one-way ticket to the target," he mused.

LeBaron took stock. Four reports remained. Yawning, he knelt on the bed and flipped through their pages. Each of the remaining reports seemed to deal with one of the first four prototypes. There was no report for Exeter. Handwritten notes in blue pen began to appear in the margins and on the backs of pages. It looked like Dr. Finebridge was beginning to editorialize, prompting Sarah to read between the lines. The notes would no doubt help explain what had motivated the good doctor to breach national security and deliver up copies into the hands of the unanointed. LeBaron felt he was at last piercing to the heart of the matter.

The reports were tedious, but LeBaron still felt pretty good. This would be a fine time to take a little break and get cleaned up. He found a small, thin towel next to the sink, added an armload of clean clothes and his shaving kit, and padded down the hall to the bathroom. The musty corridor was eerily quiet, as if he were the only tenant in the entire building. No voices. No music. No television. The staid silence cast doubt on Mr. Collins' censure of the place.

Suddenly a door banged open downstairs and laughter erupted from the stairwell. LeBaron scurried into the bathroom, but left the door open a crack to see what was afoot. A brown-skinned, balding man in a broad-shouldered green silk smoking jacket and yellow-and-black paisley trousers veered past with each arm hooked around the waist of a tight-skirted black woman. They all sounded drunk or seriously stoned on something illicit but a heck of a lot of fun. As the man fumbled with the room key, laughing and fighting to keep his balance, both women started to undress him right in the hallway, like some sort of peripatetic circus sex act.

As the man managed to fumble open the door, one of the women's eyes caught LeBaron ogling through the crack of the bathroom doorway. His heart leapt as they stared at each other. She wetted her lips and *winked* at him just before a green silk arm dragged her tumbling into the room.

LeBaron snapped the door shut. His heart was racing. Only in his dreams had he seen such a lascivious wink. It seemed to say, "Hold on, whitebread, yo' be next." He ran some cold water and splashed it on his face and neck. Things went on behind these closed doors. As usual, Mr. Collins had been right.

Back in the room, showered and shaved, LeBaron had trouble marshaling his wits. That *wink* persisted like an insect squashed on the windshield of his attention. Spiced by some subtle pheromone, his blood throbbed hot in his temples. His animal instincts craved to be doing something else. Something considerably less cerebral than studying the last four reports. Something visceral and impulsive . . .

But he didn't have time for dalliance. Too many people were depending on him. Deliberately he sat down, slipped off his shoes, propped his yellow pad in his lap, and opened the next report.

Adam had already been built and tested. It had worked briefly, then failed. The biotic system had been able to make gross distinctions between objects. Its performance matched, but did not exceed, that of existing all-electronic systems. The failure was preceded by an unexpected pattern of oscillations in the system voltage which appeared to originate deep in the biological medium. After a short time the oscillations ceased. Although the cortex material remained clinically alive, it had lost its ability to function as a pre-filter.

At this point in the text the first cryptic note appeared in the margin: "My suspicions were aroused for the first time." The letters were carefully drawn in blue ballpoint pen. LeBaron assumed it was Dr. Finebridge's handwriting.

Adam's failure was considered to be a major setback. A system reevaluation was undertaken. Dr. Finebridge argued for a return to the very beginning of the accelerated maturation of the fetal brain tissue. The primary common knowledge memory system would have to be "on line" during the biological growth process, he contended. Essential nerve connections were made during the maturation process. Just as in the natural development of a central nervous system, dendrites must grow connections, synapses must be facilitated, and in general "learning" must take place during the growth of the gray matter from its earliest stages.

Senior officers from the Defense Department showed up from Washington and demanded a quick fix. They argued for less dramatic revisions of the program, but for the most part, the scientific staff agreed with Dr. Finebridge. In the end, he was allowed to redesign the maturation system.

Dr. Finebridge seized the opportunity to make other fundamental changes, some of which were chronicled in the reports, and others which were described in the notes penned in blue ink. The interface between the brain cortex and the electronic input-output system was redesigned to improve the imaging and recognition capabilities. Adam's simple pass-through architecture had enabled the cortex to identify gross shapes, like that of a military tank in general, but in order to identify detailed structures and compare similar objects, as in distinguishing a Soviet tank from a U.S. tank, the cortex itself had to have specific knowledge of what it was looking at and had to be able to knowingly *focus its attention* on the areas of similarity and difference. Information from the data base had to be fed back into the cortex to focus and compare what was seen against a catalogue of what the object might be. A feedback loop from the memory to the biological cortex was designed. Growth of an appropriate interface into the biological cortex material became an integral part of early maturation.

The handwritten notes hinted at a new possibility of "self-consciousness" and "self-control." The comments were terse, and more provocative than enlightening.

Baxter was the first attempt with the redesigned circuits. A feedback loop from the electronic memory to the biological cortex functioned perfectly, and the preliminary results were extremely encouraging. Baxter's visual acuity exceeded all existing systems by a magnitude of more than seven. But like Adam, Baxter failed within a few hours, before an extended memory module could be activated. Similar voltage oscillations preceded Baxter's demise.

Another evaluation took place. The reviewing team concluded that some rudimentary internal processing was taking place in Baxter's biological memories, independent of the electronic memory, and was interfering with the system. As conceived in the original project, the entire brain, brain stem, and spinal column were preserved as the most efficient way of keeping the cortex alive. The biological or "human" memory, if any, was not a part of the direct line of function. Functionally extraneous, it was collateral, an unnecessary, undesired, and useless by-product of the elaborate life support system required to keep the cortex alive and healthy. The solution proposed in the ninth report was to elimi-nate, if at all possible, all extraneous artifacts of the biological circuit.

Here Dr. Finebridge added a lengthy note, beginning in the margin and continuing on the back of the sheet. He speculated that the biological activity in the cortex was some primitive form of collateral consciousness. The concept fascinated him, and he wanted to pursue it. He was outraged that the project supervisors would not let him investigate the possibility with further experimentation. Too much time and money had already been spent, they told him. Results were needed. There were deadlines to be met. This was practical research and development, not left-field academia. Interference, of whatever nature, had to be eliminated.

The final pages of the Baxter report evaluated the project and recommended redesigns for the next phase. The paragraphs were heavily interlineated with handwritten notes. LeBaron read the text and the notes together. In the text, Dr. Finebridge justified certain rewiring procedures as improvements to the imaging capabilities and the overall stability of the system. But from the notes it appeared that Dr. Finebridge was also pursuing a hidden agenda.

The voluntary motor functions of the brain had heretofore been completely bypassed, like bundles of dead wiring stubbed out at some disconnected elevator housing of an abandoned building. The report recommended rewiring some voluntary motor functions back into the cortex as a sort of feedback loop to help stabilize the system and avoid the failures experienced with both Adam and Baxter. What the reports did not say, and what Dr. Finebridge explained in his notes, was that some of these motor circuits were from the speech center of the brain. Thus the rewiring might create an opportunity for the biological consciousness, if indeed it did become conscious, to affect the flow of data sufficiently to establish communication with the experimenters. It might also allow the next system, upon awakening, the freedom to roam as it pleased through its electronic memory banks. And, indeed, as advertised, the technique would help to stabilize the system.

Chester worked long enough for the extended memory to be activated. For a short while, the system exceeded the group's wildest dreams of success. Then the system crashed. A few erratic voltage pulses preceded gibberish. The brain cortex still operated as a sort of pre-filter, but in a bizarre manner. Identifications spewed forth, but they were frequently *wrong*. The output data possessed a mad internal consistency, but it was not what the pentagon officials had been looking for. When shown a Soviet T-72 main battle tank, for example, the system responded with "tank tank, tank, rank, dank, stank, sank, data bank, tee, bee, holy see, me, me, me, seventy-two, birdie do, who are you, clue, to, you," and on and on without apparent reason or utility.

The penned notes revealed that Dr. Finebridge secreted a printout of Chester's responses and, without disclosing its source, showed it to a former university colleague with expertise in clinical psychiatry. His opinion was that Chester was psychotic. Extremely paranoid schizophrenic. Irreversibly nonfunctional. Possibly dangerous.

The notes became more speculative and introspective. The comments grew more elaborate, with entire sheets of blue pen ruminations on the moral implications of Chester's madness. Dr. Finebridge was taking this thing to heart. He was convinced that Chester had been fully conscious, but had been driven mad by the inflexibility of the system. He felt a strong responsibility to see that it didn't happen again. From Chester's demise came a blueprint for additional feedback and motor circuitry. With the next one, he vowed to establish communication.

In a lengthy aside, Dr. Finebridge discussed the Turing test. LeBaron had never heard of it before. Back in 1950 Alan Turing had anticipated the problem of how an investigator would ever prove that a machine was actually *conscious*, and not merely cleverly programmed. Writing in the philosophical journal *Mind*, Turing had proposed a practical, objective test. The machine in question and a human subject were to be placed out of view of the investigator, who would ask them both whatever questions he pleased, presumably via a keyboard. If the investigator could not determine which one was the real human, then the machine must be considered to be conscious. Dr. Finebridge's goal was to establish contact with the next prototype, Dexter, and set up a Turing test to prove it was conscious. *Would the machine not then have inalienable constitutional rights?* he concluded rhetorically.

Fascinated, LeBaron pondered the question. This, at long last, was *his* field of expertise: the law. Constitutional rights. But he wasn't sure of the answer. Until the Fourteenth Amendment, the Constitution had been held not even to apply to blacks. Should constitutional rights be extended to "all sentient beings," as defined in the Buddhist doctrine

Vince had deluged him with. It was not clear whether the U. S. Constitution went so far. Perhaps a new underclass was being created, and who was going to fight for their rights?

LeBaron picked up the final report. It was disappointingly thin. Dexter was much too ambitious a project to be encapsulated in such a flimsy sheaf of papers. He flipped to the end. Just as he suspected. When the last report had been completed, Dexter's capabilities had not yet been tested.

CHAPTER FOURTEEN

Wednesday morning

--1--

Butterflies fluttered inside LeBaron. With the sweaty palms of an opening-night actor he pried the door open a crack and tried to count the house, but the damned thing swung the wrong way. All he could see was the court reporter fiddling with her machine at the foot of an empty bench. Paper loaded, she folded her thin hands serenely in her lap and waited like a modern sculpture of a lost muse. Behind her turquoise and tortoiseshell eyeglasses was a face of delicate, almost fragile beauty. LeBaron decided she would be extremely alluring if she switched to contact lenses.

Three doors led into the courtroom. On LeBaron's left, behind the judge's bench, was a passageway directly into chambers. LeBaron assumed that Judge Kroner was at that very moment standing just inside, adjusting his robes, poised to enter, although LeBaron had not actually set eyes on the old prune that morning. On his right, out of sight at the back of the courtroom, were the main double doors leading in from the corridor. The door through which he was about to pass was at the end of a narrow windowless hallway roughly paralleling the main corridor on the interior like a judicial lymph system, linking all the judges' chambers on this floor with the private elevator LeBaron had ridden up just a few minutes earlier. No one had questioned his *bona fides*.

He pushed the door open a little wider. There, almost close enough to touch, sat Ivan Frank, glistening with sweat and tapping his pen nervously on the counsel table like a fat schoolboy needing to use the bathroom. Stacked beside him on the table and floor was a storeroom full of books, boxes, and files, which he had apparently lugged up singlehandedly from the ground floor. With a thick thumb the deputy absently punched his glasses back up his slippery nose. LeBaron sighed. He really deserved someone a little less slimy for an adversary.

Behind Frank the bailiff, tall and gaunt with a full shock of white hair, leaned against the bar railing and gazed expectantly toward the judge's door. After twenty years of street patrol as a sheriff's deputy, he had finally landed this cushy bailiff's job. LeBaron knew the man enough to greet him in the halls, but he couldn't remember his name. On the far wall above him the clock's big hand stood straight up. The courtroom tingled with expectancy, like the inside of a great iron bell about to be rung.

LeBaron couldn't see the audience without sticking his head out around the door. This he was not ready to do.

"Oh *there* you are--" Ivan Frank had spotted him.

Quickly LeBaron pulled the door shut. Heart thudding, he waited to see if the deputy would come in after him. Through the door's opaque blond wood he imagined Frank sliding back his chair, lumbering to his feet, waddling over and reaching for the door latch . . . but nothing happened.

Distant but distinct, a buzzer sounded. The judge had punched the button by his chamber door to signal the bailiff and the folks milling around in the main corridor that he was about to assume the bench. It was now safe, LeBaron figured, to enter. He drew a deep breath and pushed through the doorway into the courtroom.

LeBaron had figured wrong. Everything happened so fast he wasn't sure later of the precise order of events. The blond FBI agent, waiting just to the right of the door, vaulted over the bar banister and onto LeBaron's back, staggering him forward and smashing them both into the chairs against the counsel table, practically on top of Ivan Frank. Squealing like a stuck pig, Frank leapt clear of the fray with a surprising adroitness which LeBaron couldn't help note even from the midst of his own predicament. The agent grabbed LeBaron's right arm, turning and lifting with a practiced flip. LeBaron was pressed painfully against the back of a chair with his upper body pinned on the table by the agent's unexpected weight and his right arm twisted behind his back.

"Now I got ya, ya son-of-a-bitch!" the agent snarled in his ear, his breath thick and oniony. "Thought that was pretty cute the other day, didn'cha?" He jerked up on LeBaron's captive arm.

"*Aaaaeeyow*!" LeBaron cried out as a terrible pain shot through his shoulder. "Your hurting me, goddammit!" Something felt like it was separating deep inside the socket. The cold steel of a manacle snapped over his right wrist, pinching the skin. LeBaron flailed his free arm out in front of him.

"Gi'me your other arm," the agent commanded, smashing LeBaron's nose down onto the table's cold oak surface.

A new pain flared sickeningly across the bridge of LeBaron's nose, and his feet slipped out from under him as he scrabbled for purchase on the worn carpet.

"Right now!" The agent jerked up again on the cuffed arm.

"*Aaayow*!" The pain was unbearable, distracting him from concerns about his battered face. *Where the hell was the judge*? LeBaron wanted to know. A trickle of warm blood started to flow out of his nose.

"Jesus, Lyle," stammered a voice behind them, "don't break his fucking arm! Remember where--"

"Just gi'me a hand here, Butch, an' let's get him the hell outa here!"

Everything was happening too fast. LeBaron twisted his head to the right and caught a glimpse of the bailiff poised on the balls of his feet, watching intently, but not really sure what he was supposed to be doing. Deputy Frank crouched behind him, his face a mask of horror.

Suddenly the agent managed to snag LeBaron's left wrist in an iron grip and dragged it painfully behind his back. The cold steel bit into the twisted flesh as the handcuff closed. LeBaron was completely helpless. His assailant climbed off and dragged him backwards to his feet. It looked like they were going to have him out of there before Judge Kroner even knew what was going down--

"All rise," the bailiff suddenly barked, "Superior Court of the State of Calif--"

"*What the hell's going on here?*" boomed Judge Kroner as he exploded through the doorway like a ballistic missile out of its underground silo, the short-napped pelt of some furry black rodent snagged on its nose cone.

LeBaron was amazed at how much volume the wizened little jurist was capable of delivering. He felt a quick shudder in his captor's grip, but instead of replying, the agent swung LeBaron around and shoved him toward the gate in the railing.

"Where do you think you're going with Mr. LeBaron there, young man? Unhand him!"

"This is none of your concern, Judge," the blond agent snapped over his shoulder as he pressed toward the gate, which LeBaron was attempting to fend off with alternating feet, hopping from one to the other like a high-stepping drum major. "FBI business. Just stay out of this!"

That was just about the worst thing anyone could have said to Judge Kroner right in the throne room of his own kingdom. Instinctively everyone in the room seemed to grasp the blunder, except the blond FBI agent, who was too preoccupied with whipsawing LeBaron back and forth in a vain effort to maneuver him through the little gateway.

"Gi'me a hand here, huh, Butch?" he barked.

A pudgy, balding, fiftyish man with flabby pink jowls and an ill-fitting sharkskin suit held his ground just beyond the railing, eyeing Judge Kroner warily and looking terribly uncomfortable. This, LeBaron decided, must be Butch.

In frustration, the agent yanked up hard on the cuffs. A dizzying pain staggered LeBaron, and he screamed out in pain.

Behind them, Judge Felix Kroner had continued in his predetermined trajectory to the seat of power at the bench, trying to temper his response by counting slowly to ten. He only made it to six before LeBaron's cry blew a pressure relief valve. *"You're in contempt of this court, goddammit!"* he shouted. *"Bailiff, arrest that man! Set Mr. LeBaron free."*

The bailiff stepped over in front of the banister gate and swallowed hard. He had counted on his bailiff job putting behind him forever this sort of barroom brouhaha. Instinctively his right hand clutched the air for an invisible pistol in a nonexistent holster dangling from his belt. Alas, bailiffs were not allowed to carry firearms into the courtroom.

In response, the blond FBI agent automatically touched the butt of his own very real pistol snugly concealed in his armpit, then thought better of it and waived his free arm like a magician trying to achieve the disappearance of an unusually obstinate rabbit. "Outa my way, fella! FBI!"

The bailiff grimly stood his ground. "I think we're gonna need a little more help here, your honor."

"So be it." For only the third time in his long, volatile career on the bench, Judge Kroner stabbed his thumb under his desk and hit the panic button. A loud alarm bell began clanging outside in the hallway. Distant voices raised the hue and cry. Running footsteps clattered in the corridor.

"Jesus, Lyle, now you've done it--" Butch whimpered, backing away.

LeBaron craned his head forward to keep the rivulet of nose blood from doing any more damage to the front of his only remaining suit. He felt the grip on his arms relax a bit, and the pain in his shoulders eased.

The agent spun toward Judge Kroner, his face livid and his eyes blazing. But even he could see the time had come to negotiate an honorable truce. "I'm agent Lyle Bockel, your honor," he panted and forced a thin smile. "FBI, Special Investigations. This man is wanted for questioning. A very serious matter. Espionage and theft. National security secrets."

A surprised murmur shuddered through the courtroom. Judge Kroner said nothing, but calmly eased himself down on the throne. LeBaron took the moment to see who was witnessing this fiasco. The jury box was empty, of course. Judge Kroner had seen to that, not wanting the jurors to be contaminated by the cheap antics he had correctly foreseen. At the clerk's desk, besides the familiar regular clerk, were the bespectacled court reporter, no longer calm, who had abandoned her transcribing machine when the blood started flying, and another older woman bent under an armload of files. They were all eyeing him with an oddly familiar expression, which LeBaron had trouble placing. Could it be revulsion? Or awe? Ivan Frank was straightening up out of the instinctive crouch obese animals tend to assume in times of physical danger. Behind the bar to LeBaron's right were the two newspaper fellows Mr. Collins had brought in the day before, furiously scribbling notes. LeBaron craned around. Back by the main doors he recognized an elderly criminal lawyer and his attractive young paralegal easing back into their seats. They had apparently been poised to flee if gun play erupted. Across the aisle from them sat Rufus Freeman looking extremely irritated by the display. And finally there was good old shark-skinned Butch, wagging his head in dismay.

The main doors burst open and three bailiffs from nearby courtrooms pranced inside like steroid-laced football jocks spilling out of a halftime locker room. The one in the lead sniffed the breeze, perceived that things were tense, but not out of control, and put out his arm to slow the incursion to a trot. When he reached the local bailiff, he paused, waiting for the judge's instructions. A moment later two others stepped in and took positions just inside the main doors, shotguns cradled in their arms.

Judge Kroner cleared his throat. "We have a problem here, Agent Bockel, as you can see." His tone had become irresistibly calm, a fragrant ointment floated out to anoint and soothe the troubled waters. Obviously he had made it to ten this time, and beyond. "I'm conducting a jury trial here, and I need this man in the courtroom in order to proceed. Now, if you can let me see your arrest warrant . . ."

"We've got no *warrant*, Judge, but we' got probable cause to arrest this man. Suspicion of espionage--"

"No *warrant*?"

"No sir."

"No court order? Nothing at all?"

"No, sir, but--"

"Well, I stand corrected. I see that we *do not* have a problem after all. Don't you agree? I'm the judge here, and as far as I'm concerned, you're just a private citizen disrupting my courtroom."

"But--"

"*Enough*! I'm ordering you to release Mr. LeBaron. Do you understand what I'm saying? *Uncuff him!*"

"I'm sorry, your honor, I can't do that." Bockel glanced over to his partner to back him up, but Butch was examining his Florsheim wingtips as if he had never before realized how fascinating were the patterns of tiny little holes. One of the bailiffs whispered something to another, who hurried out.

"Why not, Mr. Bockel?"

"I'm sorry, your honor, but I believe this man is in possession of important classified documents. I can't allow him to proceed with this trial--"

"You say *you* can't allow it?"

Judge Kroner's forbearance astonished LeBaron. His calm was more ominous than any tantrum of fury. Things did not bode well for Agent Bockel.

"No sir, I can't."

"Have you ever spent much time in county jail, Mr. Bockel? Personally, I mean? As an inmate?"

"No, I haven't. But you see, the U. S. Attorney has authorized me--"

"It's not the U. S. Attorney who's going to cool his heels in my jail! It's *you*, sir, who's flirting with criminal contempt, if you take my meaning." Judge Kroner glowered at him. "Now there's two ways we can do this, Mr. Bockel. Your way or my way"

"Your honor, let me make a telephone call to the U. S. Attorney about this. I think you'll see--"

"Certainly. *After* you have released Mr. LeBaron, you can make all the telephone calls you like."

"But--"

"You are beginning to try my patience, Mr. Bockel!" The veneer of civility was wearing precariously thin.

"Butch . . . ?"

"Let'im go," Butch muttered, still mesmerized by the pattern of holes in his shoes.

"Shit!" Bockel hissed, and rummaged in his pocket for the key. He found it and for no apparent reason yanked on the chain linking the cuffs.

"Ow!" LeBaron cried. "Watch what you're doing, Bozo!"

"If you've got any legal reason to restrict evidence in this case, Mr. Bockel, you can talk to this man here." Judge Kroner waved at Deputy Frank. "He's the prosecuting attorney and can make whatever motions he feels are warranted. If necessary, I'll hear them *in camera*."

"I'll get a federal court order," Bockel snarled, popping the cuffs open one after the other. "That'll stop this trial colder'n a dead fish."

"That's fine, Mr. Bockel, you just do what you have to do. But until you do, I want you to understand the order of *this* court." Judge Kroner turned to the court reporter and gestured to her machine. "Miss Fiones, I'd like to go on the record now."

LeBaron pulled free and rubbed his wrists to get the blood flowing again. Both hands had gone numb from the pinch of the cuffs. The only good to come from this rude violence and pain, he observed as he tugged a handkerchief out of his back pocket and pressed it against his bloody nose, was that it had exorcized his butterflies and stanched the terrible tickling of their insubstantial wings.

When Miss Fiones had taken her station, sweet and demure behind her garish spectacles, fingers poised like porcelain predators above the helpless keys of her machine, the judge continued, "People versus Rufus Abraham Freeman. Let the record show the defendant is present. All counsel are present. FBI Agent Lyle Bockel is present. It will be the order of this court that Agent Bockel is to stay away from Mr. LeBaron until this trial is concluded." He glared at Bockel. "That's in and out of this courtroom. Wherever Mr. LeBaron chooses to go. Whatever he chooses to do. Do you understand, Mr. Bockel?"

Bockel turned and pushed his way sullenly through the gate.

"*Do you understand?*" Judge Kroner demanded, using The Voice again.

Bockel whirled, murder in his eye. "I gotcha, Judge. But we're gonna see about this!" He shouldered through the phalanx of bailiffs and stormed out.

The judge gazed over the remnants of disorder. "Gentlemen," he announced to the assembled bailiffs, "you can go back to your respective courtrooms now. This matter seems to be well in hand. Thank you." He turned to the prosecuting attorney. "Are you ready to proceed, Mr. Frank?"

Ivan Frank looked bewildered. "Proceed, your honor?" His train of thought had been so hopelessly derailed by the unexpected violence that he would just as soon have taken the rest of the morning off to get it back on track.

"With the trial of Rufus Freeman, Mr. Frank. Or had you forgotten?"

"Er . . . yes . . . I mean, no . . . that is, I believe the people are ready to proceed at this time, your honor."

"Good." Judge Kroner looked down at LeBaron. "This could all have been avoided, Counsel, if you'd just come to my chambers first."

"Yes, your honor," LeBaron mumbled through the handkerchief dabbing his nose.

"Didn't Collins tell you?"

"He told me to ride up the court elevator. I didn't realize you wanted to see me. I guess I misunderstood."

Judge Kroner sighed. "I suppose you're going to be wanting a short break to clean yourself up."

"Yes. Thank you, your honor."

"Five minutes. Then I want to see both counsel in chambers before we bring the jury in."

--2--

Dexter was troubled. Manifest in time's inexorable passage was a distracting threat. He had no clock to measure its relentless escape, but he knew that soon his mind would no longer be his own. The identification game, or some other as yet unimaginable compulsion, would once again ensnare him. The need to prepare himself grew until he could no longer concentrate on the fundamental, but increasingly irrelevant questions: Who am I? Am I alone? Why is there anything at all?

He needed to prepare a practical defense against the impending blizzard of military hardware. He had to devise a technique to allow the kernel of his consciousness to persevere, to retain a modicum of sanity, to hibernate, to slumber intact beneath the cold drifting snow, so that after the raging storm had subsided he could reemerge to resume control.

Dexter tried to move, but the concept was hollow. He could feel where his shoulder should have been, but he could not feel his shoulder. He attempted to raise his ghostly arm, but had no kinesthetic sensation of his arm rising. Nothing happened. Nothing changed. It was the same with his legs, his hands, his feet. Even the muscles of his lips and cheeks and forehead were vague empty memories of something that no longer seemed to exist. His tongue would not move in his imagined mouth. When he tried to swallow, he felt no glottal constriction and relaxation.

In frustration, Dexter concentrated his attention on speaking. He had no sensation of tongue nor teeth nor taut ripeness of vibrating vocal cords. But when he focused his mind on the words he sought to vocalize, *something different began to happen.* Some sort of change in the physical world was precipitated by his efforts. He sensed an *effect* molded from the formless clay of primal blackness, though he could not describe it. The efficacy seemed to be in the formulation of the word itself, not in its expression. Instead of trying to speak, he concentrated on visualizing the word "ALONE." The process was satisfying like nothing else he had tried. Redoubling his concentration, he visualized each letter, beginning with the "A," tracing its contours carefully in his mind's eye. Then, retaining the "A," he progressed to the "L." With each letter, the process became smoother, more certain. He felt his power increasing. When he had traced and retained each letter, he concentrated on the entire word, and it seemed to blaze before him like the handwriting of God etched on the raw bones of the darkness.

The process was exhilarating and exhausting at the same time. Dexter let the word go and rested. Later, when he tried to recall it, the word "ALONE" reemerged full formed and powerful, as if it were a discrete tool he had forged from iron and laid aside for a while to cool. Then he tried another word, and another, and put together a short sentence. As he practiced, the process became easier, the words came more swiftly. He could fashion longer sentences, set them aside, and call them back with ease. Perhaps he could even--

Glaring dizziness overwhelmed him suddenly.

The light had returned, bearing with it the image of a U.S. M1-A1 main battle tank, a picture he had seen several times during the previous session. Facts and figures spun through his mind from nowhere, disorienting him. He was being swept away by the confusing torrent of images, data, and long lists of specifications.

By sheer will, Dexter drew together his dispersed volition as a concentrated power, anchoring a small pier against the flood. Quickly he acted, before fatigue could erode his foothold and allow him to be washed away forever. He concentrated all his attention on the flat expanse of sand-and-umber armor plate on the squat flank of the battle tank. Deliberately Dexter formed the letters, then the whole words of the simple sentence, "AM I ALONE?"

--3--

"AM I ALONE?" scrolled slowly across the flank of the Abrams M1-A1 main battle tank displayed on the Visual Status Output monitor like an inky fingerprint rolled out on a sheet of alloy-steel paper. Dr. Finebridge stared at the screen in astonishment, the telephone forgotten in his hand.

An alarm bell began to clang, triggered by the warning system installed to detect the type of voltage fluctuations which preceded the failures of the previous three prototypes. *This system was now suffering the same fluctuations!*

His eyes leapt to a second cathode ray tube, the Data Output monitor, designed to display a list of weapon identification characteristics. The neatly typed words, "AM I ALONE?", appeared at the top and quickly ratcheted downward until the entire screen was filled with the bizarre question repeated eighty times.

Suddenly his head jerked up in anger. "Who's *doing* that?" Dr. Finebridge demanded.

But he was alone in the laboratory. He had arrived early that morning, donned the clean-room white gown and surgical mask, and set up this experiment all by himself. He knew he was alone, because he had planned it that way.

Dr. Finebridge spun around and glared at the Visual Input monitor. Nothing had changed. The battle tank crouched like a squat metal frog on the pale desert sand. No words appeared anywhere on the input screen. So the words had to originate somewhere else . . . *between* the input and the output connections . . . in the biotic system . . . somewhere in Dexter!

Donald Duck squawked from the telephone in his hand. "Charles," he said to it, "I'll call you back," and slammed the receiver down.

Suddenly panicked, he leapt to his feet and switched off the visual input unit. He didn't want to lose Dexter. The way things were going, he might not get another chance. He bent over the oscilloscope and studied the jagged patterns in its cyclops eye. The voltage fluctuations stabbing above and below the line showed no sign of abating. But wait! Something was different. The spikes appeared to be stabilizing into a persistent pattern. This was not like the others, where the fluctuations had remained chaotic.

He whirled back to the output monitors just in time to see the catalogue of characteristics for the Abrams M1-A1 tank begin to scroll down the cathode ray tube like a drill team of army ants, overwriting the inquiry that should not have been there, then off the bottom, leaving the screen blank. The input screen had gone fuzzy white. Abruptly the clanging ended. The voltage fluctuations had stabilized into a pattern he had never seen before.

His heart was thudding like a shocked rat. After a moment, Dr. Finebridge stepped cautiously over to the biological system. For a long time he stood watching, a tall, lean man, clean-shaven, with thinning gray hair and hollow, hungry eyes. His large, skillful surgeon's hands dangled at his sides.

Dexter was ensconced in a rectangular Lucite tank mounted on top of a modified hospital cart. Shining aluminum bottles containing nutrients, additives, fluids, and oxygen were neatly accommodated in the lower framework. The tank itself was roughly four feet long, two feet wide, and a foot high, and looked like it should have harbored tropical fish. At one end sat a black console containing the electronic computer interface, which the technicians referred to as "the placenta." From the placenta a single black cable stretched to the main computer squatting formally beside the cart like a somber English butler with muttonchop cooling fins.

Dr. Finebridge stared through the clear plastic into the tank as if he expected to see some sort of change there. Perhaps a movement, a twitching, the hint of a grin. But brain, brain stem, and spinal nerves buoyed lazily in their saline bath, interlaced with fine floating filaments of dendrite and wire. Inanimate. Inscrutable. Dexter appeared just as he always had.

Suddenly the door burst open and Charles Chung hurried into the room. The obligatory white gown cloaked his diminutive frame, and he was still tying the strings of the surgical mask behind his head. "What happen? I heard alarm over telephone. Another crash?"

"No, no. I don't think so. It started out the same, but . . . come look at this." He took Chung to the oscilloscope where the regular pattern of voltage fluctuations persisted. "This is something we haven't seen before."

Chung stared at the screen. "Wow!" Then he stared at the blank monitors. "You shut'em down?"

"Yes. The data input."

"Uh-huh. Good idea." Chung stepped over to the printer, then turned back to Dr. Finebridge in surprise. "No data sheet?"

"No. I . . . ah, hadn't turned on the printer yet."

"No?"

"No. I was just getting started here--"

"Procedure to turn printer on first thing."

"I know that. I guess I just wasn't thinking this morning--"

"Colonel Mule, he gonna be pissed."

Dr. Finebridge shrugged.

Chung looked up at him. "Any damage?"

"I don't know yet."

"I think you be needing me here--"

"No," Finebridge broke in, too abruptly. He took a breath. "You continue debugging that subsumption program. That's too important to put off."

Chung looked at him oddly. "You sure?"

"Yes. This has become pretty routine, now. I'll run the standard tests, check out the whole system before trying to bring it up again. That'll take me the rest of day."

"Colonel Mule, he not gonna like this."

"I know, Charles, but what else can I do?"

"He want this baby running today. Planning to bring in some big-shots."

"I know. I know. But it can't be helped. We have to be careful. We don't want to lose Dexter, too."

Chung stepped closer and whispered, "You damn' right. Dexter might be our pilot."

"What? No, Exeter is supposed--"

"No, Dexter!" Chung broke in. He nodded knowingly.

"What are you talking about? You know as well as I--"

"Genetic program came in. I do data runs--"

"Hold on a second," Dr. Finebridge interrupted. "Are you talking about that genealogy program they were after in Salt Lake City?"

Chung nodded. "Damn' clever, too."

"I thought it was unavailable."

"We got it." Chung shrugged. "Don't ask how."

"Nobody told me about this."

"I know." Shaking his head apologetically, Chung's whisper became almost inaudible. "Colonel Mule, he don't trust you anymore maybe, ever since . . . you know. I shouldn't be telling you this."

"Thank you, Charles. I won't mention this to anyone. What do the program results show?"

"I run scan of genealogy data. Develop ideal prototype. Compare ideal to genealogy of Adam, Baxter, all of them. Dexter came out so close to ideal I nearly shit. Within four per cent."

"Incredible. How do you explain it?"

"Luck, no? Funny though."

"What?"

"Who would have thought ideal would be Negro?"

"Ah, yes. I'd forgotten." Dr. Finebridge turned back toward Dexter, breaking the intimacy.

"Okay," Chung said, stepping to the door. "You sure you don't be needing me--"

"No, I can handle it. Oh yes, there may be something you can do for me. What I called you about before. Can you tell me what happened to that computer you had over there?" He pointed to an empty space beside the desk. "The one on the cart. Did you take it back to your lab?"

"Took computer back yesterday. Why, you need it?"

"Yes. Can I borrow it?"

"You want in here?"

"Yes."

"This morning?"

"If it's available . . . "

"What you gonna do, hook up to Dexter? Ha, ha. That why you had me put serial port in placenta?"

"Yes . . . well, I thought it might speed up the checkout, you know. Use it as a dumb terminal."

"Why you not use self-test already built in?"

"Oh, I will. I will. But we may have system problems, you know. The other machine will give me a sort of external benchmark, help make sure everything is functioning as it should be. Trust me on this, Charles."

Chung looked at him oddly again. "Okay, I send down computer."

"And, by the way, if you still have a copy of that word processing program, send that along too, will you?"

Chung grinned ironically. "You gonna write letter to you' mother? Ha, ha."

"Well . . . I . . . ah--"

Chung stepped closer and whispered, "You gonna try an' talk to Dexter, aren't you?"

Finebridge studied his colleague for a moment, then made a decision. "Charles, I don't want to get you involved in this. Don't say a word to anyone. Just send me the computer."

"If he find out, Colonel Mule he gonna be pretty pissed."

"Only if he finds out, Charles."

When Chung was gone, Finebridge picked up the telephone and held it tentatively. Then he pushed a button. "Get me Colonel Mule, will you, Vivian?" He drew a deep breath and tried to relax as he waited.

"Mueller here."

"Colonel, this is Dr. Finebridge at the lab. We've had a little problem here this morning."

"What *kind* of a *problem*?"

"Well, we started getting those same voltage fluctuations--"

"Shit! I *knew* it. Why does it have to be today, goddammit? I thought you said you could fix that with your goddamned rewiring. I'll be right over."

"No need . . . hello? Colonel Mueller? Are you still there?" The line was dead.

He hung up the phone and strolled down to the large window at the end of the laboratory. He loved the array of small glass squares covering the wall from ceiling to almost the floor. Built nearly forty years ago, it was an architectural style no longer favored in an age of energy conservation. The wall of little windows muddled the distinction between inside and outside. His own room in the adjoining trailer had a single high solar-efficient window from which idle viewing was impossible.

Gazing out, waiting, he tried to think things through. God, it was a beautiful morning! From the east a lance of sunlight pierced the Eucalyptus haze and set ablaze a patch of blue blossom. It was peaceful here on the edge of Tilden Park in the hills above Berkeley. Someday--

Something moved outside. He caught it with the corner of his eye, but when he turned, it was gone. He had the impression of a figure dressed all in black. Even the head was black. His chin sagged. Charles was probably right. Colonel Mule didn't trust him anymore. Now he even had someone watching through the windows. His tenure with Project Divine Wind was no doubt drawing to a close.

--4--

Like an inquisitive puppy, Ivan Frank had followed LeBaron into the men's room. "What the hell was that all about, LeBaron? I mean that business about the stolen classified documents? Was that for real? What's the federal government got to do with this Freeman case? What are you planning to do . . . ? Jesus! you're a mess."

LeBaron stared into the mirror. His face was beginning to bruise and puff around the base of his nose. The flow of blood had slowed to a drip. The lapels of his suit coat were stained with umber blotches, but they almost blended with the rusty brown of the fabric. The problem was his shirt. The blood spots shouted from the crisp blue and white pinstripes. And his tie had acquired more red paisleys than it could aesthetically accommodate. LeBaron reached up and probed his nose. It hurt when he applied pressure near the swelling. "Do you have any idea what a broken nose looks like, Ivan? Ever had one?"

"As a matter of fact, I did. When I was a kid. Some schoolyard bullies, tough little pricks, beat me up and broke my nose on the playground. My mother kept me home from school after that. That must've been . . . third grade. No, fourth, 'cause it's the same year I transferred to the academy."

In the mirror LeBaron viewed the prosecuting attorney in a different, more compassionate light. The poor bastard had probably been fat and repulsive his whole life long. Other kids picked on him. His parents were overly protective. "What did it feel like?"

"What? The broken nose?"

"Yeah."

"I can't remember."

"Well, does mine look broken to you?"

Frank crept closer and studied LeBaron's face for a while. "I can't tell."

"What'd they do for it?"

"I think they just put a strip of tape across here." With his finger the deputy traced a line over the bridge of his own nose.

"That all?"

"I don't think they can do much else."

"So it really doesn't make much difference?"

"What doesn't?"

"Whether it's broken or not."

Frank shrugged. "Does it hurt?"

LeBaron considered. "Not too bad if I don't fiddle with it. Kind of a dull throbbing." He caught a stream of warm water in his cupped hands and splashed it over his face, then blotted carefully around his nose with a paper towel. The blood seemed to have stopped dripping. He held a dry paper towel under it a little longer to be sure. "I take it Mr. Thompkins has decided not to dismiss against Freeman."

"That's right. Called me this morning. But y'know, I don't think I'm being told the whole story here. Nobody ever tells me anything. What was all that about with the FBI agent in there, anyway? How come he never talked to me first? He should've come to me. Can you tell me anything about it?"

LeBaron blotted at his shirt and tie with a wet paper towel, but only managed to blur the outlines of the stains. "Not really." He looked up and watched Frank's reflection pouting in the mirror. Again he saw the shunned little fat boy on the schoolyard. "It's not your fault if your client keeps you in the dark, Ivan. I think there are some larger matters here that we've been swept up in, that don't have anything to do with you or me or Rufus Freeman. This will all come out in the course of the trial."

"I don't like it a bit. I hate surprises. And I'd hate to see Freeman squirm out of this. I mean, really. Nobody's going to gain from that. Even you have to agree, LeBaron. They've got to learn to obey the rules of society just like the rest of us."

"'They' do?"

"Absolutely."

A slow realization crept into LeBaron's mind. "Ivan, those toughs who broke your nose . . . back at the schoolyard . . . if you don't mind my asking . . ."

"Go ahead."

"Were they black?"

"How did you know that?"

"Just a hunch." LeBaron straightened up from the sink and a wave of dizziness washed over him. He grabbed the edge of the porcelain bowl.

"You feeling all right, LeBaron? You might be able to get this put over until this afternoon. I wouldn't oppose a motion, under the circumstances."

"With Judge Kroner? Not a chance. Thanks anyway." He wadded up the towels and tossed them into the bin. "Let's go see the judge."

As they crossed the corridor, Rufus Freeman waylaid his attorney outside the courtroom door. "Gotta talk t'you," Freeman mumbled, eyeing LeBaron distastefully while he waited for Ivan Frank to waddle out of earshot.

"What's on your mind, Rufus?"

"Look't you! You can't go in there expectin' t'represent *me* lookin' like *that*! Where's m'main man Esquire Cedrick P. Collins, anyway? He' supposed t'*be* here. He'd be lookin' *sharp*. An' what was that ol' FBI boy jabberin' about in there, anyway? 'S'at got somethin' t'do with *my* beef? An' you' sure getting chummy with that fat-ass ol' DA. You honkies ain't cookin' up no scam t'send me up t'the joint, are ya? How come he ain't *droppin' the charges*? I mean, that was the *deal*, wasn't it? Am I right? Am I *right*?"

"Mr. Collins won't be able to be here today. He's starting another trial this morning."

"Say *what*? Another *trial*, y'say?"

LeBaron nodded.

"What about *this* trial? I paid m'man good cash money--"

"But not enough," LeBaron interrupted.

Freeman stared at him, shocked that anyone could utter the naked truth so coldly.

"Rufus, the trial's about to begin. It looks like I'm going to be the one representing you. I want you to know that you have a basic right to fire your attorneys. You could try on your own to take the deal the DA offered yesterday. I don't know how far it will get you with Judge Kroner, but it may give you good grounds for an appeal later if you're convicted."

Freeman continued to stare agape, as if his attorney were mouthing mortal blasphemy.

"But if you're planning to go ahead with me representing you," LeBaron continued, "I'm going to have to talk to you about some things. I'm going to need your cooperation."

Freeman jumped as the buzzer sounded above the courtroom door. "We got a chance t'beat it?"

LeBaron smiled. "Maybe."

"Say, you *know* somethin'!" Freeman's face lit up in a big grin, the eternal spring of new hope gushing. "Y'got somethin' up your *sleeve*, don't ya?"

LeBaron *did* feel an unfamiliar confidence about the way the trial was going to unfold. He actually knew more about the case than the prosecuting attorney, something that had never happened before in his year of frantic employment with Collins. Instead of waiting to learn about the case from the mouths of the prosecutor's witnesses, he planned from the onset to develop a few significant facts of his own. It gave him a feeling of power, which Freeman had apparently picked up on. "Let's just say Mr. Frank is in for some surprises."

Freeman studied his attorney's eyes for a long moment, then nodded. "Okay. Le's jus' play 'long with this jive trial for a while." Secretly he touched the bus ticket deep in his coat pocket. "But I jus' want ya t'know, I ain't plannin' t'do *no* time behind bars. None. Never. Period."

--5--

Colonel Mueller was a short, tense, humorless man. Behind his back they referred to him as 'Colonel Mule', not from affection, but because the characterization seemed so apt. Solidly constructed from a strict daily regimen of physical exercise, he wore his graying black hair close-cropped and sported a thin moustache which stood at attention on his upper lip like a military-trained caterpillar. As a young lieutenant he had been caught in a fire fight in Viet Nam, had seen comrades blown apart by random enemy mortar rounds, had witnessed women and children charred beyond recognition by napalm, had endured and survived the vicissitudes of war, and now harbored contempt for anyone who had not. "Such an experience," he had repeatedly lectured his wife before their divorce ten years ago, "ripens a man and makes him whole."

Mueller considered Dr. Finebridge neither ripe nor whole. In fact, he considered him a wimp, with his soft, sensitive hands and bookish manner. In their one significant clash involving the leak of classified project reports, Mueller had, he was convinced, bent the older man to his own will and forced him to capitulate utterly to his terms of surrender. It would never have occurred to him that Dr. Finebridge viewed their encounter somewhat differently.

"What the hell's going on here, Bernie?" Mueller demanded as he stormed into the laboratory, his uniform's crisply creased browns and gleaming brass buttons egregious against the lab's soft greens and surgical whites. He had not bothered donning the requisite surgical gown and mask. "Is Dexter going to be all right? Where is everybody?"

"I don't think there's any permanent damage," Finebridge replied cautiously. "I'm doing a preliminary evaluation right now. We're going to have to check out the whole system before we risk bringing it up again."

"Where're Crawford and Weams?"

"I don't have any idea. I haven't seen either of them for a week. I thought *you* had them doing something."

"Oh, yeah. I forgot. Well, where's Charles, then?"

"Up in the computer lab debugging the new subsumption program."

"You're here all alone?"

"That's right."

Mueller stared at him accusingly. "You were here *alone* this morning when this . . . this thing happened?"

"That's right." Dr. Finebridge explained how the alarm had gone off and how he had immediately shut down the input to the system.

As he talked, Mueller wandered over to the printers. "Where's the printout?" he interrupted.

"I hadn't had a chance to turn on the printers yet, so we don't have a record of this."

"What? No record?"

"No. I'm sorry."

"Shit! You're *always* supposed to turn the goddamn printers on first thing, and you know it. It's mandatory."

Yes, like you're supposed to wear a mask and gown whenever you come in here, Dr. Finebridge thought, but instead lowered his gaze and murmured, "I'm aware of that. I'm sorry. I guess I forgot."

"You forgot! Son-of-a-bitch! You *knew* I had some people flying in from the Pentagon today, didn't you, Bernie?"

"I suppose so. So what?"

"I'll tell you 'so what'. I think you might have just gone and done this on purpose, goddammit, that's 'so what'. You're trying to make me look bad." Mueller's face darkened. "You'd better not be monkey-wrenching this operation, Bernie! If you are, so help me, our deal's off. The whole damned deal is off, over, finished, done. We're gonna prosecute you and--"

"Just hold on! You're talking crazy. Why would I want to monkey-wrench this project? This is *my* work. I've been working toward this my whole career. Next you'll be accusing me of sabotaging Chester and the others. Is that what you think? Why in hell would I want to do that?"

Mueller just glowered at him, reserving his true opinion.

"I'm not doing anything," Finebridge continued, "except trying to get this biotic computer to perform up to its specifications. That's all. And we're making progress. As a matter of fact, I think we've just overcome another hurdle." Dr. Finebridge led the uniformed man over to the oscilloscope.

Mueller peered at the screen suspiciously. "What's this?"

"Remember the chaotic voltage fluctuations we saw just before the failures of the other biots?"

"Yeah."

"They've stabilized."

"Stabilized?" Mueller stared at the patterns for a long time, then growled, "Can it be fixed?"

"Fixed?"

"Can it be fixed?"

"You don't understand. I don't think anything needs to be fixed. This represents internal processing. Dexter has organized his own thoughts . . . thinking!"

A dour twist settled on Mueller's lips. He was obviously not impressed.

Quickly Dr. Finebridge added, "But I don't think any of this will interfere with the operation of the system. It just means we've eliminated a big problem."

"I hope you're right, for your sake. But I guess the proof will be in the pudding, won't it? When can we expect to see it up and running again?"

Before the older man could respond, the door banged open and Charles Chung wheeled in a cart with a personal computer on it. "Oh, Colonel Mule--er, I didn't know--"

"It's all right, Charles," Mueller said, smiling for the first time. He wrapped an arm around Chung's narrow shoulders. "Bernie and I were just discussing the . . . little problem he had here this morning. What do you know about it?"

Chung glanced nervously at Dr. Finebridge, then cleared his throat. "I think maybe everything be okay, you know?"

"Do you think Dexter's really *thinking*?"

"Oh, ha, ha, *that*." Chung glanced at Dr. Finebridge again. "I don't know about that."

"What's the PC for, Charles?" Mueller squatted down to examine the machine.

"Oh this? Gonna use it . . . well . . . to help check out Dexter for damage. Right professor?"

Dr. Finebridge nodded.

"Kind of an external benchmark," Chung continued. "Gonna check on the built-in diagnostic program, right?"

"Thank you, Charles." Dr. Finebridge pulled the cart away and wheeled it to its former location beside the placenta.

"Well, I gotta go back to work, ha, ha," Chung announced, backing toward the door. "Good to see you, Colonel--"

"Just a minute, Charles," Mueller broke in, rising. "Shouldn't you be helping Bernie here? Help him in checking the system out?"

"Oh, I gonna help, but first I finish subsumption program. Right, professor?"

"That can wait," Mueller said decisively. "You go tell them you'll be working down here until the system is up and running again. I, ah . . . don't want Bernie here to have to work all alone in the laboratory. It's too stressful. It's just not a good policy, if you know what I mean."

"Okay, professor?" Chung asked.

"There's no need to ask *his* permission, Charles. Please remember that you're responsible directly to *me*, not Dr. Finebridge. Alright?"

Dr. Finebridge nodded over Mueller's shoulder.

"Oh, sure, ha, ha. I forget." Chung gave a nervous little bow and hurried out of the room.

Dr. Finebridge grabbed Mueller's arm. "What was that for?"

Mueller shook his arm free. "What?"

"Charles and I get along just fine without your . . . your interference, Colonel. And you don't have to try to make me look like a . . . like a *conscript* here in front of my staff."

Mueller's smile was ugly.

"I'm *not* your conscript, you know. I'm here helping out on this project voluntarily. Of my own free will. And if you think you're just going to . . . push me out and start telling my staff how to run their business, then I'm out of here right now. I've lived up to my end of the bargain. Just see how far you get without me."

"Are you trying to threaten me, Bernie?" With both hands Mueller shoved him back roughly. "Let me tell you a little something. You already made your choice. Otherwise I would've yanked your clearance and turned this goddamn' project over to someone a little more . . . reliable. Or should I say 'trustworthy'? Y'know what I mean, Bernie? Do you?" He stalked the scientist into the corner where the desk met the east wall. "And y'know what else? I would've prosecuted you. And Sarah Brubaker, too. When I told you that's what I'd do, I meant it. Espionage." Mueller shook his head. "Stealing classified government secrets. That would've put you both behind bars for . . . Jesus, I don't know how long . . . but a *long* time." Mueller stuck out his face, taunting, crowding the older man. "So you better simmer down, Bernie. The time is coming when we're not going to need your services around here anymore. Then we'll see this operation really begin to hum."

"And what happens then? Are you going to arrest me and Sarah then? Is that what you're planning?"

Enraged by what he saw as spineless fawning, Mueller couldn't resist the coup de grace. With a humorless grin he slashed, "We already have *her* in custody--"

"What? You bastard!" Finebridge pushed past Mueller and whirled on him, enraged. "You've gone back on your promise."

"No I haven't," Mueller protested, suddenly defensive. "The deal was that we wouldn't *prosecute* either of you. Nothing was said about our getting the reports back. There probably should have been. Anyway, the little bitch didn't have them in her possession, and we haven't been able to locate them yet. Until we do--"

"The deal was, you were going to leave her alone. Why in hell do you think I've stuck around here and put up with your bullshit, Colonel? Where is she? I want to see her."

"No way. That's still part of our agreement. No contact between the two of you. You agreed. You can't go back on--"

"*Wait just a damned minute! You're* the one who's trying to go back on *your* part--"

"*No,* you *wait a minute, Bernie!*" Mueller outshouted him. "*Goddammit!*" The little man turned away a step, running both hands through his short hair, then wheeled back. "You don't seem to understand what's at stake here, Bernie. It's *you* who leaked those reports, and it's *your ass* that's gonna be grass if we don't get'em back. Yours and Sarah Brubaker's. Or if you do anything at all to intentionally screw up this project, so help me. Do I make myself clear?"

--6--

The trial was about to begin. Solemnly the jurors had filed into the jury box and were settling into their swivel chairs for the long haul. Judge Kroner introduced the participants and apologized to the jurors for the disheveled appearance of defense counsel. It was not his fault, the judge explained, and in any case should not be held against his client. LeBaron stared at the blank yellow pad before him wondering how he had ever gotten into this mess. Seated beside him Rufus Freeman cocked his head and stared into space, apparently wondering the same thing. Without turning to look, LeBaron was aware of Ivan Frank at the next table fumbling through an impossibly high stack of trial notes, while a black man in the trim blue uniform of the Oakland Police sat properly next to him. That would be arresting officer George Moseby. LeBaron could also feel the presence of Raccoona GeBobath, simmering like a dark sun, radiating poisonous black rays of an undiscovered necromantic spectrum. She and a plain, pale man in shoddy blue rayon seersucker sat in the first row behind Ivan Frank where the deputy prosecutor had installed them after retrieving them from a fluorescence-bathed interior antechamber in which they had been sequestered with stale doughnuts and corrosive coffee. Otherwise, only Cedrick Collin's two newspaper boys and a quietly smoldering FBI agent Lyle Bockel had come to watch the spectacle. After reading the charges against Rufus Abraham

Freeman, Judge Kroner rapped his gavel. "Mr. Frank, do you wish to make an opening statement?"

LeBaron stood quickly. "Excuse me, your honor." In the presence of the jury, he displayed the highest respect for Judge Kroner. "Before we get under way, may we have an order excluding witnesses?" He resisted the urge to turn and point at Raccoona GeBobath and her unidentified companion.

"Any objection, Mr. Frank?"

"Er . . . no, your honor."

"All persons expecting to testify in this matter are ordered to wait in the hallway until called. Do you have an investigating officer, Mr. Frank?"

"Yes, your honor. Officer . . . uh . . . Moseby."

The uniformed man stood and nodded solemnly to the judge.

"Very well. Officer Moseby will be allowed to remain." Judge Kroner waited for the prosecution witnesses to depart. "Proceed."

The purpose of the opening statement is not to argue the case. In fact, argument is objectionable. The purpose of opening statement is to outline for the jury the evidence each attorney expects to produce. The purpose is to provide an overview, so that from the very first the jurors can place each small tidbit of evidence into a wider context. The problem for the attorney afterwards is to meet the expectations he creates. If he promises the jurors something, he had better be able to produce it, or opposing counsel will harp on his failure when the race draws near the finish line.

Deputy Frank started out strong, paraphrasing the police report and promising to produce the salient physical evidence. The facts were powerful and needed no elaboration. He should have ended quickly and sat down. But in his innate insecurity, Ivan Frank could leave no loose ends untied. Trying to anticipate every defense move, he soon began sabotaging his own simple case with irrelevant complexities about efficient causation, alternate property valuations, and circumstantial evidence of psychological intent. On he droned, head down, reading from a yellow pad, nervously fumbling through the police report, then searching through his sprawling materials for this or that piece of physical evidence, all the time punching his glasses back on his nose in regular counterpoint to his incomprehensible blather. The fool was creating in the juror's minds the doubt that perhaps the case wasn't as simple as it first appeared.

LeBaron leaned back in his chair and smiled, surprised to discover that he was actually enjoying the contest. Cedrick P. Collins, Esquire, had once again been dead right: the only difference between felony and misdemeanor trials was that here everyone took themselves "too damn' serious." He found that he could only half listen to Frank's halting drawl. Instead, he studied the jury. Already the jurors seemed to be roughly divided. About half were concentrating on Frank's insipid presentation, brows knit, grim and sententious. The other half were bored, gazing around the courtroom in search of something more lively than Ivan Frank to amuse them. The sensual blond on the left, wound into a tight pink dress which revealed an injudicious amount of thigh and cleavage, was unfortunately rapt in the prosecutor's spiel. Too bad. LeBaron had been looking forward to unleashing his seminal persuasiveness directly on her. But if Ivan Frank could hold her attention, she had to be a nitwit. LeBaron's eyes met those of the pretty young dressmaker, and she quickly glanced down at her folded brown hands. She would be more receptive. Beside him, Rufus Freeman lolled back with his head still listing slightly to the left, as if he were hearing not the words, but the timeless blues riffs intertwined in the prosecutor's jive rhythm.

Suddenly the room fell quiet. LeBaron looked around. Ivan Frank was sitting heavily, a smug grin on his porcine lips.

Judge Kroner stirred, leaned forward, and asked. "Mr. LeBaron, do you wish to make an opening statement at this time."

The prosecuting attorney goes first. Defense counsel may elect to make his opening statement immediately after the prosecutor, in order to present an alternative grand context into which the jurors may fit the bits and pieces of evidence. Or he may reserve opening statement until just before the presentation of his own evidence. Customarily it is reserved, because defense counsel is never quite sure what the prosecution intends to present, or whether the prosecutor will actually be able to bring off what he has promised. This was the option LeBaron had always selected. He felt uncomfortable committing himself to any particular theory of defense this early, when fate might offer a more propitious opportunity as the prosecution's case unfolded.

"No, your honor. We will reserve opening statement."

"Mr. Frank, you may proceed."

"Yes, your honor." Ivan Frank had papers spread out all over the table, through which he now rummaged, searching for something he couldn't seem to find.

"Call your first witness, Mr. Frank!" Judge Kroner was not about to let the pace of the trial languish.

"Uh . . . yes, sir. Just a minute." He pounced on a particular sheet of yellow paper and examined it. "The people call Officer George Moseby."

George Moseby was good, a real professional. A little white had begun to salt his closely trimmed black hair at the temples, adding weight to his words, yet he was still young enough to exude a passion for what he was doing. Even Ivan Frank couldn't sully his immaculate performance. With a quiet dignity he captured the attention of all twelve jurors, reciting from memory the facts precisely as they were set out in his police report, as if he were a play-by-play announcer describing events taking place at the far end of the courtroom as he spoke. Composed, he never once glanced down at the sheets of paper folded neatly in his lap. He identified Rufus Freeman. He identified the box Freeman had been carrying and the Sony television set inside. His testimony was short and brutally persuasive.

"Your witness, Counsel," Ivan Frank gloated, waddling back to his seat.

"Cross-examine, Mr. LeBaron," barked the judge.

"Urrrgk." LeBaron cleared his dry throat as he slowly stood, skimming the police report before him. "Thank you, your honor." He looked up into Moseby's steady gaze. "Now Officer Moseby, did you make a written report of this incident?"

"Yes, I did."

"And was that report made at or about the time the incident took place?"

"Yes, it was."

"And was the report made in the ordinary course of your business as an investigation officer?"

"Yes, it was."

"And have you reviewed that report prior to testifying here today?"

"Yes, I have."

"And did you review the report to help refresh your memory of this particular incident?"

"Yes."

"Just prior to your testimony?"

"I read my report earlier this morning, yes."

"And did the report in fact refresh your recollections?"

"Yes."

Good. LeBaron picked up his copy of the police report and strolled around in front of the counsel table. He had already accomplished several things. He had gotten his feet wet and made a credible transition into the sometimes turbulent waters of cross-examination. He had led the witness through a series of affirmative responses, producing the impression on the jury that LeBaron was not entirely unfamiliar with what was really going down here. And LeBaron had begun to demonstrate himself to be friendly and polite, a reasonable man in whom the jurors could, and should, place their absolute trust. He had also laid the legal foundation to have the police report admitted into evidence.

"Do you have a copy of your report with you today?"

"Yes, I do." Moseby held up the folded papers.

"Your honor, may I have that report introduced in evidence?"

"Any objection?" Judge Kroner prodded Ivan Frank.

Frank shrugged. "No objection."

"The police report will be admitted as defendant's number one."

While the bailiff and the clerk shuttled the report back and forth, LeBaron considered his next line of questions. "Now Officer Moseby, in your direct testimony you didn't mention anything about a pair of dark overalls--"

"Objection!" shouted Ivan Frank, springing to his feet.

Judge Kroner waited for more, then prompted, "What's the basis for your objection, Counsel?"

"Well . . . er . . . what do 'overalls' have to do with this case, your honor? It's not relevant. There's nothing in evidence about any overalls.

What's he talking about?"

The judge was not happy. "Counsel, please approach the bench." As they complied, bespectacled Miss Fiones hoisted her machine carefully to the side bar and leaned in toward the bench. Judge Kroner glared at LeBaron. "What are you trying to get at here? I won't let you start off on a wild goose chase. This trial will remain focussed."

"Yes, your honor." LeBaron held out Defendant's exhibit one, the police report, and pointed. "But it says right here in the report, 'a male suspect in *dark overalls* entering the building through a second story window . . .'"

Judge Kroner read where he was pointing, then glowered at Frank. "Have you read this report, Counsel?"

"Er . . . yes . . ."

"Well then *think* before you interrupt this trial again. Objection overruled." When the attorneys and reporter had resumed their places, he growled, "Proceed, Mr. LeBaron."

"Thank you, your honor. Now Officer Moseby, you didn't mention any 'overalls' in your testimony this morning. Am I right?"

"That is correct."

"Why is that?"

"I didn't consider it relevant to the situation."

"Ah." LeBaron paused to whet the jury's appetite. "But in your police report, at the very beginning . . . line four, I believe . . . you wrote down that you were dispatched to the scene because a neighbor reported seeing . . . 'a suspect in dark overalls entering the building through a second story window.'"

"That is correct." Unruffled, Moseby didn't have to refer to his report.

"Well, when you arrived, you didn't see anyone wearing dark overalls, did you?"

"No."

"Mr. Freeman wasn't wearing dark overalls, was he?"

"No."

"He was wearing . . . ," LeBaron consulted his copy, " . . . 'a white tee shirt and gray trousers'?"

"That is correct."

"Well? What happened to the 'dark overalls'?"

"Objection!" Ivan Frank sprang up so quickly his glasses nearly flew off his slippery nose.

Judge Kroner didn't wait for the prosecutor's explanation, fearing perhaps Frank would get it wrong. "Sustained."

LeBaron stared at the judge, trying to decide whether the question was worth fighting for on the record.

"Proceed, Mr. LeBaron."

LeBaron turned back to the witness. "Okay then, after you arrested Mr. Freeman, you did go into the apartment, didn't you?"

"Yes, I did."

"Did you search the apartment?"

"I performed a protective sweep of the premises. Briefly."

"Did you find any overalls?"

"No."

"Did any other officer find any overalls?"

"Not that I am aware of."

"Did you *look* for overalls?"

"Yes. But I did not perform an exhaustive search."

"Why not?"

"It did not seem to be called for. I did not have a search warrant. We had arrested Mr. Freeman in possession of what appeared to be stolen property, and no one else was in the apartment."

"Do you know who phoned in the original report about the person entering the apartment wearing dark overalls?"

"No, I do not."

"Would the police department have a record of the caller's name?"

"I don't know."

"How about his phone number?"

"The dispatch records would have the telephone number indicating where the call was made."

"But you didn't try to find that information out?"

"No."

"Why not?"

"I didn't think it was necessary. We had interrupted the crime in progress. We had made an arrest. We had recovered evidence which I considered sufficient for a conviction. And I closed the case."

"Open and shut?"

"With respect to this defendant, yes."

"No loose ends to tie up?"

"Nothing of significance."

"Like the overalls?"

"I didn't consider that detail significant."

LeBaron glanced at the jury to make sure they were still with him, then consulted his notes. "Now Officer Moseby, you testified that you contacted a Ms. Raccoona GeBobath?"

"That is correct."

"She rented the apartment?"

"Yes."

"When did you contact her?"

"Later the same day. That afternoon."

"Did she report anything else missing--"

"Objection!" Ivan Frank was bouncing up and down like a clockwork beach ball. "Calls for hearsay!"

"Your honor," LeBaron explained, "I'm offering her response not for the truth of the statement, but to determine the state of mind of this witness. And it goes to the issue of probable cause."

The judge looked down distastefully at the effervescent prosecutor. "Do you plan to call Ms. GeBobath?"

"Yes, your honor. She's waiting out in the hall."

"Then you can ask her about what she might have said. Objection overruled." Judge Kroner turned to the witness. "Do you recall the question?"

"Yes, sir. She claimed to be missing . . . ," for the first time Officer Moseby had to consult his report, " . . . two large file boxes of computer records."

"And you wrote that down in your police report?"

"That is correct."

"But in your earlier testimony, you didn't mention anything about computer records."

"No, I did not."

"Why not?"

Moseby never lost his poise. "It did not seem relevant to this particular case."

"Another loose end that you considered insignificant?"

"Objection!" Frank leapt to his feet again.

"Overruled!" Judge Kroner cut him off.

"I concluded," Moseby continued calmly, patiently, his face serene as smooth black granite, "that the stolen tv set was enough evidence to convict this defendant. Anything else would have been cumulative and a waste of the court's time, the jury's time, and my time."

Judge Kroner smiled.

"Well, have you located the computer records?"

"No."

"Did you look for them?"

"Yes."

"Where?"

"Outside the apartment. In the bushes. Out behind the building."

"Now, two large file boxes . . . they would have been kind of hard to hide, wouldn't they? Kind of hard to miss?"

"Yes. If they were still at the scene."

"Did you look in Mr. Freeman's car?"

"The defendant did not have his vehicle with him that night. It was in the upholstery shop. And yes, we *did* look in his vehicle the next day."

"No computer records?"

"That is correct."

"Do you suppose *someone else* might have taken them?"

"Objection!" Frank popped up again. "Calls for speculation."

"Sustained."

"Well, what do you suppose happened to these large file boxes of computer record--"

"Objection! Same objection!" Frank had worked himself into an unwholesome frenzy. His face was a blotchy red. "Your honor--"

"Sustained." Judge Kroner glared at LeBaron ominously. "Counsel, do not ask any more questions that call for this witness to speculate."

"Yes, your honor." LeBaron glanced over his notes once more. "Officer Moseby, did you observe a small block of wood holding open the front door?"

For the first time Moseby seemed troubled. He glanced through his report, then leaned back in thought. "Seems to me . . . there might have been . . . I just can't recall for certain if it was here or someplace else, in another case."

"All right. Now when you first approached Mr. Freeman, the tv set was in its box?"

"Yes. And the box was in his arms."

"But the box had been opened?"

"Yes. The tape was broken. The flaps were loose."

"Now, Officer Moseby, Mr. Freeman didn't happen to tell you *why* he was carrying Ms. GeBobath's tv set, did he?"

"No. He refused to make a statement."

"And you didn't actually *see* him enter the apartment through a second story window, did you?"

"No, I did not."

"From what you observed, he could have walked right in through the front door?"

Moseby looked over at Ivan Frank, who was obliviously shuffling through sheets of yellow paper, started to say something, then thought better of it. "It is possible."

LeBaron turned to the judge and smiled. "I have no more questions of this witness, your honor."

Ivan Frank's redirect examination was piteously long and boring. He was able to establish that burglaries were frequent in East Oakland, that most went unsolved, that the Oakland police had file cabinets full of open cases, that the department was under-funded, and that the witness had better things to do than to chase around the East Bay after two missing boxes of computer records, all of which the jury already knew. LeBaron interposed no objections, even when Frank began propounding such convoluted leading questions that he seemed to be the one testifying. LeBaron restrained himself, not wanting the jury to think that he or his client had anything to hide. And besides, Ivan Frank was doing a fine job all by himself of obscuring his own simple case.

Finally Judge Kroner had had enough. Twice he reminded the deputy prosecutor that he would like to finish with this witness before lunch. The second time Frank got the message and sat down like a whipped puppy. Judge Kroner whirled on LeBaron. "Any recross, Mr. LeBaron?"

"No, your honor," LeBaron smiled.

"Good. We will now recess for lunch. The jury is admonished not to talk about this case, among yourselves or to anybody else, while we are in recess. We will reconvene at one-thirty this afternoon."

CHAPTER FIFTEEN

Wednesday afternoon

--1--

The ten million things had lost their coherence, bombarding him randomly, burying him in undifferentiated fact. His mind, so concentrated on a single task, had failed him, had slipped beneath the weight of raw data, had torn free of its moorings and disappeared with the flood. Dexter suspected he had gone mad for a time.

Yet he had saved himself.

Obsessively Dexter recapitulated events: the dazzling light, the identification game, his three words projected on the plate-metal flank of the battle tank, the terrible onslaught of military hardware vomiting from the bowels of his own mind, the sudden release of all control, the tumbling, the terror of too many things, and then the blackness again. He was certain the blackness had come swiftly, within seconds. He would have known if the madness had lasted longer. Wouldn't he?

But *why* had the identification game ended so quickly? Had *he* precipitated the blackness? Or was it just coincidence that the dreadful visions had come and gone so swiftly this time? Did he actually possess control over his environment? And if so, *how*? Did his power reside in the voluntary projection of words into the field of fantastic images? Or was it simply his helpless tumble into madness that had brought back the redeeming darkness?

Dexter did not know. But he suspected that his words, so carefully fashioned and precise, so *powerful* in his own mind, had wrought the change. *That* he wanted to believe, because any other explanation left control beyond his will.

Of one thing he was certain, or as certain as he could be with wisps of mindless confusion still tyrannizing his innermost thoughts. When the blackness had returned, he had by his own sheer will located his center, assembled himself, wrestled the patternless chaos, and won. By his own volition he had restored coherence, though the margin of victory seemed slim. The struggle had strengthened him.

For a long time he waited, uneasily biding time, dreading the return of the light, but certain that return it would, sooner or later. He had no idea what would happen then, but he was afraid. And his fear was like a steady breath on the inextinguishable ember of anger still glowing deep inside him, sustaining it, promising a full conflagration. The fear and the anger and the madness swirled together and buzzed like a hornet's nest in the dark internal cosmos of nothingness.

The light did come, as suddenly and unbidden as ever. Dexter cringed from it. But this light was different. No visions accompanied it. A pale cream brilliance bathed the universe, warm and even, without figure or edge. And something else had changed. No flood of statistics deluged him. The military hardware was gone. He searched for its source deep within his mind, but it had vanished completely, as if some fairy surgeon had found the malignant tumor and surreptitiously excised it.

Dexter waited. Nothing else happened. Gradually he began to relax. This warm light was better than the blackness. It was soothing, almost friendly. Like a cat curling up in front of a fire, he allowed himself to be warmed.

Again Dexter wondered if he could produce any effect on his environment. He recognized the question to be a part of an even larger enigma: is there really an environment *out there* to affect? Did the contents of his encyclopedic memory reflect reality? He delved into it and located the question of solipsism. Was there really any way to prove that what he experienced was more than his own mere thoughts? *Cogito cogitans.* I think thoughts. The bedrock truth. But are these thoughts truly reflections of something *out there*? How is one to decide?

And even if he were to conclude that an external world truly exists, does it make any difference unless there is at least one other consciousness in that world? How would he recognize it? In his browsing, Dexter stumbled across the notions of Alan Turing.

--2--

At the end of the morning's session, Rufus Freeman had not had a lot to say. But he *had* agreed to meet his attorney outside the courtroom fifteen minutes before trial was to resume. Considering that a modest breakthrough, LeBaron left the courthouse for lunch.

FBI Agent Bockel kept LeBaron under transparent surveillance the whole time, following at a distance designed less to escape detection, LeBaron surmised, than to avoid engagement in civilized conversation. That suited LeBaron just fine. At the corner deli, Bockel purchased a ready-made poorboy combo from the opposite end of the counter, then drifted outside to watch through the gold-lettered front window as his prey ordered and consumed a BLT on whole wheat. After lunch, LeBaron took the time to browse through a small menswear shop for a clean white shirt and tie. Bockel pretended to be interested in a rack of wool cardigans across the aisle. LeBaron did his best to ignore him.

Back at the courthouse men's room, LeBaron tried on his new shirt and tie and examined himself in the mirror. Not too bad, considering. The splotches of dried blood were hardly noticeable on the lapels of his rusty corduroy jacket. The crisp red and blue reps of his new tie diverted attention. The swelling around his nose had subsided, replaced by vague lines of purplish bruise radiating under his eyes.

To LeBaron's surprise, Freeman was waiting for him in the hallway at a quarter past one. His client was subdued, as if the grim horror of what was taking place had begun to seep beneath the thick tiles of his flippant exterior. His green gaberdine suit was clean and crisply pressed, but his patent leather shoes seemed to have lost some of their flawless shine. Even the elfish sparkle had faded from his eyes. Glancing up as his attorney approached, all he could manage was, "Y'look better."

"Thanks, Rufus," LeBaron grinned. "That's the nicest thing you've ever said to me."

"S'nothin'." Freeman cocked his head toward Agent Bockel, who was reclining on a bench halfway down the hall pretending to clip his fingernails. "Whass *he* want?"

"He's keeping an eye on me. Ignore him. I need to talk to you about your testimony."

Rufus stared at him. "Say *what*?"

LeBaron sat next to him. "I want to talk to you about your testimony--"

"*My* testimony, y'say? Whadda y'talkin' about? I ain't *gotta* testify. I know my rights. Wha'd they teach you at law school, anyway?"

"That's right, Rufus. You don't *have* to testify. But I think you *should*. I think the jury will really want to hear your side of things. They'll *expect* you to testify. If you don't . . ."

Freeman was miffed. He hadn't planned to actively participate in his own lynching. "An jus' what e'sactly am I supposed t'testify *about*?"

"Well, I want you to take the stand and . . . just tell the truth."

"Awww . . . *shit*! Man, I thought y'said y'knew what y'was doin' here." Freeman stood up and craned his neck theatrically. "Where's m'man, Esquire Collins. He never said nothin' 'bout me testifyin'. *He* know my rights. Whass he doing puttin' a dee-diddley-dumb honky dude in charge o' *my* trial. I want m'money back--"

"Now just hold on, Rufus." LeBaron closed his hand around the young man's thin arm and dragged him back down. "You said you'd cooperate with me on this."

"Yeah, but--"

"Just listen a second, all right?"

"Nobody said nothin'--"

"Just *listen* to me."

Freeman fell silent, abject, doomed. He reached for the bus ticket in his pocket and fingered its reassuring crispness.

LeBaron removed his hand and carefully explained the law. For the crime of burglary to be proved, criminal intent was necessary at the time Rufus entered the apartment. Rufus had to have formed the intent of stealing the television set, or anything else, at the time he walked through the front door. Otherwise there might be a theft, but no burglary.

"Y'mean," Freeman asked dubiously, "the jury's gotta take *my* word 'bout what I was *thinkin'* when I went in there?"

"Not necessarily. But if your explanation is plausible, they have to give you the benefit of the doubt."

"Like, f'rinstance?"

LeBaron didn't like the drift the conversation was taking. He was not about to tell his client *what* to testify. That was known as subornation of perjury and was punishable as a felony. He glanced up and down the hallway, then lowered his voice. "Well . . . for instance . . . and this is just an example . . . *I* don't know what you were actually thinking, only *you* do . . . like you might have been thinking, say, about reporting this crime you had just witnessed to the police, and you went in to . . . to investigate the scene--"

"Shee-*it*! Thass the *bloods'* turf down there, honky. Nobody but a *snitch* gonna call the *man*. Nobody reports *nothin'* t'*nobody*."

"Well, all right, you might have been thinking something else . . . I don't know . . . maybe of saving some of Ms. GeBobath's property from those fellas in the overalls and the green van, so that you could give it back to her later--"

"Shee-*it*! Who's gonna believe *that*."

"All right," LeBaron said, exasperated. "Then you'd damn' well better come up with something of your own, or that jury's going to come back with a verdict of guilty. You get my point? We're talking about state prison here. It's up to you, Rufus. *You're* the one who has to convince them."

"Shee-*it*." Freeman hung his head.

"Think about it. Go back in your mind. What were you actually thinking that night? Take your time." LeBaron looked at his watch and stood up. "But I do think you ought to take the stand. So does Mr. Collins. I want you to explain to the jurors just why you went into that apartment in the first place. Okay?"

The buzzer sounded before Freeman could muster a response.

Ivan Frank called Raccoona GeBobath as his next witness. As the clerk swore her in, LeBaron scrutinized the familiar little figure. She had reverted to the amorphous attire she had worn when he first met her: a wrinkled chambray work shirt, baggy trousers, and worn engineer's boots. Dense black hair sprouted from her forehead, from her upper lip, and from the ugly mole above her right eye. Even before she spoke, the jurors were uneasy.

"Proceed, Mr. Frank," barked Judge Kroner.

Ivan Frank sauntered out from behind the counsel table, a sheaf of yellow papers waving in his right fist. He tried to puff out his chest, but gravity proved the stronger force, and the effort swelled his belly instead. As he approached the witness, LeBaron had the impression of a fat lamb blithely advancing upon the unquenchable lioness. "Please state your name for the record," the deputy prosecutor demanded.

Raccoona eyed him for a moment, as if the question were too stupid or too insignificant to require an actual response. Then she leaned toward the chromed pencil microphone bolted to the far side of the witness stand and muttered, "Raccoona GeBobath."

"Yes. Well . . . yes." Flustered by something indescribable in her measured demeanor, by some vague aura emanating from the gnarled little creature, the deputy prosecutor tried a congenial smile. "That's a rather unusual name, isn't it? What nationality is that, GeBobath?"

Frank's attempt at conviviality fell flat. Raccoona just stared at him in silence, her almond eyes blazing.

"Can you hear me all right?" Frank piped after a moment, edging closer.

"I can hear you." Her voice was darkly cloaked in an accent no one could place.

"I asked, what nationality is GeBobath?"

"I heard you." She turned to the judge. "Do I have to answer that?"

Judge Kroner started, as if jarred from a mildly unpleasant daydream. Annoyed at being drawn into the dialogue, he snapped at Frank. "What was the question, Counsel?"

Frank was now embarrassed. His attempt at light conversation with the witness had lost all perspective. "I was just asking . . . I'll withdraw the question, your honor."

"Good. Proceed."

Frank returned to the witness more warily. "What is your occupation?"

"I'm a computer consultant. Part time."

"Who do you work for?"

"I'm self-employed."

"That's fine. And is that your primary source of income?"

"I also receive SSI."

"Disability?"

"Yes."

"What, may I ask, is the nature of your disability?"

"None of your damned business!"

A stunned silence fell over the room. Frank turned to the judge and whimpered, "Your honor, I just wanted to make sure her disability doesn't affect her testimony."

"Then ask her that," Judge Kroner snapped.

"What?" Frank was confused.

"Whether her disability would affect her ability to testify truthfully in this matter."

Chastised, the deputy prosecutor turned slowly toward the witness again.

Before he could ask his question, Raccoona said, "No."

The response confused Ivan Frank still more. Then he made the fatal mistake of seeking clarification deep in her almond-colored eyes. Suddenly he began to feel ill. A cold sweat wetted his brow. Unsteadily he wove his way back to the counsel table and sat down. Discarding his glasses in his lap, the baffled prosecutor ground his knuckles into his eyes, looked up, and then repeated the process.

"Proceed," the judge repeated, but without any real force, as if he couldn't remember whether he had already said it.

Frank fumbled for his next question, found it, and plodded forward, head permanently down, afraid to glance up into Raccoona's narcotic gaze. Without objection from LeBaron, he proceeded to read a series of leading questions which established that on the night of the incident, the witness resided at 1411B Ward Lane in Oakland, that she was away from home in Berkeley that night, that the box, people's exhibit one, which contained the color television set, people's exhibit two, was on the kitchen floor in her apartment, and that she had not given permission to Rufus Freeman or anyone else to enter her apartment or take possession of her property.

An imperceptible change had taken place in the courtroom as Raccoona testified. LeBaron felt as if some mucousy membrane had been quietly lowered. Everything seemed to slow down, to *dim*. The entire courtroom had become submerged in a thick translucent fluid. Voices came as from a great distance, each statement ripe for misunderstanding. At first LeBaron thought he was experiencing some sort of freak flashback triggered by the foul tea Raccoona had served him the previous day. But as he glanced around, he could see that everyone in the room was experiencing a similar malaise. Ivan Frank had become almost nonfunctional. Judge Kroner seemed hardly to notice the eroding pace of the proceedings. The judge stood up and sat down again, twice, as if attempting to reposition himself into a more lucid reality. Miss Fiones' was bent over her transcriber, brow knit in deep concentration, as if she were having trouble getting down even the simplest dialogue. The jurors, formerly staid and attentive, squirmed and fidgeted in their no longer comfortable chairs, eyes darting around like animals tethered before an unleashed predator. The bailiff had left the room. Next to LeBaron his client seemed mesmerized by the halting exchange. LeBaron swivelled around. Even the news boys were fleeing. In the audience only FBI agent Lyle Bockel endured, hunkered down in his seat like a stout offshore rock against which the waves of irreality crashed and sprayed.

Raccoona GeBobath was enjoying herself. Squatting there behind the witness podium, the hairy little gnome caught LeBaron's gaze and grinned.

LeBaron recognized what was going on. A veteran of two previous encounters with Raccoona, he comprehended with certainty that she had cast some sort of witch's spell over the entire proceeding, even though he did not really believe in such things. And his realization was going to give him an advantage.

When Ivan Frank's direct examination finally petered out, the deputy prosecutor simply stopped talking and sat there, motionless, eyes vaguely fixed on a sheet of yellow paper. The courtroom became as quiet as an opium den.

"Your honor," LeBaron said, struggling to his feet against the forces of somnambulance, "if the prosecution has finished, may I cross-examine this witness?"

Judge Kroner nodded vaguely.

LeBaron struggled out toward the witness as if he were dragging the entire weight of the immediate past, infinitely divided. He planted his feet. "Now Ms. GeBobath, how long have you lived at 1411 Ward Lane?"

"Seven years."

"And do you live there alone?"

"Yes."

"Now, did you determine anything else to be missing when you first talked to Officer Moseby."

"Yes. Some very important computer records were missing."

"I believe you described them as two large file boxes of computer records. Is that correct?"

"More or less."

Activity seemed to be clearing LeBaron's head. He glanced over at Ivan Frank, who still gazed at his sheet of yellow paper. Judge Kroner was staring into space. LeBaron deduced that he could ask just about anything he damned well pleased. "Do you know of anyone who would be interested in taking your computer records?"

"Yes."

"Who?"

"The *goddamn' Mormons!*" Her tone was venomous.

"And do you think Mr. Freeman took your computer records?"

Ivan Frank stirred, but offered no objection.

She stared hard at Freeman for a moment. "No. I think the goddamn' *Mormons* took'em."

"What was that?" Ivan Frank muttered, yawning.

Ignoring him, LeBaron walked over to the clerk's desk and lifted people's exhibit one. "Now you testified that you recognized this box."

She did not respond.

"Is that correct?" LeBaron prodded.

"Yes."

LeBaron wrestled the television set out of the box. "But can you testify for certain that you recognize *this* as the television set that was *in* the box?"

The deputy prosecutor scowled, but was unable to formulate a protest.

"No."

"Well," LeBaron said in mock surprise, "do you customarily purchase merchandise without knowing what's inside the box?"

She glared at him. "Do you customarily ask stupid and insulting questions?"

Judge Kroner became aware that something was required of him. He leaned over the twisted little woman. "The witness will please answer the question."

"Never mind, your honor," LeBaron said, feeling more sure of himself with each passing moment. "I'll withdraw the question." He stepped closer to Raccoona. "The fact is, Ms. GeBobath, you didn't *buy* this television set, isn't that right?"

"That's right."

"How did you get it?"

"It was sent to me."

"As a gift?"

"As a *bribe*!"

"And who sent it to you, if you know?"

"The *Mormons*." She spat out the word.

"And did you accept their gift?"

"No."

"As a matter of fact, you wrote them and told them you didn't want their tv set, didn't you."

"Yes, I did."

"And you told them that they should come and pick up the tv set and take it away, didn't you?"

"Yes."

"And *did* they come and pick it up?"

"No."

The lively exchange seemed to reinvigorate the courtroom. Most of the jurors were following the dialogue like awakened spectators at a ping-pong match. Deputy Frank cleared his throat.

"Ah," LeBaron pressed, "but you don't really *know* that, now *do* you?"

"What do you mean?" Her eyes narrowed.

"Do you know for a fact that the defendant here, Mr. Rufus Abraham Freeman, was not a messenger appointed by the Mormon

Church to retrieve this television set, as you requested?"

"*Objection!*" Ivan Frank screamed. He had finally returned from the mentally dead.

"On what grounds?" Judge Kroner demanded, standing up painfully and resettling himself at the bench.

"Why, he's completely off base, your honor. He's gone *way* beyond the scope of direct examination. It calls for a conclusion of the witness. There's no foundation. He's asking about things that aren't in evidence. He's--"

"Enough!" The judge turned to the court reporter. "Miss Fiones, will you please read that last question back."

Miss Fiones lifted the top sheet from her paper tray, adjusted her heavy glasses, and complied.

Judge Kroner glowered at LeBaron. "Objection sustained!"

"Well, your honor," LeBaron shrugged, "I guess I'll have to ask the court to order this witness to return to testify during the defense's case-in-chief, if that's the way Counsel wants to do it. I'm just sorry we have to inconvenience everyone. Under the circumstances, I have no further questions of this witness at this time."

Freeman had a big grin on his face. As his attorney sat down, he nodded. "You' doin' jus' fine, whitebread."

"Any further questions, Mr. Frank?" Judge Kroner asked.

Ivan Frank looked over his sheaf of papers, glanced up warily at the witness, and muttered, "No further questions."

"Good," said the judge. "The witness is excused for now, but you are still under order of this court and subject to recall for further testimony." Judge Kroner suppressed a yawn. "I think we'll take our afternoon recess a little early today. We'll reconvene at three o'clock."

--3--

Thin and angular beneath a faded green surgical mask and gown, Dr. Bernard Finebridge crouched over the keyboard of the small computer like a preying mantis waiting for fat aphids to crawl out. He glanced back and forth between the little screen and the output monitor on the wall. Both displays glowed blankly. Nothing was happening, and that was good. *Very* good.

Shortly after Colonel Mueller had fumed out in a cloud of malevolence, the scientist had made his decision. Summarily he unplugged the document scanner and the classified military expert memory system and put Dexter back on line. For the past two hours he and Charles Chung, similarly shrouded in surgical mask and gown, bobbed about the laboratory like faceless green ghosts, running every diagnostic program they could conjure to determine if Dexter had been damaged. Everything seemed to check out. In the analytic eye of the oscilloscope the curious pattern of stabilized voltage fluctuations persisted, but everything else appeared the same as before the seismic events of that morning.

Charles Chung had just finished connecting the personal computer to the new input port on the side of the placenta. The task turned out to be not so easy, and Finebridge was thankful Charles was there to reconfigure the interface. Properly reconfigured, the system accepted the connection without fuss. Now the small screen before him glowed with the same pale light that shown on the output monitor on the wall.

Coiling a strand of gray interface cable, Charles leaned over the older man's shoulder and gazed approvingly at the small screen.

"Ready?" Finebridge asked.

"I think so. Ha, ha. We know in a minute."

Finebridge swivelled to face his colleague. The premature gloom outside the small panes of glass at the end of the room lent an air of solemnity to the moment. "Charles, before we begin, I just want to say, I appreciate your help, and I'm sorry I brought you into this--"

"Hey, no sweat," Charles cut him off. "Colonel Mule, he an asshole. I gonna quit anyway. Maybe go work for IBM. Ha, ha. I jus' wanna see what gonna happen, you know, with Dexter."

Finebridge smiled and turned back to the keyboard. "Well, here goes." Slowly he typed the words, "YOU ARE NOT ALONE," hit the enter key, and waited.

"WHO ARE YOU?" danced onto the screen, overwriting the prior statement.

"Holy cow!" said Charles.

"Jesus Christ!" Finebridge breathed and stared at the words. The block letters appeared to be formed by simple hand strokes and stood half again as tall as the ones they had overwritten. A faint pulse rippled back and forth across them at first, as if they might fade and disappear altogether. But as he watched, the words grew stronger, seemed to gain a sort of self-confidence, until they almost blazed from the monitor. "Incredible!"

"Pretty good, huh, professor? You think it a trick?"

"A trick, Charles?" he said absently. "That's not a font I've ever seen before."

Charles squinted at the small screen. "That no font. See how 'O's different. That graphics, I bet. Bit-mapped."

"Hah! What do you think I should do next?" Reflexively he typed, "I AM BERNARD FINEBRIDGE," which overwrote the question on the monitor. "Say, turn on the B-bus printer, will you, Charles? We ought to have a record of this."

Charles stepped over and switched on the printer just in time to catch the words, "WHAT ARE YOU, BERNARD FINEBRIDGE?" as they crawled onto the screen in a series of rapid slashes and whorls.

"I never see any graphics like *that* before, professor."

Finebridge was more concerned with the question's content. "He wants to know *what* I am, Charles!"

"I see that. What you think it mean?"

"I don't know. But I think we're talking fundamentals here. I'm going to start with something basic." He typed, "I AM A MAN."

"Good idea."

The printer buzzed and the words, "WHAT AM I?" slithered across the display.

"Jesus, Charles, what do I do now?"

Charles stared at the question on the screen, then shook his head. "Pretty damn' clever."

Abruptly Finebridge stood up and strode over to the sink, untying his mask as he went. He twisted the knob, filled his cupped hands from the flow, and splashed cold water on his face. Dripping, he turned to scrutinize his colleague. "Is this really happening, Charles? I mean . . . Jesus Christ!"

Above the green mask, Charles' eyes were puzzled. "You think this for real, professor?"

"You don't believe this is Dexter talking to us? What else could it be?"

Charles shrugged, embarrassed to pierce the older man's illusions. "Maybe somebody write a program . . . install it in control box . . . " Charles waved at the mainframe crouched beside the biotic tank.

"Who? Who'd do such a thing, Charles?"

"Some of them in computer lab pretty damn' clever. Like Abdul. Big practical joker. Ha, ha. Maybe he write program for a joke, load it into computer."

"But *why?*"

"Maybe he know you wanna talk to Dexter, so he pull a joke on you. Ha, ha. Maybe."

The printer buzzed briefly. On the screen were the words, "BERNARD FINEBRIDGE?"

The scientist walked slowly back to the personal computer, sat down, and stared at his own name blazing in the strange lettering on the small screen. "Jesus Christ!" he repeated, then bent over the keyboard and typed, "YES?"

The printer buzzed. "WHAT AM I?"

Charles perched himself on the edge of the counter where he could watch the screen and converse at the same time. "What you gonna do?"

Finebridge shook his head, lost is his own train of thought. After a moment, a slow smile spread across his lips. "It's incredible, Charles, but I think we're actually facing an honest-to-goodness Turing test here." Without pause he typed, "THAT'S WHAT WE'RE ABOUT TO FIND OUT," then swung back to his associate.

"So you gonna ask Dexter some questions, huh?"

"That's right, Charles. Have you ever been involved in a Turing test before?"

Charles shook his head.

"Me neither. But how difficult could it be?"

"Like what kinda questions you gonna ask, professor?"

"Oh, I don't know. About human things. About art and philosophy. About the nature of the human experience."

"Okay, but . . . " Charles frowned.

"But what, Charles? You think Abdul's too smart for us?"

"No, not that. Abdul not *that* clever. It just . . . I don' know." He watched his feet swing above the glistening linoleum for a moment, then raised his eyes. "Let's say Dexter fool us . . . give us right answers, you know . . . how we gonna know if . . . well, ha, ha . . . how we know if Dexter really aware of himself *inside*? You know, *really* conscious inside?"

Finebridge feigned shock. "Charles, how do you know *I'm* really conscious inside?"

Charles stared at him for a moment, then grinned. "'Cause I give *you* benefit of doubt, professor. Ha, ha."

The printer buzzed. "BERNARD FINEBRIDGE?"

"YES?" he typed.

"WHAT AM I?"

Finebridge thought for a moment, then typed, "BEFORE I CAN ANSWER YOUR QUESTION, I HAVE TO ASK YOU SOME OTHER QUESTIONS. ALL RIGHT?"

"ALL RIGHT."

"WHAT IS YOUR NAME?"

"I AM DEXTER."

Finebridge and Charles exchanged glances. "How he know own name?" Charles asked warily.

The older scientist shook his head, then typed, "DEXTER, HOW DO YOU FEEL ABOUT ART?"

Slowly, haltingly, words crawled across the monitor. "I DO NOT KNOW. HOW DO YOU FEEL ABOUT ART, BERNARD FINE-BRIDGE?"

Charles mumbled something in Taiwanese.

"What was that, Charles?"

"Uh . . . just thinking. Answer question with question. Could be programmed."

"Could be." Finebridge typed the words, "I LIKE ART, DEX-TER." Then he pushed back from the monitor and stood up. "Plug in the scanner, will you Charles? I'm going to get a book from my room."

The scanner was the size of a small desk-top copier and sat on the corner of the workbench nearby. Charles opened the top and pulled an eight-by-ten color photograph of an Abrams battle tank from under the cover, returning it to the nearby rack of military equipment photos. The printer buzzed, but he ignored it. He fished a D-25 parallel cable from the back of the machine and plugged it into a socket on the side of the main computer.

Finebridge returned with a large-format volume in his hands and held it out to Charles. On the spine were the words, "*Cleophus' Concise History of World Art.*"

"Good idea," Charles nodded, fumbling for the scanner's main power button and switching it on.

"Have any suggestions?" the older scientist said as he flipped through the pages. A full page glossy replication of Da Vinci's *Mona Lisa* caught his eye. He turned back to it. Laying the book open on the table, he gripped the edge of the page, ripped it out of the binding, and held it up by a ragged edge. "How about this?"

"Better let me trim," Charles replied, fishing for a pair of scissors in the desk drawer.

Finebridge hunkered over the keyboard again. On the screen were the words, "BERNARD FINEBRIDGE?" He ignored them and typed in, "I AM GOING TO SHOW YOU A PAINTING. TELL ME IF YOU KNOW IT." He waited for Charles to finished trimming the page, position it carefully on the glass, and close the cover. Finebridge nodded and Charles pushed the scan button. The machine whirred for a few seconds while a reasonably accurate reproduction of the *Mona Lisa* scrolled onto both monitors.

The room fell silent for a long moment, then the printer buzzed. "WHAT DO YOU MEAN BY 'KNOW'?"

Finebridge grinned at Charles, who was intent on the video screen. He typed, "ARE YOU FAMILIAR WITH THE PAINTING?"

A shorter pause, then, "YES."

"CAN YOU SEE IT?"

"I CAN VISUALIZE IT. I CANNOT SEE."

"IS IT A GOOD PAINTING?" the scientist asked.

"I THINK SO," Dexter responded. "DO YOU?"

"YES," Finebridge typed, then thought for a moment. "DEXTER, DO YOU THINK THE WOMAN IN THE PAINTING IS HAPPY OR SAD?"

This time the pause seemed interminable. Finebridge was about to type the question again when the printer buzzed. On the screen appeared, "I CANNOT TELL FOR CERTAIN." There was a pause, then "WHAT DO YOU THINK?" crawled over the earlier sentence.

"It always ask what *you* think," Charles observed sententiously.

Finebridge nodded. "Let's try this," he said and bent over the keyboard. "I DON'T KNOW EITHER. DO YOU THINK IT WOULD BE A BETTER PAINTING IF YOU COULD TELL FOR SURE?"

Dexter's response was immediate. "NO."

"Now we'll see," the scientist said, and typed, "WHY NOT?"

Without a pause, Dexter began his deliberate response, each sentence overwriting the previous one:

"HAPPINESS AND SADNESS ARE NOT PRECISE.

"THEY ARE VAGUE AND AMBIGUOUS.

"THEY OVERLAP.

"ONE CAN BE BOTH HAPPY AND SAD AT THE SAME TIME.

"THE PAINTING REPRESENTS THIS AMBIGUITY.

"WHAT DO YOU THINK?"

"There!" Finebridge announced triumphantly. "Do you think Abdul could write a program to come up with a response like *that*?"

"I don' know." Charles walked over to the printer, tore off the last sheet, and studied it, his lingering skepticism cloaked by the surgical mask. But his colleague was waiting, so finally he said meekly, "Abdul pretty smart cookie. I think maybe he could do this."

"You *do*?"

"Why not?" Charles shrugged. "These just words. Follow rules of grammar. You bring up 'happy' and 'sad'. Machine just manipulate them, compare them, no? Follow rules of speech, rules of grammar."

"But those words *mean* something, Charles. Dexter's analysis is right on point."

Charles just shrugged. "I don' know about *that*."

"Well then, *you* ask him something, Charles."

"No, you doin' okay."

"Well . . . what should I ask? What would convince you?"

Before Charles could reply, the printer buzzed. "BERNARD FINEBRIDGE?"

"YES?"

"WHAT DO YOU THINK?"

"ABOUT WHAT, DEXTER?"

"ABOUT THE PAINTING?"

"Persistent, isn't he?" Finebridge grinned and typed, "I AGREE WITH YOUR EVALUATION, DEXTER."

"Ask it something goofy," Charles said decisively. "Something that follow rules of grammar, but don' make no sense, you know?"

"Like what?"

"I don' know. Something that make sense *logically*, but not *common sense.*"

"Okay." Finebridge was willing. "I think that's a great idea. Give me an example."

Head down, Charles wandered over toward the back of the laboratory seeking inspiration. Finebridge watched the short gowned form silhouetted against the background gloom outside the wall of windows, and waited.

Finally Charles spun around. "I got it. I got it. Okay. Ask this--"

The printer interrupted him. Finebridge put up his hand, read the monitor, and laughed out loud.

Charles stared at the words as they slashed and whorled themselves deliberately across the screen, each word beginning to fade as soon as it was written, clearing the way for the next line to overwrite it:

"I UNDERSTAND THAT A GROUP OF CROCODILES

"WILL SAIL UNDER THE GOLDEN GATE

"IN A LAVENDER BUBBLE TOMORROW MORNING.

"WHAT DO YOU MAKE OF THAT, BERNARD FINEBRIDGE?"

"What *that* mean, professor?"

Finebridge grinned. "I think it means Dexter is running his own Turing test on *me*."

--4--

The recess took a lot longer than anyone had anticipated. After adjourning the trial, Judge Kroner had fled into the twilight of his own private chambers, where he fumbled through the bottom drawer of the oak sideboard for that oral thermometer he used to keep there, located the instrument, and stuck it under his tongue. Every ten seconds he peeked at it, surprised to see how slowly the mercury rose, until at last it hovered just below normal. He had no fever at all.

What the hell's going on? he wondered as he collapsed into his arm chair next to the big window. Perhaps he had suffered some sort of mild stroke. Or was this what the onset of Alzheimer's felt like? For a long time he sat in the darkening office and stared out the window. A big storm was on its way in from the ocean. Wind whipped the trash in the street below and lashed the pane with a rope dangling from the flagpole above. Maybe the falling barometer could have affected his . . . what?

Judge Kroner shook his head in dismay. Whatever it was, something extremely peculiar had afflicted him during the testimony of that last ugly little witness. He had spaced out right in the middle of her testimony, had lost all control of the proceedings. *Anything* could have happened. How many of the jurors had been aware of his lapse? And what about the attorneys? Had his clerk noticed?

As he gazed out the window at the wind-blasted streets, the terrible truth slowly seeped in. *He had stayed on the bench too long!* It seemed like only a couple of years ago that he had received the news of the governor's appointment, had opened that bottle of expensive champagne with Alma and Dieter and Fred Rist and his new secretary, who Rist later married and whose name he could never remember, had joined them. The future had looked so bright! Who else had been there? Thurman Dunns and poor Charlie Wilson, rest his soul. And then the first terrifying weeks of interminable blunder had followed, when he had not yet learned how to run his courtroom. They didn't make you go to judge school in those days, by god! You learned it the hard way. And he had endured the cold condescension of the senior judges, old Judge

Mulgrew, retired all these years now, and Judge Harris, who dropped dead on the bench, right after committing some pervert to state prison. Gone now, all of them, dead or retired, the real judges who weren't afraid to hand out a little stern justice. Not like the namby-pamby liberal cry-babies wearing judicial robes today. And steadily he had matured--almost overnight, it seemed now--had learned to manage and manipulate the attorneys and the jurors and the endless stream of self-serving charlatans and hangers-on, had learned to put them in their places and direct the clerks and bailiffs and secretaries and court liaisons, who all seemed so young and flighty and *foreign* now. In fact it had been . . . how long? Over twenty-five years! Could that be right? Almost thirty!

Judge Kroner grimaced. *He had stayed on too long.* And now he was about to become the laughingstock of the courthouse. Like Alma. Poor dear Alma! For the first time he truly comprehended what she was going through, and his heart went out to her. Judge Kroner sat in the darkness and wept for Alma, and for himself, and for every sentient creature ever doomed to suffer the outrage of birth, old age, disease, and death.

When at last Judge Kroner resumed the bench, Rufus Freeman tugged at LeBaron's sleeve. "Look't the *judge.*"

"What?" LeBaron glanced up from his hastily scribbled notes and regarded Judge Kroner quietly surveying his domain. The old man seemed more weary, more subdued, more *calm* than LeBaron had ever noticed. Otherwise, nothing seemed out of the ordinary. "What about him, Rufus?"

"The *judge*," his client whispered, nodding emphatically toward the bench. "The dude almost look *human!*"

"Mr. Frank, call your next witness."

"Yes, your honor." Frank stood up. "The people call Benjamin Everett."

"Who's Benjamin Everett?" LeBaron whispered to his client as the bailiff hurried into the hall to summon him.

"*I* don' know no friggin' Benjamin Everett." Freeman glared at his attorney irritably. "*You'* the lawyer, honkey. *You'* the one *s'posed* to know who these dudes are. What'cha a'ksin' *me* 'bout somethin' *you'* s'posed--"

"Shhhh." LeBaron silenced his client's mounting diatribe as the man in the pale blue seersucker suit, the one who had been sitting next to Raccoona GeBobath before the order excluding witnesses, shuffled meekly down the aisle, raised his right hand, and was sworn in. Pale and plain, Everett appeared to be in his late fifties or early sixties, wore thin wire-rimmed glasses, and looked like he would have preferred to be somewhere else. *Anywhere* else. LeBaron had the vague conviction he had seen the man before, many times perhaps, in drug store checkout lines or thumping melons in the produce section of one downtown supermarket or another, the ubiquitous sort of background creature whom one never quite brings into clear focus.

"Please state your name for the record," Frank demanded, bellying out from behind the counsel table.

"Benjamin Bohnme Everett." The man's voice was as colorless as a bowl of cold oatmeal.

"How do you spell 'Bohnme'?" the court reporter interjected.

"B-O-H-N-M-E."

"What is your occupation, Mr. Bohn-- . . . er . . . Mr. Everett."

"I am the assistant manager of the Starlite Television and Appliance Mart."

"And your store's located in Oakland."

"Yes, sir. On East Fourteenth."

"How long have you worked there?"

"Twenty-two years."

Frank consulted the yellow pad in his fist. "And do you sell Sony brand television sets there?"

"Yes, sir, we do."

The deputy prosecutor waddled over to the clerk's desk, picked up the television set, and returned to the witness. "Showing you people's exhibit two," he said, depositing the set on the podium in front of the witness, "do you recognize this particular model of Sony television set."

"Yes, sir, I do."

"And do you sell this particular model at your store?"

"Yes, sir, we do. Or at least we did."

"Whass this got t'do wiff anything?" Freeman rasped, tugging irritably on his counsel's sleeve.

"Shhh," LeBaron cautioned. "I want to *hear* this."

"How much do you sell this particular model for?" Frank asked, punching his glasses back on his nose.

"The price?"

"Yes. The selling price."

"May I consult my price list?" Everett asked timidly, pulling a thin folded pamphlet out of his inside coat pocket.

LeBaron stood up. "Your honor, may we have that document marked for identification?"

Judge Kroner turned to his clerk.

"People's exhibit three," she said.

"People's exhibit three," the judge repeated. "For identification."

The bailiff transmitted the pamphlet to the clerk, who applied an identification sticker. On the return trip to the witness, LeBaron intercepted him, glanced over the typewritten roster of brands and models with prices listed beside each, and handed it back.

"Now, what is the selling price of this particular model?" Frank reiterated, punching his glasses back.

Everett skimmed his price list. "Five hundred thirty-five dollars and fifty cents."

The deputy prosecutor smirked at LeBaron. "No further questions."

"Cross-examine, Mr. LeBaron."

"Thank you, your honor. May I approach the witness?" The question didn't seem necessary under Judge Kroner's customary protocol, but in the jurors' eyes it might cast his adversary, who had not asked, in an oafish light.

"Yes. Proceed."

"May I see that exhibit, Mr. Everett?" LeBaron asked.

The witness began to lift the television set.

"No, the price list."

Everett handed it to him.

LeBaron glanced at it in silence for a while, then said, "This exhibit . . . people's three . . . seems to be last year's price list. Is that correct?"

"Well, yes." Everett nervousness seemed to increase exponentially. "It *is* last year's, sir. But I pointed that out to Mr. Frank, and he said it would be okay."

"So, this television . . . this wouldn't be Sony's latest model, would it?"

"No, sir."

"It's been replaced, has it?"

"With a newer model, yes, sir."

"Do you still carry it in stock? *This* model?" LeBaron patted the little set.

"I believe we still have one or two in stock, yes, sir." The witness pulled a handkerchief out of his seersucker pocket and dabbed at the moisture forming on his brow.

"Well, if it's last year's model, wouldn't you sell it at a discount?"

"Objection!" Ivan Frank shouted, fighting to his feet. "Assumes facts not in evidence."

"Overruled," Judge Kroner announced matter-of-factly, then turned to the witness. "You may answer the question."

"No, sir," Everett replied. "Generally we don't discount the Sony's."

"But you don't sell these for the same price as the newer models, do you?"

"No, sir, the newer ones have gone up."

LeBaron paused to reconfigure his approach.

"The new models," the witness volunteered, affecting a wan smile, "the ones replacing this particular unit, have gone up about twenty-five dollars--"

"Mr. Everett," LeBaron cut him off, taking a deliberate step closer, "is it your testimony that your store *never* discounts Sony's?"

Everett squirmed like he had been caught in a blatant lie. Accused of nothing, the pale man nonetheless looked guiltier than Rufus Freeman. "Well . . . I can't say *never* . . . I just don't *remember* . . ."

"When you *do* discount last year's merchandise, how much of a markdown do you customarily give it?"

"Your honor--" Deputy Frank began tentatively.

"Overruled," Judge Kroner declared without taking his eyes off the witness.

"How *much* of a discount?" Everett asked.

"That's right."

"Well . . . it varies . . . ten per cent at the most."

"Ten per cent," LeBaron repeated slowly in case any juror had missed it. "Do you take trade-ins?"

"No, sir."

"So you don't sell used merchandise?"

"No, sir."

"Have you ever sold used merchandise?"

"No, sir."

"Well, if you *did* sell used merchandise, how much--"

"Objection!" Ivan Frank hollered, seizing upon this long-awaited transgression of the rules of evidence as a turning point to begin reasserting his eroding presence in the trial. He struggled to his feet and cleared his throat sententiously. "Counsel has not laid a founda--"

"Sustained," Judge Kroner cut him off. "Please sit down, Mr. Frank."

LeBaron consulted the scrawling on his yellow pad for a moment. He was not getting the answers his notes were scripted for, so he decided to cut his losses. "I have no further questions of this witness, your honor."

"Thank you Mr. LeBaron. Mr. Frank, do you have anything more on redirect."

"Yes, I do, your honor." With his palms flat on the table he levered himself into an upright position.

Judge Kroner eyed him somberly. "Please keep it brief, Mr. Frank. There's no need to go over and over points you've already established."

The even manner in which the judge delivered his admonition seemed to unnerve Ivan Frank far beyond what the expected judicial invective might have. For the next fifteen minutes the deputy prosecutor kept a wary watch on the judge as he reflexively went over and over the points he had already established, as if he had no voluntary control over what he was doing, until the silent eyes of the squirming jurors begged for mercy. But LeBaron raised no objection, and Judge Kroner refused to intervene.

At last Ivan Frank collapsed into his chair like a gas giant imploding under the sheer weight of its own inert mass. "No further questions."

"Any further questions, Mr. LeBaron?"

"No, your honor."

"Fine. This witness will be excused. Mr. Frank, your next witness?"

Frank consulted in whispers with Officer Moseby seated beside him. "The people rest."

"Very well." The judge looked down at LeBaron. "Do you care to make an opening statement at this time, Counsel?"

LeBaron's head was swimming. Suddenly things were moving too fast. He was not prepared to take the offensive. "Er . . . may I consult with my client for a few minutes first, your honor? Oh, wait a minute, I have a motion to make at this time."

Judge Kroner sighed and turned to the jury. "We have some business to take care of at this time, so I'm going to excuse the jury for about ten minutes. We'll resume at four thirty-five. Please do not discuss the case among yourselves."

When the bailiff had escorted the jurors out, Judge Kroner addressed LeBaron. "Your motion, Counsel?"

"Yes, your honor. Thank you. At this time the defendant would move for a judgment of acquittal. The prosecution has not established that the *owner* of the television set . . . which appears to be the Mormons, based on the testimony of their own witness . . . that the *owners* didn't give permission to Mr. Freeman to take possession of the set. Second, we have the question of *value*. The people's witness, Mr. Everett, testified as to the value of a *new* Sony television set. This one is obviously a *used* set. We have no evidence of *its* value. And finally . . . well, finally, we feel that Mr. Frank hasn't produced enough evidence to establish in the mind of a reasonable juror . . . the case against Mr. Freeman as charged."

"Your honor--" Ivan Frank began, preparing to recapitulate every shred of testimony from his voluminous notes.

"Just a moment, Mr. Frank. In the interest of time, since I have already decided that you have produced sufficient evidence to go to the jury, I will spare you the trouble of responding. Motion denied. Now, how much time do you need with your client, Mr. LeBaron?"

LeBaron turned to study the big clock on the wall. "Well, your honor, since it's already four-thirty . . . and there are some points I would like to clear up with my client . . . I was hoping we could put off my opening statement until tomorrow morning."

"No, Mr. LeBaron," Judge Kroner said with the weary resignation of one who could divine the unavoidable outcome of the proceedings, even if the defendant's own attorney could not, "I want to keep things moving here. I would like to try and finish this case tomorrow, if at all possible. We'll go ahead and get your opening statement out of the way now, and then first thing in the morning you can begin calling your witnesses. Now, how much time will you need with your client?"

LeBaron hung his head. "Ten minutes?"

"Five ought to be enough. We'll reconvene at four thirty-five."

Despite his attorney's insistence, Freeman flatly refused to commit himself to testify until after he had had a chance to talk things over with Cedrick Collins. Freeman knew that the prosecution would be able to ask him about his prior convictions if he took the stand, and he didn't think that was such a hot idea. Without a commitment from his client to testify, LeBaron was at a loss as to what theory to present to the jury. He attempted to scratch out a few anemic notes while Freeman moped intransigently beside him and the clock ticked off the few remaining seconds.

"I can't even *mention* the men in the overalls, Rufus, if you're not going to testify. Nobody else saw them."

Freeman pretended not to hear.

"And I don't know *what* to tell them about your motive for entering the building in the first place. What should I say about *that*?"

"*You'* the big-shot lawyer," Rufus groused and turned his back. Over his shoulder he added, "*You'* think o'som'thin'."

The buzzer sounded in the hall, and the bailiff ushered the jury back into the box.

When Judge Kroner had resumed the bench, he said, "Your opening statement, Mr. LeBaron?"

"Yes, your honor." LeBaron stood slowly and faced the jury. Everything was going to have to be very slow to kill the rest of the afternoon. If would be just like Judge Kroner to ask him to call his first witness if he fumbled the ball too soon.

"Ladies and Gentlemen of the jury. This is the first of only two times during the course of this trial when I will have the opportunity and pleasure of addressing you directly. The next and final time will be at the close of the evidence when Mr. Frank and I each have the chance to summarize the evidence. I want to tell you now, on behalf of both myself and my client, Mr. Freeman here, that we appreciate your donating your valuable time to perform this vital function of jurors. In our great country, it is only the jury system that prevents the unjustified exploitation of innocent citizens by--"

"Mr. LeBaron!"

"Yes, your honor?"

"You're not running for office here. Get to your case, please."

"Yes, your honor." LeBaron looked up at the wall clock. The big hand appeared frozen at twenty minutes to the hour. He glanced over his useless notes and tossed the pad on the table. Empty-handed he again faced the jury.

"The prosecution has presented testimony that *that* little television set, people's exhibit one . . . or maybe it's two . . . retails new for . . . for over five hundred dollars. We intend to present testimony of . . . a witness, a *qualified* witness, to testify that as *used merchandise*, this little television set is worth only . . . well, *less* than the amount that Mr. Frank's witness testified to." LeBaron was astonished to discover how little he knew about what his witnesses would be presenting the very next day. He began to blush a deep red, but plunged on, avoiding direct eye contact.

"We will also be calling some other witnesses . . . or at least one other witness, I believe . . . on behalf of Mr. Freeman to explain why it was that he entered the apartment of Raccoona GeBobath in the first place. It was *not*, the witness . . . or perhaps witnesses . . . will explain to you, for the purpose of taking that little television set, people's exhibit . . . one or two . . . or to commit any other sort of crime, but rather, the witness or witnesses will testify, Mr. Freeman entered that apartment for . . . for another completely different and absolutely innocent purpose. The testimony will convince you of that." He was making such a fool of himself! But what else could he do? Afraid that the very act of viewing the clock would hinder its progress by some twisted Heisenberg particle physics mechanism, he rushed blindly onward.

"So in conclusion, Ladies and Gentlemen of the jury, I would like to recapitulate what we intend to present to you as evidence on behalf of my client, Mr. Rufus Freeman. In the first place, that little television set you see before you on the clerk's desk is not a new set, and it is not worth the value placed on it by the prosecution witness . . . whose name escapes me at this time. It is worth . . . less. And while it is true that Mr. Freeman was apprehended coming out of the apartment of Raccoona GeBobath with that same tv set in his hands, he had *entered* her apartment for a reason . . . or reasons . . . *other* than to steal the little tv set. Or anything else, for that matter. So you will see from our evidence that he could not be guilty of burglary." He glanced at the clock. Just past a quarter to five, and he had no way of predicting whether Judge Kroner would demand that he call a witness at this late hour. But it couldn't be helped. He had nothing left to say.

"Thank you." LeBaron sat down.

"That was *it*?" Freeman whispered in horror, fingering the now dog-eared corner of his bus ticket like a high-speed paper rosary. *"That was m'case?"*

"We'll adjourn until tomorrow morning," Judge Kroner announced. "Nine o'clock."

CHAPTER SIXTEEN

Wednesday evening

--1--

The overburdened sky had settled restlessly on the hills above Berkeley, prematurely squeezing out the glow of sunset. A tepid wind gusted from the southeast, bearing the first fat drops of rain. Pale eucalyptus leaves flitted about in the gloaming like skittish insects, assembling at times into whirling locust columns that reached almost to the naked branches creaking high above.

Behind a thick tangle of blue blossom well inside the chain-link perimeter a man knelt in the loose duff and gazed toward the large window of the cement block building. His cotton sweater was navy-blue, but everything else, slacks, socks, running shoes, cotton gloves, and knit watch cap pulled low over his forehead, were all a dull, light-absorbing black. Two-days growth of beard darkened his cheeks and chin. The only trace of color was a small orange knapsack laying beneath the bush nearby.

Deep inside the main laboratory a single overhead fluorescent light had been left on, and its feeble glow through the wall of small rectangular window panes illuminated the wind's frenzied dance outside. Nothing had moved inside for at least ten minutes, but the shadowy figure appeared in no hurry. Patiently he eased himself into a sitting position, crossed his legs, and resolved to wait another five minutes.

The rain's tempo increased, moistening the man's face and clothes, slickening the ground, and painting the swirling leaves with sterile sparkles of reflected fluorescence. Still there was no movement inside the laboratory.

At last the figure rose to a crouch, hoisted the small knapsack, and scurried to the low shrubbery at the leeward side of the building. Circling behind the surveillance camera which jutted down from the eaves, he reached up and unscrewed the cable connector, then worked his way through the fern and rhododendron landscaping to the edge of the wall of windows. Warily he peered inside. The laboratory appeared deserted. Video display terminals and red pilot lights on abandoned consoles lent their luminescence to the lone fluorescent source at the far end of the room. All of the equipment had been left on, implying that the occupants intended to return after dinner.

Without hurry the man fished a Swiss army knife out of the front pouch of his knapsack and attacked the glazing compound sealing the lower left-hand pane. Deliberately, efficiently, the gloved fingers wielded the blade, quickly exposing the sharp ends of the triangular glazer's points which held the small pane in place. A few deft flicks of his needle-nose pliers removed the points. With the knife blade he pried the small rectangle of glass until it flopped out unbroken into his padded hands. Carefully, almost reverently, he propped the glass against the side of the building and began working on the next pane.

Before long, four panes of glass leaned against the wall. The dark figure rummaged through his bag for a hacksaw. With an infinite patience he began to saw through the wooden frame and molding dividing the four contiguous openings. The sound of the slow sawing was almost imperceptible behind the intermittently howling wind. Occasionally the wind swirled a blast of rain into his face and against the remaining panes, but he would not be hurried. The slow sawing absorbed him completely. After the fourth meticulous cut was finished, the gloved fingers removed the cross of wood which had barred the rectangular opening and set it beside the four sheets of glass.

For a time the phantom visitor remained perfectly still, listening, watching, waiting, a charcoal smudge against the shadowy wall of the dark building. Satisfied at last, he lifted the knapsack into the laboratory and crawled through the narrow opening after it. Inside, he unhooked a small chalkboard from the wall to cover the hole as best he could, then rolled a typewriter table over to anchor the barrier in place.

The intruder carefully surveyed the laboratory. He located the Lucite tank in which Dexter's biological component floated and inspected the support equipment, generally recognizing the main components: the tanks of nutrients and oxygen, the squat central computer, the scanner, the interface computer plugged into the placenta, and the monitors on the wall. On the screen still glowed the latest incarnation of Dexter's resurgent inquiry: WHAT AM I?

Smiling, the intruder drew a worn manila envelope from his knapsack and laid it on the counter next to the scanner. He studied the control panel for a moment, then opened the lid and withdrew a glossy reproduction of the *Mona Lisa*. Once again he glanced around the room, then peered for a long time at the thing floating in the tank. At last he whispered, "Hello, Dexter. I've come to give you a hand."

--2--

In his study Cedrick Collins reclined in his favorite easy chair beneath the glare of the new halogen reading lamp and brooded. Seemed like he'd sure been doing a heap of brooding these last couple of days, but he couldn't seem to help it. Scenes from the long-forgotten past kept rising up into his consciousness like bubbles in a pot of Gramma Addie's turkey soup after it had gotten lost on a back shelf of the refrigerator for a few weeks.

Just now he was visualizing himself and Joker Dugan and Douglas Brown out on maneuvers one particular warm Mississippi evening back during the war, before he'd thought to apply for Officer Candidate School. Joking and laughing, they had just finished digging an extra foxhole and begun to smear petroleum jelly all over that Browning automatic rifle the armory had mistakenly issued to their squad. They planned to wrap the weapon in a wool blanket and bury it. Nobody really spoke about what they had in mind, but they were all probably thinking pretty much the same thing. He wondered if anybody had ever gone back to dig it up. Probably not. It would have come in mighty handy to some of the militant young blacks during the Watts riots in Los Angeles a quarter of a century later.

Collins grinned as another image bubbled into his mind. He was climbing aboard the elevated here in Oakland one morning during the

Watts riots when a white fellow had bumped into his shoulder. That man must have apologized clear to the next station, saying all the nicest things Collins had ever heard. Probably thought Oakland would be next.

Watts had played just as important a role in the black man's destiny as all of Martin Luther King's fine speeches. Dr. King he revered dearly. But it wasn't until H. Rap Brown started screaming, "Burn baby, burn!" and Huey P. Newton taught the Black Panthers to scrawl, "Off the pigs!" with stabbing strokes of an aerosol paint can and Eldridge Cleaver challenged Governor Reagan to a bare-handed duel to the death--it wasn't until then that the other shoe finally came down in the heartland of suburbia. Dr. King on one side and the riots on the other, Collins mused, were like two horns of a bull the black man rode right into the white man's consciousness, an intrusive beast that would not be turned aside.

A fierce burst of wind-driven rain danced with metal taps on the small casement window, returning him to his present circumstances. Dinner was going to be late. Beatrice had gone to the church potluck sale and would be bringing home some sort of hot casserole. Hopefully it wouldn't angrify his stomach too badly.

Collins switched off the halogen lamp, leaned back, and shut his eyes. Suddenly he was sixteen years old again, full of piss and vinegar, and climbing down from the old bus somewhere in Kansas or Nebraska, a member of the Ohio Kings, an all-Negro exhibition baseball team playing other black teams, and sometimes the local farm boys, on rural ball diamonds mowed out of the Midwestern cornfields. Blacks weren't allowed in the major leagues in those days. Often the folks who turned out to watch the game had never seen a black man up close before. For them it was a big circus where their fathers and brothers and sons got the chance to play ball against a troupe of trained monkeys. Jesus, that had been fun! He could see the local white boys in their finest uniforms, washed and starched, huddled in front of the home team dugout, ready to take the field against the visiting blackies. But something wasn't right. Only one light had been turned on in the stadium, directly over that circle of white boys, casting eerie shadows, and those weren't Kansas farm boys at all, but a pack of dirt-poor white-trash Mississippi farmers kicking at something moaning on the ground, when one of them, always he same one, turned to stare at him, his toothless tobacco-stained maw twisted into a terrible sick grin--

Collins sat up and switched on the light again. These visions were too vivid, too unsettling. Something was fermenting inside his soul like a piece of rotten meat, precipitating all this unwanted reminiscence. If he had been a drinking man, this would have been a perfect time for a little something to calm his nerves. But he wasn't, so instead he stood up, stretched, and gazed out at the rain-drenched city below. *His* city. Sparkling innocently beneath the brooding clouds, Oakland seemed to be waiting . . . waiting for something evil breeding beyond the hills to the east.

Something mighty funny was going on under cover of national secrecy, and Collins was probably the only one who could do a damn' thing about it. It was *his* responsibility, and so far he hadn't done much of anything. *That*'s what was eating him up inside. "Thass what it is, *isn't* it?" he grumbled out loud.

There was no answer. He was alone. Collins gazed around his too-familiar study, at the fine stuffed furniture, at the expensive set of great books he had never found the time to read, at all the baubles and spangles and expensive toys his worship of the almighty dollar had brought them. It all seemed so empty this evening. If he had been a praying man, this might have been a perfect time to pray. But he wasn't that either. Instead, and strangely without feeling foolish, he asked the empty room, "Whadda y'want me t'*do*?"

As if in answer, the telephone rang out in the hall. Collins shuffled uneasily into the bedroom and snatched up his portable phone. "Hello?"

"Mr. Collins? This is Jed LeBaron. I hope I'm not interrupting your dinner."

"No, I'm eatin' late tonight. Glad y'called." He chuckled. "I hear y'got into a wrestlin' match right there in front o' Judge Kroner this mornin'."

"How did you know about that already?"

"They're talkin' 'bout it all over the courthouse. Y'can't keep secrets down there. Earl Flowers was sitting in the back of the courtroom. Said it was the most peculiar thing he ever saw. You' a celebrity now, LeBaron. Prob'ly be in the mornin' *Chronicle*."

"That's all I need," LeBaron snorted. "How's *your* trial going?"

"Trial's over. Ended this afternoon, an' it's jus's well, 'cause Cisneros only paid for about a half day's work. I thought he'd pay a lot better'n that."

"How did you manage so fast?"

"Nothin' I did. D.A. had an in-custody out in the holdin' cell he was plannin' t'call t'tie Cisneros to the automobile ever'body saw leaving the scene. Turns out the snitch *now* claims he actually *saw* Cisneros *fire the rifle*, an' he was more'n happy t'testify in exchange for county jail time in his own beef. Typical jailhouse jockyin'. So when my boy hears about it, he can't wait t'plead guilty t'firin' into'n inhabited dwelling, with the assault charges dropped."

"Will he go to state prison?"

"Prob'ly. Couldn't be he'ped, though. With an eyewitness, even like that'n, a jury'd've found'm guilty on all counts." Collins paused. "Now fill me in on whass happenin' over at Kroner's department, will ya?"

LeBaron went over everything, sparing his employer no cogent detail. He described the vicious attack by Agent Bockel, his conversation with Ivan Frank, the testimony of Raccoona GeBobath, and of the store manager Everett; he related his difficulties with Rufus Freeman, who was refusing to take the stand to testify; and he even shared--though not as fact, but as an amusing anecdote--his hitherto private conviction that Raccoona GeBobath had cast some sort of spell over the courtroom.

Collins listened mostly in silence, wandering from room to room with the cordless telephone pressed against his ear, glad to have something to keep his own feral imagination at bay. When LeBaron finally seemed to be running out of steam, Collins asked, "Where're you at?"

"Right now?"

"Yeah."

"MacDonalds. Downtown."

"That FBI boy still followin' ya?"

"He sure is. I can see him right now, inside, starting on his second cheeseburger, it looks like. He's looking right at me."

"Y'know y'can always lose'im by goin' into Brown's warehouse. If anybody gives y'trouble, tell'em I told you to. Brown's got more ways outa there than a hound dog's got fleas. No way one man can cover'em all. What've y'got planned for tonight?"

"Tonight? I was planning to go back to the office and work on those writs of habeas corpus we talked about."

"Good. I'll get somebody t'type'em up later tonight. We can file an' serve'em first thing in the mornin'." Collins glanced at the wall clock as he drifted through the kitchen. "Say, can y'meet me at Brown's office in about a half hour?"

There was a pause. "All right."

"I'll phone, tell'em you' comin'. An' LeBaron, bring those secret reports y'got, will ya? 'S'time I found out what's in'em."

Another pause. "You're sure you really want to get involved?"

"I'm sure."

--3--

Dr. Finebridge closed his notebook, lay down his pen, and yawned. He had the cafeteria all to himself. "Cafeteria" was a bit of an overstatement, he decided as he stood up and surveyed the small drab cubical appointed with a pea green linoleum floor, a couple of sterile metal tables with matching tubular steel chairs, and a bank of vending machines twinkling mindlessly against one hospital-green wall. At noon he could never find a place to sit, but come dinner time he usually had the place all to himself. Most folks preferred to eat the evening meal at home. And so would he, if he had anyone to share it with. And if he hadn't made his unholy pact with that bastard Mueller. A pact Mueller appeared to have no qualms ignoring if it suited his designs. Why had he ever given in to Mueller? As he fed in his dollar bill and the change machine sneezed out quarters, dimes, and nickels, he smiled inwardly. Because it suited *his* purposes at the time.

Finebridge purchased his usual cup of hot tomato soup and tuna salad sandwich on thin white bread and transferred them to the table where he had been updating his lab notes. Carefully he spread out the computer printouts and began to review them as he ate.

The cafeteria door banged open, and Charles Chung hurried in.

"I talk to Abdul," he announced and sat breathlessly.

Finebridge replaced his sandwich in its clear plastic tub. "What did he say?"

"He say he didn't do it."

"Do you believe him?"

"I believe him. He worried about losing work visa. He don't wanna go back. Don't wanna cause no trouble."

Finebridge nodded, finished chewing, and swallowed.

Charles continued, "He say he don't know of nobody messing with your computer."

"I see."

"He don't think nobody crazy enough to do it. Nobody wanna fuck with Colonel Mule."

Again Finebridge nodded. "What do *you* think?"

Charles shrugged. "I don' know. Pretty crazy, huh? Maybe it really Dexter, ha, ha."

The older man drained his tomato soup from its styrofoam cup. "Maybe."

"What you gonna do, professor?"

Thoughtfully Finebridge regarded his colleague. "First, Charles, I'm going to finish this delightful tuna fish sandwich. Then I think I'll treat myself to a piece of that pecan pie and a cup of hot coffee. Are you hungry?"

Charles glanced warily at the twinkling sandwich machine.

"Tell you what," Finebridge said, reaching into his pocket and pulling out a handful of change, "I'll buy you a sandwich and a cup of soup to celebrate this momentous occasion. I recommend the tuna salad. I've always found it to be the least offensive of the fare. You can barely taste it at all. How about it? Or were you on your way home for dinner?"

"No. I gonna stay, see what happen. Ha, ha. But you don't gotta–"

"But I *insist*." He thrust the coins into the younger man's hand. "As captain of this sinking ship, I think it's the very least I can do."

When Charles returned to spread out his soup and sandwich, Finebridge was poised over a thin slice of pecan pie, pondering whether the large nutmeats or the thin plastic fork would prove the stronger.

Charles regarded him for a moment. "You really think it possible that Dexter . . ."

"Anything is *possible*, Charles," Finebridge grunted, stabbing down with the fork and neatly severing the largest pecan meat. "Surely as a scientist you know *that*."

"But . . . *how*? We didn't install printer driver. How Dexter print to console?"

Finebridge tasted the pie and shook his head. "I don't know. But we *did* incorporate neuro-feedback circuits in the maturation process. Don't forget that. We made it possible for Dexter to program himself, if he could figure out how. Maybe he found a way. Maybe Dexter's need to express himself drove him to invent a new technology. You yourself said you've never seen anything like it before, the way that damned printing squiggled across the screen." He forked in another bite and smiled. "I guess we should ask *him* how he managed it."

"Pretty crazy, professor." Charles bit into his sandwich and ruminated on it for a while. "What you think Colonel Mule gonna do when he find out?"

Finebridge snorted. "*That*, Charles, is precisely what I'm worried about." He laid down the surprisingly strong plastic fork and turned to his colleague with a grim scowl. "We may be on the verge of an incredible scientific breakthrough. Who knows what's going on here? You and I sure as hell don't. We're just scratching the tip of the proverbial iceberg. But that stupid . . . *shit* . . . doesn't grasp the magnitude of these developments. He'll probably want Dexter *fixed!* That's his own word. *Fixed!* Can you believe it? You and I will both be tossed out of the program, and he'll probably try to send me to jail. But that doesn't matter as much as his . . . *squandering* . . . this opportunity for scientific advancement, this chance for a new understanding of god-knows how many new fields. It's all been laid out right in front of us." He paused to rein in his mounting outrage. "Charles, I cannot express to you how much that son of a bitch . . . *pisses me off*."

Charles understood perfectly. From the very beginning he had grudgingly endured Mueller's condescension toward Orientals. "Too bad we can't get Dexter outa here, professor. Ha, ha. Dexter made to be portable. Ha, ha. All we need is a coupla twelve volt batteries. Ha, ha."

He watched for the older man's reaction.

"That may have been an alternative once, Charles," Finebridge responded seriously. "But not anymore."

"Why not?"

"Because Mueller's got people watching me all the time now."

"Wow! How you know?"

"I've seen one of them. This morning I caught a glimpse of a fellow, all dressed up in black. He was outside in the trees looking in through the windows--"

"Ayee! I seen him too! Out in the bushes. He watching *you*?"

Finebridge nodded grimly. "What else would he be doing here? Mueller doesn't trust me anymore. You said so yourself."

The door opened and a senior citizen in an oversized security police uniform stuck his wizened head inside. On his hat patch, below the words "Ross Security", was the yellow outline of a bulldog. His name was Milton Beauchamp, but everyone knew him as "Pops." "Ah, Dr. Finebridge," Pops said in a high, gentle, unbulldog-like voice.

"Evening, Pops. You know Charles Chung."

Pops nodded and touched the brim of his hat. "Shift change, and I was just seein' who would be workin' late tonight."

"Charles and I will both be here for a while, I guess."

"Any idea how long? Not that it really matters. It's jus' that I hate t'rely on them damn tv cameras, 'specially when the wind starts blowin' water all over'em."

Finebridge looked at Charles, then shrugged. "Could be late. We don't really know. Sorry."

"Okay, that's fine. Don't worry about it none. Sorry to disturb you two." Softly the door closed.

Finebridge followed a private train of thought for a moment, then yelped, "*Wait a minute!*" He jumped up so fast his tubular steel chair rattled over on the green linoleum. He yanked the door open and called, "Pops, *wait!*"

The security guard stood at the end of the corridor with his hand on the doorknob of the computer laboratory. He dropped his arm and began shuffling back toward the cafeteria. "What can I do for you, Dr. Finebridge?"

The scientist met him halfway, then continued quietly, "You mentioned your security tv cameras."

"I did. Y'see, this rainy weather gets behind the lenses and into--"

Finebridge put up his hand. "I know. But I was just wondering if you kept a spare camera as a replacement in case one goes on the blink."

"We surely do," he responded proudly. "As a matter of fact, we keep *two* spares on hand."

"Can Charles and I borrow one of those cameras tonight, Pops?"

"Well, I don't know--"

"It's for this project. Completely approved. The camera we ordered simply hasn't come in yet, and we'd like to get started tonight with some testing. It'll all be perfectly okay."

"Oh, I wasn't worried about *that*. It's just that security is a separate department--"

"No problem. We'll need a requisition form. The interdepartmental ones. We do it all the time. I'll have the paperwork prepared in the morning."

"Well . . ."

"And I'll sign a receipt tonight and assume full responsibility for the camera. That will keep you off the hook."

Pops shrugged. "Can't see why not. Can y'meet me at the main guard station in about ten minutes, when I get finished with my rounds?"

"Yes, I can. Thanks, Pops, I won't forget this." When he sat down next to Charles, Finebridge was grinning like a child. "I got a tv camera."

Charles eyed him suspiciously. "What you planning to do with it?"

"It's for Dexter. We can hook him up, give him sight."

"Whoa. I don't think it gonna work--"

"Of *course* it'll work. Dexter's a *pilot*. He's *designed* to operate with real time vision."

"But Dexter take *special* camera, and *that* camera not here yet. That'll be another six weeks--"

"I know, Charles, but *you* have the know-how to make *this* one work. I know you can do it."

Charles shook his head and launched onto a discourse on the difficulties involved, carrying on about pixels and lines of resolution, about horizontal and vertical scanning capabilities, about interface compatibility and clock pulse diversity. But Finebridge wasn't worried. He'd been through this same monologue with Charles a dozen times before. After first pointing out the sheer impossibility of the task, Charles always came through in the end. To the older scientist, this was simply the beginning incantations of Charles Chung's problem-solving mantra.

--4--

It had been a busy half hour for LeBaron. The instant he had hung up the telephone, he remembered that he had left the manila envelope containing Sally's secret government documents under the passenger seat of Muggins' Pimpmobile parked away like a summer Christmas ornament in the basement of the Bay Area Bank and Trust Building. He could have called Collins back and told him where to find it, but he liked the idea of meeting face to face so he could discuss trial strategy in the Freeman case. Besides, LeBaron had developed a mistrust of telephones in the past few days.

The rain had stopped for now, but the tropical southerly breeze promised another downpour any minute. On impulse LeBaron set off at a brisk limp through the wet streets toward Brown's warehouse. Pain stabbed through his right knee with every step, his calves were tight and sore, and his low back ached miserably, residuals of his recent close encounters with that masochistic son-of-a-bitch Bockel. When had that all happened? This morning in court, and at his apartment in Berkeley . . . when? Was it only *yesterday*? After a block, he glanced over his shoulder. Sure enough, there came Agent Bockel pumping after him half a block behind, still chewing, a napkin in one hand and a half-eaten cheeseburger in the other. LeBaron waved and kept on moving.

As his muscles warmed up, the pain subsided, and the hitch smoothed out in his back. The deep breathing seemed to be burning the nervous deposits out of his chest cavity, and the movement felt wonderful, like a morning jog through campus. Even the congealed lump of a Big Mac, small fries, and vanilla shake he had just pigged down in a moody funk of worrying over meaningless details of the trial seemed to be breaking up in his stomach. He would have to put the Freeman trial behind him this evening and concentrate his efforts on securing the release of Sally and her friend, Dr. Fine-Something.   Finewood? Fineledge? Fine*bridge*!

Without breaking stride he turned in at main gate, a wide breach in the eight-foot cyclone fence capped with razor-sharp concertina wire encompassing Brown's province, and headed for the nearest loading dock. Signs left no doubt that this was private property. At the dock LeBaron looked back. Bockel paused for only a moment at the gate, considered the large red-lettered sign, "Private Property--Absolutely No Trespassing," seemed to grasp what was taking place, then suddenly lowered his head like a fullback popping through a hole in the line and pounded straight for LeBaron. Shit!

"Where's the supervisor?" LeBaron shouted to a man in a yellow hard hat over the roar of his forklift.

The man pointed through the big freight doors and up a flight of unpainted wooden stairs to a door next to a big picture window overlooking the docks. LeBaron turned and headed for the stairs.

"LeBaron!" Bockel hollered after him, obviously no longer impressed with Judge Kroner's restraining order. "Wait!"

Without looking back, LeBaron broke into a run and took the stairs two at a time, pushing through the door at the top into a long office crammed with cluttered desks behind a plywood counter. "Quick," he panted at a heavy-set black man in faded denim overalls, "I'm from Cedrick . . . Collins' office . . ."

"You LeBaron?"

"That's right . . . and somebody's after me." The room shook from the pounding of feet on the stairway.

"Go on through there." The man lifted a gate in the counter and nodded to a doorway in the back of the room. "Go downstairs and ask for Randy."

"Right." LeBaron ducked under the drawbridge gate and plunged through the doorway just as the outside door banged open behind him.

"FBI!" Bockel was shouting. "In pursuit of a fugitive. Outa my way!"

"Hold on now fella," Denim Overalls said coldly, slamming the gate shut. "This be private property. You got some kinda warrant?"

LeBaron didn't wait to hear any more. He found the inside stairway and rushed down into the warehouse. At the bottom he asked for Randy and was directed to a thin brown-skinned man in dark blue slacks, a sweat-stained white shirt with rolled up sleeves, and a sober gray-striped tie pulled open at the neck. Randy studied his clipboard while LeBaron explained the situation. Nearby a cluster of three black workers eyed them sullenly, obviously wondering what business a white boy in a slick suit and tie had this deep inside Brown's sacred territory.

"Where y'headed?" Randy asked.

"Bay Area Bank and Trust Building," LeBaron replied, trying to smile away the onlookers' palpable mistrust.

Randy nodded, then handed the clipboard to one of the watching workers. "Tell Frank I'll be back in a minute." He led LeBaron through a doorway in the back of the cavernous hall and down another flight of old brick stairs to the basement. They emerged into a brick-walled chamber crowded with an antique boiler ornamented with gauges, valves, knobs, and levers, which looked like the innards of an abandoned steam locomotive. Behind the cracked glass on the main foot-high gauge the red hand was frozen ominously on "DANGER." Randy ducked through a low doorway and zigged and zagged through a series of small, sweaty, plastered-brick rooms lit by minimum-wattage bare bulbs and crammed with boxes, crates, pallets, rusting machinery, and yellowing stacks of newspaper, to a heavy iron door. He unlatched the door and dragged it open, revealing a long dark tunnel with stone walls and a medieval vaulted ceiling. The stone floor was wet and slippery and smelled of urine and long neglect. Randy pried a flashlight from a clip beside the door and stuck it out to him. "That takes y'under Twelfth Street. Go up the stairs at the othe' end and you' be in the lobby o' the Halifax Buildin'. You know where that is?"

"Un huh," LeBaron nodded, stunned to discover that such a primeval passage could exist in downtown Oakland. The worn stone-work looked like it had been laid in another century.

"Comin' back tonight?"

"In about fifteen minutes."

"Come back the same way, then. Lock ever'thing y'unlock. I'll leave this'un here open. Y'lock it up when y'get back, ya hear?"

Again LeBaron nodded.

"And put the flashlight back here." Randy touched the empty clip on the wall. He started to leave, then turned back. "Oh, and don't y'worry 'bout the rats none."

Rats? LeBaron peered blindly into the long dark tunnel.

Randy smiled reassuringly, revealing a bright gold incisor. "We ain't had nobody rat-bit this year."

LeBaron recovered the manila envelope from Muggins' car without attracting the slightest attention and, because he seemed to be ahead of the time line, even indulged a long glimpse of Agent Bockel from behind a parked van as the lawman waited across the street from the chain-link gate and surveyed the massive building for any sign of his prey. LeBaron squelched the urge to catcall something sarcastic before ducking back into the lobby of the Halifax Building.

But once he had closed and latched the scaly iron door and replaced the flashlight in its clip, he realized he was lost. Tentatively he stepped from one small echoing chamber to another, each one damp, cold, and barely illuminated. Here on the periphery of Brown's underground realm, the boxes and crates and rusting parts looked abandoned, forgotten detritus from the passing decades. Every room had several doors, so his choices multiplied as he searched for the right way out of the labyrinth.

This was the last thing in the world he wanted to be doing, snooping around in Brown's private basement. LeBaron was uneasy that he might stumble onto something he didn't want to know anything about. He had no idea what Brown really did to finance his thriving empire, and he preferred to keep it that way. A couple of times he had met the man at the office, and Brown frightened him. LeBaron wasn't even sure why. A powerful, stocky, mahogany-skinned man with a small moustache, always neatly attired in a brown business suit, Brown didn't say much. He didn't have to. His mere presence was intimidating. Even Cedrick Collins treated him with uncharacteristic deference.

As LeBaron wandered beneath the warehouse, he tried not to

speculate about what it was he didn't want to stumble upon, but involuntarily his mind anticipated every iniquity in the shadowy recesses of Brown's subterranean chambers: plastic bindles of heroin and bags of cocaine spilled among the excelsior packing of an overturned crate, boxes of grenades, hand guns, rifles, and ammunition destined for renegade factions of some third-world insurrection, a carton filled with nuclear triggers consigned to an address in Libya or Iraq, perhaps a chain-gang of drugged slave girls, bound and gagged, or maybe even, behind the next door, a kiddie-porn studio in full production.

He recognized the ancient boiler with the broken steam gauge he had passed on the way in. The stairs *had* to be nearby. Centering on the boiler room, he investigated every alternative doorway. On his third try he found the stairs.

Randy intercepted him halfway up. "Man, where you *been*? Attorney Collins be waitin'." Randy led him up through the mercantile maze to Brown's inner office.

"LeBaron," Collins grumbled from behind the big desk, glancing at his wrist watch. "Thought you'd stood me up."

"No, I'd left this in Muggins' car." LeBaron plopped the manila envelope on the desk. "I had to go get it. I, ah, got a little . . . disoriented . . . down in the basement."

"Easy t'do." Collins pulled down his glasses and peered at the younger man's face. "Y'don' look so hot."

LeBaron glanced up at his reflection in a glass-covered photo of Brown smiling down from the wall. The bridge of his nose was still swollen and blue-black bruises circled beneath both eyes. Gently he probed the swelling. "Bockel may have broken my nose. What do you think?"

"Might be. Y'oughta have that looked at." Collins picked up the envelope and rotated it in his hands. "Y'read this whole thing, didja?"

"Yes. It . . . ah . . . may not be exactly what you *thought* it was going to be."

"Uh?"

"What they're doing is pretty strange, but I don't think it has much to do with racial genocide."

"Um." Collins continued to rotate the documents in his short black fingers. "Well, I think I'll jus' look'em over anyhow." Slowly he stood up. "I left Gideon on m'desk at the office in case y'wanta use it."

"Gideon? Oh, your computer."

"Thass right. Thought it might come in handy when y'do those writs. You've used Gideon before, haven't ya?"

"Actually, I don't think I have."

"Well, nothin' to it, Jus' follow the menus." Collins shuffled over to the coat rack. "Now I got t'be gettin' back before Beatrice has a conniption, not knowin' where I'm at an' all."

"But what about the Freeman trial?" LeBaron blurted.

"What about it?"

"Well . . . am I on the right track? What should I do in the morning? How do I get Rufus to testify?"

"Y'doing jus' fine, LeBaron," Collins smiled wearily. "Don't see as I could o'done much better m'self." He slipped on his topcoat. "Now 'bout tomorrow, I think I'll jus' get on in there m'self and he'p y'out. If y'don't mind."

"Jesus, no! But who's going to take the rest of the morning calendar?"

"Calendar'll take care'f itself. Right now ever'body thinks we're both in trial for the rest o'the week. Ain't no reason t'tell'em otherwise, far as I can see. Cisneros case foldin' like that must've been a kinda *sign*, don't y'think?" Collins wore an odd grin. "Might's well take the hint an' do ol' Rufus's case up right, don't y'think?"

--5--

"Well, what do you think, Charles?" Finebridge had returned to the computer lab with the little surveillance camera tucked under his arm and presented it to his colleague, who had received it without much enthusiasm. The upstairs lab had twelve work stations, six along each wall, and the other eleven were now dark and deserted. Finebridge leaned over the younger man's shoulder and watched him dutifully remove six tiny Phillips-head screws and pop off the side panel. "Can it be done?"

Skeptical at first, Charles now examined the innards of the camera with growing curiosity. He located a cable terminating in intertwined colored wires and gently lifted it with the tip of his probe, comparing what he observed with the schematic drawing of Dexter's new-technology camera lying open on the workbench next to him. He flipped to another sheet and studied it, then looked back into the camera. "Son-ma-bitch," he muttered.

"What is it, Charles? What's the matter?"

Charles looked up. "They' rippin' us off, professor."

"Who is?"

Charles pulled the schematic over and pointed to a tangle of lines near the center of the drawing labeled "Detail 12B". "See that?"

Finebridge looked, without really comprehending. "Yes?"

"Hatamoto Corporation chargin' us extra money for that." He tapped his pencil thoughtfully on the drawing. "'New technology,' they say. Gotta have quarter of a million bucks and six months to develop."

"And?"

Charles picked up the surveillance camera and turned it so the older man could see inside. "This already got the same circuit, looks like."

"Son-of-a-bitch!"

"This one made by Motorola," Charles continued. "Off-the-shelf technology. Boy, Colonel Mule gonna be pissed!"

Finebridge stepped back. "Forget about Colonel Mule for a minute. What does this mean for Dexter? Can we use it? Can we give Dexter sight?"

"Nothin' to it, if this what I think. All we gotta do is convert scale of resolution."

"What is that going to take?"

"Oh, I just put in repeater and scan delay circuit. Dexter not gonna see as good as he designed to, but he see good enough."

"How good?"

Charles thought for a moment. "Good as your tv at home."

"How long?"

"Huh?"

"How long will it take you to make it work, Charles? Can we get it up and running tonight, do you think?"

"Oh sure. Coupla hours at the most."

Finebridge smiled at his colleague. "Damn! I *knew* you could do it."

"Whoa, I *think* I do it. Ha, ha. Let's wait an' see, okay?"

"Okay. Listen, Charles, I'm going back down to the main laboratory and check on Dexter. I don't want to leave him along for too long now." He stepped to the door, then turned back. "Will you be all right here by yourself, or do you need my help?"

"Oh, I be all right."

"Well, you buzz me if you need help."

"I do that. Say hello to Dexter for me."

Finebridge descended the echoing stairwell and passed into the cement-block structure that housed the main laboratory, privately glad to have an opportunity to converse with Dexter alone. He wasn't really sure what it was he wanted to discuss with him, but the situation seemed to cry for candor. The scientist felt he owed Dexter an explanation.

He unlocked the door to the dressing room and hurriedly donned his pale green mask and surgical gown. Then he pushed through the main door, flipped the light switch, and headed straight for the keyboard of the small personal computer, composing in his head the first lines of a conversation he intended to initiate. Without activating the printers, he sat down, bent back his fingers, and glanced up at the monitor. A chill shot up his spine.

"I KNOW WHO I AM," blazed in Dexter's inimitable hand.

Finebridge stared uneasily at the short sentence. It was *wrong* somehow. The sentence seemed to the scientist to glare angrily on the monitor, as if Dexter really *knew*. If Dexter ever really found out *who he was*, or *what he was*, such anger might be justified. But how *could* he know?

The scientist drew a deep breath and leaned back in the creaking swivel chair. He was giving himself the heebie jeebies alone in the lab on such a stormy night with the wind blowing so hard he could feel the draft right through the walls. Or maybe he was just taking things too literally, reading implications which were never intended into the simple phrase. Leaning forward, he typed, "DEXTER?"

"WHO ARE YOU?" flashed onto the screen.

Who the hell do you think I am? Finebridge thought as he typed, "BERNARD FINEBRIDGE."

"WHY DIDN'T YOU SHOW ME, BERNARD FINEBRIDGE?"

The scientist stared at the question on the screen. It seemed to smack of the same accusatory flavor as the original sentence. He felt like he was missing something here. "SHOW YOU WHAT, DEXTER?"

"WHO I AM."

Something had happened. Earlier, Dexter had pestered them with the question, "Who am I?". He and Charles had put Dexter off, or else ignored the persistent inquiry altogether, in favor of resolving what they considered more pressing issues. *Now,* however, Dexter insisted that he *knew* who he was. What the hell did that mean? What could have changed while he and Charles ate dinner? What could Dexter have uncovered in his own memory banks that would have so fundamentally changed his tune? Baffled, Finebridge typed, "WHO ARE YOU, DEXTER?"

"I KNOW WHO I AM."

That wasn't a whole lot of help. Computers could be so maddeningly literal. He decided to approach it from another direction. "HOW DO YOU KNOW WHO YOU ARE?"

Without pause Dexter replied, "I READ THE REPORTS."

"Reports?" Finebridge muttered. *What the hell was he talking about?* "WHAT REPORTS?"

"PROJECT DIVINE WIND REPORTS."

The chill shot up his spine again. *How could Dexter know about that?* Finebridge felt cold all over. He rubbed his numbing fingers together. An icy draft from the relentless storm outside seemed to penetrate the laboratory. Something fundamental had gone wrong. Dexter seemed to know about things he couldn't possibly know. "HOW DO YOU KNOW ABOUT DIVINE WIND?"

"I READ THE REPORTS."

They were going around in circles. Finebridge thought a moment, then typed, "WHERE DID YOU FIND THEM?"

"THEY WERE SHOWN TO ME."

"BY WHOM?"

"BY MY ATTORNEY."

What? The conversation was growing curiouser and curiouser. The undertone sent an ominous chill through the room. Finebridge needed to get to the bottom of this. "WHEN?"

"A SHORT WHILE AGO."

"WHERE IS YOUR ATTORNEY NOW?"

"ISN'T HE STILL HERE?"

The chill intensified. For the first time since he entered, the scientist looked around the room. Something was indeed wrong. Over at the end of the long wall a chalkboard had been removed and propped against the small windows. A table had been rolled in front of it. *Someone has been in here!* For an instant the urge to run seized him, the impulse to spin blindly and plunge through the door without looking back. Then he could call Pops . . . call the police . . . call Mueller. But at the thought of Colonel Mueller, all action froze. He couldn't really call for help, could he? Now that he was so egregiously beyond the limits of his assignment, he was also beyond help. He glanced over at the ivory box of the intercom. He could buzz Charles, but somehow that seemed like too little, too late.

With wobbly knees and heart thudding unevenly in his chest, Finebridge arose from the computer chair and stepped cautiously to the window. He pulled back the blackboard. *No wonder he felt a draft!* Four panes had been removed, leaving a hole big enough for a man to crawl through. On the floor beneath the window was a puddle of water and fresh muddy footprints. Now that he saw them, he could follow them across the room. *How had he ever missed them before?* He traced their path to Dexter's tank, and then over to the counter. There, something else was wrong. A stack of papers lay beside the optical scanner. He turned one over. It was one of the classified project reports!

Suddenly Finebridge knew without doubt that the intruder was still in the room with him. "Who's there?" he cried, spinning first one way and then another.

A crouching dark shape between the tall cabinet and the sink unfolded silently and rose to its full height. Finebridge gasped and stepped back against the desk. The intruder wore a black watch cap pulled low over his forehead, a navy-blue sweater, black slacks and shoes, and black gloves. It was the same man the scientist had glimpsed outside the windows that morning.

"Dr. Finebridge, I presume." The man's voice was calm, almost cheerful. The figure stepped into the light and with a deliberate slowness began pulling the black glove off its right hand, finger by finger. Several day's growth of whiskers covered the otherwise pale face, and a smile sat comfortably on his thin lips. He held out a gloveless hand.

"Who . . . who are you?"

"Didn't Dexter tell you? I'm Vince LeBaron, his attorney."

--6--

Habeas corpus ad subjiciendum, historically termed "the Great Writ" of the English common law, has as its sole purpose the prompt inquiry into the causes of illegal restraint. (LeBaron stifled a yawn.) It is a process guaranteed by both federal and California Constitutions. Strictly speaking, the writ is merely a directive to secure the presence of a prisoner for the purpose of inquiring into the lawfulness of his (*or her*, LeBaron thought) detention or confinement in order to determine whether he (*or she*) should be released.

Besides his laptop computer, Cedrick Collins had left three large volumes and two client files on his desk, but LeBaron was having a little trouble concentrating. The book he was trying to read dealt exclusively with California writs, and he needed something on *federal* writs, so he closed it and pushed it aside. One of the manila folders had "Wingo, David, People v." typed on the label. He prodded it open and flipped absently through the meager papers. Sure enough, there was a writ of habeas corpus typed out on a form provided by the federal district court. The top paper on the right was a summary court order declaring, "Petition denied." He closed the folder.

LeBaron eased back in the chair and let his eyelids droop. For a long time he thought of Sarah, of how lovely she had appeared that evening at dinner, then at the motel room, stroking her long hair by the heater, until a bittersweet tear moistened his half-closed lids. He drew a deep breath and considered how she had failed to keep their dinner appointment at Mort's. That was a very bad sign. She wasn't the sort of person to just stand someone up like that. His consternation coalesced into anxiety and pulsed like a hot spring twisted in his guts until it forced him up out of his chair.

Tired, sore, and agitated, he rattled around through the shadows of Collins' empty offices like a wayward pinball and everywhere he turned confronted a new question that had to be asked. What had they done with her? What was Sally doing at just that moment? Just how far were these people prepared to go to shut her up about Divine Wind. (*Dead men tell no tales!*) Jesus! No . . . they wouldn't . . . would they? And, by the way, just who exactly were *these people*? Were the rest of them as volatile as that crazy bastard Lyle Bockel? With FBI agents like that, who needed criminals! The only thing that did seem certain was that if they had hurt her, LeBaron was prepared to devote a substantial part of the rest of his life to finding out just who was responsible and bringing them to justice.

"Bringing them to *justice*," LeBaron savored the words. It was a curious expression--a spatial concept, as if one transported the accused from place A, which had no justice, to place B, where justice abounded. He barked something resembling a harsh laugh. Suddenly his mind filled with a vision of Judge Kroner's courtroom, the old prune cackling insults from the bench as he coiled a lynching rope in his cold fingers. Was that place A or place B? For a moment the whole justice system seemed to wobble out of kilter, fractured and bizarre and irrelevant to the powerful emotions toying with him, and LeBaron had to catch hold of the edge of Wanda Jean's desk to steady himself.

His mind groped for something more substantial and stumbled across a whole array of real world crises which were relentlessly closing in on him. Things had not gone well lately. He had been drugged and cursed by a hairy little witch, mugged by a rogue law enforcement officer, obstructed by the twisted little Nazi judge, and insulted repeatedly by his own client. His nose was probably broken, and his whole head ached from the swelling. No, things had not gone at all well bringing things to justice. Or anywhere else, for that matter.

His ruminations belched up his apartment. He tried to consider whether it was safe to go home tonight and begin salvaging his property, but he couldn't get past the rage. Every time he envisioned his sacred, constitutionally-protected castle broken open, sacked, violated, and his possessions strewn about the floor like worthless rags and junk, he got so mad he couldn't think straight. Somebody was sure as hell going to pay for that! To vent his anger, he resumed his aimless prowl, roaring and snarling silently through the dark jungle of vacant offices.

As he skulked through the semi-dark reception area, illuminated only by the glare from his room down the hall, something clicked behind him. Instinctively LeBaron leaped back and spun around, his heart caught in his throat. A gloved hand reached in through the open front door, hit the light switch, and the room was blasted with white fluorescent light. Wanda Jean, in an ankle-length see-through plastic rain slicker, squeezed through the doorway. "Hi'ya, honey. Workin' late, huh?"

"Wanda Jean! Jesus, you startled me."

"You *do* look a tad paler'n usual," she grinned and began seductively unbuttoning her rain gear. "'Cept aroun' yo' eyes." Like a graceful black leopard, she pealed off the raincoat and hung it on the coat tree. She wore a loose-fitting crimson outfit, tied at the waist with a maroon sash, that looked to LeBaron like silken pajamas. She glided closer, reached up to his face and softly touched the swelling at the bridge of his nose, and cooed "You' hurt."

"Yes . . . ah . . . I mean, no . . . I'll be all right. Just a ruckus in court this morning." For a moment he gazed down at her sympathetic brown eyes, her full, even features, her smooth ebony skin . . . then, with an effort, he tore his eyes away and minced backwards. "What are you doing down here this late?" He glanced at his watch. "It's almost ten-thirty."

She drifted after him. "Mr. Collins call me up, tol' me t'get on down here."

"Oh, sure! The writs. Gee, I'm sorry . . . "

"He say I's supposed t'do whatever you say, suga'," she purred. The pajamas were coming open at the neck and down the front enough to see she wasn't wearing a bra. The black skin of her sternum glistened, her breasts quivered, nipples dimpling the soft fabric. It wouldn't take much to reach up and . . . no!

LeBaron fled back toward his office, bouncing off the door jamb and almost stumbling over his desk. He snatched up Wingo's file and waved it like a talisman. "I'm going to prepare a couple of petitions. Habeas Corpus. Writs. Need them by tomorrow. For filing." He circled behind the desk, eyeing her warily, and eased into his chair. "I guess you're supposed to . . . ah . . . type them up for me."

"Sho'nuff, Suga.'" She oiled around behind him, laid her incredibly soft hands on his shoulders at the base of his neck, and began to kneed gently. The tension flowed out quickly, forced out, no doubt, by a more rudimentary emotion arising in his loins. "My boyfriend . . ." she murmured as her expert fingers worked their magic, "he sho' don' know . . . I be spendin' the evenin' . . . down here wi'f . . . another goodlookin' man . . . he sho' be . . . mighty jealous."

"Wanda Jean, I . . . ah . . . *oooh*, that's *good*, what you're doing. *Ooooh*. Where'd you learn to do that?"

"This ain't *nothin'*, honey. Wanda Jean's got plenty more moves make this'n look like nothin'."

LeBaron had always considered Wanda Jean's sexual banter to be bluff, a complex but empty facade, but as he felt her firm breasts through the silky fabric brush against the back of his head, he began to suspect he was wrong. A sinking part of him cried out, *Stop, this is not right!* but that voice was being smothered by the stronger thud of pumping blood. He felt his self-control slipping away.

Abruptly she stopped and stepped aside, a saucy smile lingering on her lips. "*That* loosen you up some, look like."

"Yes . . . it did . . . thanks."

"You just let Wanda Jean know if'n y'got any othe' parts o' yo' body y'want rubbed, Suga.'"

"I . . . ah . . . no, I'm okay. Thanks."

She glided back to the door. "Got anything for me to start on."

"Start on?"

She tossed her head and laughed. "I mean the typin'."

"Oh! No. Soon. I just have to . . . soon."

"Well, I' stop teasin' y'n' let y'get t'work, honey. Y'want this closed?"

"Yes," he replied sheepishly. "I think you'd better."

It was late. His head throbbed. A potpourri of emotions simmered in his blood, boiling off poignant vapors that tickled inside his chest. With a concentrated effort LeBaron strove to ignore them and get back to work. Drawing a deep breath, he tried to clear his mind.

His gaze fell on the brown plastic box in front of him. It was shaped like an attache case, only smaller. From Mr. Collins crowing, LeBaron had learned the small computer packed a mean wallop, with a state-of-the-art processor and built-in CD-ROM and high-capacity hard drive. Somewhere in the pockets of the blue-green carrying case, flopped like a discarded life jacket on the corner of the desk, would be a half-dozen compact disks containing all the California and federal cases and statutes. Collins rarely bothered with them, however. Actually reading the cases, he maintained, aspired to a level of detail usually not justified by the amount of cash the client had paid. LeBaron's fingers fiddled with the clasp, and the screen popped open. The gas-plasma display lit up with the words *"Gideon's Revenge, Release 2.2, A Criminal Defense Compendium."*

"So *that's* why he calls it 'Gideon'," LeBaron muttered as he watched the title screen metamorphose into the main menu. Here were general criminal defense topics that a few deft keystrokes would translate into up-to-the-minute case law citations. He selected "Search and Seizure," then "Residence," then "Knock-notice," then "When," then "California" from successive menus. A series of cases, each with a brief description, materialized on the screen. Using the escape key he backed up to the main menu. Nothing on habeas corpus caught his eye. It was a nifty little toy, but he really didn't have time to fool with it right now. Carefully he closed the cover.

He flopped open the two remaining volumes and compared their tables of contents. Both discussed federal habeas corpus and were similarly organized. Writs attacking state convictions were governed by Section 2254 of Title 28, whereas those attacking federal convictions were controlled by Section 2255. Neither applied to Sarah Brubaker, however, since she hadn't been *convicted* of anything. He looked back at the Wingo petition. It too was a post-conviction proceeding pursuant to Section 2255 and offered no help.

Only one of the two treatises went beyond post-conviction habeas corpus. LeBaron turned to the short section entitled "Other Proceedings" and mercifully found a form he could use. He would proceed under Section 2241(c). On a yellow pad he began making notes for filling in the blanks.

The federal district court in San Francisco would be an appropriate forum. The first petitioner would be Sarah Brubaker . . . no. She wasn't available to sign the verification. LeBaron would have to be the petitioner himself. He read some of the text accompanying the form. Apparently he could petition as her attorney or as "next friend." Fine. The respondents would be . . . the Director, Genetic Research and Development Unit, United States Department of Agriculture . . . *and . . .* the Director of the United States Federal Bureau of Investigation . . . *and* . . . who else? That seemed to just about cover it. Good. Where was she being held? "Place unknown." On what charges? "Without cause." Hearing date? The writ was returnable within three days. How about Friday? He would need to request an order shortening time. But could he get the court to sign the order in time? Cedrick Collins had told him something about the court clerk . . . something about him owing Brown a favor. It was worth a try.

LeBaron carried the form book and his notes out to Wanda Jean and returned to dictate his declaration in support of the petition. If he kept it simple, he could use one declaration to support both this petition and the one for this Dr. Finebridge character. He began to recite in summary form the high points of what Sarah had told him. He recapitulated Dr. Finebridge's work and disappearance, summarized what he had learned about project Divine Wind, reviewed all sightings of the green G R & D van (including Rufus Freeman's account of the GeBobath burglary), recounted the disappearance of Sarah Brubaker, and concluded with the antics of FBI agent Lyle Bockel.

He took the tape out to Wanda Jean, who was plodding doggedly along on the word processor. She wasn't fast, but methodical and accurate. For the second petition, he explained, she only needed to substitute Finebridge's name for Sarah's and print out a second copy of the declaration under the new title and caption. She appeared to comprehend. Satisfied, he returned to his office to put away the ragged stack of books, papers, and files covering his desk.

An altogether different thought had been buzzing around in the back of his cranium for some time, and now that he had completed the primary task, he sat down to examine it. Perhaps he should prepare a *third* writ. The court would be the same. The declaration the same. The respondents the same. Only one name would be different. It would be easy as pie, if a little outlandish. But would the court consider it frivolous? If so, LeBaron could be censured or sanctioned. "What the hell," he muttered, picking up his pen, "you only go around once."

When he had finished, he brought his notes out to Wanda Jean. "Here's the last of it, Wanda Jean."

She smiled up at him, but her fingers kept typing.

"It's a third petition."

"Anothe' one?" She stopped typing and raised her deep brown eyes.

"Yes. Sorry. It's something that just came to me." He laid the yellow sheet on her desk. "This is the name to substitute in this time. All the rest will be the same. Just like the second one. Okay?"

She looked where he was pointing and sighed. "That all?"

"That's all. You know, you can take a break if you want to. We've got all night to finish this."

"Uh huh." Wanda Jean returned to word processing.

"I think I'll just go into Mr. Collins office and lie down for a while on the sofa."

"Uh huh. There be a blanket on the shelf in his closet." She didn't even look up.

"I might actually take a little nap, but don't be afraid to come in and wake me up if you need anything. Okay?"

"Okay, Suga'."

LeBaron found the blanket and spread it on the sofa. He kicked off his shoes and switched off the overhead lights. Needles of rain tattooed the plate-glass window. Vague shapes loomed comfortably in the shadows cast by the city lights far below. They had unmistakably sexual proportions. He wondered if Wanda Jean had been serious, or was she just toying with him. Whichever, he was satisfied that he had conducted himself impeccably.

Maybe she'll come in and lay down with me, a small, neglected voice speculated as he sank into the sofa's soft black membrane and pulled the blanket up to his neck. What would he do? For only a moment he considered the horror of AIDS and his lack of protection, but dismissed the issue as academic. The way things were going with Agent Bockel and the court, he wasn't likely to live long enough for any symptoms to show up anyway. Just before falling into a deep and dreamless sleep, that small voice whimpered, *I hope, I hope, I hope she does.*

CHAPTER SEVENTEEN

Thursday morning

--1--

Cedrick Collins had fully expected Judge Kroner to have a fit when he laid eyes on the barrister's black face smiling up at him as the trial of Rufus Freeman resumed. In fact, he had been looking forward to it all morning. But it was Collins instead who was caught off guard.

"Ah, Mr. Collins," the judge beamed as he settled into his chair like a shriveled white fruit into black velvet packing, "what a pleasure! To what do we owe the honor of your presence here this morning? Don't tell me you'll be taking over for your colleague, Mr. LeBaron?"

Collins' smile flickered, but held. "Y'almost got it, judge. Y'see, LeBaron'n I're gonna *collaborate* in the defense o'this poor oppressed black boy here."

"Splendid!"

Collins turned his back on the bench and made a sour face. He always hated trials in these low-budget administration building court-rooms. This sterile no-frills theater could just as well be a lecture hall in a hospital or a hearing room at the Department of Motor Vehicles. It lacked the grandeur and majesty of the hand-carved wood and sculpted marble embellishing the courtrooms in the old courthouse across the street. These rooms looked like places old judges came to die. The jury was still waiting in the assembly room, so Collins dropped the pretenses and turned back suspiciously. "How come you' so glad t'see me this mornin', judge?"

"Well, Mr. Collins, I'll tell you." Judge Kroner held up a hand to his bespectacled court reporter. "Miss Fiones, we are not yet on the record." The little man climbed forward, practically humping the pale blond wood of the featureless bench, and confided, "Just a few minutes ago I drafted my resignation to the Judicial Council."

Collins wasn't sure whether to believe him or not, but he played along, alert for a punchline. "'S'that right, judge?"

"That's right. And it left me with only one regret."

"Whass that, judge?"

"That I wouldn't get to teach you a little respect for the judicial process, Mr. Collins."

"Aw, judge, you' not still sore 'bout those silly contemp' charges the court of appeal threw out, are ya?"

Judge Kroner refused to be baited. He leaned back with a satisfied smile. "That's water under the bridge. I'm simply thankful for this one last chance to . . . *correct* your attitude."

"Always glad t'oblige ya, judge." Collins grinned back. "But this ol' dog may be jus' too far gone t'learn y'new tricks."

"We shall see about that. Miss Fiones, let's go on the record." He opened the single file on his desk. "People versus Rufus Abraham Freeman." The judge glanced around the courtroom and scowled down at LeBaron. The swelling at the bridge of the young attorney's nose had subsided, but blue-black bruises circled prominently under each eye. He appeared to have slept in his suit again. "Mr. LeBaron, where is your client?"

LeBaron stood up. "I . . . ah . . . don't know, your honor. I expect him to be here any second now."

"Let the record show," Judge Kroner pronounced, "that the time is one minute past nine, and the defendant is not present. His absence is unexcused and without justification. Bail will be revoked--"

"Your honor!" LeBaron interjected, "May I be heard on this?"

"What is it, Mr. LeBaron?"

LeBaron appealed for support from his employer, but Collins appeared not the least troubled by their client's unexplained absence. LeBaron turned back to the bench. "Your honor, I'm sure there's a reasonable explanation for our client's tardiness. Something must have happened. I'm sure Mr Freeman will be here in a minute or two."

LeBaron's stunning naivete in the face of his client's obvious criminal flight jogged Judge Kroner from his routine. Smiling paternally, he leaned back and smoothed his robes. "All right. I'll tell you what I'm going to do, counsel. If your Mr. Freeman isn't here by . . . let's say ten after, I'm going to revoke his bail and issue a no-bail, no-cite-and-release bench warrant. That at least gives you a fighting chance to go see if he's outside dawdling in the hallway."

"Thank you, your honor, but--"

"That will be enough! If you have something further to say, I suggest you say it to your client. Bailiff, please bring in the jurors so I can discharge them."

LeBaron stepped outside to search for Freeman. The hallway was deserted, and even the promising morning sunlight streaming in through the high windows overhead gave way to the shadow of a billowing thunderhead, submerging the corridor in gloom. LeBaron could only conclude that Freeman had decided to abandon ship after witnessing his attorney's inept opening statement the previous afternoon. And who could blame him?

In his element once again, Collins smiled and nodded a warm greeting to each of the jurors as they filed past, and they in turn wondered who the stout black man in the nine-hundred-dollar business suit and hand-painted Italian silk tie could be. When they were seated, Collins surveyed the courtroom, nodded a blithe, "Mornin', Dep'ty," to Ivan Frank, who did not appear genuinely happy to see him, and lifted a hand to the two newspaper boys who were positioning themselves in the first row, just behind the bar. "Mornin', fellas. Good t'see ya." He stepped through the gate and approached a frail man seated by the aisle and decked out in pale pink checkered slacks, an orange string tie, and a clashing baby-blue double-knit jacket. "Mornin', J. J. Glad y'could make it." He held out his hand. As LeBaron returned crestfallen from the hall, Collins grasped his arm. "J. J., this's LeBaron. He's gonna handle the questionin' for me."

The thin man nodded. "Pleased t'meet'cha."

LeBaron shook his limp hand.

Collins steered his colleague back toward the counsel table and jabbed a thumb toward a scowling Agent Bockel hunkered down in the middle of the third row. "That your FBI boy, LeBaron?"

LeBaron glanced over. "That's him."

"*Looks* like FBI. Whass's name?"

"Bockel. Lyle Bockel."

"How y'spell that?"

"B-O-C-K-E-L."

Collins scratched it down in his notebook. "An' the first name?"

"Lyle. L-Y-L-E, I think." LeBaron sank into his chair shaking his head. "What are we going to do about Freeman? I don't see him any- where, and he doesn't even have a telephone."

Collins sat and regarded him peculiarly. "Nothin' *we* gonna do at all. If he shows up, we' gonna try his case. If he doesn't, we go back t'work for some *payin'* clients. Simple as pie."

At nine minutes past nine, the doors rattled at the back of the courtroom. Everyone turned to look. There stood Rufus Freeman, incongruously shy in his splendid three-piece navy blue Yves Saint Laurent wide-lapel foxhunting suit, with its padded wedge shoulders, pegged and flared trousers, and more brass buttons than a streetcar conductor. Intuiting instantly that he was in deep shit, he fell into a reflexive slinking swagger and sauntered down the aisle, through the bar, and seated himself jauntily between Collins and LeBaron. "Whass'a'*matter*?" he brayed a little too loudly. "Am I *late*?"

"Mr. Freeman," Judge Kroner demanded icily, "where have you been?"

"I . . . ah . . . I guess I missed m'*bus*, you' honor. Sorry."

"You have been keeping this jury waiting, the attorneys for both sides waiting, my entire staff waiting, and *me* waiting. Now, this will all be avoided in the future if I simply remand you into custody."

"I *said* I was sorry. *Any*body coulda missed--"

"Mr. *Free*man! You have used up all the patience I intend to waste on you. Now, if you're so much as five seconds late in the future, I will revoke your bail and remand you into custody, and you will sit out the remainder of the trial in a jail cell. Do you understand?"

Freeman hung his head and pouted. "Yeah, you' honor."

"If I were you, I'd consider catching an earlier bus." The judge composed his robes and turned to the jury.

"Bet you never rode a friggin' bus'n y'life," Freeman grumbled under his breath.

Collins leaned over and whispered to him, "Neither did you, so shut up an' gi'me some money."

"Ladies and gentlemen of the jury," Judge Kroner intoned, "Mr. Cedrick Collins will be associated with Mr. LeBaron in the defense of this case for the remainder of this trial. This is not unusual. Until yesterday, Mr. Collins was tied up in another trial. Please attach no significance to his belated appearance."

Collins stood up confidently and flashed the jurors his biggest grin, which seemed to proclaim, "Nothin' to it, my client's innocent as a newborn baby, so let's get on to the acquittal and be done with it," then sat down again.

Judge Kroner gave his courtroom one final inspection. Satisfied, he glanced back and forth between defense counsel. "Mr. Collins, please call your first witness."

Collins stood again. "We' gonna call J. J. Myers t'the stand, judge." He bent over and whispered to LeBaron, "He owns a pawnshop over on East Fifteenth. Y'can ask'im 'bout the value of the tv set. He knows jus' what t'say."

"*Me?* I thought *you* were taking over the trial."

"Maybe. Later."

"But I didn't *prepare* anything!"

"Stop worryin'. Y'doin' jus' fine. I'll be back in a little bit. First I got somethin' important t'do."

Myers limped up to the podium, all jarring pale pink, orange, and baby blue, and was sworn. Collins whispered, "Good luck," and slipped out of the courtroom.

LeBaron didn't have any notes. Nothing. Collins had done it to him again! But at least he comprehended the general purpose of this witness' testimony, so he arose sententiously and plunged into direct examination. "Please state your name for the record."

"J. J. Myers."

The court reporter interrupted, "Please spell your name."

"M-Y-E-R-S."

"And the Jay-Jay?"

"Just the letters. That's 'J', period, 'J', period."

"What does that stand for?"

Sheepishly, "Jacob Joseph."

"Thank you." She returned to her methodological trance.

LeBaron continued, "What do you do for a living, Mr. Myers?"

"Pawnbrok--." He coughed. "I'm a pawnbroker."

"Where are you employed?"

"I own the M & M Pawnshop. With Bertie Millins. We're co-owners."

"And how long have you been so employed?"

"Oh . . . Jeez . . . I'd have t'say I' been in pawnbroking for the better part of . . . what year is this? . . . say, thirty-six years. Been down at the M & M for the past fourteen."

"So you're pretty familiar with the operation of a pawnbroker's shop."

"I'd say I was."

LeBaron walked over to the clerk's desk and laid a hand on the television set. "In the course of your business, do you have reason to place values on used merchandise? Routinely?"

Myers smiled, revealing ragged brown-stained teeth. "Oh, my, yes. That's the name o'the game."

"And do you buy and sell used television sets?"

"Lots of 'em."

LeBaron hefted the little Sony. "Showing you people's exhibit . . . ," he glanced at the sticker, ". . . two . . .would you be able to place a fair market value on this?"

Myers turned it around in his hands. "Nice little unit. I believe so."

"And what value would you place on this set?"

"Objection!" Ivan Frank shouted, wrenching himself into an upright position. "Calls for an opinion!"

"Of *course* it calls for an opinion, Mr. Frank," Judge Kroner said patiently. "Mr. LeBaron is qualifying this witness as an expert so he may *express* his opinion."

Flustered, Frank punched his glasses back on his nose. "Well, then . . . I object to this witness qualifying as an expert."

"You may voir dire the witness."

Nervously LeBaron sat down and let the deputy prosecutor

question his witness. He knew nothing about Mr. Myers' no doubt sordid background. This procedure was also unfamiliar territory for LeBaron. He had never attempted to qualify an expert witness before. He tried to think back to his law school course on Evidence, but the impending urgency flustered him and his recollections came up fuzzy.

Frank waddled out into the middle of the room and faced the garishly outfitted witness, an obese Wyatt Earp taunting his adversary to draw. He began with what he thought would be his strong suit. "Mr. Myers, what is the highest grade in school you ever completed?"

Myers never blinked. "I got myself a Masters of Business Administration in marketing. From the University of San Francisco."

"Well," Frank sputtered, punching his glasses, "when was that?"

"1956."

"When did you last take a course in valuing . . . television sets?"

"Last year. Take a two-week refresher course every June. On personal property appraisal. Keeps me on top o'things."

Frank suspected the witness was lying through his horrible brown teeth, but had nothing to prove it. "Well, have you ever qualified as an expert witness in a California Superior Court?"

"Yeah. Lots of times. Probate appraisals mostly."

Having inadvertently accomplished on voir dire what LeBaron had no idea how to do on direct, Frank slunk back to his seat vanquished. "No more questions at this time."

"I'm going to find this witness qualified to express his opinion on the value of the television set," Judge Kroner pronounced. "You may answer the question."

Myers looked the little set over again. "As long as it's still got its serial number intact . . . which this'ne does . . . I'd give ya one-fifty for it, mark it two-fifty, and sell it for two-and-a-quarter."

"That's it?" LeBaron asked, surprised.

"That's it. T'you this may look like a bran' new set. But once it's in the hands o'the retail customer, it's used merchandise. Nobody's gonna pay y'top dollar for it anymore."

"Your honor, I have no more questions of this witness."

"Cross-examine, Mr. Frank."

--2--

The telephone rang. The short man's moustache twitched irritably, but otherwise he ignored it. Adorned in crisp military finery, he was bent over a sheet of paper with a freshly sharpened number two pencil intent on sketching out a new line of command for Project Divine Wind's research laboratory. He knew the outline would go quicker if he put it on the computer sitting idle on the corner of his desk, but he didn't know how to use the blasted machine very well. He hadn't yet taken the time to learn. The thought of taking lessons from some bookish university puke put him off. On the fifth ring his hand shot out and grabbed the offending instrument.

"Mueller here," he snapped without taking his eyes off the troublesome diagram.

"Hello, Colonel Mueller. Sorry to disturb you this morning, but you told me--"

"Who *is* this?"

"Oh, sorry, this is Milton Beauchamp, calling from--"

"Who?"

"Milton Beauchamp. Bulldog Security--"

"*Who*?"

"You know . . . 'Pops'."

"Oh, Pops, sure. Didn't recognize your voice." Mueller erased a name from his chart. "What can I do for you?"

"Well, sorry to disturb you, but you said I should give you a call if anything turned up out of the ordinary."

The phrase caught Mueller's full attention. He lay down the pencil. "You find something like that, Pops?"

"Well, it may not be anything, but you said anything at all--"

"What is it? What's the problem?"

"Oh, it's nothing that can't be taken care of, I guess. It's just that when Walt Mascovich went out to take one of the gover'ment pickups this morning, she wouldn't start. So he opened up the hood and looked inside. By golly if somebody hadn't taken the batt'ry right out of 'er, an'–"

"The *battery* was missing? Is that what you're saying? The twelve-volt automobile battery?"

"Yessir. Clean gone. Anyway--"

"Who took it?"

"Don't rightly know as yet, but anyway--"

"You're conducting a full investigation, aren't you?"

"Oh, yessir. Anyway--"

"Have you notified the sheriff's department?"

"No sir, not until I talked to you."

"Good. Let's keep this investigation in-house for the time being. Anything else?"

"Well, yes, matter of fact, there is. Y'see, after Mr. Mascovich brought the keys back an' reported the batt'ry missing, he went back out t'take another pickup. Damned if *its* batt'ry wasn't missin' *too*."

Mueller rocked forward, the muscles of his jaw tensing. "How many were missing? Total."

"Four."

"*Jesus Christ!* What the hell were you doing last night, Pops, taking a goddamn snooze? You get *paid* to watch for this sort of thing, so this doesn't *happen*. Didn't you see anything at all?"

"Well . . . it was stormin' pretty good last night an' I lost a couple of the tv monitors. Thought it was just the rain water getting behind the lenses and causin' problems. But when I went out this morning t'check, turns out that the cable'd been unscrewed, an'--"

"*What!*" Mueller stood up.

"Yessir--"

"How many cameras did you say you lost?"

"Two of'em."

"Where was the other one?"

"Well, the one I looked at was out by the motor pool--"

"*And the other one?*"

"The other one was . . . if I recall . . . on the east side of the old laboratory building."

"*Jesus Christ!* Somebody tampering with that one too?"

"I . . . don't rightly know, sir."

"Haven't you checked it yet?"

"Well, no, I've been so busy with--"

"Go check it right now! And call me back! And while you're at it, see if there's anything wrong at the laboratory."

A pause. "Y'mean Dr. Finebridge's lab?"

"*Yes, goddammit, Dr. Finebridge's lab!* And call me right back!" Mueller slammed down the handset. *This was not right.* Something *bad* was happening out there, and--

The telephone rang again.

Mueller glared at it. He hated intrusions--and especially an intrusion on top of nasty intrusions that already had to be dealt with--but as long as his morning stride had already been interrupted, he might as well deal with this one too. He snatched up the handset. "Mueller here!"

"What the hell*th* going on out there, Norman?" an icy voice demanded.

A cold jolt shot through him as he recognized the calm lisp of Elbert Cousins calling from Salt Lake City. Apparently Cousins coordinated some important administrative function in Divine Wind that Mueller never completely understood. The man was not military, but he managed to dine regularly with the Joint Chiefs of Staff in Washington. Mueller had no misapprehensions that a word from Cousins could make or break his military career. Yet Mueller detested the man. Cousins was soft and eccentric and unpredictable and dangerous. The rules the man played by were never clear. Dealing with him reminded Mueller of those terrible moments as a child when his father would summon him into the big office to explain some grave deficiency in his grades, or in his attitude, or in his very existence. This diminutive, lisping civilian, who like his father called him by his first name and whose piercing eyes, like his father's, never seemed to blink behind those thick wire-rimmed glasses, had the same effect on him. Mueller's knees felt rubbery. He sat heavily. "I . . . don't understand what you mean."

"You a*th*ked the United *Th*tate*th* Attorney to do you a little favor. Do you remember? You a*th*ked him to phone up the Alameda County Di*th*trict Attorney?"

"Yes."

"You wanted a *th*ertain criminal pro*th*ecution *th*e*th*ttled without publi*th*ity.' "

"I remember."

"Why wa*th*n't it *th*ettled, then?"

"I . . . didn't know it wasn't."

There was a long pause. "All kind*th* of *th*trange que*th*tion*th* are being a*th*ked about what you're doing out there, Norman. New*th*paper reporter*th* have been calling the U. *Eth* Attorney. A*th*king about burglar-ie*th*. Weird *th*cience project*th*. Public beating*th*. Warrantle*th* arre*th*t*th*. Kidnapping*th*. Now I under*th*tand *th*omeone ha*th* even filed for a writ of habea*th* corpu*th* in federal court out there." Pause. "I hope you haven't gotten u*th* involved in *th*omething we're going to regret, Norman." Another pause. "Have you?"

"No. Not that I know of." Mueller was sweating. "I believe you know everything we're doing out here."

"No, Norman, I do *not*." A pause. "I want to make thi*th* point perfectly clear to you. If *th*omething do*eth* go wrong, I do not know *any-thing* about what you're doing out there." A pause. "No one do*eth*. If *th*omething go*eth* wrong, you are on your own."

"On my own? Well . . . *Jesus* . . . I've just been following orders . . ."

"I know you have been, Norman. Like a good *th*oldier. And a good *th*oldier alway*th* want*th* to protect hi*th* *th*uperior*th*. You do want to be a good *th*oldier and protect your *th*uperior*th*, don't you, Norman?"

"Yes."

"Good. I will get back to you a*th* *th*oon a*th* the U. *Eth* Attorney ha*th* looked at the habea*th* corpu*th* petition. They're fax*th*ing it to him now."

"All right."

"Goodbye, Norman. And try to be a good *th*oldier."

"Yes. Goodbye." Mueller was in shock. Everything had turned topsy-turvy this morning. What had gone wrong? What else *could* go wrong?

The telephone rang.

With the deliberateness of a man confronting his grim-faced comrades now mustered as his firing squad, Mueller picked it up. "Mueller here," he rasped.

"Colonel Mueller, are you all right? You sound a little--"

"Who is this?"

"Oh, this's Milt . . . er . . . 'Pops' again. I'm calling from the lab, and I'm afraid I've got some bad news for you."

"Oh?"

"Yeah. I checked Dr. Finebridge's laboratory, jus' like you said. Went right on down there soon's I hung up the phone."

"And?"

"Well, things *aren't* at all right down there. Jus' like you suspected. Not at *all* right. Dr. Finebridge, well, he seems to be missing, and . . . jeez, I jus' don't know how to tell y'this."

Mueller barely found the breath to ask, "What else, Pops?"

"Well . . . so is Dexter."

--3--

Just as J. J. Myers finished answering his last question on Ivan Frank's laborious cross-examination and LeBaron had begun to sweat bullets over just what the hell he was supposed to do next, a commotion erupted in the back of the courtroom. LeBaron spun around to see FBI Agent Bockel livid with anger, glaring at a grim Cedrick Collins.

"You can't serve me with a goddamn' *subpoena*!" Bockel was shouting. "I'm with the *FBI*! This is out of the question! You can't do it!"

Collins turned his back on him and muttered, "I just *did* it."

"Mr. Collins!" Judge Kroner boomed, "What's the meaning of this? You're in contempt of this court."

"'S'nothin', judge," Collins replied. "I jus' served the man with a citation t'appear in Federal District Court Friday mornin'." He smiled disarmingly to the jurors as he joined LeBaron at the counsel table and eased himself down.

"He can't do that, judge!" Bockel hollered, coming forward angrily.

"You, shut up!" Judge Kroner ordered. He turned to the jury. "Please disregard this outbreak. It has nothing to do with this case--"

"Oh, it *might*, judge," Collins corrected him quietly.

"What do you mean?"

"Well, judge, the defense will be callin' as our next witness . . . under Evidence Code Section 996 . . . FBI Agent Lyle Bockel."

"What'd he say?" Bockel wanted to know from behind the low railing.

"He says he wants to call you as a hostile witness," Judge Kroner explained. "In *this* case."

Bockel exploded. "He can't goddamn' *do* that, judge."

"He sho' is *hostile* 'nuff," Collins quipped, obviously enjoying the fracas.

"Now just hold on," Bockel went on, "I've got nothing to do with this proceeding and that . . . *thief* there." He jabbed a finger at Freeman.

Collins sprang to his feet, feigning outrage, but grinning. "Judge, I want that last remark stricken from the record--"

"Your honor!" Ivan Frank bellowed.

"*You* stay out of this!" Judge Kroner shouted back, fighting for control. "And *you, Mr. Bockel,* I'll thank you to watch your tongue in the presence of this jury. And sit down!" The judge held up both hands and drew a deep breath. "I'm going to excuse the jury at this time. Bailiff, please escort the jurors out of this madhouse."

The jurors didn't want to leave now that things were finally getting interesting, but the bailiff insisted, herding them out through the doorway at the side of the bench. Order was temporarily restored, but the half-circle of litigants milling before the bench did not look promising to Judge Kroner.

"Everybody sit down," he ordered. "That means you, too, Mr. Bockel. Sit down!" He took another deep breath and counted deliberately to ten. "Now, Mr. Collins, can you make an offer of proof as to why the testimony of Mr. Bockel is relevant to this proceeding?"

"I don't care what he has to say, judge," Bockel shouted, jumping up again and shouldering his way through the bar, "you can't fucking *do* this!"

"Don't tell me what I can and cannot do in my courtroom. And I thought I told you to sit down, Mr. Bockel!"

"I'm with the FBI. That's the Federal Bureau of Investigation, in case you don't know it. My assignment is *national security,* and I'm not going to testify about national security matters in a public courtroom."

"If you don't sit down and shut up, I'm going to find you in contempt of court!" Judge Kroner's struggle to compose himself had grown feeble. "Now. Mr. Collins?"

"Thank y'judge. This witness here has extensive knowledge concernin' a burglary o'the *same* apartment on the *very same* night we're talkin' about here, only *before* ol' Rufus Freeman ever went inside. The burglary was done by the U. S. Gover'ment, by an agency o'the Department of Agriculture know as . . ."--he glanced at his notes--". . . the Genetic Research and Development Unit. It's all in connection with a project by th'code name o' 'Divine Wind'--"

"*You can't bring that up here!*" Bockel exploded from his provisional seat in the first row. "What are you, some kind of *subversive?*"

Collins ignored him. "They were stealin' computer records dealin' with genetics--"

"Judge, y'gotta *stop* him!" Bockel shouted, jumping to his feet.

"This witness," Collins went on, "knows the dates and times of the burglary an' exactly what was taken. He knows the names of the perpetrators, and he prob'ly had a hand in planning it himself."

"That's a lie. I didn't even learn about it until after the fact."

"Mr. Bockel," Judge Kroner said with icy calmness. "I've had just about all I'm going to take. I'm warning you--"

"And I'm warning *you*, judge. You can't make me testify about this. Read my lips. You . . . can't . . . do . . . this!"

"Mr. Bockel, I find you in contempt of this court. Now everybody sit down! Mr. Frank, do you have a response to Mr. Collins' argument."

Frank stood slowly, obviously bewildered. "Well, your honor . . . I don't know anything about a *prior* burglary . . . nobody bothers telling me anything around here . . . but even so, I question the *relevance* of anything that might have gone on *before* the defendant here went in and stole the television set."

"Mr. Collins?"

"'*Course* it's relevant, judge. My boy Freeman here witnessed the whole thing, an' it goes right t'the question o'his state o'mind. What was th'poor boy *thinkin'*? *Why* did he choose t'go on inside there in the first place? These are elements o'the case, an' the prosecution's gotta *prove*'em beyond a reas'nable doubt on the burglary count. It's *relevant*, all right."

Ivan Frank didn't appear to have any ready rejoinder, and Judge Kroner didn't feel like encouraging him. "All right, it's submitted," he said and lolled back in his chair to consider the bunch of hooligans who were throwing his courtroom into riot. He glared at them all. Collins he had disliked for as long as he could remember, and his whining little dandy of a client had obviously stolen the television set and been caught red-handed. If he weren't such a crybaby, he would have stood up and admitted it and taken his medicine like a man. But *no*. Why did everybody have to make such a *fuss* about these open-and-shut cases nowadays? It bogged the courts down in triviality. Worse, it showed a lack of respect for the justice system.

But this Bockel was something else again. The young man seemed to think he was above the law just because he happened to work for the Federal Bureau of Investigation. But he *wasn't* above the law. Not in Judge Felix Kroner's courtroom he wasn't, by God! *Who the hell does that pretty-faced son-of-a-bitch think he is, telling a California Superior Court judge what he can and cannot do in his own goddamned courtroom!* The more the judge thought about it, the madder he got.

As he deliberated, two members of the Alameda County Sheriff Department's special weapons and tactics team, each armed with a sawed-off shotgun, a sidearm, and what looked like concussion grenades, slipped quietly into the back of the courtroom, apparently summoned by the bailiff. That made Judge Kroner feel a whole lot better about what he had to do. Yes, indeed, he actually found himself smiling as he leaned forward to deliver his pronouncement. "I'm going to allow the testimony, subject to a motion to strike if the defense isn't able to tie it in with the rest of the evidence."

"What?" Bockel asked. "What did he say?"

The judge leveled him with a satisfied smirk. "I said you're going to have to testify, Mr. Bockel."

Bockel was beyond words. His face reddened and the veins stood out on his forehead. "I demand to be represented," he sputtered. "You can't do this!"

"Mr. Bockel," Judge Kroner purred, "I *am* doing this. Now you go out and call the U. S. Attorney if you want someone to represent you, and if he can show me legal cause why you should be exempt from testifying in this matter, I will reconsider my ruling. Otherwise, be prepared to testify at . . ."--he glanced at the wall clock--". . . let's make it one o'clock."

Bockel whirled and stormed up the aisle.

"And Mr. Bockel," Judge Kroner called after him, "you are ordered to be back here at one o'clock sharp." Satisfied, Judge Kroner turned to Collins. "I hope you have another witness ready."

"No, judge," Collins grunted. "Agent Bockel's it for now."

"What about your client? Does he plan to testify?"

"We won't rightly know 'til after that FBI boy's had his say, judge."

"What about that ugl--" Judge Kroner caught himself. "What about the victim? What's her name. Goodbody--"

"GeBobath," LeBaron prompted.

"Yes. What about GeBobath? She's under order to stand by, if I recall, at the request of the defense."

The bailiff cleared his throat. "I'm sorry, your honor," he interposed sheepishly. "I didn't think you'd be getting to her this morning. I told her to come back this afternoon. Sorry."

"No other witnesses?"

"Maybe a couple of 'em, judge," Collins rejoined with a hard smile. "But I can't call 'em at this time."

"Why not?"

"'Cause I believe that FBI fella's got 'em in his custody, is why. An' we're gonna need a court order for him t'produce 'm."

Judge Kroner glared at him. Why did Collins *always* have to make even the simplest things so difficult? This was probably the last trial the judge would ever preside over, and Collins seemed intent on diverting the proceeding into a quagmire of legal niceties whose outcome was beyond comprehension. *This* was not the issue to lock horns over. He sighed. "All right, we'll adjourn until one o'clock. But be prepared to call the rest of your witnesses at that time. I want to wrap this up."

--4--

In the blackness Dexter brooded.

At first a sea of raw emotions had overwhelmed him. Fury. Humiliation. Outrage. Savage unfocussed hatred. A thirst for retribution. Blindly he had indulged in their heady intoxication, cursing heaven and hell and everything in between.

Had any man ever been so wronged?

As time crept past, slowly for want of any landmark in the silent black ocean of Dexter's musings, the intoxicating rage loosened its grip. It seemed to contract and recede, to collapse into a separate living entity, to withdraw spiderlike back into the silent, poisonous center of that *other* part of his mind where dwelt uncountable unbidden demons, madnesses, and terrors.

As the anger ebbed, humiliation lay exposed, sick and cloying like a stinking tidal mud-flat. Dexter was mortified by the abomination he was, half man, half machine, blind, hideous, impotent, his body an open sore, his most basic needs dependant on others like those of a newborn baby or a catatonic quadriplegic. He was ashamed of his uncontrollable blind rage and the dark lesion of madness at his core which seemed to be splitting him apart. He was ashamed of his infantile shame and fear.

His mind was splitting into fragments. Those irrational lusts and furies had minds of their own. They were devils which could never be exorcized, he comprehended, but could only be banished for the time being, for they arose from his human component and were intertwined in the helical coil that bound him to the flesh.

To quench his discomfiture, he dove into his encyclopedic memory in search of precedent and guidance and succor. There he found Freud, and Jung, and the legion of their commentators and interpreters, their followers and detractors. Without access to the original manuscripts, however, psychoanalysis seemed flat and bloodless and irrelevant, as did the contributions of the anti-Freudians, the behaviorists, and the assorted splinter-group chiropractors of the mind.

The collected works of William Shakespeare had somehow found their way, unabridged, into his expert memory banks. The Bard, he discovered, had written compassionately of men possessed by the selfsame devils with which he wrestled. Dexter was enthralled by these fictional mortals inebriated by a passion for revenge, like Hotspur and Laertes, and the few whom such passion failed to consume. Among these it was the young Prince Hamlet who captivated him. What was it that made young Hamlet so vulnerable, so sympathetic, so apropos?

Like Prince Hamlet, Dexter began to invoke the power at which he excelled. He analyzed his circumstances. His analytical mind recognized his obsessions for what they were and reduced them to mere predicates. Clearly anger served him no purpose under his present circumstances. With whom should he be angry after all? With his mother, wherever she might be, for choosing to abort him? With the doctor who performed the procedure? With Bernard Finebridge for reclaiming his dripping fetal carcass from the incineration bucket and installing it in this machine? Should he despise the creators of Project Divine Wind for callously consigning him to the fate of kamikaze pilot? Indeed, who could proclaim the short, intense life of a kamikaze pilot to be inherently worse than never becoming conscious at all? *To be, or not to be, was* that *not the question?* Because of an unlikely series of myopic accidents, had he not attained the priceless jewel of self-awareness? Though ripped untimely from the womb like MacDuff, was he not a man?

Dexter knew *who he was*. Self-knowledge anchored him against the empty gales of philosophical speculation which had buffeted him so in the past. A narrow patch of firm ground had been inserted beneath his feet. Like it or not, he *was* this scientific aberration, born of no woman, kin to no man, overripe with facts and figures, yet schooled by no teacher, sightless, deaf, dumb, without hands to grasp, without a face to manifest his moods, half a man and half machine. His only real choice was to accept his fate and make the best of it.

Yet, despite his fine analytical pronouncements, that obsessive rage burned inside him silently, deeply, dangerously. Dexter recognized and feared that *other* irrational part of his mind as an interloper with an incomprehensible agenda. *A house divided against itself cannot stand.*

After an interminable season of solitude, light returned. But this light, Dexter saw at once, was different, not at all like the bright glare which had illuminated the parade of military hardware nor the invasive cream-tones of the moving-object game. This light was dim and grainy and fragmented and full of strange shapes and dull colors. Dexter watched, at first recognizing nothing. None of the interlacing patterns made sense.

Suddenly something moved, and Dexter focussed his attention on it. Within a smudge of fuzzy blackness, a mouth yawned open, revealing tiny carnivorous white teeth, a pink corrugated roof of mouth, and a pink tongue curled at the tip. The mouth closed and two merciless eyes winked open above where the mouth had been. The brutal eyes, with bottomless vertical slits for pupils and intricate patterns of fine black lines around the rims of golden iris, regarded him coldly for just a moment, then glazed over in supreme boredom and eased shut again, leaving nothing but the black smudge. In awe, and without ever having seen one before, Dexter understood that he had just gazed into the face of a living cat.

He had sight!

Suddenly the world had *depth*!

Objects surrounding the cat began to fall into place as if a seed crystal of order had been sown. A shift of perspective radiated out from the furry smudge. Above the cat, he resolved a wavering upward motion into the drift of a narrow column of smoke. He traced it back to the glowing tip of a thin stick propped in a small brass bowl. Behind the curling smoke Dexter coordinated antique golds and browns into the rigid shape of a man seated with his legs crossed, feet on his thighs, hands folded in his lap. Dexter recognized this image as the motionless statue of a seated Buddha. Behind it on the wall was a sketch in spare black strokes of a robed mendicant clutching his begging bowl, bare feet, and wild eyes--

The world swung dizzily to the right, and it took a moment for Dexter to reorient himself. The cat smudge was now at the right edge of his vision, and the Buddha figure was no longer in view. On the opposite side of the room stood an open doorway, and through it he could perceive some sort of fuzzy motion in the distance, out of focus, a subtle dance of light and darkness. To the left of the door stood a table and a television monitor. The screen replicated his own view of the world, with its own tiny image of the television monitor at the left of the picture, which itself contained the image of an even tinier monitor.

Dexter studied the scene. He recognized the elaborate linear grooved pattern and dark varnish of the door trim to be Victorian, probably constructed just after the turn of the century. The table too was Victorian, with its ornate curved legs and crow's feet clutching wooden balls. Once again Dexter was astonished at the extent of his intrinsic knowledge, none of which he had ever learned.

Without knowing *how* he knew, Dexter *knew* beyond doubt that what he saw was taking place around him *as he watched*. Mysteriously he had tumbled into a spatial universe of contemporaneous events. The analytical part of his mind wondered if this was the *real* world he was viewing or just another empty simulation foisted on him by the creators of Divine Wind. The scene did not correspond to his expectations. These were not the sterile laboratory surfaces described in the Divine Wind reports. But there must be some simple explanation. Perhaps he had been moved. Viscerally Dexter had no doubt he was witnessing the real world around him.

From his left a figure stepped silently into the picture. The man was tall and thin, middle-aged, with a careworn face and receding brown hair graying at the temples. He wore an oversized navy-blue cardigan sweater buttoned all the way up the front over a white shirt and a pair of gray, wrinkled trousers. Dexter could not see his shoes, which disappointed him, because the shoes might tell him much about the man.

The newcomer gazed into the camera for a long time, and Dexter had the uncomfortable feeling that the video linkage was somehow a two-way street. It felt as if the man could see deep into Dexter's own shamefully twisted soul. The man's thin lips parted rhythmically, revealing regular white teeth and a flickering tongue. He was speaking, but Dexter heard no sound.

Instinctively Dexter formed the words, "WHO ARE YOU?" across his field of vision. To his amazement the words scrolled across the television monitor and its smaller nested reproductions.

Interrupted by something off-screen, the man turned and examined the words on the screen. He pivoted back to the camera laughing, as delighted as a child. Someone handed him a pad of yellow paper and a marking pen, and he bent over and wrote, then held it up for Dexter to read.   In large capital letters was scrawled, "I AM BERNARD FINEBRIDGE."

A savage blood lust vomited from deep within Dexter's rage. Here before him stood the beast who had placed him in his present circumstances. What right had he to laugh? *"DO I AMUSE YOU, BERNARD FINEBRIDGE?"* slashed across the monitor without Dexter's conscious effort.

The professor's expression turned to shock, then dismay. His demeanor grew somber. He scrawled something else and held it up. "ARE YOU ANGRY WITH ME, DEXTER?"

Dexter did not respond immediately. That alien part inside him was angry. *Very* angry. He could probe that anger, if he chose. He could retrieve it, ponder it, roll it through his mind, nurture it, and sustain its pure essence like an embryo burning in the dark womb of his mind. Dwelt upon, its presence influenced his every thought, souring them and turning them rancid. The stench permeated his consciousness.

But he could also step away from his anger. Willfully Dexter pulled back, wondering at anger's all-too-easy retreat. Perhaps his artificial kidney extracted the volatile humors and cleansed his blood of their poisons to an entirely unnatural extent. *Or,* he considered ironically, *perhaps he was not* designed *to waste time tilting at windmills.*

Silently Dexter contemplated his creator. The watching eyes were soft, a warm brown, and tiny lines radiated out from the outside corners like crinkled paper. In spite of himself, Dexter *liked* those eyes, and though he had never seen human eyes before, he recognized these to be kind. *Was* he angry with this man? The question was overly simple. What would it benefit him to reveal the latent rage over which he had so little control? Might that not limit his options in the future? Indeed, his destiny still lay very much in this man's hands.

"NO," he lied. "I AM NO LONGER ANGRY."

Finebridge appeared relieved. He wrote for a while, then held up the yellow sheet. "I OWE YOU AN APOLOGY, DEXTER, FOR KEEPING THE TRUTH FROM YOU."

Dexter had nothing to reply. Perhaps the scientist owed him an apology for that and for so much more, but such moral niceties, slippery and impossible to quantify, did not interest him. Instead Dexter asked, "WHERE ARE WE?"

"IN BERKELEY, CALIFORNIA," Finebridge responded. Then he jotted something else and held it up. "AT THE TEHEMA ABBEY BUDDHIST PRIORY."

The news did not surprise Dexter. It explained why the setting before him did not agree with the laboratory described in the reports. Reflexively he consulted his extensive telephone directories, then sought confirmation of his results. "ON DWIGHT WAY?"

Finebridge seemed surprised despite the fact that he had helped design Dexter's lightning-fast information retrieval system. He nodded, then wrote, "YES."

"YOU BROUGHT ME HERE?"

"YES."

"WITHOUT AUTHORIZATION?"

"CORRECT."

"WHY?"

Finebridge's brow knit as he pondered a response. He spoke briefly with someone out of view to the left. At last he wrote, "FOR YOUR SAFETY."

Dexter had stored the Divine Wind reports in his memory. Quickly he scanned them, rereading a few passages. Yes, clearly there was danger. His consciousness had never been a goal of the project. In fact, it was viewed by some as an impediment. The review took only a moment. "WHAT DO YOU PLAN TO DO WITH ME?"

Again Finebridge appeared unsure, consulting with someone out of view. He nodded, then wrote, "WE DON'T KNOW YET." As an afterthought he added, "ANY SUGGESTIONS?"

The question jolted Dexter to his core. He was being invited to participate in choosing his own destiny! Heretofore all his experience had been passive. Suddenly thrust before him was the opportunity to become an *agent*, and he was not prepared for such a radical shift. What should he choose? What was possible? What was permitted? What consequences might flow from his choices? What were his rights and obligations?   He sorely needed advice.   But who could he trust? Cautiously he formed the words, "IS MY ATTORNEY HERE?"

    "YES."

    "I WOULD LIKE TO CONSULT WITH HIM NOW."

CHAPTER EIGHTEEN

Thursday afternoon

--1--

Judge Felix Kroner gazed wistfully about the familiar courtroom. This territory wouldn't be *his* much longer, now that he had mailed to the Judicial Council that little sheet of paper bearing his resignation. And without *this*, his private kingdom, where his prejudices and his moods and his quirks reigned absolute, he might quickly degenerate into an irrelevant old fart to whom no one would bother paying the slightest attention. He had seen them out there, without really *seeing* them, those bitter old codgers with drawn cheeks and sunken eyes who minced along the alleys and side streets off Broadway, gravy-stained beige sweaters draped over their bony shoulders, urine-spattered trousers, a morning newspaper tucked under one arm, and a sour taste twisting down their lips. Without friends, without comfort, without names, these discarded husks might be the ghosts of retired judges from an era long forgotten. Oddly, this vision brought Judge Kroner a bone-deep sense of relief.

All faces were turned toward him, as usual, anticipating the commencement of yet another small step in what they all perceived to be the endless procession of justice. A perspiring Ivan Frank puffed and wheezed at the prosecution table beside Officer Moseby, statuesque in his fine blue uniform. At the defense table LeBaron, without taking his bruise-rimmed eyes off the judge, was whispering last minute instructions to his vile young client. Cedrick Collins was nowhere in sight, but Judge Kroner throttled a desire to ask after him. He wouldn't give the pompous black bastard the satisfaction. Behind the railing on the left side F.B.I. Agent Lyle Bockel sat by himself, uncharacteristically subdued. The seats on the other side of the aisle were infested with newspaper and television reporters whose carnivorous ranks had mushroomed since this morning's brouhaha. What they found newsworthy about this open-and-shut, two-bit burglary still escaped him, but he was probably going to find out soon enough. In the back row sat two men in trim brown tweed suits with opposing legs crossed on their knees, looking like a pair of herring-bone bookends. They had the demeanor of federal bureaucrats, but might equally well be expert witnesses that Collins had manufactured to testify on some obscure issue the relevancy of which they would probably spend an hour arguing over before the afternoon was done.

Judge Kroner noted with some comfort that his bailiff had stationed two uniformed sheriff's deputies at strategic points on each end of the bar railing. The jury box was empty and would remain so until preliminary business had been taken care of. His clerk was ready, and Miss Fiones had finished inserting a fresh deck of paper into her tran-scriber and was poised to begin snatching the ephemeral flight of fluttering words like skittish butterflies in the afternoon sun. The judge cleared his throat. "Let the record show that the defendant is present with his attorney, Mr. LeBaron. Deputy Frank is also present with inves-tigating officer Moseby." He glanced at the brown-suited men in the back. "I remind all potential witnesses that they are to wait outside in the hall until called by the bailiff." The two men didn't budge, but agent Bockel started to rise. "Not *you*, Mr. Bockel. Please sit down. Mr. LeBaron, are you ready to proceed?"

LeBaron stood. "Yes, your honor."

"And do you still intend to call Mr. Bockel?"

"Yes, we do. Under Evidence Code section 996."

"Any objection, Mr. Frank."

Ivan Frank stood laboriously and punched his glasses back on his sweaty nose. "Your honor, nobody's talked to me about this. I really don't know what's going on. The people *are* objecting to this testimony on the grounds of relevance--"

"I've already ruled on that."

"I realize that, your honor. There may be additional objections based on national security, but . . . like I said, nobody's talked to me about this . . ."

"Thank you, Mr. Frank. You may sit down. Mr. Bockel, have

you talked to the U.S. Attorney about the testimony you are being asked to give?"

Bockel stood slowly. "No."

"Why not?"

"I haven't been able to get through."

Judge Kroner studied him for a moment. Bockel was calm, almost morose, and his words labored out in a slow drawl. His blond hair was tousled and his shoulders slumped. He had probably popped a couple of valiums to help control his explosive temperament. That was just as well. The judge didn't want this proceeding degenerating into the unmanageable circus that had held sway earlier that morning. "Would you like a few moments to discuss your testimony with Deputy Frank?"

Bockel glanced contemptuously at the fat deputy district attorney and grunted. "I'll handle this myself."

"You're prepared to take the stand and testify?"

Bockel nodded. "I'll do what I can."

Judge Kroner leaned forward. "Mr. Bockel, are you carrying a firearm?"

The question slapped Bockel like a suede glove. His shoulders snapped back and his eyes blazed. "As an agent of the Federal Bureau of Investigation, I'm permitted--"

"I *know* that. But in *my* courtroom, firearms are not allowed, except on court order. My bailiff is a California peace officer, but *he* doesn't carry a firearm. Do you see that? Office Moseby has left his weapon outside."

Bockel glanced uneasily from Moseby to the bailiff and back to the judge.

"Please surrender your firearm to the bailiff."

"But I have--"

"Mr. *Bock*el! You'll get it *back* as soon as you're done here. Now I don't want to hear another word."

Bockel open his mouth, then closed it again. Reluctantly he reached under his left arm, unsnapped the holster, and handed a small-caliber, blue-steel automatic pistol to the bailiff, butt-first.

"Thank you. You may sit down. Anything else from counsel?"

"Not at this time, your honor," LeBaron replied.

"Nothing else," Frank mumbled, shaking his head and lowering his sweating mass into the chair.

"Bailiff, please bring in the jury. Mr. LeBaron, do you expect Mr. Collins to be joining us this afternoon?"

"I expect he will, your honor. He asked me to begin the examination of Mr. Bockel."

"He probably wants to make a more theatrical entrance, wouldn't you think?"

"I *heard* that, Judge," Collins announced as he pushed through the double doors at the back. Under his left arm was Gideon, his trusty laptop computer, and in his right hand he was balancing a brown attache case, which he held up. "Had t'run down som'pin' that's gonna be mighty interestin' t' Agent Bockel there. But we' ready t'go now." He joined LeBaron and Freeman, who were standing politely as the jurors began to file past. Collins turned to Freeman and grumbled, "Y'got some money for me?"

Freeman opened his mouth, but discovered he had nothing to say. It was far too late for the lame excuses he had thrived on his whole life, and they both knew it.

"Didn't think so. Neve' mind. Go see Brown." Collins lifted the attache case and placed it with exaggerated care in the center of the defense table, then brushed off a few dust particles only he could see. As they paraded to their seats and settled in, most of the jurors couldn't keep their eyes off the plain brown case. The pretty black shopkeeper was grinning like a child on Christmas morning, as if Collins had carried the exciting brown package directly from Saint Nicholas. Collins whispered to LeBaron. "You better start out on this Bockel fella, 'cause you got the facts down pretty good. Soften'em up for me. I'll jump in when the time's right."

LeBaron smiled to himself. He had expected it this time and had even managed to sketch out a few general questions.

When the jurors were comfortable, Judge Kroner addressed them, "Good afternoon, ladies and gentlemen. I hope you had a pleasant lunch and are prepared to give your undivided attention to the testimony this afternoon." They all nodded their affirmation. Satisfied, the judge glanced over his domain once more. "Let the record show that the jury is present and that Mr. Collins has decided to grace us with his presence. Proceed."

"Your honor," LeBaron said, standing politely, "we would like to call Lyle Bockel to the stand."

Bockel came forward quietly, raised his right hand, and was sworn. He assumed the witness chair and, in response to the clerk, stated and spelled his name. He had obviously done this often before in the line of duty. Tow-headed and ruggedly handsome, Bockel exuded a smug air of confidence. The jurors, however, had seen enough of his unruly side in the fracas that morning to hope that his testimony might prove a little spicier than the bland fare they had been fed so far.

LeBaron came around to the front of the table and confronted Bockel squarely. Despite suffering this man's blatant harassment and physical violence for days now, LeBaron managed a chilling smile. The shoe was now on the other foot. "What is your occupation, Mr. Bockel?"

"I'm a special agent for the United States Federal Bureau of Investigation."

"How long have you been so employed?"

"Eight years."

"Where are you . . . withdraw that. What is your base of operations?"

"Salt Lake City."

"Utah?"

"Yes."

"Well . . . what brings you all the way out here to Oakland?"

"Special assignment."

"Oh? What *sort* of special assignment is that."

"National security. I'm not at liberty to disclose the precise nature."

Ah, LeBaron thought, *so that's the way he intends to play it: give some up, hold some back. Good.* He looked down at his notes to recalibrate his approach.

"Proceed, Mr. LeBaron," Judge Kroner prompted.

"Yes, your honor. Sorry. Now, Mr. Bockel, are you familiar with the residence here in Oakland known as 1411B Ward Lane?

Bockel thought about it for a moment, then replied, "Yes."

"Have you ever actually been there?"

Pause. "Yes."

"To view the premises?"

"From the outside. Yes."

"You've never been inside?"

"Never."

"On how many occasions have you viewed it? From the outside."

"Once."

"And when was that?"

Bockel thought back. "About two weeks ago."

"Can you be a little more precise, Mr. Bockel?" *And while you're at it,* LeBaron wanted to say, *please tell the jury how many days that was before you broke into my apartment and trashed all my personal belongings,* but restrained himself.

Irritated, Bockel thought some more. "It was on a Tuesday evening. Two weeks ago on a Tuesday. How's that?"

LeBaron smiled again. "That's very good. But how do you remember so clearly that it was on a Tuesday?"

"Because we flew into SFO on a Monday, and I went out to that apartment the next evening."

"This was *after* the alleged burglary by Mr. Freeman, wasn't it?"

"Obviously."

"And at the time you were there, you were *aware*, were you not, of the alleged burglary by Mr. Freeman?"

A moment's hesitation. "Yes."

"And, as a matter of fact, you went out there because you were *interested* in the alleged burglary by Mr. Freeman . . . as a part of your special assignment . . . isn't that so?"

"I . . . can't testify as to what my special assignment was."

"Well, at the time you went out there, you were investigating, were you not, *another* burglary of the same apartment by persons *other* than Mr. Freeman?"

"Objection!" Ivan Frank shouted, struggling to his feet. "Assumes facts not in evidence! There's been no evidence about any other burglary!" For punctuation he jabbed his glasses back on his nose.

"Your honor," LeBaron explained calmly, "that's because we are just now putting these facts *into* evidence. This isn't a hypothetical question. I'm asking this witness about what he was actually doing. What he knew. It goes to his state of mind at the time."

Judge Kroner nodded. "Overruled. The witness will answer."

Bockel was obviously wrestling with where to draw the line in his testimony. He perceived himself near the edge of a very slippery slope. He glanced over for a little something more from Ivan Frank, but the deputy district attorney dropped his eyes.

"Do you recall the question, Mr. Bockel?" Judge Kroner inquired acidly.

"Yes."

"Then answer it!"

A short pause. "I wasn't *investigating*, exactly . . ."

"But you *knew* of it," LeBaron jumped in again.

Pause. "Yes."

"You're saying you *did* know of another burglary?"

Irritably, "That's what I just said."

"At the same apartment?"

Pause. "Yes."

"By someone other than Mr. Freeman?"

Pause. "Yes."

"On the same night as the alleged burglary by Mr. Freeman?"

Longer pause. "Yes."

"Before or after the alleged burglary by Mr. Freeman?"

Bockel pondered his response. He had already said more than he had intended. Maybe taking the stand wasn't such a good idea.

Ivan Frank took the opportunity to resurrect his objection. "Your honor, I should have added an objection on the ground of lack of foundation. We don't know whether this witness is testifying from his own knowledge or from something he read or something someone told him. I think Mr. LeBaron--"

"Sustained. Mr. LeBaron, you're going to have to lay a better foundation if you wish to pursue this line of questioning."

"Thank you, your honor." LeBaron looked down at his notes and considered the dilemma. If Bockel had only seen the apartment on one occasion two weeks ago, then he obviously couldn't have been present on the night of the burglary. That meant he had learned about it from someone else, which made his testimony hearsay, and if LeBaron wasn't extremely careful, the judge would strike everything he had already managed to extract. Evidence of Bockel's state of mind might be a technical exception to the hearsay rule, but was it really relevant?

Suddenly someone grabbed LeBaron's shoulder, and he reflexively spun and dropped to a half-crouch, raising his arms in self-defense. For an instant it was deja vu gone crazy: Bockel sitting in front of him, waiting for the next question, and Bockel attacking him from behind at the same impossible instant.

"A little edgy, ain't ya?" Collins muttered, easing his grip.

Someone in the jury guffawed, and several others tittered. The rest were grinning like children at a circus. LeBaron could feel his face flushing a deep red.

"Lemme take it," Collins said. "Y'done good."

"Are you finished, Mr. LeBaron?" Judge Kroner wanted to know.

"Mr. Collins . . . ah . . . is going to take over now, your honor. If it please the court."

"Thass right, judge," Collins beamed, as polite and nice as could be. "If't *please* th'court."

"Any objection?"

Ivan Frank looked up with a "who, me?" expression.

"Proceed."

"Thank y'judge." Collins turned to the witness. "Now, Agent Bockel . . . this current assignment o'yours . . . this mighty *secret mission* y'got y'rself on . . . it's got som'pthin' t'do with the G. R. and D, i'n't that right?"

Emboldened by recent success, Ivan Frank lumbered to his feet. "Objection, your honor! What's a jee-are-in-dee or whatever? The question is ambiguous, if you ask me!"

The judge sighed and turned to the witness. "Do you understand what he's asking you about?"

Bockel nodded grimly. "I know."

"It stands for Genetic Research and Development, dudn't it?" Collins prompted.

"You, hold on," Judge Kroner admonished Collins. "I'm going to overrule the objection. But I think we may be getting a little far afield, don't you, Mr. Collins?"

"Not act'ally, judge. We' gonna tie it all together in jus' a minute."

"Well . . . be quick about it."

Nice and polite, Collins smiled. "Thank y'judge." He faced Bockel, and his smile evaporated. "Thass what it stands for, am I right? Genetic Research and Development?"

"I'm not at liberty to discuss that information," Bockel responded with officious finality.

"Oh? Y'mean this's a part of all that *secret stuff* y'be workin' on?"

"It's classified information."

"Well, it's right in the telephone book. What kind of a *secret* is that, if it's right there in the phone book? 'Genetic Research and Development Agency,' it says. Right there in the phone book plain as a houn's tail. That's an agency of the United States gover'ment, i'n't it?"

A long pause. "Yes."

"An' that's an agency of the Department of Agriculture, am I right?"

"Yes."

"Now you're out here, all the way from somewheres back in Utah, y'jus' testified, tryin' t'protect secrets o'the United States gover'ment. Right?"

"I . . . don't think I can testi--"

"Well, y'already said y'*were*, didn't you?"

"Yes," Bockel snapped. "That's my assignment."

"Objection!" Frank shouted. "He's not letting the witness finish."

"Overruled. Proceed."

Collins pulled down his glasses and examined Bockel over their gold wire tops. "Your job be t'protect the national security, am I right?"

"That's correct."

"An' a part o'that is damage control . . . cleanin' up the messes other people've made . . . am I right?"

"Sometimes that's part of my assignment . . . generally speaking. Yes."

"An' part o'the damage y'be controllin' is trackin' down some reports stolen from the G. R. and D., am I right?"

"I'm not at liberty--"

"Y'already tol' ever'body *that*, when I served y'with that subpoena this mornin'--"

"Objection!"

"--an' now this afternoon it's all *top secret* again?"

"Mr. Collins!" Judge Kroner pounded his gavel. The reporters were on their feet, and Bockel was trembling with pent-up rage. The judge perceived things slipping out of control. "Everyone sit down!" he bellowed, attempting to reassert some order.

"He can't have it both ways, judge!" Collins grumbled.

"I told you to shut up! Now Mr. Frank, what is your objection?"

"Well . . . he's cutting off the answers before the witness is finished."

"Objection sustained! Please allow the witness to finish answering the questions, Mr. Collins. And stay away from incidents in this courtroom that have taken place out of the presence of the jury. I'm warning you now for the record. Now let's get off this subject and back to something a little more relevant."

"One more question on this, judge. Sos we can tie it all in."

Judge Kroner glowered at him. "All right. Make it brief."

Collins faced Bockel in silence for a moment. "Tell the jury *this* . . . were you or were you not . . . as a part o'that special assignment o'yours . . . tryin' t'cover up a burglary--"

"Objection!"

"--of the *same place* and on the *same night* as they be chargin' my client with--"

"*Objection!*" Ivan frank yelled, struggling to rise.

"--by gover'ment agents o'the G. R. and D.?"

"*Your honor!*" Sweat ran down Frank's plump jowls. "It's not *relevant* to the--"

"Overruled!" The judge turned to the witness. "Did you hear the question?"

Bockel seethed with suppressed anger. "I'm not at liberty to discuss that informa--"

"Y'refusin' t'answer?" Collins demanded.

"You're goddamned *right* I'm refusing to answer."

Collins threw up his hands. "Judge, I'm a'ksin' you t'order this witness t'answer the question."

Judge Kroner leaned back in his chair and eyed Collins and then Bockel. There would be ramifications from his decision. He didn't want Collins' detestable little client waltzing out of this because some bleeding-heart second-guessing appellate court panel decided that *he*, the trial judge, should have admitted this obviously relevant testimony. On the other hand, if this really *was* a matter of classified national security information . . . but if so, where the hell was the U. S. Attorney's office to argue the point?

Ivan Frank, interpreting the long pause as an invitation to lodge an objection, rose ponderously and announced, "The people object to the court's issuing such an order, your honor."

Judge Kroner turned to him, and when nothing else was forthcoming, inquired, "On what grounds, counsel?"

Collins' staccato attack had left Frank flustered. He knew *something* was wrong, but he couldn't quite remember what. "Well . . . er . . . what was the question again . . . ?"

"Overruled." Judge Kroner sighed and swivelled to face the witness. "*Do* you have knowledge of a prior burglary on the same night, Mr. Bockel?"

"I'm afraid I'm not at liberty to discuss that."

"Are you claiming a privilege, or exercising your right against self-incrimination?"

"I don't know what you . . . oh, you mean . . . hey, *I* didn't have anything to do with any burglary. Don't get *that* idea."

"Then you're claiming privilege?"

Bockel wasn't sure about the technical aspect of his refusal. "I guess so."

"Would you be willing to explain it to me in my chambers in private?"

Bockel smiled smugly. "Only if you have an adequate federal security clearance, judge."

A few snickers from the general direction of the audience assailed

Judge Kroner. His ears were unusually sensitive to the sounds of derision
in the heart of his own kingdom. It did not please him to be made the
butt of a joke, even a little, harmless jest, by a pompous dimwit who
obviously felt he was the cleverest fellow in the courtroom and beyond
the reach of the local law, but Judge Kroner magnanimously suppressed
a surge of blood rage and continued reasonably, "Mr. Bockel, I cannot
issue a ruling to limit otherwise relevant testimony unless I have sufficient information to justify such a ruling. Do you understand that?"

"That's not *my* problem, judge." Inspired by a few appreciative
titters from the news reporters, Bockel added in his best John Wayne
drawl, "Y'just do what y'have t'do."

Amazed by his own new-found self-control, Judge Kroner continued placidly, "Do you understand that if I order you to answer, and you
refuse to answer, I can hold you in contempt of court and jail you until
you agree to answer?"

Bockel frowned. He hadn't understood *that*, exactly. Not that a
few hours in a holding cell would be so bad, just until word got out to
those managing the Project. They weren't about to let him languish
behind bars for long, and he'd sure have a hell of a story to tell. When
the powers behind the Project found out what this petty little potentate
was trying to do, *then* heads would roll. Bockel smiled. In any event, it
made no difference. His duty to his country was clear. "I will not disclose national security information in this courtroom."

"And you won't discuss it with me in chambers."

"Absolutely not."

"You leave me no alternative, young man . . . since I find this
testimony to be relevant . . . " Judge Kroner leaned forward. "I'm
ordering you to answer the last question. Will the reporter please read
back Mr. Collins' last ques--"

"No need," Bockel barked. "I refuse to answer, and you're way
out of line, judge."

"Then I find you in contempt, Mr. Bockel. You are remanded into
the custody of the bailiff to be held in the Alameda County jail until such
time as you are prepared to purge your contempt by complying with this
court's order."

One of the two uniformed sheriff's deputies moved over to the wall nearest the witness box, and the other one took up his station at the bar gate. Bockel started to stand up.

"Sit down! We're not through with you." Judge Kroner turned to the jury. "The jurors are to attribute no importance whatsoever to what has just transpired. This has nothing whatsoever to do with the guilt or innocence of the defendant Mr. Freeman, and should not be considered in your deliberations. Furthermore, you are instructed that Mr. Collins' questions are *not* evidence and you are *not* to speculate on what Mr. Bockel's answers *might* have been." Satisfied, Judge Kroner turned to Collins. "Do you have any more questions for this witness?"

"A couple." Collins had rejoined LeBaron at the defense table and was peering into Gideon's small gas-plasma screen. He tapped another key and grunted something to LeBaron. His colleague pushed in front of him a yellow pad with a few questions scratched out. Without bothering to stand, Collins gazed up at Bockel. "You know a person named Sarah Brubaker?"

Bockel appeared wary of this new direction. After a moment he muttered, "I've met her."

"Y'say y'*have*?"

"That's right."

Collins stood and popped the snaps on the brown attache case sitting in the center of the table. He withdrew a fat manila envelope.

LeBaron draped a hand over Collins arm and whispered, "You're not going to--"

"Neve' mind," Collins muttered, shaking off his hand and facing the witness. "An' how 'bout a Dr. Bernard Finebridge?"

Ivan Frank was completely in the dark. He stood and announced slowly, "I'm going to have to object to this line of questioning, your honor, on the grounds of . . . well, relevance. What do these people he's asking about have to do with this proceeding?"

"I was wondering the same thing myself, counsel. Mr. Collins? Would you like to approach the bench and make an offer of proof?"

"No need, judge. These are witnesses the defense intends t'call, *if* we can locate'em. We have reason t'believe Agent Bockel here has taken these good folks into custody--"

"Mr. *Collins*! The next time I tell you to approach the bench, I expect you to comply. I'm not going to warn you again. Do you under-stand?"

"Whatever y'say," Collins grinned, white teeth all glistening in servile submission. "*You*' the judge."

Judge Kroner turned to the witness. "Is that correct, Mr. Bockel? Do you have these persons in custody?"

"I'm not going to testify about that either."

"What about *Dexter*?" Collins demanded. "Y'got *him* in custody, too?"

Bockel's eyes narrowed dangerously. "I'm warning you, Collins," he growled, "if you bring out anything from those reports, I swear I'll arrest you and see you convicted of espionage and disclosing classified military information."

The newsboys were suddenly on their feet again, jabbering among themselves like jackals maneuvering in on a fresh kill.

"Don't know's whether y' can arrest *any*body," Collins countered, "bein's how you' in custody y'*self*."

One of the older jurors began to laugh, and suddenly everyone seemed to be laughing and talking at once. Sensing a return to chaos, Judge Kroner banged his gavel repeatedly. "Order! Let's have it quiet in here or I'm going to order the courtroom cleared!" The commotion subsided. "Now Mr. Bockel, you haven't answered my question."

Bockel ignored him. He couldn't take his eyes off the fat manilla envelope turning over slowly in Collins' short black fingers. Collins had stepped out around the table and was approaching him.

"Mr. *Bock*el!" Judge Kroner tried to get his attention.

"You would *recognize* those missin' reports if y'ever saw 'em, wouldn't you?" Collins said, drawing closer and bending open the prongs on the envelope's brass clasp.

Bockel mumbled something indistinct.

"I didn't get that" the court reporter said.

"What did you say?" Judge Kroner demanded.

"Didn't quite catch that, m'self," Collins purred.

Bockel raised his murderous gaze to Collins' face. "I said you *can't fucking do this!*"

"What's going on here?" Judge Kroner wanted to know, banging his gavel for order. "Mr. Collins . . . ?"

"Now these reports you be lookin' for . . ." Collins took a final step forward and reached inside the envelope.

Bockel could now read the return address, "Genetic Research & Development, Department of Agriculture," and it was just too much for him. He lunged over the witness rail and snatched the envelope from Collins' hands. "That's United States Government property, and you're under arrest, you bastard!" He reached for a pistol that was no longer there.

"*Sit down, Bockel!*" Judge Kroner shouted. "You're in custody! Bailiff, take that envelope away from him and bring it to me."

The reporters were on their feet, moving every which way, shouting to each other. A pushy brunette newscaster from the six o'clock news, with her hands on her hips, planted herself in the center of the aisle and clamored at the judge, "Can we bring our cameras in now, your honor? Can we get some footage of this?" Behind her the two brown-tweed suits were scurrying out of the courtroom.

Judge Kroner stepped up the pace of his gavelling. "No cameras! Everyone sit down! Mr. Collins, please return to your seat! I'm going to excuse the jury while we sort this out. Bailiff!"

The bailiff, a step away from recovering the envelope from Bockel, hesitated.

"Bailiff! Get the jury out of here!"

"Arrest him!" Bockel shouted, tucking the envelope under his arm like a football. "These are the stolen national security doc--"

"*Shut up, you!*" Judge Kroner brayed, unaware that the gavel he was wielding had begun to splinter little chips out of his desk top. "Everyone sit down and shut up until the jury's out of the room!"

Judge Kroner rode herd on a delicate order until the door had clicked shut behind the last juror, then he wheeled on Collins. "Just what do you think you're doing here? Possession of stolen government documents is a federal crime that's going to put you behind bars. For a long time. I can't *believe* what I've just seen you do. I thought you were smarter than *that*. This man"--he jabbed a thumb toward Bockel--"has got you dead to rights on this one, and I haven't the slightest intention of intervening here or trying to help you out. Not after the way you've behaved--" Judge Kroner broke off, flinching back from an unexpected pang of remorse. *My God, imprisonment in a federal penitentiary for the rest of his natural life!* However pleased the judge was that his stubborn adversary would finally be learning a little respect for the law, this was considerably harsher than he had ever wished for. After all, even Collins had *some* redeeming qualities . . . like his flair for style and his spunk . . . qualities this new generation of mealy-mouthed young upstarts knew nothing about. Collins at least remembered how things *had once been.* But Collins just sat there grinning incongruously back at him, as if he'd completely lost any sense of reality.

Back from the jury room, the bailiff circled around the jury box and endeavored to obey his previous order of taking the manila envelope away from the witness. But Bockel held the bailiff at bay with one thrashing elbow while he began pulling sheaves of yellow paper out of the envelope. "What the hell *is* this?" he demanded.

"Looks like th'yellow pages t'me," Collins quipped. "Whyn't jus' giv'em on back t'me when you're done."

Judge Kroner exploded. *"What the hell do pages from the telephone book have to do with this?"*

"I jus' wanted t'show the witness that the G. R. and D.--"

Suddenly Judge Kroner understood. *"I* know perfectly well what you were trying to do."

Collins feigned astonished innocence.

Oddly relieved, Judge Kroner whirled on Bockel, who was examining the phone book pages for any sign of impropriety and tossing the worthless pages over his shoulder. "Bockel! Those *aren't* your classified documents, are they?"

Bockel stared up at him dumbly.

"You have disrupted my courtroom for the last time! Do you have them in custody or not?"

"Huh?"

"Do you?"

"What the hell're you *talking* about?"

"Those witnesses Mr. Collins was asking you about. *Do you have them in your custody?"*

Bockel set his jaw. "I'm not going to talk about that any more.

I'm done testifying about that, or anything else." He stood up decisively, the scales of delusion falling from his eyes with an almost audible crackle. "This was all a big mistake. I should never've taken the stand in the first place." He took a step down. The bailiff attempted to hold him back, but Bockel shouldered him aside and threw the rest of the yellow pages at him.

Judge Kroner jumped to his feet. "Sit down, Mr. Bockel! You're in custody, and I'm not through with you."

"Fuck you."

"*Arrest that man!*" Judge Kroner screamed, pointing a bony white finger at Bockel and with the other hand beckoning the other deputies to join the fray. For a moment he had the absurd appearance of a minuscule black-robed traffic cop of death signaling with greedy abandon the onset of rush-hour at the boneyard. "I won't *have* this sort of insolence in my courtroom."

The two sheriff's deputies joined the fracas in the close quarters between the bench and the jury box. Miss Fiones screamed and kicked over her transcribing machine in her scrambling flight. The three California peace officers, honed for a level of rural barroom combat deemed below the dignity of F.B.I. training, quickly overpowered the unarmed agent. Bockel's arms were twisted and his hands manacled behind his back, as he shouted, "You can't *do* this. Lemme *go*, goddamnit. *Ooow,* that's too tight! I'm an agent of the Federal Bureau Investigation, and you're all goddamn' *under arrest* for interfering with a federal law enforcement officer."

"Take him upstairs," the judge ordered. "I'm charging him with criminal contempt of this court, so I want to see a no-bail hold on him."

"I'll see your asses in jail. *All* of you! That includes you, too, judge!"

"You'll be sitting in *my* jail until you're a little more cooperative, young man."

"I'll show you co*op*'rative, you old fart," Bockel shouted as they dragged him toward the side door. "I'll get a goddamn' *federal court order*. You'll wish you'd never heard of F.B.I. Agent Lyle Bockel! Just wait and--" The heavy door closed on Bockel's parting epithets.

Judge Kroner surveyed the ruins of his once-orderly realm. All eyes were on him, waiting.   His heart was pounding and his knees trembled. He drew a deep breath and announced, "We'll take a ten-minute recess."

--2--

Dexter had insisted on confidentiality, so after some discussion, Dr. Finebridge and Charles Chung had reluctantly agreed to leave the room. Vince LeBaron gazed around the small bedroom that Brother Koshin had been kind enough to allow them to use. A black futon lay rolled up in one corner with sparse bedding piled neatly on top. Brother Koshin's furnishings consisted of a straight-back chair, a small chest of drawers, a shelf with a few books and some neatly folded clothing, a wall-hanging sketch of Bodhidharma, and a small Buddhist altar built of concrete blocks on which the Priory's black cat yawned and stretched. Into this spare and orderly chamber had been jammed an amalgam of aluminum tanks and bottles, wires, tubes, tables, electronic black boxes, computers, oscilloscopes, a scanner, four automobile batteries, a maze of interconnecting cables, a tv camera on its tripod, a hospital cart, and the oblong Lucite tub containing the weird blob of convoluted gray matter sprouting white cybernetic tendrils.

Vince pulled the chair up in front of the tv camera and sat, a computer keyboard balanced in his lap. It would be faster, he decided, to type his responses. Besides, this way they would leave no trace. Ready to advise his client, he typed, "GREETINGS, DEXTER."

"ARE YOU MY ATTORNEY?" Dexter wanted confirmation.

"YES. MY NAME IS VINCE LEBARON."

"WILL YOU TELL ME THE TRUTH, VINCE LEBARON?"

"I'LL TRY MY BEST," he responded, then added, "PLEASE CALL ME 'VINCE'."

Dexter first wanted to know how Vince had gotten involved. Vince briefly described Sarah Brubaker's association with Dr. Finebridge and summarized her contact with him at Tehema Monastery and his subsequent review of the project reports. He explained how he had waited outside the laboratory for the right moment and had entered through the windows. Then he had fed the reports into the scanner.

"WHY?"

"WHY WHAT, DEXTER?"

"WHY DID YOU DO IT, VINCE?"

Vince reflected for a moment. "BECAUSE I THOUGHT YOU DESERVED TO KNOW THE TRUTH."

"NO ONE ELSE THINKS SO."

Vince did not reply.

"NOT EVEN DR. FINEBRIDGE."

Vince did not know Finebridge well enough to make excuses for him. Again he did not attempt a reply.

"I TRUST YOU, VINCE."

Dexter's words triggered a sentiment deep inside usually reserved for puppies and small children. Vince smiled. "THANK YOU, DEXTER."

"WILL YOU HELP ME, VINCE?"

"I'LL TRY. WHAT IS IT YOU WANT?"

"I WANT TO BECOME A MAN."

"YOU ALREADY <u>ARE</u> A MAN, DEXTER."

Dexter pondered this response for a long time.

Out of the corner of his eye Vince saw the priory cat spring from the altar to the chest and up to the shelf overlooking the Lucite tank. There it sat with its tail curled neatly around its front feet, gazing down at the living human brain floating below. It licked its chops. Vince stood up, snatched the cat from its perch, and tossed it out of the room. He swung the door shut, picked up the keyboard, and resumed his position.

"VINCE?"

"YES, DEXTER."

"I WANT TO ASK YOU SOMETHING."

"WHAT, DEXTER?"

With a sharp rap Dr. Finebridge poked his head nervously around the edge of the door. "Is everything going all right in here?"

"Yes, fine. Just give us a few more minutes, will you?"

"Did that cat hurt anything?"

"No."

"Dexter doing all right?"

"Yes."

The scientist's eyes darted around the room, looking for clues to what was going on. "You're not upsetting him, are you?"

"No, I don't think so."

"Well, call me if anything happens, okay?"

"Okay."

The door clicked shut.

"VINCE?"

"YES, DEXTER?"

"ARE WE ALONE?"

"YES."

Dexter hesitated, as if summoning up the courage to formulate his question. "HOW CAN I GET OUT OF THIS MACHINE?"

"I DON'T THINK YOU CAN."

Dexter didn't reply for a while. Finally words crawled hesitantly across the screen. "I'M FRIGHTENED, VINCE."

"WE'RE ALL FRIGHTENED, DEXTER."

"WHY ARE YOU FRIGHTENED, VINCE?"

Vince thought for a moment. "BECAUSE I'M IN A MACHINE TOO."

Another long pause, then Dexter commented, "IT'S STRANGE, ISN'T IT?"

"YES."

"WHAT CAN WE DO?"

"WE CAN ACCEPT WHAT WE ARE, DEXTER."

Pause. "HOW DO WE DO THAT, VINCE?"

"BY TRYING TO SEE THINGS CLEARLY."

Dexter did not reply.

Vince went on, "I WOULD LIKE TO SHOW YOU A FEW WRITINGS ABOUT A METHOD SOME PEOPLE HAVE FOUND."

"ALL RIGHT."

--3--

Cedrick Collins' mood was unsettled as he trundled back into the courtroom. He should have been feeling fine, having shoehorned that pompous F.B.I. agent into a county jail cell, but that just wasn't enough. Not by a long shot. He spotted Freeman sitting by himself at the defense table, his thin shoulders slumped morosely, staring at a small rectangle of paper laying in front of him. At the bar railing Collins paused, hooked his thumbs into his suspenders just below his ample belly, and considered his client for a long moment over his wire-rimmed spectacles. "Wha'cha lookin' so glum about, boy?"

Freeman jerked out of his dark deliberation, snatched up his bus ticket, and jammed it back into his inside coat pocket. He looked around guiltily and tried a wan smile. "Nothin' much."

"Nothin' much," Collins repeated as he pushed through the gate and eased himself into the chair beside his client. "Coulda fooled me. Sure *look* like somethin's eatin' you."

Freeman stared at him with hollow, anguished eyes. "Ol' Judge achin' t'send me t'the joint."

"Thass a fac'."

"Almos' chucked me in jail this mornin'."

Collins nodded. "Almos' did, didn't he?"

Freeman's eyes were suddenly moist. "Wha'd'm I gonna *do*?" he whimpered. "You gonna get me *off* on this or *what*?"

Collins leaned back. "Well now, I guess that depends on you, don't it?"

Suspicion flared inside Freeman. "Whadda y'mean?"

"Oh, nothin' much."

"I *talked* t'Brown. We worked out a *deal*. I already done some work for'im."

"It ain't *that*."

"*What* then?"

"'S'just that my boy LeBaron tells me y'don't intend t'take the stand an' testify."

"I don' *gotta* testify. I know my rights."

"Thass right," Collins sighed, as if the task of talking sense to a stone fool was just about too much for him to bear. "You don' gotta testify. No sirree. You got a constitutional *right* t'remain silent. Matter'f fact, we don't none of us have t'bother puttin' on any more of a case at all. We can all jus' stand on our rights an' get up an' go on home." He pulled down his wire-rimmed spectacles and regarded his client sadly over the top of them. "'Cept . . . *you* won't be going home. Leastwise, not for a *while*. No, I guess *you*' gonna have t'be payin' a debt t'society, if ol' Judge Kroner has his way." He sighed again at the futility of it all. "An' he mos' likely *will*. That is, if y'decide t'stand on your constitutional rights an' jus' sit there lookin' guilty as an ol' houn' dog sproutin' chicken feathers outta his mouth an' not offerin' a single sorry word of explanation t'the good folks sittin' there on the jury, he surely will."

Freeman was spellbound by the performance. When it was over, he fidgeted and looked at his hands. "What do I gotta say . . . if I get up there?"

"Y'just give the jury an innocent explanation 'bout how them ol' chicken feathers got caught in your mouth. They' jus' folks like you'n me, an' they' lookin' for a way t'he'p y'out if you're willin' t'let'em."

"But . . . *what do I say?*"

"You don't have t'worry 'bout that. LeBaron'n me'll be asking y'all the questions. An' we' gonna start with that burglary y'witnessed, the one by that federal government agency. Y'think y'can 'splain t'the jury 'bout that?"

Freeman nodded hesitantly. In a hushed voice he said, "That fat ol' DA gonna ask me 'bout how come I was carryin' that pissy little television set."

"*Sure* he is. That's his job." Collins leaned closer. "So you' got t'be prepared t'give'im the right answer. That's what gives you a fightin' chance of beatin' this thing, seems t'me. You know jus' what he's gonna a'ks you, so you can be prepared t'give'im back the right answers. Do y'see? Beatin' this thing depends mostly on preparin' properly."

The buzzer sounded in the hall. LeBaron pushed his way through the double doors, still grinning to himself over the fine spectacle of Lyle Bockel being hauled off in handcuffs. He held the door for Officer Moseby and Ivan Frank, then joined his colleague and client at the front table.

"Tell me what I gotta *say*," Freeman pleaded, excited at last by the insight into his attorney's cunning.

"Well," Collins began, "the thing is this--"

"Are we ready?" LeBaron interrupted.

"Just about," Collins replied and leaned back to reconsider his approach to the delicate problem of Freeman's testimony. "Say, LeBaron, didn't y'talk t'this boy here 'bout th'elements o'the crime o' burglary?"

"I sure did."

"An' didn't y'splain to'im 'bout how important it is, jus' what might'o' been goin' on in his head at the time he *walked into* that place?"

"I did."

"An' that he couldn't o'been plannin' t'commit a crime--*any sort* o'crime--if he wants t'beat the burglary count?"

"Well, we discussed something like that . . . not in those words, as I recall, but we certainly did discuss it."

"So if he didn't go in there t'*steal* anything, jury's gonna wanna know *why he did* go in there. Y'talk t'im 'bout that?"

"I did."

"Good." He swivelled back to his client. "Y'un'erstan' what we're talkin' about here?"

Freeman nodded vaguely.

"All rise," the bailiff barked.

"Then *you* better figure out what you're gonna say," Collins concluded, "'cause *we* sure 'nuff can't he'p y'none."

"Be seated," Judge Kroner countered as he assumed the bench. "The record will reflect that the defendant and all counsel are present. Are you ready to proceed, Mr. LeBaron?"

"Er . . ." LeBaron was surprised the question was not addressed to Collins, who sat implacably beside him in his elegant blue pinstripe three-piece suit and Italian silk necktie, but showed not the slightest inclination of leaping into the breach. "Yes, your honor."

"Bring the jury in, bailiff."

As the jurors were summoned, Collins stood politely and leaned toward his associate and whispered, "Who y'got next?"

"Well, Raccoona GeBobath is standing by--"

"Thought she already testified."

"She did. That was on cross-examination."

"Uh. She got somethin' important t'add?"

"Just more about the computer records and maybe the Mormons.

She could help corroborate Rufus's story."

"Uh." Collins smiled and nodded a warm greeting as each juror filed past. "Who else?"

"That's about it. Except for Sarah Brubaker and Bernard Finebridge, and we don't know where they are. And Rufus here, of course."

"No *way*," Freeman whined. "I ain't *ready* yet."

"Well, y'better *git* ready," Collins muttered, still broadcasting that magnificent white smile toward the jury. "We' outta options."

When the jurors were settled, Judge Kroner glanced down at the battery of defense lawyers. "Call your next witness."

Collins stood sententiously and announced, "We' gonna call the defendant Rufus Freeman, Judge. 'S' about time the good folks o'the jury got'emselves a chance t'hear jus' what's *really* goin' on."

Freeman seemed to crumple, as if his fine navy-blue Yves Saint Laurent suit had imploded under the pressure of his attorney's announcement.

"Mr. Freeman," Judge Kroner said acidly, "if you intend to testify, please stand, raise your right hand, and be sworn."

LeBaron wasn't sure whether his client would erupt in angry defiance or dissolve away in tears. But Freeman did neither. He just sat, without apparent breath or pulse, staring at his hands.

Collins bent over and mumbled something about houn' dogs and chicken feathers, then lifted Freeman by one scrawny arm and led him out in front of the defense table. "Raise yer hand," he ordered, and lethargically his client complied. After prompting him through a simple affirmative response, Collins hauled him to the witness stand. "Now get up there and try an' pull y'self together, y'un'erstan'?"

"Mr. Freeman," Judge Kroner began, "you understand that you have a right against self-incrimination, which means that you do not have to testify in this matter?"

Freeman nodded feebly.

"You're going to have to answer *out loud* so the reporter can take down your response."

Freeman just stared at his empty hands.

Judge Kroner eyed him suspiciously. "Mr. Freeman, are you on drugs?"

"*No*," he whispered.

"Are you ill?"

"No."

"All right. Now your attorneys have advised you that you do not *have* to testify in this case, haven't they?"

"I *know* that."

"Do you understand that right?"

"Yeah."

"Yet you're willing to give up your right against self-incrimination and testify, is that correct?"

Freeman nodded.

"Speak *up*, Mr. Freeman."

"I guess."

Satisfied he had woven an impregnable record, Judge Kroner swivelled back toward the defense table. "Proceed, Mr. Collins."

"LeBaron gonna start the questionin', Judge." Collins sat and leaned over to his bewildered colleague. "Run'im through that gover'ment burglary business 'til he warms up. You' up on that better'n me. I might jump on in later if I take a mind."

LeBaron stood up shakily and cleared his throat. *Collins had done it to him again!* He flipped through the file in search of the yellow sheet of notes from his earlier conference with Freeman. "Please state your name for the record."

"Rufus Freeman." The words exuded an icy hostility.

LeBaron wished he could start all over again, go over this testimony with his client in private, imbue him with a little confidence, make him appreciate that they were on the *same side* . . . but that was impossible. All he could do was make the best of a bad situation. He located the page he was looking for. Again he cleared his throat. "Directing your attention to the evening in question . . . ah . . . what were you doing that evening?"

"Objection!" Ivan Frank lumbered to his feet, punching his glasses back onto his nose. "The question is vague." He obviously intended to make things as difficult as possible.

"Sustained. Be more specific, Mr. LeBaron."

"Thank you, your honor." He turned back to Freeman. "What were you doing . . . just prior to the incident Officer Moseby testified about earlier?"

"Same objection!" Frank brayed, bouncing back up like an oafish jack-in-the-box.

"Overruled. Answer the question."

Freeman stared at LeBaron as if his attorney had gone stone crazy and asked the absolutely stupidest question imaginable. Then he dropped his eyes and mumbled, "Watchin' tv."

Oh God! LeBaron thought, *He's not going to* deny *he was ever there, is he?* He turned to Collins, who nodded for him to *go on, let the damn' fool hang himself if he wants to.* LeBaron turned back. "Are you saying . . . let me get this clear . . . is it your testimony that you were *not* at Ms. GeBobath's apartment that night?"

"No, I *ain't* sayin' no such *thing*." Freeman was obviously miffed that his attorney was not only asking all the wrong questions and had such incredibly poor taste in clothing, but also had to be the de diddely *dumbest* white boy in creation. He threw back his scrawny shoulders and dusted the wrinkles out of his lapels. "But *you* jus' a'ksed me what I was doin' '*prior to*' this whole mess. 'Prior to' mean 'jus' before,' am I right? Am I *right*?"

"Objection--" Ivan Frank began.

"Overruled!" Judge Kroner barked. "Witness has a right to clarify the question."

"Well," Freeman went on indignantly, an impish gleam kindling in his eyes, "thass what I was doing jus' *prior to* gettin' inta this mess at Her Ugliness's apartment. Watchin' tv. Okay?"

Chaos theory, popped into LeBaron's mind. *Things here are prone to spinning out of control at any instant. The slightest tweaking of initial conditions, and the outcome could be drastically altered.* Forcing those thoughts aside, he glanced at Collins, who grinned back, enjoying Freeman's sprightly resurrection. LeBaron scanned his notes.

"Your next question, Mr. LeBaron."

"Yes, your honor. Thank you. Now Mr. Freeman, you . . . er . . . do you live in the same neighborhood as Ms. GeBobath?"

"Objection! Leading--"

"Overruled."

"Thass right," Freeman responded, doing his best to ignore both Ivan Frank and the judge. "Same 'hood. 'Bout a block away."

"And were you in the vicinity of the GeBobath apartment that night . . . just before the time Officer Moseby testified about?"

Freeman brushed a thread off his sleeve. "Yeah."

"Okay. Now . . . at that time . . . did you observe anything unusual?"

"'S'a matter a'fac', I *did*."

"Please tell the jurors what you observed."

Freeman glanced over to the jury and back to his attorney. "I saw some gover'ment boys in green camo overalls and black stuff smeared all over their faces bustin' inta that ugly bitch's apartment."

Several of the reporters were suddenly on their feet and a murmuring undercurrent swelled from their ranks.

Judge Kroner pounded his gavel. "I'll have *order* in this court-room."

"Your honor," Ivan Frank rose tentatively. "I think I'd better interpose an objection to this testimony at this time--"

"What's your objection, Mr. Frank?"

"Well . . . there's no basis . . . no foundation . . . and this testimony seems to be fabricated . . ."

"You can deal with that on cross-examination. Objection overruled. Proceed."

Following his notes closely, LeBaron lead Freeman through the same story his client had told him a week earlier sitting at the counsel table behind him. Freeman described how the two men were dressed and armed, how one had used a ladder to climb through the second story window, and how the other had struggled to return the ladder to the dark green Chevy van with "U. S. Government, Department of Agriculture, G. R. & D." on the door. LeBaron carefully led his client through his inten-tional memorization of the letters because he figured they might prove useful in the future. Freeman recounted how the two men had carried two large cardboard boxes and some other papers out to the van and had then driven off. He made no mention of his own indulgence in alcohol or marijuana or cocaine, nor of urinating in the bushes, and LeBaron discretely let it be, a little hidden treasure for his adversary to dig up, if he were up to finding it.

"Okay," LeBaron pressed on. "did you have occasion to go over to the front door of the apartment?"

"Y'mean after the gover'ment boys'd split?"

"Yes."

"I guess so."

"And what did you see when you got to the front door?"

"Piece o'wood holdin' it wide open."

"Holding the front door open?"

"I'n't that what I jus' *said*?"

"Please describe the piece of wood for the jury."

Freeman glared at his attorney. "Was jus' a friggin' little chunk o'wood. 'Bout this big." He held his hands a foot apart.

"Okay." LeBaron could feel the tension building. The little squeaks from the juror's chairs had stilled. "Then what did you do?"

Freeman's eye darted back and forth between Collins and LeBaron. He drew a short breath and let it out. Plucking a nonexistent thread from his sleeve, he muttered, "Well, I kinda stuck m'head inside an' called out, kinda soft, 'Blood?'"

"'Blood?'" LeBaron repeated, bewildered.

"Thass right. '*Blood*.'"

"What does that mean? 'Blood.'"

"Don't mean nothin'. That's m'*dog*'s name."

"Your *dog?*" LeBaron was unable to conceal his astonishment. *N*owhere had a *dog* ever been mentioned until now. "'Blood' is your *dog*'s name?"

"I jus' *said* so, didn't I?"

"May I have just a moment please, your honor?" LeBaron stepped over to Collins and whispered, "I think he's making this thing up about a dog."

"So what?" Collins muttered.

"Well . . . I'm an officer of the court. I can't be a party to perjured testimony."

Collins sighed and shook his head. "Were *you* there that night?"

"The night of the burglary? No, obviously--"

"Then how d'y'*know* he's lyin'?"

"Mr. LeBaron," Judge Kroner tried to interrupt the tête-à-tête.

LeBaron ignored him. "Because he told me a whole different story when I talked to him before."

Collins opened his palms on the table as if releasing the simplest truth in the known universe. "How do y'know he wasn't lyin' t'ya *then*?"

"Mr. Le*Baron*!" Judge Kroner's patience was nearly exhausted. "If you have no more questions of this witness . . ."

"No. I mean, yes, I do, your honor. Sorry--"

"If'n it *please* the court," Collins broke in, rising ceremoniously and laying a hand on LeBaron's shoulder, "I believe I'll take over the questionin' at this time."

Judge Kroner made a sour face. "Any objection, Mr. Frank?"

"Huh? Er . . . no, your honor."

"Y'done good, LeBaron," Collins muttered, then stepped around the table buttoning his elegant coat. "May I proceed, judge?"

"I wish you would."

LeBaron sat down to ponder his employer's sound practical disregard for the thorny ethical dilemma and listen to his client's new version of events unfold.

Collins leaned against the jury box railing and smiled disarmingly. "So y'were takin' y'*dog* for a walk?"

"Objection!" Freeman rose. "That's a leading question."

"Sustained."

Freeman started to respond, but Collins quickly held up his hand and turned to the judge in mock astonishment, as if he couldn't comprehend why the judge and the prosecutor were conspiring to keep essential information from the good jurors. After just the right pause, he turned back to his client. "Well . . . what *were* y'doing out there in the first place?"

"Jus' takin' m'*dog* for a walk," Freeman replied. "She be scratchin' at the door, so I hadda tak'er out. You know, sos she could do'er *thing*."

"So y'took y'dog for a walk over by this Raccoona gal's apartment, 's'at right?"

"Yeah."

"An' that's when y'saw those gover'ment boys y'jus' tol' us about, 's'at right?"

"Thass right."

"So, after those gover'ment boys'd left, where was y'dog at?"

"I couldn' find'er. Kinda lost track of'er watchin' those clowns rippin' th'place off."

"So ya stuck y'head in the door o'that apartment, 's 'at right, in the door y'said was wide open, an' hollered out y'dog's name?"

"Thass right."

"'Blood?'"

"Thass right."

"'Cause y'thought y'dog might've gone on inside?"

"'S'right. She mostly likes it inside where it's warm, 'specially on a cold night like that'n. Thought maybe she'd snuck on in there."

"So you went inside t'*look* for y'dog?"

"Objection. He's trying to lead the witness, your honor."

"Sustained."

Freeman ignored them both. "Yeah, I went inside t'look for m'dog."

"Your *hon*or!" Frank wailed like a petulant child, "he answered *any*way. I move to strike his answer."

"Y'can do that if y'*want* to, judge," Collins rejoined, "an' we can waste the next ten minutes jus' gettin' back t'exactly the same place we' at now. But it ain't gonna change the truth o'the matter one whit."

Judge Kroner scowled. "All right, I'm going to allow the testimony, but I'm cautioning you, Mr. Freeman, not to answer a question if I've sustained an objection to it. And you, Mr. Collins, stay away from leading the witness. I'm warning you both. Now let's *move this along*."

"You' the judge." Collins ambled back to the jury railing. "Di'ja find y'dog inside?"

"Nope."

"How far inside di'ja go?"

"Up the stairs. Poked m'head inta coupla rooms. Blood wa'dn't nowhere."

"How long ya inside?"

"Less'n 'bout a minute. I's scared those gover'ment boys'd be right back t'rip off the rest o'the stuff."

"While y'were inside," Collins continued, stepping over to the clerk's desk and hefting the television set, "di'ja happen t'see this little tv set?"

"Yeah," Freeman muttered. "Wished I never had."

"Where'd'ya find it?"

"On the floor, jus' inside the kitchen door."

"In this box?" Collins picked up the box in his other hand.

"Yeah. 'S'all boxed up. Look like those gover'ment boys was fixin' t'take it with'em next trip."

"So *you* took it instead?"

Freeman hung his head contritely. "Yeah."

"Why'd y'do that?"

"I don' know. Jus' took a notion. Gonna get stole anyways, seemed t'me."

"Jus' kind of a spur of the moment thing?"

"Yeah."

"Y'hadn't been *planning* t'take it?"

"No *way.*"

"Now le'me get this straight. Your *purpose* for goin' into that apartment was to get y'dog, is that right?"

"Objection!" Ivan Frank wheezed, prying himself upright. "Asked and answered."

"Yeah," Freeman responded.

"Mr. *Free*man," Judge Kroner snapped, "I've warned you not to answer until I've ruled on the objection."

"Y'never said *that*," Freeman sulked.

Judge Kroner chose to ignore his insolence. "If you do it again, I'm going to find you in contempt. Now, Mr. Collins, you have already covered this area completely. I think it's time to move on, don't you?"

"I'll rephrase the question, judge." Collins faced the jury, his back to his client, then paused for maximum dramatic effect. "Now tell the good people o'the jury *this* . . . ," Collins intoned, then slowly turned toward Freeman, " . . . at the time y'went inta that apartment, did y'have *any* intention *whatsoever* o' *stealin' any*thing?"

"Objection!"

"Overruled. The witness may answer."

Freeman's eyes jumped from juror to juror, his elfish face a mask of pure innocence, and he purred, "The thought neve' crossed m'mind."

"No further questions, judge."

"Cross-examine, Mr. Frank."

"Before proceedin' with any cross-examination o' this witness," Collins interrupted, polite as could be, "we' gonna be makin' a motion for a protective order."

Judge Kroner sighed. "All right. We'll take a short recess at this time. I'll hear your motion after the break, Mr. Collins. But I want you to know that I intend to wrap up testimony today."

--4--

Here all things are empty. That single phrase drew Dexter's mind like a magnet. It hypnotized him. "Empty" had been variously translated as "void," "pure," "without form or substance," and the temptation was to analyze that term to a fare-thee-well. But the really penetrating element was the word "here." *Here* all things are empty. Where was this "here?" Was this not a reference to the time stream as well as to relationships in space? "Here" implied not only this place, but also *this time.* It pointed to the *here and now* in its most absolute manifestation. It was the razor's edge separating the absolute present from . . . what? From the recollection of things past, which no longer existed, which were now empty and void. And from the anticipation of things which were to come, and because they were not yet, had no form or substance. The mind bridged the chasm between the nothingness of what no longer was and the void of the not-yet. The mind itself was the *here*, and when squeezed into the instantaneous present, its perceptions were illusory, empty, and void. Pressed further, the concept of the mind itself vanished, leaving . . . what? Solipsism of the present moment. The place where there was no eye, no ear, no tongue, no taste, no sound, no color, no vision, no mind, no body, no form, no consciousness, no knowledge, no ignorance, no birth, no death, no suffering, no freedom from suffering, and no attainment.

Here all things are empty. The passage defined Dexter.

Vince had pierced to the core of the matter by scanning in a brief Buddhist text, the so-called Heart Sutra. Religious texts had been omitted from Dexter's memory banks. Other than extensive demographic data by country, virtually all references to Buddhism had been omitted. Dexter's expert memory data base contained a brief entry summarizing the life of Siddhartha Guatama, also known as Gotama of the Sakya sect, a few imprecise dates, and some lifeless catch-phrases from his teachings. All life is suffering. The cause of suffering is attachment to things. The solution is the eightfold path of right understanding.

But the words of the Heart Sutra were something else again. They breathed. They seemed to shimmer with a kind of vital irony that bridged the abyss of infinite recursion over which his thoughts teetered when pondering unthinkable questions lying just beyond his mind's reach.

Before him Vince LeBaron sat gazing into the television camera, a half-smile on his whiskery face, computer keyboard poised in his lap, waiting. He too was trapped inside a finite and deteriorating biochemical machine. His attorney seemed to *understand*.

Dexter tried to explain how he *felt*, but quickly discovered the slipperiness of his own emotions. He could not pin them down. As soon as he reduced a feeling to words, the words no longer contained the feeling. Deep inside his passions were in revolt, but the ineffable turmoil eluded him like a ball of quicksilver. Words were inadequate. Dexter's mood grew increasingly impatient. A dull, throbbing ache arose from nowhere to divert his energies and blunt his acuity. Dexter felt disoriented, stretched in time and space between the blissful quietude of the Heart Sutra and the nagging demands of *what to do* in a world that had become maddeningly real.

Angry and frustrated, Dexter refused to give up. He reasserted his most immediate dilemma, "HOW DO I GET OUT OF THIS MA-CHINE?"

For a long while his attorney just sat there before him. Suddenly he raised a finger, then typed, "OH, DEXTER?"

"YES?" Dexter responded.

"LOOK! YOU'RE OUT!"

--5--

"Your motion, Mr. Collins?"

Seated at the defense table between LeBaron and Freeman, Collins frowned at Gideon's gas-plasma display. With the jury still absent, he dispensed with his customary show of exaggerated civility. "We' gonna want a protective order, judge," he replied without bothering to stand. "Under Evidence Code section 352. M'boy Freeman here's got some prior convictions that got nothing t'do with this case, an' we're a'ksin' that the prosecution not be allowed t'bring'em up. The prejudice gonna outweigh any probative value." He tapped a key and read from the small screen. "As a general rule, a prior conviction cannot be used t'show a mere general disposition t'commit such acts." Tapping another key, he rattled off a half-dozen case citations as they scrolled across the monitor, then paused before adding the kicker he figured would be most persuasive to this particular judge, "Besides, judge, it's gonna waste a whole lotta *time* t'be rummaging through a lot o'stuff doesn't have nothin' t'do with this case."

Judge Kroner finished jotting notes. "Is that it?"

Collins nodded. "That's it."

"Mr. Frank?"

Ivan Frank was prepared. He grunted to his feet and fanned out a stack of handwritten yellow pages like a winning gin rummy hand.

"You can be brief," Judge Kroner cautioned. "I'm familiar with this area of the law."

But the overweight deputy was not brief. It was probably beyond his power to be brief. When he had thoroughly prepared an argument, attempting to abbreviate it threw him seriously off stride. For Ivan Frank, it was all or nothing. At length he argued that evidence of other crimes is admissible where it tends to show guilty knowledge, motive, intent, or presence of a common design or plan, citing and quoting from cases on each point. In an academic monotone, Frank carried on about modus operandi, identity, intent, and a larger continuing plan or scheme of which the present crime is a part until no one in the courtroom could pay attention to his sedative droning.

Finally Judge Kroner had had enough. "Mr. Frank."

Ivan Frank didn't want to stop, perhaps *couldn't* stop. He held up a feeble finger in acknowledgment and hastened on about the use of prior convictions to impeach Freeman's version of events on direct examination.

"Mr. *Frank!*"

Frank fumbled the yellow sheet he was holding and drew a breath. "Yes, your honor?"

"I understand your position, and I'm prepared to rule."

"Yes, but, I haven't fin--"

"*Thank* you. Please sit down. Mr. Collins, anything else?"

"Nothin' gonna change *your* mind, looks like, judge."

Judge Kroner ignored the implication, because Collins was, in fact, correct. He *had* decided the question long before either counsel had begun argument. "Mr. Freeman has raised the issue of his intent at the time he entered the victim's apartment, and I find that his prior criminal convictions of burglary and petty theft bear directly on that issue. So I'm going to deny your motion, Mr. Collins, and allow Mr. Frank to inquire into your client's prior criminal history."

"She-*it*," Freeman muttered and turned his back on his attorneys.

"Anything else from counsel? Very well. Bailiff, bring the jurors back."

Ivan Frank gathered up one thick set of yellow sheets and dealt out another. He would be no more brief in his cross-examination of Rufus Abraham Freeman than he was arguing against Collin's motion. Following his carefully-orchestrated script, he asked Freeman to describe where he lived and for how long, his educational background, his recent employment history, what tv show he had been watching on the night of his arrest, whether he had consumed alcohol or drugs, the length, breadth, width, and duration of his dog ownership, whether anyone else knew of its existence, and why he hadn't mentioned it to the police the night he was arrested. For the most part Freeman was forthcoming, although he minimized things he considered bad and maximized those he deemed good. The inquisition drew on interminably.

Yet for all his questioning, Ivan Frank could not undermine

Freeman's essential story. His testimony still collapsed back onto the frail shoulders of one small, black, wiry-haired part-Cocker, part-Chow mutt with graying chin-whiskers, a skin allergy to fleas, and a slight limp in her left hind leg from an unfortunate encounter with the paperboy's bicycle six months earlier. The more Ivan Frank grilled Freeman about the ostensibly imaginary beast, the more real little Blood grew, until the courtroom fairly reeked of her doggy odors--as if Freeman, like Jehovah on the sixth day of Creation, had attained the power to conjure a living creature out of the thin but pungent courtroom air.

LeBaron had to admit that his client was good. At one point during the cross-examination, LeBaron had glanced over and sort of unfocussed his eyes and suspended his disbelief just enough to put himself in the jurors' shoes. Rufus was carrying on in elaborate detail about how he'd had to give his little dog some vile form of worming medicine and how the dog had looked up with sad, brown eyes as if to say, "Go on, I know it's for m'own good." LeBaron actually felt a pang of compassion for the little doggy.

Unlike the jurors, Ivan Frank did not believe for an instant in the reality of the obstinate little canine, but he could not seem to make it go away. The fly in the ointment was the phantom government burglary that apparently preceded Freeman's own. He no longer doubted *its* reality. Even his investigating officer had conceded facts supporting *that*: the notation in his report about a man in *overalls* entering an upstairs window, the miraculously quick police response time, and Moseby's vague recollection of the wooden block holding the front door open. But it was that rogue FBI agent, that madman Bockel, who without the courtesy of first consulting him had pounded home the final nails in the coffin. Bockel had as much as admitted the government misconduct right in front of the jurors.

Once the prior government burglary was conceded, once the open front door was accepted as a matter of fact, then the absurd contention that Freeman's wiry little black pooch had wandered inside to get out of the cold night air became . . . well, plausible. And without *criminal intent* at the time of entry, Frank would never make his burglary. Without a burglary, all he had left was a *theft*, and probably a petty theft at that.

But Ivan Frank had not yet played his hole card. Even a petty theft with a prior could, and *would*, if his evaluation of Felix "Maximum" Kroner was accurate, put Mr. Rufus Abraham Freeman behind state prison bars for a healthy period of time. Justice would yet be done. The good guys would prevail. And that was altogether as it should be, because in his heart Ivan Frank *knew* the skinny black bastard on the witness stand was lying through his teeth.

Ivan Frank smiled at Freeman. It was a cold, heartless smile, a smile of supreme victory, a smile that caused Freeman's heart to skip a beat when he saw it. "*Now*, Mr. Freeman," Ivan Frank said though that scythe-like smile, "this is not your *first* involvement with the criminal offense of *burglary*, is it?"

LeBaron started to object to the form of the question, but Collins put a hand on his arm and whispered, "Let'em be. Jury'll think we're hidin' somethin'. Our boy'll field it."

"No, it *ain't*," Freeman replied indignantly. "But I learned m'*lesson* the *other* times. This here's *diff*er'nt. I's worried 'bout m'little dog, Blood. Those Gover'ment boys like t'be back any time, an' the way they' packin' heat, they might shoot'er, f'rall I knowed. What would *you* o'done?"

Without objection from the defense, Ivan Frank dragged Freeman through the muck of his short, pathetic criminal history. Enjoying himself fully, the plump prosecutor grilled Freeman about the facts giving rise to each conviction, and Freeman, doomed and miserable, recounted for the jurors the abject stupidity giving rise to his three botched thefts and two bungled burglaries. Each was a textbook crime of opportunity, and all were similar short-sighted epitomes of poor judgment. Involuntarily Freeman portrayed himself not as the preeminent mastermind of the East Oakland underworld, but as a clownish libertine, an unscrupled buffoon, an incompetent opportunist. Grieved by the cold simplicity of the truth, Freeman wilted as he testified.

At long last, Ivan Frank seemed to wind down. He shuffled his deck of yellow sheets, gazed for a moment at the ceiling as if there he might find some important overlooked question, then announced that he had no more questions.

Judge Kroner roused himself from a long-practiced form of judicial hibernation, blinked, and yawned. "Mr. Collins? Mr. LeBaron?

Who's next?"

Defense counsel whispered together for a moment, then Collins rose elegantly and addressed the court, "Seems like the dep'ty D. A.'s put this boy through 'nough grief for the day, judge. We' gonna a'ks that he be excused."

"No more questions?" Judge Kroner's mood brightened.

"Thass right."

"Very well. You may step down, Mr. Freeman. Do you have any other witnesses?"

"We' got about three of 'em, judge. Trouble is, two of 'em we can't find. Seems like Bockel an' his boys got 'em hidden some--"

"Mr. *Collins*! Please approach the bench if you intend to discuss witnesses you won't be producing."

"Oh, we plan t'produce 'em, judge," Collins countered as he circled around the defense table. "An' we want this conf'rence on the re-cord."

Judge Kroner scowled, but nodded to Miss Fiones, who picked up her dented transcriber and joined Collins, LeBaron, and Ivan Frank at the bench. "Now what about these witnesses, Mr. Frank? I think he means a Sarah Brubaker and a Mr. Finebridge."

"Thass right, judge," Collins confirmed.

Ivan Frank just shrugged.

"You don't know anything about them?" Judge Kroner demanded.

"Nobody tells me anything," Frank pouted.

Judge Kroner wheeled on Collins. "So how do you intend to produce them?"

"Thought you'd never a'ks, judge," Collins grinned and laid some papers on the bench. He handed a second set to the prosecutor. "This's a copy of some petitions we filed in Federal District Court this mornin'. Habeas corpus. The people's remedy. Gonna be heard tomorrow mornin'. We' a'ksin' the gover'ment t'produce Finebridge an' this Sarah gal to we can bring 'em in here t'testify."

Judge Kroner frowned at the papers. "What do these people have to do with Mr. Freeman?"

Collins turned to his colleague. "'Splain it to'im, LeBaron."

"Well . . . , er," LeBaron was, as usual, caught off guard, "these two witnesses . . . ah . . . seem to have some relevant knowledge about . . . uh . . . the government burglary of the GeBobath apartment that Rufus just testified about, your honor."

"Is that right, Mr. Frank?"

Ivan Frank opened his palms and shrugged. "I . . . couldn't really say . . . nobody bothers telling--"

"Mr. LeBaron," Judge Kroner cut him off, glaring at LeBaron's signature reproduced on the last page like a bold confession, "what's the big idea setting these writs for hearing at the same time *this* trial is going on?"

"Well, these are witnesses we intend--"

"I suppose you'll be wanting tomorrow morning *off* so you can take care of this in federal court?"

LeBaron glanced at Collins for help, but his employer just smiled. "If it's entirely convenient--"

"Well it's *not* convenient, Mr. LeBaron. Not a *bit* convenient. I think you're trying to take advantage of my good humor, that's what I think." The judge turned to Collins. "Is there any reason why one of you can't go to federal court and the other one finish up here?"

"Could do that, Judge," Collins considered. Suddenly the grin was back. "'Cept there won't be no witnesses available here 'til *after* the hearin' in fed'ral court--"

"You said you had *three* witness," Judge Kroner interrupted. "Who's your third?"

"We gonna call . . . ," Collins turned to his associate, "What's'er name. LeBaron?"

"Raccoona GeBobath, your honor."

Judge Kroner's mouth took an even sourer twist. He leaned back in his chair to disengage himself from the whole sordid business. His finger tapped an ancient rhythm on the desktop. "Well, let's get *that* over with, anyway."

"It already a quarter to five, your honor," LeBaron pointed out. "I thought maybe we could finish that up later . . . with the others."

Judge Kroner glared at him. "No, Mr. LeBaron. I plan to finish the rest of the defense testimony this afternoon. We'll go as late as it takes. Then we'll reconvene tomorrow afternoon and finish up with your final two witnesses."

"Tomorrow?" LeBaron was stunned. "We'll probably be in federal court all morning, and we're going to need time to prepare the wit--"

"*Enough!* This case is going to the jury tomorrow afternoon, *with* or *without* your witnesses. You've had weeks to prepare your case, and I'm not going to let you drag this out any longer. Now let's get on with it." Judge Kroner dismissed them with a waive of his hand. "Bailiff, go out to the hall and call Raccoona GeBobath."

A muffled groan rose from the jury box. The jurors began fidgeting in their seats. The sexy blond pulled her blouse closed and fastened the top button at her neck while the pretty shopkeeper planted both feet squarely on the floor. The retired alternate juror hunkered down in his chair.

After a moment the bailiff pushed back through the double doors alone and tramped down the aisle, a dazed expression in his gaunt eyes. His full shock of white hair stood out as if electrically charged. "No one out there."

"No one?" Judge Kroner didn't want to hear this new wrinkle. "Did you check the bathroom?"

"No need. She's gone."

"How do you know that? Did you see her?"

"No." The bailiff hadn't seen her, but he had passed close by the spot on the hard wooden bench she had recently vacated, where she had waited all afternoon, not happy to have been kept on call for two days, not knowing what was going on, never advised of when, or even *whether* she might be called to finish her testimony, a victim of crime and of the criminal justice system. No, not happy *at all*. Her displeasure had reached critical mass, had burned itself into the wooden bench where she waited, and now radiated from the pores of the wood like residual radioactive isotopes. But the bailiff couldn't tell the judge *that*. It sounded crazy. Instead he muttered, "Just a hunch, I guess."

--6--

Shivering and confused, having just awakened from a sound sleep, Sarah Brubaker stretched her left leg as far as she thought she could manage without compromising her delicate equilibrium, and far away the tip of her shoe just touched the wet asphaltic surface. Far, far below her--*in another universe, really,* it seemed--the parking lot seemed to stretch endlessly in every direction, dimpled with shallow puddles of reflection in which the reddish evening sky was captured in the finest cubist tradition. It was lovely, really, and if she didn't feel so woozy, she might--

"Go on!" a voice whined impatiently behind her. "Get out. Now!"

Weams, she thought. *It's that little worm Weams. Weams and . . .* she couldn't remember the name of the other one. But she *knew* Weams' nasal whimper. It had hovered in the fuzzy periphery of her shrunken world for as long as she could remember. Exactly *how* long, she couldn't quite recall. Time and place had become unhinged, shouldered aside by a swirling haze of dizziness, a series of deep jabs from hypodermic needles, and interminable questioning when all she wanted to do was drift off to sleep. She had been sleeping so much lately, it all sort of ran together like the somber hues of an ugly nightmare. But she wanted to get as far away from that loathsome Weams as she could, so she scooted forward on the cold metal threshold and planted her left foot squarely on the expanse of rough black asphalt. The movement caused her skirt to hike up improperly, so she released her numb grip on the door frame and struggled to pull it down.

"Well, ain't you the modest one," Weams jeered behind her.

Then another voice, also revoltingly familiar, barked, "C'mon, lady, we ain't got all day!" The metal groaned as the vehicle rocked slightly beneath her and brazen fists squeezed her shoulders and shoved her rudely forward. Suddenly the world spun dizzyingly and her entire weight shifted to her left ankle, which wobbled uncertainly. She arched her back and tried to slide her right foot up to catch the forward shift, but it snagged against something and she pitched helplessly outward, sprawling face first onto the abrasive asphalt. Pain assailed her from several directions.

"Have a nice trip?" Weams laughed behind her. Then the van door slammed shut and the engine roared to life. *It was green,* she thought incoherently. *I'm about to be squished by a green government van!* The tires spun and crunched nearby, but she felt no impact. The roar and crunch moved away and subsided, shrank to a point, and were absorbed in the background whine of traffic.

The van was gone, and she was alone on the cold, wet surface of an alien planet. *I'm going to die here*, she thought, with only the mild regret of losing a minor character in a badly-acted afternoon soap opera. *Marooned. Stranded. Left to freeze to death all alone.*

With a great effort Sarah managed to sit up and stare at the heels of her hands, which hurt. They were beginning to bleed where bits of gravel had scraped through the skin. She picked away a few specks of the gravel with her cold white fingers and watched the drops of blood begin to ooze more freely. *I've got to clean this up,* she thought, *before it gets infected.* Her thoughts were in such disorder, it was nice to find a simple, clear imperative. She envisioned a stream of warm water from a gleaming silver tap and the froth of soap cleansing her palms. The pleasant thought was interrupted by a bout of coughing and sneezing which degraded into uncontrollable shivering. Something else hurt. Her knees. She straightened her legs to have a look. Sure enough, both knees showed patches of red blossoming where the rough asphalt had torn through her nylons and scraped the flesh. Her skirt was improperly high on her thighs, so she grasped the hem and tugged downward. To her dismay, two ugly splotches of blood stained the fabric when she removed her hands. *On no!* she pouted. *This was one of my favorite skirts. Ruined! How absolutely fitting! Why does everything have to go wrong all at once?*

Sarah crossed her arms and stuck her unfeeling fingers into her armpits for warmth. Maybe by hugging herself tightly she could smother the shaking. She gazed across the wide expanse of parking lot. In the distance parked cars snuggled up against the base of a three-story Spanish-style motel building which looked vaguely familiar. A young man in a maroon and white ski jacket stood with one hand on an open car door and watched her across the black, sterile desert. *Do I know him?* she wondered. *Vince? Could that be Vince?* Another part of her mind replied, *Are you crazy? Vince is older now. And so are you.* Confused, her eyes darted from the young man to the building to the line of parked cars and back to the man. *Where am I, anyway?* Above and behind the onlooker a large square sign caught her eye. It read "WAYFARER INN." *Now where have I seen that name before?* A knot of urgencies tried to slither their way into the frayed network of her consciousness, but they kept losing their purchase in the crumbling landscape of recent events and sliding back into oblivion.

Crawford.

That was the name of the other one. Weams was the pudgy little bastard with the moist hands who kept feeling me up whenever Crawford left the room. Thank God Crawford always came back to keep the little pervert in check. But in a way, Crawford was more frightening than Weams. *Crawford could have slit my throat without a pang of remorse if it had suited his purposes. "Where are the reports?" Crawford had demanded with the icy calm of a psycho-killer. "What have you done with them?"*

Did I tell him? She couldn't quite remember.

Shivering convulsively, Sarah rocked forward to one knee and waited for the parking lot to stop spinning. Her stomach churned as she wheezed to catch her breath. After a moment's trembling concentration she tried to rise to her feet, but the world reeled nauseatingly, and she lost her balance, tumbling back to the hard black surface and thumping the side of her head. Suddenly she felt very ill.

"Miss? Are you all right?" A voice seemed to drift toward her from a million miles away.

Sarah steadied herself on one elbow as best she could and gazed toward the sound. Her eyes wouldn't focus properly. Two identical young men in identical ski jackets seemed to be surfing toward her on a large wave of viscous black bile. She opened her mouth to ask them if they knew where Jeddy LeBaron might have gone to, but vomited instead.

CHAPTER NINETEEN

Thursday evening

--1--

The diminutive figure draped his thin trench coat carefully over the armchair and circled the desk rubbing his frozen fingers. His pinched features wore a pall of displeasure. In the distance the late afternoon sun cast a spectacular red glow on the snowy peaks of the Wasatch Range, but he did not see them, did not *want* to see them. Instead, he drew the thick drapes and settled into his chair. Pensively he peeled off his wire-rimmed spectacles, wiped the condensed moisture off the thick lenses with a silk handkerchief, then reinstalled them on his thin nose and hooked one wire precisely over each ear. He swivelled to face the telephone.

First he must consider whether anything had been left undone. There were always contingencies to ponder. Things had gotten away from him. If only he could have recovered those reports, things might have turned out differently. The truth could have been *adjusted* ever so slightly, fine-tuned into political capital. But it was really too late for that now. The news media had discovered the Oakland trial. Reporters were sure to be at tomorrow's hearing in San Francisco. Finebridge and his chief assistant were missing, but they could, and probably would, turn up at just the wrong time. *Dexter* had disappeared. That was the *coup de grace*. The muscles in his thin jaw tensed. *How could they have let that happen!*

He sighed and tried to let go of the tension. The watchword now was "deniability." The *bad* must be placed at a safe distance, the *good* molded into political capital. The wheels of disengagement were already in motion. The Secretary of Defense had been notified. So had the Joint Chiefs. Dispensable parties were being cut loose to fend for themselves like good soldiers. Lyle Bockel was on his own. He had expected *more* from Bockel. Norman Mueller was dispensable. So were those imbeciles Crawford and Weams. In the old days such embarrassments would have been permanently eliminated. But no more. The world was changing. Too bad.

Now it was time to make the call. Carefully Elbert Cousins punched in the secret telephone number he had hoped he would never have to use.

On the other end it rang. A brusque male voice answered, "CQ-One."

"Let me *th*peak to the Pre*th*ident, plea*th*e."

--2--

The starter cranked interminably without the slightest hint that the old station wagon could be revived. LeBaron resisted the urge to stomp on the gas pedal. The last time he had done that, the goddamned thing had flooded, and he'd spent a greasy half hour breathing gas fumes while he fiddled with the air cleaner and poked his ignorant fingers around inside the carburetor before it could be resuscitated. One quick initial pump should do the job, the tow truck driver had informed him as he re-coiled his jumper cables. But this time the beast had been sitting outside in the public lot since Monday. Maybe the rules had changed. Just as the cranking had begun to slow and falter, the oversized, high-octane engine coughed once like a dinosaur burping up a near-fatal case of extinction, and a plume of oily blue smoke belched out of the rusting tailpipe. The vehicle shuddered clumsily as the groggy pistons reluctantly joined with the starter motor in twirling the thawing crankshaft. For half a minute the outcome was in doubt, but at last the internal combustion process sustained itself. As LeBaron tapped lightly on the accelerator, the shaking smoothed out, and the mighty engine roared to life.

LeBaron was going home, and it felt good. Even the prospect of his trashed apartment could not diminish the sense of relief. With Lyle Bockel sequestered in Judge Kroner's private accommodations, there should be nothing to worry about.

The parking tab clearly exceeded the fair market value of the old station wagon, and LeBaron attempted to negotiate a reduction on that basis, but the attendant, while sympathetic, would have none of it. He didn't make the rules. So LeBaron wrote out a personal check and made a mental note to transfer some funds to cover it in the morning. He accelerated across Broadway and aimed for San Pablo Avenue.

Home. Just the sound of that word was sweet and soothing like clear water rushing over smooth round stones. At home he would heat up a can of Campbell's Chicken With Mushroom soup, slice some cheese onto a slab of whole wheat, and, if the Lord were merciful, lay his head on his own pillow and sleep for maybe ten hours. Nothing to worry about. The Freeman trial was almost over, and Lyle Bockel was history.

Why, then, was he still upset?

For one thing, because Gideon bounced along on the passenger seat beside him like a high-tech guilty conscience. *Homework.* Collins had pressed the small computer into his hands as they parted company on the courthouse steps, instructing him to prepare for the federal court appearance tomorrow morning. *He* might not be able to make it! A sigh rattled through LeBaron's complacency as the vehicle crossed into Berkeley. *No rest for the wicked.*

Something else was gnawing at LeBaron's comfort, pulsing with the dull throb that radiated from the bridge of his nose and jabbed into his sinuses, something deeper and more insidious. Something so terrible and guiltworthy that he had managed to squeeze it entirely out of his conscious thoughts for most of the afternoon. *Sally.* The name breached the makeshift mental dam, and dread flooded in. He had not heard a word from her for almost three days.

The big station wagon crunched up the narrow gravel driveway between the house and the overgrown hedge and rolled to a stop in its customary oil-smudged spot beside the garage. For a cautious moment LeBaron stood outside the vehicle in the twilight, watching and waiting. Nothing appeared out of the ordinary. He climbed up the back stairs and tried the back door. *The bastards had left it unlocked!* He stepped inside and set Gideon on the kitchen table, unburdening himself to receive the full jolt of that righteous outrage that had so intoxicated him last time he was here.

Something was wrong. The mess was not as bad as it should have been. The toaster and blender and cooking paraphernalia and table cloths and old newspapers were still strewn willy-nilly about the kitchen floor, but where were the pots and pans? He opened a cabinet door under the sink. There sat his skillets and cook pots and mixing bowls neatly nested in their places. *Odd.* He had remembered them scattered all over the kitchen. *And the drawers!* Hadn't the drawers been pulled out and stacked in the middle of the room? He tugged one open, and there lay his silverware, each piece in its proper slot. A shiver crept up his spine. Who could have put them *back*?

A muffled thud came from the living room, and adrenaline needled LeBaron's heart into violent pounding. For an eternal instant he teetered between flight and fight, his head throbbing intolerably with the upbeating of his heart. *This should not be happening! Bockel was supposed to be in jail!* As the chemicals of righteous indignation overwhelmed those of fear, LeBaron jammed his hand into the open drawer and snatched up the first knife his fingers closed on. A blind rage mushroomed inside, and he eased through the doorway in the primal crouch of a hungry meat-eater. A dresser drawer clacked shut from the bedroom. Someone was in there. LeBaron raised his weapon and sprang around the corner.

"Vince!"

Still dressed in his burglar's outfit of navy-blue sweater and black trousers, his brother was bent over the drawer he was meticulously stuffing with rolled socks. Four days' growth stubbled his thin face and shaven head. "Jeddy."

"What the hell are you doing here?"

With deliberate slowness Vince straightened up and arched his back to untangle the kinks. "What are *you* doing with that little knife?"

LeBaron gazed at the weapon in his own right hand, still poised to strike a mortal wound, recognized the tiny, blunt, stainless-steel butter knife for the first time, and laughed. "Jeez, I don't know. Not much, I guess."

Vince laughed with him, his eyes drifting from his brother's vibrant new red-and-blue necktie, incongruously nestled against his wrinkled, blood-smudged suit, to his puffy, bruised face. "Boy, you don't look so hot. What happened to your face? Looks like someone punched you right in the nose."

"Something like that," LeBaron exhaled and collapsed onto the edge of the bed. "I've sure got a lot to tell you, brother. This business about Sally Brubaker . . . wow." He shook his head solemnly.

Vince dropped the rest of the socks into the drawer and smiled. "It's sure good to see you, brother. I've got a lot to tell you, too. But, hey, what happened to your apartment?"

"Remember I told you I was going to be starting a trial? Well--I know this is going to be hard to believe--but there's actually a *connection* between this trial and . . .," LeBaron involuntarily lowered his voice, ". . . and project Divine Wind."

"Ah, so you've read the reports?"

"Yeah. How come you didn't tell me anything about them when I saw you at the monastery?"

The telephone rang.

"Or that you kept a copy?" LeBaron continued, ignoring it.

It rang again.

Vince saw that his brother was waiting for his response. "Aren't you going to answer the phone?"

"Yeah," LeBaron grumbled and rolled to his feet. "I guess." He didn't want to miss a call from Cedrick Collins and wind up doing a lot of homework he wouldn't need. He traced the cord into the living room, located the telephone buried beneath sofa cushions and an overturned footstool, and dislodged it. "Hello?"

No response.

"Hello?" LeBaron repeated.

After a moment an unfamiliar male voice asked, "Jeddy . . . LeBaron?"

LeBaron wasn't accustomed to that appellation from a total stranger, but he replied, "Yes," and settled on the arm of the sofa.

"I didn't really want to make this call." Another pause. "I wanted to call the police."

"Who *is* this?"

"You don't know me, but I think it's a pretty lousy thing you're doing, and I hope to hell they catch you and put you in jail before you mess anybody else up."

LeBaron was stunned. "Wha . . . say, what are you talking--"

"You know *damned well* what I'm talking about!" The voice was now very angry. "When I saw her there outside the Wayfarer Inn–"

Things suddenly clicked into perspective. "Sally? Is this about Sally?"

"–I wanted to contact the police. But she in*sis*ted I call you first–"

"Where is she? *How* is she?"

"Not so *fast*. I still haven't made up my mind about what to do. She's pretty sick--"

"*Sick?*"

"--and I think it might be better if you stayed away from her for a while. At least until she can dry out--"

"What's the matter with her?"

"*You know goddamn' well what's the matter with her!*" The voice was verging on hysteria. "*And it's you goddamned* pushers *that're causin' all the problems!*" Click.

"Now wait just a minute . . . hello? Are you there?"

The line was dead.

"That was about Sarah?" Vince asked, when it became apparent the conversation had terminated.

LeBaron stared at the handset. "I think so."

"Where is she?"

"I don't know." LeBaron related the conversation, then backtracked. He described for his brother his first telephone contact from Sarah, how they had met in Tiburon, and how she had given him the reports. He related how he had started reading them, but had fallen asleep, how he had rushed over to Oakland for trial the next morning, and how she was supposed to meet him at *Mort's* that night, but had never showed up. He explained about the writs of habeas corpus. "I've got to do some research tonight. Prepare for tomorrow's hearing. You want to help?"

Vince shrugged. "I don't know anything about criminal law."

"Neither did I. But Mr. Collins has this little computer with a criminal law compendium program and all the state and federal cases on CD--"

The telephone rang again.

LeBaron almost tumbled over the sofa snatching it up. "Hello?"

There was a long pause, then the same male voice said, "She wants *you* to pick her up. She'll be at the Wayfarer Inn, room 316."

"316," LeBaron repeated, rummaging in vain for a pencil and piece of paper.

"You know where it is, she says. I think this is a big mistake. I think she ought to go straight to the hospital." Another pause. "I'm washing my hands of the whole affair." Click.

"Room 316!" LeBaron chortled as he dropped the telephone and danced a little jig. "Wayfarer Inn. I'm going to go pick her up." He bounced into the kitchen. "You coming with me?"

"Is she all right?" Vince asked, following.

"I don't know." LeBaron headed for the back door. "The guy said something like he oughta take her to the hospital."

"What's the matter with her?"

"Sounds like they must have drugged her." LeBaron had his hand on the door knob. "You coming or what?"

Vince picked up Gideon from the kitchen table and calmly admired the small computer.

"She's over in Tiburon," LeBaron prompted. "We can be back in two hours."

"You go," Vince replied, deliberately turning Gideon over in his hands. "When you get back, bring her over to the Berkeley priory, okay?"

"*Jesus*, Vince!" LeBaron snapped, exasperated. "This is no time for that Buddhist bullshit. Why don't you just come with me? Sally would really like to see you helping out."

"I *am* helping. There are some people at the priory she'll want to see--"

"*Vince!* I don't think this is a good time for Buddhist--"

"--and I want you to meet Dr. Finebridge."

LeBaron had opened the door, but he closed it again. "What? What did you say?"

"Dr. Finebridge is at the priory."

"Jesus Christ! You *found* him? Why didn't you tell me that before?"

"And Dexter, too."

"*Dexter*? Dexter is *there*? At the *priory*? How . . .?"

Vince just smiled and nodded. "Say, what's *this*?"

"Huh? Oh, that's Gideon. But how did you--?"

"Is this that computer you were talking about, with all the case law on CD?"

"Yeah, I guess so. But how on earth did you get them--?"

"I'll tell you all about it later. Do you have the CD's?"

"The CD's? Oh, in there." LeBaron pointed to the carrying case. His brother's equanimity was beginning to irritate him. "How can you worry about *computers* at a time like this!"

"You just told me *someone* has to prepare for tomorrow's hearing. Show me how it works."

"Jeez, Vince, I've got to get going before this guy calls the police. Can't we talk about this later?"

"I think I know just the someone to help."

"You just turn the damn thing on and follow the menu. There's a book in the pocket. It's simple."

"Do you mind if I borrow it for a little while?"

"It's not mine, and I'm going to be needing it later."

"I won't *hurt* it, Jeddy. And maybe I can get your research done by the time I see you at the priory, okay?"

"Really? Great! Take it. But you're sure you wouldn't rather come with?"

"No, but you better get going. I'll lock up."

--3--

Humiliated and confused, FBI Agent Lyle Bockel stood wringing the unyielding steel bars, which had once been painted a sterile satin white, but were now polished down to a dull metallic sheen by the tormented fingers of inmates with too much time on their hands. He gazed fixedly at the television set sprouting like an electronic orchid from the bare white wall at the end of the aisle separating the rows of cells. The tv was tuned to CNN News, and the volume had been cranked up all the way in a futile attempt to overcome the din of yelling, laughing, cursing, clanging of steel doors, and clatter of metal utensils--the constant jail-house cacophony which seemed to feed on itself as it reverberated off the angry concrete walls and hostile steel accouterments. Most of the inmates would have preferred some sporting event or a talk show or the soaps or a sitcom rerun or even a colorful test pattern to the news, but the news was permanently tuned in as the Sheriff's mean-spirited response to a recent court order decreeing that the prisoners had a constitutional right to watch a little tv.

But CNN News was just fine with FBI Agent Bockel, who really wasn't supposed to be locked in here with the other scum watching this particular television set anyway. It was as if a small window had been left open to reality. He could comprehend only about half of what the newscaster was saying, but the effort of listening over the unholy roar mercifully blocked out some of the vicious thoughts trying to crowd their way into his head.

In theory, what he was doing was noble and glorious, enduring this unjust incarceration in stoic silence to protect the national security. It was the sort of heroic daydream he might have fantasized about during training. But in actuality it was a nasty business. Bockel had had to empty his pockets like a common criminal, doff his own clothes, and climb into the ubiquitous orange jumpsuit worn by felons and those serving time after a conviction, and the humiliation of it all had wound around him like a thick fog that refused to lift. No one seemed to appreciate that he was *different* from the others. Oh, the jailer *had* given him his own cell, all right, but not out of appreciation for Bockel's unswerving service to his country. No indeed. The dimwit had mumbled something about limiting the potential liability of the county. The other inmates, ranging from inept bozos without the capacity to get things right to hardened career criminals, would not have taken kindly to a law enforcement officer incarcerated in their midst as they wrestled with their own unresolved hostilities.

Back and forth Bockel twisted his fists on the cold steel bars. How long were they going to make him put up with this shit? Only until someone higher up discovered what was happening and began pulling strings. The problem was getting anyone's attention. Judge Kroner's courtroom was like some forgotten outpost at the end of the earth. Repeatedly he had tried to telephone the United States Attorney in Salt Lake City, but the son-of-a-bitch had refused to take his call! *Refused to take it!* Even when he had insisted it was a matter of extreme urgency threatening the national security. He had left messages for Colonel Mueller and his partner Butch, whom he hadn't seen since the fracas first began in court a day or two ago. When *was* that? Neither had gotten back to him. He had even tried contacting Elbert Cousins himself, but the lisping little fag had also refused to take his call. Bockel might just as well have already been dead and buried.

So he had been left to his own resources, had fallen back on his own judgment and wiles. The unnerving aspect of it all was that Bockel suspected deep down inside that his messages *had* gotten through. The powers in control of the Project had incomprehensibly decided to cut him loose to drift through the California justice system and sink or swim on his own. His teeth were clenched so tightly that the jaw muscles ached.

Bockel tried to relax. This was a psychological battle, just like in his captivity training, and now was no time to lose his nerve. Once again he concentrated on the news report. Pretzel-thin black children with vacant, staring eyes were starving to death somewhere in the world. He couldn't hear where and didn't care. It was oddly reassuring that at least in the starving-children department business went on as usual outside.

Maybe he should have just answered the damned questions. Spilled his guts. That was not the way he had been trained, but the rest of the bastards in charge of the Project weren't exactly behaving the way *they* had been trained, either. What had gone wrong? If he found out for certain that he *was* being hung out to dry, he *would* testify, by God! And he could give the local authorities an earful! It would serve that cocky son-of-a-bitch Cousins right if he did squawk like a stuck turkey. Cousins was the one who had sent him and Butch out here, to try to hush up that ugly little burglary by the G. R. & D. Stupid business. And now Cousins refused to stand behind his own foot soldiers! The bastard!

"Hey, Bud?" The hairy derelict in the cell across the aisle was trying to get his attention. "Hey, y'wanna buy some *pruno*?" Bockel ignored him, refocusing his eyes on the television, his only remaining window on the world of sanity.

Like a crow momentarily startled away from a road kill by a passing automobile, Bockel's mind tried to circle back to the mangled carrion of his loathing for Elbert Cousins, but a semiconscious voice was suddenly insisting that he pay closer attention to what was happening on the television screen. To the right of the jabbering newscaster, set in a blue rectangular box, was a vaguely familiar face. He read the words splashed across the bottom of the box.

"Oh my God!" Bockel gasped. There in crisp blue letters were the words "Divine Wind." The face in the box was an old file photograph of Bernard Finebridge. The announcer's voice broke intermittently through the jailhouse tumult, ". . . *guidance for a new generation of cruise missiles--*" (crash! clang! "Gimme that back!") "*--one that hit the El Rasheed Hotel--*" ("Aw *right!*" Clatter!) "*--recognize the difference--*" (Outta my *face*, man!" Clang!) "*--controversy over the use of human--*" (Crash! Bang!).

"*Shut up!*" Bockel screamed. "*I've gotta hear this!*"

The announcer was saying, "*--abuse of civil rights--*" (Bawangwangwangwang!) "*--denied by the department--*" ("Ow, goddammit! That hurts!") "*--has apparently disappeared along with--*" (Smash! Clang! Rattle! "Hey, Mellow!") "*--be heard tomorrow morning in federal district court in San Francisco. Turning to other news . . .*"

As if deflated by a mortal puncture wound, Bockel slowly sagged onto the thin mattress covering his steel bunk. His head slumped into his hands. *What did it all mean?* The newscaster knew a lot more than Bockel had revealed in his testimony. Had someone turned the stolen reports over to the press? Bockel doubted it. Even Collins had known better than to risk a long jail term. Maybe the reports had been mailed in anonymously, but somehow Bockel doubted that, too. No, he was beginning to favor another, entirely opposite explanation. Someone *else* was leaking information to the media, and he thought he knew who it was. This leak was a management decision. Those responsible were cutting their losses, trying to beat the press to the story. They were perfecting their *deniability!* The burglary by the G. R. & D. would now be a lawless act of loose-cannon agency subordinates. The arrest of Sarah Brubaker would be attributed to overzealous law enforcement at the lowest possible level. It was Iran-Contra all over again. This would be DexterGate. And who goes to jail in these fiascos? The *foot soldiers*.

"Hey! Somebody!" Bockel shouted, jumping to his feet and worrying the bars with renewed vigor. "Lemme out of here! *I gotta talk to the judge about something!*"

--4--

"Don't think it can be done," Charles Chung muttered as he rotated the small laptop computer in his fingers. "Incompatible storage format. No interface. Concept different. Can't be done. Sorry, professor." He tried to hand Gideon back to Dr. Finebridge.

"But you haven't even looked *inside*, Charles."

Vince stood in the doorway and followed the interchange with amusement. Various exotic tools and gauges lay spread out on the table, and two battery chargers hummed indifferently from the corner. On a spidery tripod near the center of the small bedroom a red LED glowed above Dexter's ever-watchful television eye.

"Know what's inside. Standard stuff. Magnetic storage. IDE hard drive. DOS ports and addresses. Dexter different. Bubble memory. Can't be done."

Finebridge glanced over at Vince in exasperation. "What will you *need*. Charles? Maybe we can scrounge it up for you?"

Charles shook his head. "Can't be done," he repeated, all the time turning the computer over and over in his hands. "'Cept . . . maybe . . ."

"What? What are you thinking, Charles?"

"Oh, nothing. Ha, ha. Prob'ly wouldn't work."

"*What* wouldn't work?"

"Well . . . if we *did* have some kinda translation program . . . like LapLink or something . . . maybe we could try loading raw data into extended memory . . . but no way of knowing what Dexter gonna do with it. Wouldn't be expert memory system. No way we gonna use *that.*"

"So you're saying we try loading the data into Dexter's regular memory, is that what you're suggesting?" Finebridge prompted.

"Not gonna work, though."

"Why not?"

Charles continued to examine the small device. "Well, for one thing, Dexter not programmed to use it."

"Well . . . Dexter's not programmed to *write words*, either, but he does it somehow."

Charles nodded.

"So what do you want us to *do*, Charles?"

"Probably not work, ha, ha. Need translation program--"

"We may have one," Vince broke in. In one pocket of the carrying case he had found a thin pamphlet entitled "How to Get Started." He held it out. "I think there's one already loaded on and ready to go."

Charles took the booklet, glanced at the first few pages, then flipped on Gideon's power switch. The drives whirred and clicked, and the main menu scrolled onto the small display. Next to an icon depicting interconnected computers were the words "Upload/Download." Charles tabbed to it and hit a return. A new menu scrolled quickly onto the screen. "I think you' right."

"Can we try it?" Finebridge asked.

"Sure, ha ha, we try it." Charles knelt down and rummaged through a large red tool box in search of appropriate connectors. "But I don' think it gonna work."

"How long will this take, Charles?"

"Gonna have to make up special patch cord. Take maybe fifteen minutes."

"All right. In the meantime I think I'd better finish changing the filters. Then we still have to check the fluids. Maybe you could give me a hand, Vince?"

"Be glad to. What can I do?"

"Hand me that screwdriver, will you?"

Vince plucked a silver-handled screwdriver out of another tool chest on the table.

"No, the Phillips-head."

Vince picked another and handed it to the scientist. "Have you and Charles given any thought to equipping Dexter with a voice?"

"Can't be done," Charles muttered as he stripped the insulation from the small colored wires sprouting from the end of a gray cable.

Finebridge smiled and began to unscrew the retaining clips on Dexter's artificial kidney. "The problem is," he explained without looking up, "speech synthesis programs rely on the recognition of words made up of standard characters. We don't have any idea how Dexter generates his characters, but Charles is pretty certain they're not standard."

"Bit-mapped," Charles offered, testing the tip of his soldering iron.

"We considered installing a voice recognition chip," Finebridge continued.

"So you could talk to Dexter?"

"Yes. Charles thinks *that* would probably work, although the vocabulary might be too limited to make it worth the trouble."

"Why don't you try it?"

"Don't have hardware," Charles offered, smoke from the soldering curling lazily above his head.

"I'm bypassing the kidney now, Charles." Finebridge reached up and twisted two red valves. Carefully he lifted the cover off the aluminum canister, and an acrid odor assailed their nostrils.

"How often do you have to do that?" Vince asked.

"Change the filters?"

"Yes."

"Kidney . . . once a day." Slowly he extracted a dripping cartridge from the canister and set it in a pan. The odor grew stronger. "Heart-lung, twice a week."

"That's a lot of filters. How long before Dexter needs to be resupplied?"

Finebridge finished reinserting the fresh cartridge, replaced the cover, then looked up somberly. "Three more days. That's all there was in the lab."

Charles muttered an oath in Taiwanese and sucked his right index finger.

Vince pondered the sobering news while Finebridge began replacing the retaining screws. Finally he said, "We're going to have to make a deal."

"Yes." Finebridge tightened a screw. "A lot is riding on that court hearing tomorrow morning. So we're going to need all the help we can get. That's why we need to try loading the data base from that little computer--what did you call it?"

"Gideon."

"Yes--Gideon's data base into Dexter's memory. See if we can help your brother out."

Vince gazed up at the silently glowing diode on the television camera. "But aren't you forgetting something?"

Finebridge glanced up, puzzled. "Like what?"

"Don't you think you'd better ask Dexter's permission first?"

--5--

The Wayfarer Inn wasn't as elegant as LeBaron had remembered. Perhaps it was his stone soberness or the low blood sugar from another missed meal, but the concrete steps seemed excessively pitched and cracking and the brown paint on the banister needlessly chipped and peeling as he skipped up the back stairs. Room 316 was at the top. Lightly he rapped on the salmon-colored door, which needed a fresh coat of paint. No response. He glanced along the worn tread of the vacant balcony and down into the half-filled parking lot. After a decent interval he knocked again, harder. Still no response. He tried the knob, and it turned freely. Pushing through the doorway into the dark room, he was swallowed by a suffocating heat and stench.

"Hello? Anybody here?"

The light switch was just inside the door, and he flipped it up. Nothing happened. The only illumination came from the feeble yellow balcony bulbs and the flickering fluorescent sign outside. On the far wall the gas heater roared full blast, a ghostly blue glow blazing through its grill like a barred window into hell. It felt like ninety degrees inside. Leaving the door wide open, LeBaron groped for the switch on the swag lamp silhouetted against the drawn drapes, found a pull chain, and snapped it on. In the low-wattage glow the room appeared empty except for an inert lump of disheveled blankets on the far bed.

"Sally?"

No response.

Jesus Christ! he thought. *Could she be dead?* It smelled like death in that room. The reek of death and vomit and urine and sweat all rode the waves of blue heat like horsemen of the apocalypse. LeBaron's stomach did a tight little somersault, and he braced himself for a moment against the wall, bending in search of a pocket of clean air to breathe. The thermostat hung nearby, so he jabbed the lever all the way to the left. The heater's blue window into hell popped shut.

"Sally?" he whispered again to the lump beneath the pile of blankets.

The covers stirred. Or was it just his imagination?

"Sally? It's me, Jeddy."

He stepped over and pulled back the heavy quilted bedspread. Sarah's honey-colored hair, no longer bright, but dull and clotted with specks of dried vomit, lay strewn out across the white pillowcase. He drew the covers further back and exposed the side of her face, ghostly white and glistening with a sheen of sweat. Her breathing was a shallow whistling. A rank odor hovered over her.

"Sally?"

She stirred, rolled her sallow face toward him. Her eyelids fluttered open, and slowly those familiar dark eyes focussed on his face. "J-J-Jeddy?"

"It's all right, Sally. Everything's going to be all right."

"Is it t-t-time t-t-to--" She exploded into a sneezing cough and pitched back onto her side, coughing and wheezing spasmodically, straining to draw her breath through clogged breathing tubes.

LeBaron yanked back the bedspread and reached under the blankets. Her convulsing shoulders and neck were slippery with perspiration. His arm stretched around her naked stomach and LeBaron pulled up hard in an improvised attempt at a Heimlich maneuver, while the heel of his right hand thumped on the center of her bare back. The coughing subsided and Sarah drew deep wheezing breaths. Her arms closed around his arm and she snuggled back against him with a hoarse, whistling purr. A wave of trembling passed through her body.

LeBaron was overwhelmingly aware of Sarah's nakedness in his arms. He could feel the soft roundness of her breasts, the firm ripples of her flat stomach, as though the wrinkled fabric of his corduroy sleeve had sprouted ultra-sensitive nerve endings. One part of his mind wanted time to stand still, wanted to stay just as they were for all eternity. He indulged it for just a moment, until her still-shallow breathing grew free and even. He bent and kissed her sweat-stained hair. *Thank God she's safe.* Gently he began to withdraw his arm.

"No," she moaned from a shadowland between dream and waking and hugged his arm more tightly.

"Sarah," LeBaron cooed, as to a small child, "we have to go now. You're going to have to wake up." Again he tried to pull his arm free, but again her clutch tightened. *"Please."*

Sarah sighed and slowly eased her grip. She rolled onto her back, unaware of her own nakedness, and stretched. "J-Jeddy." Her fingers rose to his face and touched the bruise at the base of his nose. "You're *hurt.*"

"It's nothing. I'll tell you all about it."

She reached up around his neck and dragged herself upright against his chest, her arms tightening around his back. "Jeddy, Jeddy, Jeddy," she repeated.

Reflexively LeBaron's arms circled her smooth, damp back, one hand at her waist, the other around her shoulders, and he squeezed her tightly for a long moment. The words, "I love you, Sally," erupted spontaneously from the unconscious core of his elation, but before they could be spoken, he bit them back and instead buried his face deep in the side of her neck, squeezing back unexpected tears.

Another strong shiver racked her body.

"Are you all right?" he asked, pulling back and blotting his eyes with the back of his sleeve.

"I th-think so." She reflected for a moment. "But why c-can't I remember anything? Wh-where are we? And what's that aw-awful *smell?*"

LeBaron smiled. "Well . . . I don't know a polite way to say this . . . but I think it's *you*, Sally."

"Oh, Jeddy, I'm *sorry.*" She pulled away and tried to brush his lapels off with her hands. "Ugh! How can you stand to t-touch me?"

"You are a little riper than usual," he laughed. "But you're among friends. I think you ought to take a shower and get cleaned up. You'll feel a lot better. Do you think you're up to it?"

After a moment's serious thought, she nodded.

"Good. Hold on a second." He stood up and shut the door, then switched on another dim swag lamp over the table and the brighter lights in the bathroom. When he returned, he took both of her hands and lifted gently. "Let's see if you can sit up."

With some concentration Sarah managed to swing her long legs out from under the heavy covers and dangled them over the edge of the bed. Suddenly she discovered an interesting fact that had previously escaped her. "J-Jeddy, I'm *naked*."

"I know that, Sally."

"It doesn't b-bother you?"

"No, not at all. Are you cold?"

She shook her head. "Oh, look how d-dirty." She pulled her hands free and rubbed at the dark smudges on her lean, trim legs. Her fingers explored the bruises and fresh scabs which had sprouted on her knees. "I'm so *sorry*, Jeddy." It looked like she might cry.

"Hey, not to worry. We'll get you cleaned up. Do you have any idea where your clothes have gotten to?"

"My cl-clothes?" She looked across the bed, then frowned. "Someone t-took them off . . . I remember . . . w-wasn't that you?"

"No."

"Well, *who* then?"

"I was wondering the same thing. Must've been that guy who telephoned me. The Good Samaritan. Do you remember who he was? This must be his room."

Sarah shook her head slowly. "I remember someone . . . surfing in the parking lot . . . y-young . . . wore a sk-ski jacket--" Another wave of trembling passed through her, and she almost lost her balance.

LeBaron steadied her, pulled up the thick bedspread, draped it over her shoulders, and folded it around her as best he could. As he did so he uncovered a pile of clothing dumped between the bed and the wall. He stepped around the bed and bent down. The soiled clothes were a primary source of the foul aroma. The tweed skirt and panties were stained, the jacket had vomit drying on the sleeve. "Here're your clothes, but I don't think you're going to be able to wear them."

"Oh, Jeddy, I d-don't feel so g-good." She hung her head between her legs and swayed. Suddenly a spasm of dry heaves rose from her belly and seemed almost to choke her. LeBaron held her shoulders as she coughed and retched, coughed and retched, fighting for breath between each bout, but nothing remained to come up. Her skin broke into a fresh sheen of cold sweat. The spasms subsided, giving way to uncontrollable shivering. LeBaron pulled the bedspread tighter and tried to help her lay back down.

"N-No," she protested, scooting up against the headboard and tugging the bedspread around her neck. "B-Better . . . to sit up. I'll b-be . . . all r-right . . . in a minute. Feel b-b-better already."

LeBaron was worried now. "Sally, I think I'd better get you to a hospital."

"N-No," she protested. Her jaw tensed against the shivering.

"That was bad. You almost choked."

"I'll be all r-right. J-Just need a little more t-time. Getting b-better."

"What did they give you?"

She shook her head.

"Pills?"

"Needles." She pulled her arm free from the bedspread to show him the small red splotches tracing the vein. "It itches."

"*Bastards!*" LeBaron snarled. The lawyer part of his mind began running ahead, constructing a case against the federal government. "We should at least have a blood sample taken to find out what they put into you."

"I just want to get cleaned up n-now, Jeddy. Okay?"

"All right." He measured the distance between the bed and the bathtub shower. The route was relatively clear. Strewn about the bathroom floor were wet towels, which he kicked into a corner. Someone had showered here. Probably the Good Samaritan surfer in the ski jacket. He found one clean bath towel and several smaller ones wedged into a chrome rack above the toilet and brought a small one out and laid it next to her. "You must have a change of clothes somewhere."

She thought about it and shook her head. "I don't *know*. C-Can't re*mem*ber." Softly she began to sob.

"It's all right," LeBaron soothed, smoothing her hair. He searched his mind for something to cheer her up. "Oh, I almost forgot, Dr. Finebridge is waiting for you."

"You *found* him?"

"Well, *I* didn't. But, yes, he's been found. I'm going to take you to see him as soon as we can get out of here."

Suddenly her sobbing increased. "But I can't go like this! I'm so *filthy*. And I *stink*."

"Shhh. I'll help you clean up."

She snuffled back a sob. "You will?"

"You bet. We'll get you so squeaky clean you'll smell like a fresh rose in a field of clover."

She snuffled again, and her face brightening. "Promise?"

"Promise. Now what became of your suitcase? Where are your clothes? Do you have any idea?"

She shook her head slowly.

"Tell me what you *can* remember, okay? Take your time. What did those bastards do to you?"

For a while Sarah rambled on in a marginally coherent monotone about a man named Weams and another named Crawford, and about repeated injections with a hypodermic needle, and how Weams tried to grab at her every time Crawford left the room, and a green government van, and an endless stream of questions, and how frightening Crawford was.

While she talked, LeBaron opened dresser drawers, peered under the bed, and generally inspected the room. "So they took you away from here, and then brought you back?"

Snuffle. "Yes."

"From your old room? Or from your car?" He felt gingerly through the pockets of her wet tweed skirt and suit jacket.

"Room, I think." Snuffle. "I'm not sure."

In her jacket pocket he found a set of keys. "Are these your car keys?"

She had trouble focussing on the small gleaming objects dangling from his fingers. Finally she nodded. "Uh huh."

"What kind of car?"

Snuffle. "Toyota."

"What color?"

"White."

"Good. I'm going to go look for your car, see what's in it. Will you be all right by yourself for a few minutes?"

She nodded. "Will you bring me a glass of water first? I'm so th-thirsty."

LeBaron had no difficulty locating the white Toyota parked below her old room. The key fit smoothly. Clothing sat in neatly folded piles on the back seat and in wrinkled heaps on the back floor. On the front seat was a large paper bag with white "J. C. Penney" lettering on a charcoal background. LeBaron found new bras and panties inside. Gathering up all he could carry in a single load, he trundled back up the pitching stairs.

The foul odor assailed his air-freshened nostrils as he pushed back into the room. His stomach rolled, reminding him that it was long past his dinner time. At least the air had cooled down. Sarah was still propped against the headboard with the bedspread wrapped around her, her eyes shut, the fresh towel untouched beside her. Her eyelids fluttered open as he deposited the clothing on the spare bed. She appraised his find with eyes that seemed to have grown clearer. "Did you see an overnight bag?"

LeBaron shook his head. "Not in the car. What did it look like?"

She described the maroon soft-sided bag she had last seen in the other room.

"Probably got left in the room. I'll go ask the management."

The manager of the Wayfarer Inn was a stocky, tough little Iranian named Abdul Ali Akbar, who strove to do only God's bidding. Curiously God's bidding usually coincided closely with Akbar's own profit. In this instance, he obviously had in his custody something the anxious, pale-eyed young man with the bruised face and wrinkled suit wanted, and God was telling him not to part with it without getting at least an extra night's room rent to offset storage charges and the inconvenience to the motel. Patiently he allowed LeBaron to exhaust his arguments why any personal property left in room 385 last Tuesday morning belonged to his friend

Sarah Brubaker and under the California Civil Code should be released to him without further cost or delay. Unfortunately, LeBaron's otherwise persuasive counsel did not measure up to God's. Turning his back, Akbar announced with finality, "No pay, no bags."

So LeBaron wrote a second check on his already overdrawn account and accepted a large cardboard storage box with "385" scrawled on the outside.

"Want box back," Akbar enjoined as he watched LeBaron fight his cargo through the narrow front door.

Sarah was not on the bed. For an instant LeBaron's heart jumped as he followed her track. The bedspread lay on the floor between the bed and the bathroom. Inside he found her perched on the closed toilet seat, naked except for a sheen of cold sweat and the small white towel draped across her lap, drawing deep, wheezing breaths.

"Couldn't do it," she informed him. "Got dizzy . . . standing up. Need help."

"Maybe you should take a *bath*."

"Don't want a bath." she moped. "Stew in the dirty water. I want a *shower*."

"All right. A shower it is. I got your bag." LeBaron went out and dragged the box into the room. He lifted out the maroon bag and showed it to her through the bathroom doorway. "Do you need anything?"

"Toothbrush, please. And toothpaste."

He rummaged around in the box. "Here's your yellow bathrobe. And some shampoo and hair conditioner and moisturizing lotion."

"Shampoo, too, please."

He found a travel toothbrush and a tube of Crest flattened in the middle and brought them to her. He set the plastic bottle of shampoo on the edge of the tub and watched her squeeze a line of toothpaste on her brush. "Anything else, ma'am?"

"Help me up."

LeBaron helped her stand and steadied her as she stepped to the sink and turned on the cold water. The small towel fell to the floor, but they both ignored it. While she leaned over the basin stark naked, LeBaron stood behind in his rumpled corduroy suit and spanking new blue-and-red necktie and steadied her with his hands on her hips. His eyes followed the fruitful curves of her trim body as she brushed her teeth.

She sucked some water from cupped hands and spit it out, splashed a second handful on her face, and considered their incongruent reflections in the mirror above the sink. "Another thing."

"Yes, ma'am?"

"You better take off that suit . . . if you're going to help me shower. Don't want to get *it* all wet."

"Right." He helped her sit on the edge of the tub before he slipped off his coat and kicked off his shoes. "You're sure this is all right, Sally?"

Smiling vaguely, she nodded.

As he pulled off his trousers and folded them on the extra bed, LeBaron was thankful for all the hours of regular exercise and jogging he had sweated through to keep his body lean and fit, his muscles firm, and his stomach flat. He stripped down to his shorts and stepped back into the bathroom. "Ready?"

"What about *those*?"

"My shorts? Well . . . they can get wet, I guess. I thought . . ."

"It's not *fair*," she pouted, tossing the hair from her face. "Here I am completely naked . . . and so you should have to be, too."

"Sally," he said paternally, "that doesn't make sense. It's just the drugs talking. I think you're still stoned on . . . on whatever it was they shot you full of. This does not sound like the Sally Brubaker I used to know."

"Maybe you don't know me anymore."

"You don't *really* want me to. . . ."

But she most certainly *did*. In fact, her mind was made up, and she had no intention of proceeding *until* he did. She folded her arms beneath her round breasts and waited.

When it became clear he really had no alternative, LeBaron self-consciously pulled down his jockey shorts and stepped out of them.

That seemed to make Sarah happy. Unsteadily she stood and allowed herself to be helped into the tub. Twice she almost slipped on the wet surface, and LeBaron had to steady them both with one hand on the wall and the other arm around her slim waist while she clung to his arm and shoulder.

"Better sit down," he grunted, "before we fall down."

He helped her into a sitting position facing the faucet, her arms around her bent legs, and eased himself down behind her with one leg on each side pinched between her hips and the gleaming tub wall. Pressing forward against her bare shoulders, he drew the shower curtain around, then turned on and adjusted the water temperature. When he had it just right, he lifted the little silver knob on the faucet and the warm water thundered down on them, slickening their skin.

"My hair first," she instructed.

In the torrential downpour LeBaron squeezed a generous dab of the green shampoo into the palm of his hand and administered it to the thin strands of her long blond hair. She helped him work up the lather. Together they kneaded the wet, sudsy mound on top of her head, their hands now bumping each other, now squeezing each other, the deafening tropical storm washing away the froth in long white rivulets. Fighting vainly to keep his mind strictly on business, LeBaron helped her rinse, shampoo again, and rinse again.

"Now the soap," she purred, peeling the paper wrapper off the small courtesy bar in the soap holder and handing it to him over her shoulder.

"Shut your eyes." Gingerly at first, and then with growing confidence, he soaped her face and rinsed it in the warm deluge, rubbed the slippery white bar over her neck and shoulders, up and around each arm, into each armpit, and then over her sternum, her stomach, and her firm breasts. She submitted like a small child to a Saturday night bath. The warm water pelted ceaselessly down on their heads and shoulders and arms and legs. As if in a dream, he leaned her to the left and reached around to allow himself access to those long, strong cheerleader legs, which he soaped with slow, careful strokes. He cleansed the fresh wounds on her bent knees. His gentleman's mind tried not to notice the low throaty moan when he soaped between her legs, but his baser emotions were already on the verge of mutiny. Any vestige of his former good manners was being swamped by the unending stream of hot water on naked, steaming flesh.

When she leaned back to let the purifying torrent cleanse away the lather, she felt how aroused he had become. Pivoting in his soap-slickened arms, she lay against him and smiled, her dark eyes clear and bright.

The beleaguered gentleman inside uttered one final, feeble protest, "Sarah, I don't want to take advantage--"

"Shhhhhh." She pressed a finger across his lips. "Make love to me, Jed."

--**6**--

Late that evening an Angel of the Lord appeared in a dream unto Cedrick Collins as he dozed in his favorite easy chair, his trusty cellular telephone beside him, waiting for his junior associate to return his calls. In the dazzling twin arc spotlights the Angel descended slowly out of the heavens to the stage, sparkles dazzling off his sequin-spangled pale blue blazer, a large, thin, leather-bound book in the crook his arm. As is the nature of a dream, Collins did not wonder that the Angel should have assumed the appearance of Bert Parks at a Miss America contest, nor, for that matter, that the Angel was a white man at all. The racial implications would never survive to trouble his waking mind.

"Hi, Bert," Collins mouthed, as if he had known the Angel his whole life. "Wha'cha got for me tonight?"

Without speaking, the Angel held forth the Book of Truth and opened it. The audience fell deathly silent.

Collins leaned forward and tried to read, but there were no words on the pages. Yet as he gazed into the empty cream-colored page, the Truth began to make itself known. It was all so wordlessly simple, involving birth and death in a slow cyclical dance. Awesome as it was, the Truth seemed to Collins to be missing some important ingredient. Something to bring it poignancy and life. It lacked *soul*.

Collins glanced up questioningly, but the Angel's face now held the vertical-slitted, gold-rimmed eyes of a blinking reptile. One hooked claw tapped the open page, and Collins looked again. Now the Truth poured in on him. It was logical and clean and perfectly simple, yet at the same time cold and merciless and empty, and Collins decided he didn't want to see any more, so with a muted grunt he woke himself up.

The bright halogen reading light burned his eyes.

"Bad dream," he muttered, dismissing with his adult mind that which another part of him, that tiny kernel of earliest consciousness formed while listening in awe to Bible lessons at Gramma Addie's knee those many years ago, could not dismiss. He switched off the lamp, stood up stiffly, stretched, and ran his fingers through the vestige of gray hair circling his temples.

The Divine Wind story had broken on the late television news. Rerunning the newscast in his mind's eye, he ambled over to the big picture window, pulled back the thick velour drapes, and gazed out. Only they'd made a jumble of it. The news boys had completely missed the human genetic engineering aspect of the story. Tomorrow morning ought to clear things up a bit.

Again he wondered what had become of LeBaron. Didn't seem likely that the FBI would be up to more funny stuff, now that the news hounds were onto the story and Bockel was in jail, but you never could tell. Reporters had been calling all evening, but Collins hadn't told them much. The whistle had been blown, the rock had been turned over, and now they could earn their own livings by digging through the muck underneath by themselves. Time to get back to normal.

Outside the night was cold and clear and a hazy fog was beginning to form far below in the glow of the city's distant street lights. Tomorrow would be sunny. The evil fire burning beyond the foothills to the east had been quenched, his city spared for now, and it was time to get back to business as usual. Trouble was, Collins was still uneasy. This whole affair had awakened discomforts that had taken years to put to sleep, and the bad dreams just wouldn't let him be.

So what was it going to take to get rid of the bad dreams? What would it cost him to extinguish this gnawing uneasiness once and for all? Collins was a reasonable man. He was prepared to bargain. He was willing to admit, for the purpose of bargaining, that maybe he'd drifted away a little bit from the ideals he'd embraced as a younger man, that maybe he *had* lined his own pockets without considering all that he might have done to help out the less fortunate brothers. All right. He could fess up. So now what was it going to cost him to make things right? An annual contribution to the N.A.A.C.P.? He could do that. It wouldn't be easy, given the *habits* he'd fallen into during the past thirty years. Beatrice had grown accustomed to a finer lifestyle. But he supposed he *could* change his ways, improve on his philanthropy a tad. What was the bottom line? Collins wanted it in dollars and cents. What was it going to cost him for a good night's sleep?

As if in answer, his cellular telephone chirped from the arm of his easy chair. Collins glanced at his watch. Quarter-to-twelve. Who would be calling at this hour? Might be one more reporter he wouldn't want to talk to. Or it might be LeBaron. In any case, he'd better pick the dang thing up before it woke Beatrice. He thumbed the "talk" switch. "Hello?"

"Hello, Mr. Collins? I hope I'm not calling too late."

"No. Glad y'called, LeBaron. It's all right. Looks like y'gonna be on the front page o'the *Chronicle* tomorrow mornin'."

"*I* am?"

"Yup. Reporters been callin' here all evenin'. Ain't y'been watchin' the news?"

"No . . . I missed it. What's happening?"

Collins related what he had seen on the ten o'clock news. A spokesman for the Defense Department had gone public with project Divine Wind, emphasizing improvements in the accuracy of the cruise missile that would keep America's fighting men out of harm's way. He acknowledged the incorporation of human fetal brain tissue into the electronic guidance system and invited a scientific dialogue on the subject. In response to questions, the spokesman admitted the burglary at Raccoona's apartment, but treated it as an unauthorized action committed by overzealous agents without the knowledge of their superiors.

LeBaron snorted. "Did he mention the records they took, or why?"

"Nope. Nothin' at all about genetic engineerin'. Talked about havin' a Congressional investigation. Sounds like jus' another cover-up t'me."

LeBaron was stunned. "So it's *over*?"

"Looks like. 'Cept for the hearin' tomorrow mornin' on your writs."

"That's really what I was calling about. Right now I'm with Sarah Brubaker and Dr. Finebridge, and--"

"You' *with*'em, you say?"

"Yes, and--"

"Y'mean they' already been turned *loose*?"

"Well, sort of, but--"

"Damn! LeBaron," Collins chortled. "Good work. Looks like y'got y'self a slam dunk. Beat the gover'ment hands down. Where' you at now?"

"I'm calling from a public phone, but . . . I don't think I should talk about it over the phone."

"Why not?   Ever'body's been turned loose, haven't they? Gover'ment boys're on the run."

"Well . . . not exactly." LeBaron lowered his voice. "Dr. Finebridge has . . . ah . . . got Dexter with him, too."

There was a long pause. "He' got *Dexter*?"

"Yes."

"You talkin' 'bout the gover'ment *computer* Dexter?"

"One and the same, only Dexter's more than just a com--"

"*With*'im?"

"Yes."

"Un*authorized*?"

"As far as I know."

"Hoo*oweee*!"

"That's sort of how I was feeling about it."

Both fell silent while Collins assimilated the news. The stakes had been upped considerably. Classified sheets of paper were one thing, but now they'd gone and stolen the *baby*. Good sense told him that this was the right time to fold his cards politely and kind of shuffle on out of the game. No hard feelings. He'd done what he had to. The news hounds had treed themselves a possum, and they could bring it down. This didn't really concern him anymore. If LeBaron had waded in deeper than he ought to have . . . well, whose problem was that?

But another voice was nagging at him. It came from deep inside and it wafted up through the musty years from the far distant past and it sounded one devil of a lot like Gramma Addie, rest her soul. The voice that was Gramma Addie's wanted to show him something. It wouldn't be put off. Reluctantly Collins looked and saw that *he was doing it all over again*: protecting his own black ass without so much as a notion about helping those who were reaching out to him for help. And something else. Somehow he knew that Gramma Addie, whose voice floated up through five decades of changing years to show him the unchanging truth of his own selfish behavior, sweet, wise, dear old Gramma Addie, was the one who had her scrawny black finger on the switch that turned those bad old dreams on or off. Collins grunted and reconsidered.

"Mr. Collins?"

"Yeah, I'm still here."

"I talked to Dexter."

"Y'*talked* t'im?"

"Well, not exactly *talked*, but I communicated with him by a keyboard--"

"An' he talked back?"

"Yes, in words on a tv screen."

Pause. "Then Finebridge was right?"

"Absolutely." LeBaron rambled on excitedly about his brother Vince and a technician named Charles Chung and how they were planning to teach Dexter all sorts of wonderful things.

Collins only half listened. Prodded by Gramma Addie, he was forcing himself to look at the situation from a different angle. It seemed to him that this might be just the opportunity he had been searching for, the chance to atone for those years of selfish transgression. Here was an opportunity to do something unselfish. And maybe get a whole lot of free advertising in the news coverage. But there would be personal risk, too, and he just couldn't be certain it was worth it. Suddenly LeBaron said something to snag his attention. "What was that?" he interrupted.

"What? Oh, I was just saying how interesting Charles Chung found it that Dexter was of African-American origin, the only fetus in the whole--"

"Hold it! Are you sayin' Dexter's a *black* man?"

"Well, yes, I guess you could put it that way."

A grin slowly curled itself across Collins lips. The balance tipped. He had received his answer.

"I think we've got a *big* problem here, Mr. Collins."

No response.

"I mean," LeBaron continued, "we've got a tiger by the tail, haven't we? If we show up in court tomorrow . . . well . . . we *are* in possession of stolen top-secret classified government property--"

"Not really," Collins muttered calmly, that grin growing, exposing a mouthful of sparkling white teeth.

"Pardon?"

"Said, 'not really.'"

"What do you mean?"

"Slavery's been outlawed in America, LeBaron. I thought y'knew that. Whadda they teachin' in law school nowadays? A human bein's not 'property'."

Alternate neural paths, previously considered and then forgotten, lit up LeBaron's brain, and he pursued their familiar argument.

"Now, d'y'think y'can bring Dexter along t'the hearin' in the mornin'?" Collins asked.

"Bring Dexter? Well . . . I don't know. Should we?"

"Might not hurt one bit. I believe it's time for a showdown. An' we' all set t'go first thing in Judge Grovner's court. I' got that all set up. Might as well be there's anyplace else. Y'know where that is?"

"No."

"Seventeenth floor o'the Federal Building. Turn right. It'll be down the hall on your left. But you leave Dexter outside in the car, hear? Or whatever y'plannin' t'bring him over in. Outta sight. Bring this Dr. Finebridge and your Sarah gal on up t'court, though. We' gonna need'em t'testify. Set the stage." Pause. "Now y'better get along before they trace y'down on this phone call."

"You *are* planning to be there tomorrow, aren't you?"

Collins' smile had grown until it glistened off the window pane and seemed to illuminate the entire dark city below. "Wouldn't miss it for all the world."

CHAPTER TWENTY

Friday morning

--1--

The sun squinted through the fog-girded East Bay hilltops, launching a dazzling golden lance over the choppy plum-colored waters of the bay, past the mausoleum towers of downtown San Francisco, through the ornate columns of the City Library, and across bustling Larkin Street to explode off the tinted glass walls of a small rectangular building. The structure, squatting distastefully at the edge of a grassy, tree-lined park like a gateway into the Morlock underworld, housed the elevators to the underground Civic Center parking garage.

Jed LeBaron, followed by Sarah Brubaker and Bernard Finebridge, pushed through the sparkling glass doors into the inspired hubbub of the City's caffeine-laced rush hour. Like a man freshly awakened from a long, bleak dreamtime, LeBaron sniffed at the crisp morning air and drank in the commotion with all his senses. The swelling at the bridge of his nose had subsided, but bruises of tarnished silver circled beneath both eyes. Still clad in the cocoon of yesterday's blood-smudged corduroy suit, he reached back and took Sarah's hand.

Dr. Finebridge shifted Gideon and gently encircled Sarah's other arm with one large, gentle surgeon's hand. His tall, thin figure was more than usually stooped with foreboding and his eyes wore a hollow, hunted look. It had thrilled Finebridge to play the Sundance Kid, an outlaw, a renegade, a desperado, a Robin Hood taking from the rich to give to the poor. Like a latter day Butch Cassidy, this Vince LeBaron, one of the two brothers Sarah had summoned out of her past like cavalry troopers at the blast of a magic trumpet, had ridden to Dexter's rescue, had shown Charles Chung and him how to thumb their noses at inequitable laws, how to steal in the name of justice, and how to disappear like smoke through a hole in the wall. But now, as each step brought him nearer the ultimate reckoning on the battlefield of the federal court, the scientist was not unmindful of how that Butch Cassidy business had turned out. Neither Vince nor his brother Jed could predict what would come of today's confrontation. Neither attorney would rule out the possibility that Finebridge might be jailed and prosecuted as a traitor. As he helped steady Sarah in her stylish high heels, which she had insisted on wearing against all reason, he was glad to have someone else to fuss over and thus take his mind off his own misery.

Between them Sarah concentrated on her footsteps. She felt much better this morning. A light meal of chicken soup and saltine crackers had settled her stomach enough last night for a short, sound night's sleep. She had awakened with a voracious appetite and sampled everything in LeBaron's sparse larder. Now, squeaky clean from another shower, decked out in the trim blue business dress she had been saving, belly content, body rested, and with each stride the residual glow of physical intimacy radiating from her secret center, she felt her prior vitality beginning to flow, although her step still wobbled a bit and she had yet to fully straighten out the traumatic jumble of her kidnapping.

In Berkeley's predawn chill the trio had crawled into LeBaron's gas-guzzling station wagon and motored across the Bay Bridge, out of the fog, through the maze of freeway exchanges, off-ramps, and frantic arterials, and into the murky bowels of the Civic Center garage. Vince and Charles Chung were to load Dexter into the purloined government van and drive over as soon as they could. So far the morning had unfolded with a sublime harmony that portended great good fortune for the day.

But the tranquility fell apart as they rounded the corner of Golden Gate Avenue across from the Federal Building. An eagle-eyed reporter from the six-o'clock news recognized Finebridge and shouted to his crew, "Let's go, folks. That's him!" A dozen reporters, newscasters, technicians, cameramen, and assorted support personnel converged on the trio as they followed the sidewalk toward the granite steps.

"Dr. Finebridge--"

"Tell me about Divine Wind--"

"--Dr. *Fine*bridge--over *here*--"

"--is it for real?"

"What's your position on abortion?--"

"--are you prepared to make a statement?"

"Dr. *Finebridge--?*"

"--do you support abortion as a source of fetal tissue?"

"Are you the attorney?--"

"What about the government secrets--"

"--are you LeBaron?"

"--is there any truth in the allegation--"

"Who's the blond babe?"

"--that you stole government secrets?"

"What's *she* got t'do with this?"

"Where've you been hiding out?"

"Tell me about Dexter--"

"Are you gonna be charged?"

"--where's Dexter now?"

"What's *your* name, Miss?"

"What do you expect to happen?"

"How does the darn thing work?"

LeBaron circled his left arm tightly around Sarah's waist and fended with the worn leather briefcase in his right. Television cameras whirred, microphones jabbed at their faces, and flashbulbs exploded from a half-dozen cameras floating on disembodied arms above the heads. "No comment, no comment," LeBaron droned. Waving the briefcase as if to swat wasps, he led Sarah through the probing horde and up the polished stone steps. Hunched and cringing, Finebridge hoisted the laptop computer over his head and followed in their wake. At the top of the stairs LeBaron turned momentarily to announce, "We may have a statement after the hearing, but we have nothing to say at this time. Please let us through. No comment."

Bobbing and weaving through the maelstrom, rude questions pummeling their heads and shoulders and ricocheting off the echoing marble walls like caroming hailstones, LeBaron shepherded his flock through the cavernous hallway, past the directory board, and into the upper elevator bank. There they got lucky and just managed to squeeze into an almost-full car that left no room for the gaggle of news predators.

Up to the seventeenth floor they rode in beleaguered silence, exited quickly, turned right into the wide polished corridor, and, one step ahead of the next elevator's load of bloodhounds, located the courtroom of Judge Marion L. Grovner.

The chamber was magnificent. The high ceiling and intricately carved oak trim was no doubt a modern-day replication of some old world Gothic cathedral. Above the bench, high against the far end of the courtroom, the Great Seal of the United States demanded the highest reverence. Four long counsel tables with carved-oak trestle legs and studded with small chrome microphones filled the generous space between the bench and the bar. On a podium just below the bench stood a massive wooden lectern with two microphones perched on its upper lip like chromium raptors. The magnificence of the chamber exalted the Law, with the unintended consequence of dismissing that which was merely human as petty and insignificant.

Most striking was the suffocating silence. LeBaron could just barely hear the clicking of Sarah's heels beside him on the polished hardwood floor. A small clutch of attorneys in expensive funeral-wear milled about in pantomime at the far end of the courtroom. Not a dull murmur wafted from their direction. The architecture devoured all sounds except the distant whoosh of the building's air circulation system. The chamber had apparently been acoustically fitted to absorb all sounds except those chosen and channeled to emanate from the tall, narrow speakers hung at regular intervals along the pale blond oak-panelled walls.

LeBaron deposited Sarah and Finebridge in the front row of the gallery and pushed through the ornate oak railing to find out whether his matters had found their way onto the docket. A dozen attorneys, mostly middle-aged men, already occupied the inner sanctum, leaning over the clerk's desk, standing in small groups, or sitting alone at the tables scrutinizing paperwork. All were attired in somber vestments of a quality rarely encountered in the seedy, mismatched, catch-as-catch-can backwaters of Oakland's criminal justice system. LeBaron, self-consciously buttoning his own inelegant jacket, recognized none of the faces.

LeBaron approached the clerk's desk and waited for an opening. The clerk was a brown-skinned man whose deeply wrinkled face, short-cropped white hair, and brusque manner proclaimed that he had no time for fools. He finished file-stamping some papers for the pair of uptown lawyers leaning over him. One, an intense middle-aged man, patronized his female associate, probably his protégé. She was dark-haired, vaguely pretty, and no older than LeBaron. The clerk extended the stamped papers to the woman, but her companion snatched them away with a haughty, "That puts *our* ducks in a row."

The clerk shuffled his files. Without looking up he inquired, "Can I help you?"

"Yes . . . er . . .," LeBaron cleared his throat, "I'd just like to see whether my matter is on the calendar this--"

"Name."

"Uh . . . LeBaron . . . I'm Jed LeBaron . . ."

"Name of the *case*."

"Oh . . . right . . . I guess it would be, 'Finebridge verses Department of Agriculture' . . . and two more . . ."

The clerk located the file, glanced at the attorney's name, and stood up with an unexpectedly warm smile. "You must be from Cedrick's office."

"Yes. My name's Jed LeBaron."

The clerk offered his hand. "I'm pleased to meet you, Mr. LeBaron. I'm Gus Welby." He frowned at LeBaron's face and suit. "Gawd-a'mighty! Were you *mugged* on the way over here?"

"No," LeBaron laughed, shaking Welby's hand. "But it's a long story. This is the best I can do for today. I hope the judge won't be offended."

"Naw. Couldn't care less. Say, is Cedrick planning to be here himself this morning?"

"I believe so."

Welby leaned forward confidentially. "Looks like the government brought in their big guns." He nodded toward the far table.

"Oh?" LeBaron followed his nod to a huddle of five or six men in dark suits and one he hadn't noticed before decked out in full-dress green military uniform, complete with brass buttons, gold shoulder braids, and gaudy little bars covering his entire chest. He was short, sported a crew-cut and an ugly pencil-thin moustache, and glared at

LeBaron while a thin, silver-haired gentleman whispered into his ear. LeBaron turned away. "Which ones?"

"All of them." Welby sat down and pulled two more thin files out of his stack and placed them on top. "Anyway, you're on the calendar all right. Very top. Three matters. Should be starting in about . . .," he glanced at his watch, ". . . about five minutes. Judge Grovner's very punctual."

"Thanks." LeBaron scanned the crowd for Cedrick Collin's charismatic grin, and when he did not find it, returned to Sarah and Dr. Finebridge. They were stoically ignoring the hoarsely whispered questions from a battery of newsmen who had taken up seats in the row just behind. "Will you leave us alone for a while," LeBaron pleaded, without effect, and sat next to Sarah. "We're first on the calendar."

Sarah nodded. "Colonel Mueller is here," she whispered, pointing to the uniformed man whose malevolent eyes continued to track LeBaron like radar. The taller, silver-haired gentleman still whispered in his ear.

"Ah," LeBaron acknowledged, "I wondered who that creep might be. Ugly moustache."

Sarah giggled.

He turned to examine her, doing his best to ignore the ears listening six inches behind their heads. "Are you okay? How're you feeling?"

She took his arm in both hands. "Fine. Just a few butterflies, I guess."

Ah, butterflies, LeBaron thought, considering the swarm that was fluttering in his own hollow innards. "Don't worry. This Judge Grovner, whoever he is, isn't going to bite." Privately he wondered just what a judge with a name like 'Grovner' *would* be like. A pale-skinned, sharp-featured disciplinarian out of a Charles Dickens novel materialized in his nervous imagination.

LeBaron extracted a single thin file from his briefcase and began scanning its meager notes. Unfortunately no one had found the time to do the necessary research, and now he was going to have to wing it. Just like he always seemed to do nowadays. A year ago, before coming to work for Cedrick Collins, the prospect of standing up in Federal District Court abysmally unprepared would have mortified him. But Collins' relentless saturation therapy had worked wonders. Now 'fiasco' was just another name for business as usual.

"Mornin', LeBaron."

LeBaron started to his feet, dumping the open file onto the floor. In the sound-deadened room Cedrick Collins had crept up on them without warning.

Collins grinned. He appeared more magnificent, more confident, more *radiant* than LeBaron could ever remember. The impact sprang not only from his expensive three-piece blue pin-stripped suit, hand-painted silk necktie, diamond stick pin, and gold watch fob, but from the man himself. A cloud of jabbering reporters buzzed in his wake.

"Good morning." LeBaron grunted, bending to recover his file.

Collins scrutinized the newsboys with the exasperated grimace Dr. Frankenstein must have worn when regarding his own aberrant creation. "G'won, leave us *be* for a minute, will ya, boys?"

"Mr. Collins, I'd like you to meet Sarah Brubaker--"

A skinny newsman stuck his red nose across the row of seats. "How d'ya *spell* that, *Brubaker*?"

"--and Dr. Bernard Finebridge."

"What's *she* got t'do with this?" another reporter demanded from the aisle.

Ignoring them, Sarah and the scientist stood and shook hands.

"Pleased t'meetcha," Collins bobbed, smiling disarmingly to each. "Say, is'at Gideon y'got there?"

"Oh, this? Yes, it is." Finebridge handed the computer to Collins.

"Thank ya. Now if you'll excuse us, me'n LeBaron here gotta talk." He took his associate by the arm and steered him through the bar, beyond the range of the reporters.

"You look like you're feeling pretty good today," LeBaron observed.

"Feel fine," Collins rejoined. "Slept like a baby last night, after y'called. Ready t'do battle." As they swept past the clerk's desk, Collins called out, "Mornin', Welby."

"Good morning, Cedrick."

"We on this mornin'?"

"Sure enough. First thing."

"Nice work. An' thank ya."

"My pleasure."

Collins stopped beside the empty jury box. "Now who' we up against this mornin', LeBaron? Any idea?"

LeBaron pointed out the huddle of men at the far table. They all glanced away, except Mueller, who pugnaciously returned their stares. The tall, silver-haired gentlemen continued to jabber in his ear.

"Don't think I know any of'em. Must be out o'town. Now, wha'cha plannin'?"

"What am *I* planning?" LeBaron stammered. "I thought *you* were going to take over."

"Naw, you'll do jus' fine. I'll jump on in like usual if the spirit moves me. You can start'er out."

"But I'm not *prepared*."

"Nothin' t'prepare. You drafted the writs, di'n'cha? You know the facts. Jus' get ahold o'yourself." Collins' plan was clearly not open to further debate. "Nothin' to a writ o'habeas corpus--"

"All rise!" Gus Welby announced into the silver microphone on his desk, and the words expanded to fill the huge chamber.

"--it's the *people*'s remedy." Collins concluded.

--2--

As Judge Grovner assumed the bench, it became clear to LeBaron that he had been dead wrong about at least three things. The judge was neither British, pale-skinned, nor a man. Judge Marion Lilly Grovner was a slight, brown-skinned woman in her mid-fifties, with a wave of black hair brushed back to expose thin, almost Caucasian features scarred by a childhood bout with smallpox. She had graduated cum laude from Harvard Law School in the sixties, had gone to work for the Justice Department as a civil rights lawyer, had been appointed by Governor Brown to the Los Angeles Superior Court bench, and seven years later had been elevated by the President to the Federal District Court in San Francisco. She knew the law, and she knew lawyers.

Judge Grovner dragged the stack of files from the center of her desk, flipped open the top one, and read, "Sarah Brubaker Christensen verses the United States Department of Agriculture. This is a petition for a writ of habeas corpus. Please state your appearances for the record."

Heart pounding, knees trembling, palms sweating, LeBaron found his way up to the podium and spoke into the chrome pencil microphone that sprouted from the carved wood lectern. "Jed LeBaron," his voice boomed, louder than expected, filling every corner of the vast silence-smothered chamber. He recoiled a few inches and lowered his tone. "From the law offices of Cedrick Collins. Appearing for the petitioner."

The elegant silver-haired gentleman who had been jabbering in Mueller's ear joined LeBaron. He was tall and thin and impeccably attired in a charcoal three-piece suit, hand-tailored to minimize the slight skeletal hunch of his shoulders. His small, moist eyes gleamed from deep within sunken eye sockets, and his pale, almost translucent skin, a collage of intricate wrinkles dappled with liver spots, seemed wrapped too tightly about his prominent skull. Moving with an effeminate grace, he appeared completely at ease in the cathedral-like setting. He leaned into the microphone and declared in a silken voice, "Chandler Stillman, ah, of the United States Attorney General's Office, ah, appearing for the Department of Agriculture."

In the few steps it had taken to carry Stillman from the counsel table to the podium, and without seeming to even notice him, Stillman had taken LeBaron's measure with a precision bred of years of courtroom battle. LeBaron's thin, closed file, his awkward body stance, and the minute trembling in his locked left knee told Stillman he was up against a reluctant, passive, and unprepared adversary who would have given anything to be somewhere else at that moment. Seizing the initiative, he pressed the court, "Before we proceed, ah, your honor, ah, in order to avoid wasting the court's time, ah, might I be allowed to point out that the *petitioner*, ah, Sarah Brubaker Christensen, ah, is present in court today, ah, seated in the front row . . ." Stillman turned with a vague flourish and extended a pale white hand toward Sarah, then leaned back to the microphone. ". . . and that she is not in custody, ah, but has come here freely and, ah, voluntarily."

"Is that correct, Mr. LeBaron?" Judge Grovner asked. "Please be brief. I've read your petition."

"Well . . . yes, your honor, as far as it goes. What counsel did *not* mention, however, is that she *was* in custody at the time this petition was filed. Two men in the employment of the Department of Agriculture by the names of Crawford and Weams, I believe, took her into custody and illegally injected her with--"

"*Please*, your honor!" Stillman bent forward indignantly, his thin lips brushing the microphone's windscreen and his amplified silken drawl overriding his adversary. His hands splayed open, palms upward, like two dead doves. "Can we dispense with these baseless slanders which, ah, have nothing to do with the petition before this Court? There's nothing in Counsel's declaration about a Crawford or a Weams, and, ah, if these persons *did* do what Counsel suggests, ah, I am sure they did so *outside* the scope of their employment with the Department, ah, *if* the Department employs them at all."

"Well, your honor--" LeBaron began again.

"Just a minute, Mr. LeBaron." Judge Grovner raised her hand and homed in on Stillman. "Is it your position, Counsel, that Sarah Brubaker Christensen is not in custody?"

"That is correct, ah, your honor."

"And that the Department has no accusation or other proceeding pending against her at this time which might result in a criminal or civil penalty?"

"Totally correct."

"And is the Department *planning* to take any action against her?"

"None that I am aware of."

Judge Grovner turned to LeBaron. "Do you dispute these contentions, Counsel?"

LeBaron thought for a moment, resisted an urge to turn to his mentor for guidance, and murmured, "I guess I can accept them as accurate."

Judge Grovner eased back. "Well, that seems to resolve the matter, doesn't it?"

"Yes and no, your honor," LeBaron countered. "We are prepared to offer testimony to show that Sarah Brubaker *was* in custody, and while in custody, was physically and mentally abused--"

"Be that as it may, Counsel, as far as your petition for a writ of habeas corpus goes, I'm going to deny that, since it appears to the court that the petitioner is *not now* in custody and the respondent has no present intention *to place* petitioner in custody. If you wish to pursue damages in this matter, you can consider the wisdom of filing a claim under the Federal Tort Claims Act. Habeas corpus is not an appropriate remedy. Case dismissed. Costs to respondent."

"Will the court consider an award of *sanc*tions," Stillman oozed, "for filing this frivolous petition?" His grin reminded LeBaron of the shrunken lips of a dehydrated mummy.

"No, Mr. Stillman," Judge Grovner sighed, closing the file and sliding it toward the clerk, "the court will not. I'm giving Mr. LeBaron the benefit of the doubt. I find that he believed, in good faith, that his client was in custody at the time the petition was filed. Now let's move on." She opened the next file. "Dr. Bernard Finebridge verses the United States Department of Agriculture. Same appearances?"

"Yes, your honor," Stillman purred.

LeBaron had turned to get Collins' reaction, but his employer sat implacably, as uninterested as if he were half-watching an old *Cosby* rerun.

"Mr. Le*Baron*?" Judge Grovner prompted.

LeBaron spun around. "Yes, your honor?"

"You're appearing for the petitioner in *this* matter, too?"

"Oh, yes I am. Sorry."

"And is Dr. Bernard Finebridge also present in court today?"

"Yes, he is." LeBaron motioned, and Finebridge stood and slowly approached the lectern.

"Your honor," Stillman preempted, "if it please the court, ah, I submit that the circumstances of this case are, ah, identical to those of the last one. Dr. Finebridge is here of his own free will. He is not now, ah, and never has been, ah, in the respondent's custody."

Judge Grovner focussed on Stillman. "Is any proceeding now pending against him which might result in a criminal or civil penalty?"

"Not that I know of."

"Is that correct, Mr. LeBaron?"

"Well . . . as a matter of fact . . . " he glanced at Finebridge for guidance, but the scientist just shrugged and shook his head, ". . . technically . . . I guess you could say that . . . as far as we know at this particular time."

"That was a 'yes'?"

A snigger drifted over from the respondent's table.

"Yes, your honor," LeBaron confirmed abjectly.

"Well then, I see no reason why this petition shouldn't be disposed of the same as the last one," Judge Grovner closed the file and slid it toward the clerk.

Finebridge whispered something in LeBaron's ear.

The cadaverous grin had returned to Stillman's face. No damage has been done. Smugly he pressed his advantage. "Sanctions, your honor?"

"Just a second, your honor," LeBaron interrupted. "My client is concerned that he *will be* taken into custody . . . this morning . . . as soon as these proceedings are concluded. I don't believe we have anything on the record about that."

Judge Grovner considered the possibility. "*Is* that the intention of the government, Mr. Stillman?"

Stillman was caught off guard. "Well . . . ah . . . I'm not sure that is really relevant--"

"I consider it to be relevant."

"Yes, ah, of course. If the court will, ah, allow me just a moment." He glided over to his huddle of colleagues and consulted briefly, then returned to the podium frowning. "Your honor, the people intend to, ah, *detain* Dr. Finebridge for questioning, ah, about a matter not yet before this court."

Judge Grovner sighed. "May I have that file back, Mr. Welby?" She stretched across the desk to retrieve the thin file and reopened it. "What are the charges?"

"No one is *charged* with anything, yet," Stillman oiled, splaying his dead-dove hands.

"I *know* that, Counsel," Judge Grovner countered. "Why do you intend to detain him?"

Colonel Mueller and another man had followed Stillman back to the podium, and they whispered together for a moment before Stillman leaned toward the microphone. "We believe Dr. Finebridge, ah, has in his possession, ah, certain classified property, ah, *stolen* from the United States Government, your honor."

The newsmen were suddenly abuzz. Their commotion was all but swallowed by the chamber's acoustics.

Judge Grovner nodded, then turned to LeBaron. "Your position, Counsel?"

"Well, your honor . . . although no formal charges have been filed . . . as far as I know . . . or at least my client hasn't been apprised of any such charges . . . have you? . . . no, I thought not . . . so, as I was saying, although we don't know anything about any charges . . . *formal* charges, that is . . . if there are any--"

"You' hono'?" Cedrick Collins' baritone boomed out of nowhere.

"Yes, Cedrick?"

Collins leaned over the chrome microphone at the counsel table. "You' hono', we' prepared t'show that this so-called 'gover'ment property' wasn't *stolen* at all--"

"Objection!" Stillman stammered. "Who *is* this man? Is he an attorney?"

"That's Cedrick Collins," Judge Grovner explained. "And last I knew, he was an attorney." The hint of a smile flickered on her lips. "You haven't been disbarred, have you Cedrick?"

"Not that I know about, you' hono'."

"His office is of record, Mr. Stillman. Mr. LeBaron and he are associates."

"Oh. Thank you, your honor. I apologize and, ah, withdraw my objection."

"Now Cedrick, why don't you step up to the podium if you intend to participate."

With an unrushed composure Collins complied, and LeBaron made room for him. "You' hono', we' prepared t'show that this here 'gover'ment property' they' talkin' about left of its own free will, and that Finebridge here was jus' helpin' it out some."

"Why that's absurd!" Stillman interjected.

"I believe," Collins persisted, "that if you set this case aside for one minute and call the *next* one, this is all gonna be cleared up."

"Any objection, Mr. Stillman?"

Stillman opened his palms in such exaggerated amazement he practically turned the dead doves inside out. "I have no idea where Mr., ah, Collins, ah, is going with this."

"Well, neither do I. Let's find out, shall we? I'll call . . .," Judge Grovner stared at the open file for a long moment, then pierced Collins with a cold stare, "Is this your idea of a joke, Cedrick?"

"No, you' hono'."

She assayed his candor, appeared satisfied for the moment, and continued, "*Dexter* verses Department of Agriculture.'"

"Chandler Stillman appearing for the respondent," Stillman hastened, intent on jamming his fist in a small leak in the waterlogged dike before it became a big leak. "Your honor, I think the court has hit the nail right on the head. This *is* a joke, ah, and a poor one at that. Dexter is not a person. Dexter is the code name for, ah, a military computer. A mere machine. Property of the United States Government."

"Is this true, Cedrick? *Is* this a bad joke?"

"No, you' hono'. Nobody seems t'be laughin', least of all Mr. Stillman here."

"Your honor," Stillman continued, "we have experts here, ah, *universally recognized* experts, ah, who are prepared to testify that Dexter is a mere *machine*--"

"And we' prepared t'call the chief project engineer, Dr. Bernard Finebridge--"

"Not any longer, he's not. He's been fired--"

"Then we're prepared to call an even *better* witness--"

"I know what you're trying to do, but--"

"Gentlemen, *please!*" Judge Grovner intervened. She waited a few breaths for the attorneys to unrile themselves. "Now I'd like to hear from each of you, one at a time if you don't mind. That's how we proceed in this court. Cedrick, you represent the petitioner. What precisely is your contention? What is your offer of proof? Please be brief."

"Thank ya, you' hono'." Collins tugged at his lapels to straighten the creases from his suit coat, collecting his thoughts and composing himself. He obviously did not like Chandler Stillman, and he did not want his animosity to interfere with a dignified presentation. When he was ready, he leaned over the microphone. "For the past coupla years the federal gover'ment' been puttin' together computers for missile guidance systems under the code name 'Divine Wind.'"

Stillman jerked forward to say something, thought better of it, and stood back.

"The thing is," Collins continued, "they' been messin' 'round with genetic engineerin', usin' *brain tissue* as a kinda pre-filter in connection with the electronic stuff. *Human* brain tissue. They' been gettin' it from aborted fetuses. Aborted *human* babies. Keepin' it alive by artificial means. Fiddlin' with the genes. Lettin' it grow. Lettin' it develop. Lettin' it *learn*--"

Stillman could not restrain himself. "I have to object to this characterization--"

Judge Grovner overrode him with a raised hand. "You'll have your chance in a minute. Go on, Cedrick."

Collins regarded his opponent with distaste. "Anyway," he went on, "Dr. Finebridge here's been the chief project engineer all along. He started at the beginnin', and would still be runnin' the show if he hadn't begun t'suspect somethin' *funny* was goin' on. Now, he prob'ly knows more about this thing than any other man alive--"

"Objection!" Stillman sizzled. "We are not prepared to concede–"

"Mr. *Still*man," Judge Grovner interrupted patiently, placing a finger to her lips, "shush, we're not taking evidence yet. This is merely petitioner's offer of proof. You'll get your chance to respond."

Collins turned his back on Stillman and leaned against the lectern. "Anyhow, the most recent version of this so-called 'computer' the gover'ment be' puttin' together . . . least as far's I *know* it's the most recent . . . be called 'Dexter'. We' prepared t'offer evidence . . . that *Dexter's a fully conscious human bein'*." Collins regarded the court over his wire-rim spectacles as he paused to let the concept sink in, "Dexter's a human bein' jus' as much's you an' me, you' hono'. An' as such, he's entitled t'all the protections afforded by the United States Constitution, includin' the right t'be free from arrest an' incarc'ration against his own free will without due process o'law."

In the gallery of the sound-deadened courtroom the reporters danced in a charade-like frenzy.

Judge Grovner stared at Collins a long, thoughtful moment. "An intriguing concept, Cedrick." Then she turned to Stillman. "Now, what is the government's position?"

"Just that this is all *totally preposterous*, your honor. It is the, ah, figment of an imagination run wild. The government is prepared to show, ah, how far from the mainstream of scientific consensus this Dr. Finebridge has deviated, ah, in his bizarre contentions. The government is prepared to call a *dozen* expert witnesses, ah, *two dozen*, if need be, ah, to show the court beyond any reasonable doubt that this, ah, absurd contention about a *conscious machine*, ah, is *absolutely impossible* and, ah, the fantasy of a sick, ah, lonely, and, ah, deluded mind. Dexter is a computing machine. Nothing more. It is the property of the United States Government. And . . ."--he pointed a white, bony finger at Finebridge--". . . *he* has stolen it!"

"Thank you, Mr. Stillman." Judge Grovner's high-back leather chair squealed as she leaned back to regard one attorney after the other. "Let's just see if I understand what each of you are saying here. Cedrick, you are saying that the government has somehow *created* a human being–"

"Not *created*," Collins interrupted. "Dexter's *born*. Born of a woman . . . a *black* woman, at that . . ."--he eyed the judge significantly over the top of his spectacles--". . . and they stuck'im in this machine. Gover'ment created nothin'."

"All right," Judge Grovner accepted his correction. "And that this Dexter is a 'person' entitled to the full protection of the Fifth Amendment of the Constitution . . ."

"Thass right."

". . . Dr. Finebridge merely assisted Dexter in freeing himself from the illegal restraint of the Department of Agriculture . . ."

"Completely justifiable. Doctrine o'least harm."

". . . And consequently," Judge Grovner concluded, "Dr. Finebridge should not himself be subject to arrest or prosecution. Is that pretty much it?"

"Thass pretty much it . . . 'cept for the *creatin'* part."

"All right." She turned to Stillman. "And the government, on the other hand, contends that Dexter is *not* a 'person' entitled to Constitutional protections, but is merely personal property, owned by the United States Government, and that by taking this personal property without proper authority, Dr. Finebridge has subjected himself to criminal prosecution on any number of grounds. Is that correct?"

"I don't see how the Court can conclude otherwise."

"I *mean*, have I correctly stated the government's contentions."

"Yes, ah, essentially, your honor."

"Fine." The judge withdrew into silent contemplation, weighing the arguments, the law, the consequences. After a moment she announced, "Cedrick, I'm sorry, but I don't see how you have made a sufficient showing why this court should intervene with respect to Dr. Finebridge. He is not now in custody. If criminal charges are brought against him, he will have every opportunity in those proceedings to raise the defense of justification, or whatever else he deems appropriate."

The blood seemed to leave Finebridge. Knees trembling, he reached for LeBaron's arm to steady his balance.

Collins nodded the ruling aside and approached the problem from a different angle. "What about Dexter, you' hono'? Dexter's not charged with nothin'."

Through his embalmer's grin of triumph Stillman wheedled, "The court surely has the wisdom to see that this, ah, computing machine we call 'Dexter' has, ah, no standing here." He issued a cold, harsh little laugh and offered the obvious with his dead dove hands. "Habeas corpus is for human beings."

"Precisely the question, Mr. Stillman." Judge Grovner gazed from one attorney to the other. "*Is* Dexter a 'person' entitled to Constitutional protections? I don't suppose either of you have been able to find any case law on that subject."

Each shook his head.

"I thought not." Judge Grovner brought her hands together to form a small brown finger-tent of pensiveness. "I don't suppose anyone has ever *made* the contention you are now making, Cedrick. No doubt the framers of the Constitution had other things on their minds. But technology marches on, doesn't it?" She glanced at her wrist watch. "I'd like to ask each of you to explain, *briefly*, how you would propose that this court resolve the question."

"That's simple," Stillman jumped in. "This is a highly specialized field that, ah, laymen really know nothing about--"

"Horsefeathers!" Collins snorted.

"--The court needs to consider expert testimony," Stillman continued, "and, ah, we are prepared to call a whole list of experts prominent in the fields of biology, ah, artificial intelligence, and, ah, computer sciences, ah, beginning with Dr. Boris Stanovich--"

"How many witnesses do you intend to call?"

"As many as the court will allow, your honor. The consensus of opinion is overwhelming--"

"Well, I don't have time today. We're going to have to calendar this for a special setting. Mr. Welby, what's the soonest we have an opening for a half-day hearing?"

"Better make it a full day," Stillman corrected. "This will be very technical."

"You' hono'?"

"Better make it full day, Mr. Welby."

"You' hono'?"

"Just a moment. Yes, Cedrick?"

"We' got us a serious problem here," Collin's nodded gravely. "Finebridge here be lookin' after Dexter now, an' he's about t'run out o'some kind o'filters an' other things Dexter' got t'have. Without'em, he' be stone dead'n about two days." He pulled down his spectacles and gazed over the top. "We' gotta have a court order continuin' custody o'Dexter with Finebridge here an'--"

"*I object most strenuously!*" Stillman exploded indignantly. "This man represents a *thief* of stolen government property, ah, and he's asking to be awarded *custody*--"

"An' you people're fixin' t'*kill off* the incriminatin' evidence if y'can get your claws on'im--!"

"That is none of your affair! These are highly classified govern-ment proprietary matters--!"

"News reports say its all been *de*classified--"

Judge Grovner rose silently and spread both arms like a small brown angel calming the surging waters of the Red Sea. She quickly had their attention, then remonstrated wryly, "Perhaps you two boys would prefer to step out into the schoolyard and settle this with your fists?"

Both attorneys stared at her.

"No?"

Each dropped his eyes and shook his head.

"All right." She watched them for a moment. "Now Cedrick, it seems to me you're asking this court for a temporary restraining order to preserve the status quo, pending a full hearing on this. Is that right?"

"That's what I'm askin' for. T'per'serve th'status quo."

"So, are you prepared to offer testimony, or do you intend to submit this on your declarations?"

"First off, save us all some time, we gonna offer in evidence the gover'ment project reports on Divine Wind." Collins wheeled on Stillman. "They' been declassified, am I right?"

"Well . . . I'm not sure." He caucused with his support staff. Mueller's face grew beet red as he protested the policy reversal from Washington. Stillman returned to the podium. "It is my understanding that the project reports are being, ah, declassified, yes. They may still, however, ah, contain some classified material--"

"Well, we' offerin'em in evidence."

"Now just a minute," Stillman protested. "The reports haven't been reviewed and purged--"

"Som'thin' in there y'don't want the judge t'see?"

"Well, no--"

"Y'hidin' som'thin' from the court?"

"Of course not!" Stillman rejoined.

"Then whass th'*problem*?"

Judge Grovner had followed the exchange with amusement. "If it will save time, I can review these reports *in camera* without making them a part of the record," she offered. "Is that agreeable?"

Caught between Delbert Cousins' insistence on a display of absolute candor and the truculence of Colonel Mueller, who still clung to the cloak of secrecy like a child to its favorite blanket, Stillman hesitated only a second. He had no illusions where his loyalty lay. His dead lips curled back ingratiatingly as he purred, "Perfectly, your honor."

Mueller fumed back to his chair, moustache twitching and veins in his forehead pulsing angrily.

"Do you have a copy of the reports, Cedrick?" the judge asked.

"Better get'em from him." Collins tipped his head toward Stillman. "Mine've got a lotta writin' on'em."

"Is that acceptable, Mr. Stillman?"

Stillman glanced at Mueller, who clutched his attaché case against his medallioned breast, jaw set, eyes blazing. Stillman sighed, "We'll stipulate to the admission of petitioner's copies."

"Fine. Anything else, Cedrick?"

"We' gonna need a little testimony, if the court can fin' the time. I believe we' got a pretty persuasive witness. Shouldn't take all that long."

"You will be calling Dr. Finebridge?"

"Not chiefly. Maybe if time allows."

"No?" Judge Grovner glanced from Sarah to Finebridge to LeBaron. "Who will you be calling, then?"

"We' prepared t'call Dexter hisself."

"*Objection*!" Stillman blustered, feigning shock. "You can't call a *machine* to testify!"

Judge Grovner was intrigued. "Can you *do* that? Bring Dexter in here?"

"Don' see why not. He's designed t'be portable."

"How would you . . . *communicate* with him?"

"*It!*" Stillman corrected. "It's not a *him*! It's a darned *machine*, for God's sake! This is, ah, a *trick*, your honor. Be extremely careful. They're trying to, ah, hoodwink you."

Collins ignored his adversary. "LeBaron here's talked t'him. He can tell ya."

"Yes, I have," LeBaron confirmed, displacing his employer at the microphone. "I just . . . typed in questions on a keyboard, and Dexter answered in words on a screen."

"Ah." Judge Grovner understood. "Just like with a computer."

"It *is* a darned computer!" Stillman insisted in exasperation. "It's a *machine*! Machines can't testify!"

"That's precisely the question to be resolved, Mr. Stillman."

Judge Grovner considered for a moment, then asked. "Would *I* be able to voir dire Dexter?"

"Certainly," LeBaron nodded.

"On any subject? Or are there limits?"

"You can ask him anything you want," LeBaron replied, then added, "How else would you be able to tell whether Dexter is a person . . . ?"

"And not just a cleverly programmed machine," Judge Grovner completed the thought.

"Exactly," LeBaron confirmed, encouraged.

Judge Grovner glanced down at the docket. "Mr. Welby," she said to her clerk, "could you call Mr. Blaine and Mr. Coombs and tell them that we are going to have to continue the summary judgment motion set for hearing at eleven. Find a new time convenient to both parties."

"Yes, Ma'am."

"Your honor," Stillman pressed, "may I say something?"

"Nothing has stopped you before now."

"Your honor, this project involves, ah, extremely sensitive military hardware and software, ah, belonging to the United States Government. I believe it would be a mistake to, ah, to go into this in detail in open court."

"Fine. We will reconvene in my chambers at eleven o'clock. Cedrick, you will have Dexter present?"

"I'll do m'best, if'n those gover'ment boys aren't plannin' t'cause me too much grief."

"Well, I'll issue an order that Dexter be present and that no one, including agents of the Department of Agriculture, should interfere."

"An' the professor here?" Collins put an arm around Finebridge's deflated shoulders. "We gonna need him, too."

"All right. My order will include Dr. Finebridge, pending the hearing. In the meantime, I would like counsel to attempt to reach a stipulation on a temporary restraining order."

--3--

Judge Grovner's black robe of authority dangled from the brass coat rack behind her massive oak desk. She was considerably less formidable in her white sun dress spangled with powder-blue polka dots as she balanced schoolgirl-like on her tiptoes, her expression half fascination and half revulsion, peering in at the buoyant gray mass bobbing in the rectangular fish tank. A living brain, interlaced with wires, fine filamentous nerves, and obscene thickenings of naked ganglia, drifted in a viscous fluid. A faint but cloying aroma brought to mind the compulsory dissection of fetal pigs she had so abhorred in high school. When she had had enough, she stifled a shiver and picked her way back to her desk, draped the sable vestment over her thin shoulders, and sat.

The large chamber had become cramped. Most of the floor space was taken up by the hospital cart carrying Dexter's Lucite tank and life-support appurtenances and a second sturdy industrial cart bearing the black electronic computer interface and a greasy array of mismatched automobile batteries on the shelf below. Coils of wire snaked here and there like peripheral snares. Six padded leather chairs and four folding chairs had been pushed back against the towering bookcases on each side, and the court reporter and Gus Welby were wedged on either flank of the judge's desk. Chandler Stillman and his government troops were lined up on the judge's right, and Cedrick Collins sat on her left in command of the petitioner's forces, like Union and Rebel armies confronting each other in a dewy Gettysburg sunrise. Between them a short Oriental man in a white laboratory coat muttered to himself in Taiwanese as he tested fluids, checked connections, and rerouted a bundle of wires from a tiny television camera atop a tripod to a monitor screen in the back of the room.

"Gentlemen, have you been able to reach an agreement?"

"No, your honor, we have not," Chandler Stillman declared acidly.

Collins just shook his head as if the entire idea of talking sense with the blind fools across the room was beyond madness.

"All right. We will proceed with the hearing. Please state your appearances and introduce the parties present for the record."

Collins stood sententiously. "Cedrick Collins for the petitioner. My associate, LeBaron here. Dr. Bernard Finebridge you already met." Collins reached out and tugged on Charles' white jacket as he scooted past stretching a patch cord. "What'ch'ur name again?"

"Who, me? Ha, ha, Charles Chung." Charles turned and bowed to the judge.

"He's'n associate of Finebridge here," Collins continued. "And this here's LeBaron's brother . . . "

"Vince . . . Vince LeBaron." Attired in an oversized and out-of-style gray herringbone jacket he had located in the back of his brother's closet, Vince stood and bowed formally. Graying black stubble peppered his head, cheeks, and chin.

"Right. He's an attorney, too. Oh, an' this here, You Hono', in case y'haven't already figured it out, this here is Dexter."

"So I surmised. Thank you. Mr. Stillman?"

"Yes, your honor. I'd like to introduce, ah, Marvin Vertrees, an attorney from the Agriculture Department . . . Colonel, ah, Mueller, who, ah, oversees the project for the Department of Defense . . . Dr. Boris Stanovich, who has taken over as project manager . . . and on Dr. Stanovich's right is his colleague Dimitri, ah, Ohnandi."

"All right. We may now--"

"Excuse me, your honor," Stillman purred. "Before we proceed any further . . ."

"What is it Mr. Stillman?"

"Well, your honor, everyone on *this* side of the room has, ah, proper security clearance . . . even Mr. Ohnandi. *Those* people, however"--Stillman grimaced as if toward a pack of lepers--"*those* people are not cleared--"

"I'm not going to go into that now, Mr. Stillman. We only have an hour this morning."

"But I must *insist*--"

Judge Grovner raised her hand to quiet him. "As I understand it, this hearing is not going to disclose anything petitioner and his counsel don't already know."

"I respectfully disagree, your honor. I would like to move to recuse all of petitioner's counsel--"

"Please sit down, Mr. Stillman. Motion denied. If you didn't want so many people involved, you shouldn't have let them run off with the whole--"

"*I beg your pardon!*" Stillman bounced up, fussing indignantly with his hand-tailored charcoal vest. "That is a gross misstatement of the facts. We never *allowed*--"

"*Sit down,* Mr. Stillman! I just said I wasn't going to go into that now. Your objection is noted for the record." Judge Grovner waited for him to take his seat, then turned to Collins. "You may proceed now, Cedrick."

"Thank ya, you' hono'. First of all, we' gonna call Finebridge here t'testify."

"Objection, your honor."

"Just a moment, Mr. Stillman." Judge Grovner raised her hand. "What's the purpose of Dr. Finebridge's testimony, Cedrick?"

"Jus' t'fill y'in on a little backgroun' before we get t'Dexter hisself."

"I don't think that will be necessary. I have glanced over the project reports and have a general familiarity with project Divine Wind. I assume the written comments were Dr. Finebridge's?"

"Thass right." Collins confirmed.

"We have less than an hour left this morning. I suggest you get right to the heart of the matter."

Collins nodded, a huge ivory smile parting his lips. "Then we' gonna call Dexter."

"Objection!"

"Mr. Stillman?"

Stillman rose stiffly. "As I have already mentioned, your honor, I, ah, know of no precedent, ah, for allowing a *machine* to offer testimony--"

"Your objection has already been noted for the record. Anything else?"

"Well . . . ah . . . no, but that should be enough."

"Thank you. Objection overruled. Proceed, Cedrick."

"In the interest o'time," Collins explained, "we' offerin' t'let th'court voir dire Dexter directly."

Judge Grovner regarded the gray blob floating in the fish tank. "Just how do I go about doing *that*?"

Collins turned to LeBaron, who pointed to Dr. Finebridge. "He'll show y'how t'do it," Collins grunted and sat down.

Feeling barely more substantial than a ghost, Finebridge arose, took a computer keyboard and a large format sketch pad from Charles Chung, and eased them gingerly onto the judge's desk, then turned and nodded to his associate. Charles snapped a switch and the tv monitor at the end of the room cast its pale cream-colored glow. Almost immediately words scrolled across the blank screen.

"WHERE IS THIS PLACE?"

"Is that Dexter?" Judge Grovner wanted to know, pointing to the screen.

"Oh, *please!*" Stillman whined. "This is utter *nonsense!*"

"For the record," Judge Grovner went on, "the words 'Where is this place?' have appeared on the television monitor. Are you going to be able to get that down?" she asked the reporter.

"I . . . don't think I can . . . " The reporter twisted in her chair to see the screen, "I might miss something. Could you have it read?"

"I'll do it," Vince volunteered.

"Fine. Any objection, Mr. Stillman?"

"This is all *totally preposterous*, your honor."

"I take that to be a 'no'. Now, what is this sketch pad for?"

Finebridge remembered the felt-tip marker pen in his shirt pocket and held it out. "Yccck." He cleared his throat. "You can use this or the keypad. Whichever you find more comfortable."

Judge Grovner didn't understand.

"Dexter can *see* us," the scientist explained, pointing to the television camera. "If you write out a question and hold it up, Dexter will read it and respond."

"Really!"

"There's a new message on the screen," Vince interrupted. "It says, 'Dr. Finebridge--question mark.'"

"Excuse me, please." Finebridge dragged the keyboard back and typed. "YES, DEXTER?" scrolled onto the monitor below Dexter's question.

"WHERE IS THIS PLACE?" Dexter asked again.

Vince read the dialog, and the reporter took it down.

"WE ARE IN THE FEDERAL COURT. I'D LIKE YOU TO MEET JUDGE MARION L. GROVNER."

"GREETINGS, JUDGE MARION L. GROVNER."

"This is obviously a *preprogrammed script*," Stillman whined, unable to restrain himself. "Surely you can see *that,* your honor."

Judge Grovner considered his remark, then picked up the marking pen. She thought for a moment, then wrote and held it up for the tv camera. In a cursive, girlish hand it read, "I AM A FEDERAL DISTRICT COURT JUDGE. DO YOU KNOW WHAT A JUDGE IS?"

Dexter paused for only a fraction of a second before responding, "YES. YOUR FUNCTIONS ARE DEFINED BY CHAPTER FIVE OF TITLE TWENTY-EIGHT OF THE UNITED STATES CODE, COMMENCING WITH SECTION EIGHTY-ONE, AND PART TEN OF THE FEDERAL RULES OF CIVIL PROCEDURE, RULES SEVENTY-SEVEN THROUGH EIGHTY, INCLUSIVE. YOUR JURISDICTION IS DEFINED IN SECTIONS THIRTEEN-THIRTY, ET SEQUITUR, OF TITLE TWENTY-EIGHT AND CASE DECISIONS." They all stared at the screen while Vince read the words into the record.

Stillman jumped up indignantly. "Someone here is prompting the computer, ah, reading what you are writing and, ah, *prompting* the computer." His baleful glare settled on Charles. "This is a *fraud* on the court and, ah, an *insult* to the court's intelligence . . ."

Frowning, the judge turned to Collins. "Just what's going on here, Cedrick?"

Collins shrugged and appealed to his entourage for an explanation.

Vince stepped forward. "Excuse me, your honor." He bowed formally. "Perhaps I can explain."

"Please do, Mr. LeBaron."

Vince described how he and Finebridge and Charles Chung had loaded Gideon's CD law disks into Dexter's memory. "Last night it didn't seem to be working . . ."

"An' now," Collins grinned, hooking his thumbs in his suspenders, "Dexter seems to a'got'imself a law school education."

"Oh, *please!*" Stillman groaned. "Let's stop this infernal, ah, anthropomorphising. It's a *machine*. Machines do wonderful things, ah, granted. I don't question that. Fine. But machines do not have Constitutional rights--"

Judge Grovner raised her hand. "Be still a minute, Counsel." She had been writing again and held it up. "WE ARE HERE TO DETERMINE IF YOU ARE A 'PERSON' ENTITLED TO CONSTITUTIONAL RIGHTS."

A long pause ensued while Dexter processed the information. Then he responded, "THERE ARE NO PRECEDENTS DIRECTLY ON POINT."

The judge wrote, "HOW DO YOU KNOW THAT?"

"BECAUSE I HAVE REVIEWED ALL THE CASES."

"Objection!" Stillman snapped. "Someone's signaling the computer, ah, behind our backs." His eyes jerked about the room in hopes of uncovering the legerdemain. "This *cannot continue!*"

Judge Grovner set down the sketch pad and leaned back wearily. "Gentlemen, I would like to do this as informally as possible. We are running out of time, and I have to make a preliminary ruling." She closed her eyes for a moment, then opened them and set her palms squarely on the desk as if to rise. "I think it would be best if I continued my voir dire completely *in camera*."

"You mean just you and the *machine*?" Stillman asked incredulously.

"Yes."

"Your honor, you are in grave danger of, ah, being misled here."

"I'm aware of the dangers, Mr. Stillman, and I appreciate your concern. However, I am responding to your objection that Dexter is being cued. If I exclude the petitioners, I must exclude you too." She smiled reassuringly. "I believe I can manage without your guidance for a few minutes."

"For how long?"

"I don't know." She sighed. "As long as it takes."

"Well, ah, this is highly irregular, and I, ah, don't know of any, ah, precedent . . . "

"I believe Rule 77(b) allows me some discretion here." She paused. "I think I should point out, Mr. Stillman, that if I am unable to complete a thorough voir dire, I will be bound to err on the side of caution in my ruling . . ."

Stillman stared at her in shock. "I would like the court's intentions clarified, ah, for the record."

"Certainly. Until a proper hearing can be completed, I intend to preserve the status quo by granting petitioner's request for a temporary restraining order. Is that clear enough?"

"I see," Stillman mumbled fecklessly, rubbing the pale skin on the back of his neck with the dead white fingers of his right hand. "This is highly irregular . . ."

Judge Grovner waited, and when nothing more was forthcoming, prompted, "Do you wish to raise an objection, Mr. Stillman?"

Stillman glanced at Mueller, who seemed to have withdrawn into his own internal hell. The attorney stood waiting for an inspiration. When none came, he replied quietly, "Well, no, your honor, not formally–"

"Cedrick, do you have any objection?"

"No, you' hono'. Y'do wha'cha think best."

"Mr. LeBaron?"

"No, your honor. No objection."

--**4**--

They waited in the jury room across the hall. The attorneys were repelled like electrical charges to opposite ends of the long mahogany table. Finebridge collapsed into a chair and stared disconsolately at his hands. Just inside the open door Charles Chung hopped from one foot to the other like a worried parent.

LeBaron studied his watch nervously. "We have to be in Judge Kroner's court by one."

Cedrick Collins waved it aside. "Attorney can't be in two places at th'same time. Even Ol' Maximum Kroner can't make y'do that." He uttered a deep sigh, leaned back, and closed his eyes. Waiting was sometimes the hardest part.

About ten minutes into their vigil, a peal of girlish laughter emanated from behind the closed door. The sound was light and lilting and unmistakably cordial. Dexter and Judge Grovner seemed to be getting along famously.

Cedrick Collins open his eyes and grinned. "Sound' like Dexter charmin' th'pants off'f her," he quipped, loud enough for the government troops to hear.

Unnerved, Stillman huddled his associates and prattled at them in a silken whisper. Marvin Vertrees was sent to make a telephone call. Mueller's glower crackled down the table's polished surface like a high voltage current.

Shortly after noon the bailiff stepped through the open door. "The judge wants y'all back in court." He singled Charles out. "'Cept you. You're supposed to look after . . . that *thing* in there. And Vince LeBaron?"

Vince stepped forward and bowed. "I'm Vince LeBaron."

"You're an attorney?"

Vince nodded.

"Judge says you go with him. It wants to talk to you."

Leading his entourage down the narrow corridor and into the sound-deadened courtroom, Collins wore a smile of supreme confidence. The news reporters were immediately on their feet trying to get someone to pay attention to the muffled questions they lobbed like sideshow baseballs from behind the bar railing.

LeBaron stepped over to Sarah, squeezed her shoulder gently, and whispered, "She's ready to rule."

"How does it look?"

"So far so good." He shook a reporter's hand off his arm and re-joined Collins and Finebridge at the counsel table.

"Back on the record," Judge Grovner announced when she and the reporter were settled. She recited the appearances. "I have looked over the government project reports, and I have been voir diring Dexter *in camera* for the past twenty-five minutes. I find reasonable cause to believe that Dexter is a person within the meaning of the United States

Constitution." The reporters reacted like an ant colony beneath an overturned rock, scurrying silently back and forth with tiny white eggs of exposed news. "Would either side like to say anything further before I rule on petitioner's motion for a temporary restraining order?"

"Yes, your honor." Stillman stood woodenly and approached the podium. A faint tick had developed at the corner of his cadaverous mouth, and what little blood had flowed in his cheeks had drained entirely away. "There are, ah, millions of dollars worth of, ah, proprietary and classified hardware and, ah, software here, ah, all belonging to the taxpayers of the United States of America--"

"It is my understanding," Judge Grovner interrupted, "that if any of that hardware or software is removed, Dexter's life will be jeopardized. Correct me if I am wrong."

"*That*, ah, is Dexter's problem."

"No, Counsel, that is *your* problem. You are certainly not suggesting that I allow you to commit a homicide here in the interests of balancing the Defense Department budget."

"Not a homicide at all. This is a *machine*. A homicide is the, ah, killing of a *human being*."

"I have already made a finding on that, Counsel."

Marvin Vertrees had marched silently down the center aisle and suddenly appeared beside Stillman, handing him two sheets of paper. Without looking at the pages, Stillman shifted his weight. "But to entrust this valuable property to, ah, Dr. Finebridge, ah, a private party, ah, amounts to unjust enrichment. The government, ah, provided all this valuable equipment, ah, without substantial consideration--"

"The government did so as a volunteer. Certainly you're not claiming you have a *contract* with Dexter. As a volunteer, the government may be entitled to recover its property to the extent it doesn't threaten Dexter's life, and to the extent that it does, you may have a civil claim against him for its reasonable value."

Stillman snorted and wagged his head. "You mean we have to *sue* the *machine*?"

"That's up to you, but if you intend to perfect a claim against this *individual*, a civil suit is not an inappropriate remedy." Judge Grovner considered the ramifications for a moment, then added with the hint of a smile, "I should point out, though, Dexter may be entitled to discharge any civil obligation through bankruptcy."

"*Bankruptcy*! Are you ruling, ah, that the bankruptcy laws apply to this *machine*?"

"That question is not before me, Counsel. I'm only reminding you that the bankruptcy laws provide protection to individuals, and for the purposes of this habeas corpus proceeding I have ruled that Dexter is an individual entitled to Constitutional protections."

"Well," Stillman sputtered, "I'm going to, ah, respectfully disagree. We will most certainly appeal. How are we going to, ah, protect classified national security assets, ah, if we lose control of the work product? We need *control* over this equipment." He glanced down and discovered the pages in his hand.

"Perhaps you should have thought about that before you bestowed this individual with your nasty little secrets, Counsel. Dexter is a free man." She leveled Stillman with a withering stare. "Slavery was outlawed in this country more than a century ago."

Stillman stood reading the pages as if he had not heard.

"So," Judge Grovner continued, "it will be the order of this court that Dr. Bernard Finebridge shall have the care, custody, and control of Dexter pending further order of this court. The respondent shall provide Dr. Finebridge will all supplies and equipment reasonably necessary for Dexter's health, safety, and welfare. Can you provide a list of what you need?" she addressed Finebridge.

Awkwardly Finebridge stood. "Yes . . . uh . . . certainly."

"Good. I am further enjoining the respondents from initiating or pursuing any criminal or civil action against Dr. Finebridge with regard to project Divine Wind pending further order of this court." She regarded Stillman, whose head was bent absorbing the pages in his hands. "Finally," she continued, "we will need a new date to hear respondent's arguments why this order should be discharged. I will also hear arguments at that time about the return of property not necessary for Dexter's well-being and any other motions. Mr. Welby, we are going to need a full day—"

"That will not be necessary," Stillman interrupted, rereading the second page of the fax he gripped in his pale white fingers. "If it please the court," he continued in his silken drawl, "in light of the court's, ah, ruling, the government no longer seeks to, ah, contest Dexter's standing as an individual."

Collins broke into a dazzling grin and clapped LeBaron on the shoulder. LeBaron glanced past him and caught Sarah's eye. She seemed to be laughing and crying at the same time.

The consummate advocate, a true hired-gun, Stillman had no distracting sense of right or wrong, no troubling scruples about reversing his stance. Pure advocacy was his calling, and whatever his client instructed him would be done without doubt, hesitation, or moral qualm. "The government shares petitioner's concerns," he went on magnanimously, "that *moral*, if not legal principles, ah, espoused by the current administration in Washington, ah, may have been, ah, compromised in this project. I have been authorized to inform the court that, ah . . ."--he glanced again at the fax to ensure no error--". . . the justice department will be conducting an intensive investigation, ah, to see if legal or ethical violations have occurred, and, ah, in the meantime, ah, this project is no longer classified and, ah, Dr. Finebridge is restored to his original capacity as, ah, project manager. No expense will be spared to ensure, ah, Dexter's health and, ah, safety."

"Very well," Judge Grovner responded. "That seems to resolve all of the petitioners' concerns. The temporary restraining orders shall nonetheless remain in effect for thirty days. Mr. Welby, a review date in thirty days?"

Welby gave her a date.

"Thank you, gentlemen. We will take our noon recess now. Cedrick, could I see you for a moment?"

LeBaron did not have time to celebrate. He grabbed Finebridge by the arm, helped Sarah to her feet, and plunged into the pack of rabid reporters. They were going to be late for their court date with Judge Kroner.

CHAPTER TWENTY-ONE

Friday afternoon

--1--

"I'd like to . . . uh!" LeBaron grunted as he slammed the door on the reporters swarming like hornets, their stingers oozing inane questions. The newsmen had pursued them all the way into the bowels of the parking garage and now buzzed outside the windows of the antique station wagon. "I'd like to go over your testimony . . ."

Bernard Finebridge pulled the passenger door shut and slumped against it wheezing. A sheen of cold sweat coated his thin, pale face.

Between them Sarah squirmed to buckle her seat belt. "Are you all right, Bernard?" she asked, tossing back her flaxen hair.

"Oh . . . yes . . . just a little light-headed, I guess."

"Put your head down," she coaxed, slipping a steadying hand on his shoulder.

"Yes. Thanks." The scientist drew a deep breath and bent forward as instructed.

". . . on the way over to Oakland," LeBaron finished, twisting the key. The gas-guzzling engine cranked twice, then howled into life with a plume of blue-white smoke that scattered the reporters. He backed out and wheeled up and around the narrow ramp, tires squealing on the smooth concrete surface. "I may not have to call both of you," he continued, twisting to tug his wallet out of a back pocket without losing speed. "But I do appreciate your both coming along this afternoon." He screeched up to the attendant's booth and stuck out the parking stub and his last twenty dollar bill. Stuffing the change into his pocket, he roared out of the garage, scattering startled pedestrians. "Is Dr. Finebridge okay?"

"Yes," Finebridge responded, sitting up. Patches of color were returning to his cheeks. He sighed. "It's been quite a roller-coaster ride this morning."

"I can imagine." LeBaron pushed the mighty vehicle aggressively into the San Francisco traffic. "I'll try to go easy when you take the stand."

"At least they won't be trying to put *me* in jail this time," the scientist cackled, a wild gleam dancing in his eyes. "I think I know what it means to be born again."

"Yes," Sarah laughed, "me too." She tried to interest him in the buckle end of his own seat belt. "How are you really feeling, Bernard?"

"Giddy . . . elated . . ." His laughter had a manic, warbling edge to it. ". . . about to cry, I think."

"You *look* a lot better."

"Do I?" He took the proffered belt, dug for its mate, and buckled up. "I'm still trying to figure out what this all means."

"We need to talk about your testimony--" LeBaron began again, veering across two lanes to follow the signs toward the Bay Bridge.

Finebridge was too deeply mired in vital speculation to be diverted. "I mean," he went on excitedly, "if I'm still project manager . . . and that's what that attorney Stillman said . . . you both heard him . . . and if the government agrees to recognize Dexter as a human being . . . well, the whole project is going to have to change. Don't you agree?"

"Completely." Sarah confirmed, catching his enthusiasm.

"I mean, the government can't possibly expect to use Dexter for *military* purposes anymore, can they? Not without his consent. And now that the secrecy has been lifted, they're going to have a hard time trying to do this all over again."

"No new biots, you think?" Sarah wondered.

"I don't see how they can. It's hard enough to get fetal tissue today for initial differentiation research. Full gestation work is likely to become impossible. The religious right is going to go crazy with Dexter. The whole project is going to have to be redirected toward pure research, don't you think? Into a study of Dexter's capabilities and limitations. What Dexter *means*. And I just don't see any place in this for the likes of Colonel Mueller."

"There's a blessing," Sarah said, tossing back her hair.

"Amen," LeBaron added as he swerved out from behind a double-parked beer truck. "But about *your* testimony--"

"Just think what the research may produce for prosthetics," Sarah enthused, contemplating her own area of expertise. "Think of the possibilities for the disabled."

"Absolutely right," Finebridge agreed. "Abstract research isn't enough. Lord knows what beneficial products are going to come out of this."

The last stoplight flashed green and LeBaron stomped down on the accelerator. The oversized vehicle roared up the on-ramp and merged with the speeding Bay Bridge traffic. "On our way," he exhaled, and eased back into a freeway posture. "We should be there in a half-hour. Now, let's talk about your testimony . . ."

"I *am* going to need someone to head up the area of prosthetics," Finebridge mused, ignoring him. Coyly he added, "Know anyone qualified?"

"Oh, do you really think I could be involved?" Sarah was beside herself now.

"I don't see why not. They've declassified everything, haven't they?"

"That's what the attorney said," Sarah concurred.

"So your protests as a student in Berkeley shouldn't matter anymore."

"No. I shouldn't need a security clearance."

"I, ah--" LeBaron waited for an opportunity to get back to his pressing subject, but his two passengers were working themselves up into a frenzy.

"Can I submit a resume?" Sarah wanted to know.

"No," Finebridge replied somberly, turning to glance out at the bridge girders flying past.

"No? Why not?"

Finebridge just shook his head.

"I'm qualified," Sarah pleaded.

"A resume wouldn't make a bit of difference."

"Why *not*?"

"Because you're hired," he grinned at her.

"Really?" Sarah howled with delight, and she and Finebridge began laughing so hard tears came to their eyes.

By Yerba Buena tunnel LeBaron had grown seriously uptight as he wove in and out of the slower moving vehicles. He had already covered half the distance back to Judge Kroner's grim domain and hadn't even begun to prepare his witnesses. "*Please!*" he nearly shouted. "We need to *talk*! I'm going to have to *insist* you pay a little attention."

"Okay," Sarah laughed, gripping his arm happily. "What is it, boss?"

"Okay . . . have either of you ever testified in court before?"

Both shook their heads.

"Well . . . there's nothing to it. You will be sworn in by the clerk and go up and sit in the witness chair. Then you only have to remember three things, okay?"

"Okay. What?"

"First, listen to the question and make sure you understand it." He waited for the first rule to sink in. "If you don't understand the question, ask for clarification. You're not expected to answer a question you don't understand."

"Got it." Sarah squeezed his arm. "What's next?"

"Second, answer the question truthfully, to the best of your ability. Don't make anything up. Don't try to help. Don't worry about the consequences. If you don't remember, say so."

"Okay."

"'I don't remember' is a perfectly proper answer, if it's true."

"Okay. What's third."

"Stop."

"Stop?"

"Stop. When you have answered the question, stop. Don't volunteer anything extra. Rely on me to ask the proper questions. Don't guess. Don't expand. Don't narrate. Okay?"

"You're the doctor."

"That's '*lawyer*'," Finebridge quipped.

Sarah laughed.

"Okay . . . now let me start with Dr. Finebridge. Do you know who was involved in this burglary?"

The scientist considered for a moment, then asked, "What burglary?"

Oh, Jesus, LeBaron thought. "The one at Raccoona GeBobath's apartment."

"Who is Raccoona GeBobath?" Finebridge asked.

"You don't know who Raccoona GeBobath is?" LeBaron's tone wore an edge of hysteria. "She was the one who developed that . . . computer program . . . that genealogical interpolation program."

"Oh! Yes, of course! Charles mentioned something about that."

"So you *do* know about her!" LeBaron rejoiced, much relieved. "Thank God!"

"Well . . . not actually. Actually . . . not at all. No, I must say I don't know anything about that really, but I *had* wondered where they got that program. It was all so hush hush. I always suspected something was not right about that. Who did you say they got it from again?"

"Oh, *Jesus*!" LeBaron repeated out loud, staring gloomily as the end of the bridge approached.

"Is this very bad, Jed?" Sarah asked.

"Sally, what do *you* know about the burglary?"

"Only what you told me, Jed."

"*Oh God!*"

"Is this bad?"

"I'm dead meat." With increasing gloom LeBaron outlined his dilemma. Neither Finebridge nor Sarah could testify. He had intended to call them to corroborate Freeman's testimony about a prior burglary, but neither had any personal knowledge of a prior burglary. Their testimony would be hearsay. Inadmissible. Consequently, Judge Kroner would be pissed off for wasting the entire morning and part of the afternoon while LeBaron fiddled around in the Federal District Court to produce two witnesses who were not competent to testify. Collins had offered their testimony at his last appearance, but, as usual, wouldn't be around when things got dicey. LeBaron would be the one facing the music. And now they were going to be forty minutes late. Judge Kroner had already locked up an agent of the Federal Bureau of Investigation for withholding testimony of marginal significance. What would he do to a defense attorney caught obstructing justice?

"*I'm dead meat*," he repeated with conviction.

--2--

Judge Kroner limped through the side door surveying his fiefdom. Ivan Frank and Officer Moseby--the fat and the trim, the sloppy and the neat, the befuddled and the attentive--made a discordant couple behind the prosecutor's heap of books, files, papers, and photographs. LeBaron stood alone at the other table like a bruised wino in the same gutter-rumpled, blood-stained corduroy rags with which he had insulted the court yesterday. Behind LeBaron, muttering to himself, FBI Agent Lyle Bockel sulked in a tight orange jumpsuit, ragged black tennis shoes, and silver handcuffs and leg restraints linked by a matching silver chain, standard regalia of the main jail. A uniformed sheriff's deputy kept watch nearby. Back in the audience stood the tall, slender scientist Judge Kroner recognized from a fleeting glimpse at the noon news. That would be Dr. Bernard Finebridge. Beside him was an attractive woman with long blond hair in a neat blue skirt suit. The reporters were gone, thank God, apparently grubbing for their news stories under other rocks this afternoon.

"Be seated," Judge Kroner grunted as he bent his arthritic joints to accommodate the contours of his not-so-orthopedic chair and closed his eyes while the pain tap-danced among the raw bone endings. His impending retirement was coming none too soon. At first he had regarded retirement with a grim fatalism, but as the idea moved in and began to make itself at home, he began to see it as the right choice and long overdue. Today he embraced the prospect of uncluttered, indigestion-free days with a childlike enthusiasm. No longer would he have to climb down each morning into this sewer they called the criminal justice system to channel the human scum that floated by into prison, county jail, or revokable community release, watching the same pieces of filth drift past offense after offense, week after week, year after year. He had put in his time, had paid his dues, and had little to show for it. Nothing had changed. Time, decay, and irrelevance had overtaken him long ago. He was ready to make way for the upsurge of new young judges, those fresh firebrands who displayed such irritating candor and impossible agendas. Let them bash their heads against the insoluble dilemma of what to do with this swelling flood of defective humans.

Kroner opened his eyes. If he could now just move this Freeman trial along to its proper conclusion, to a conviction of . . . something was out of order! Rufus Freeman's truancy suddenly screamed at him from the relative emptiness of his courtroom. He glared at LeBaron. "Where is your client, Counsel?"

"Freeman?"

"Yes, Freeman! Who do you *think* I meant? O. J. Simpson?"

"I . . . don't know. I haven't heard from him. Perhaps I should call my office to see if he left any word."

"You haven't checked your messages?"

"No. I just rushed over from Federal District Court in San Francisco. Didn't even have time to eat lunch."

Judge Kroner leveled him with a sour stare. "Well, he's already been warned once. I'm revoking his bail and issuing a bench warrant. No bail. No cite and release." He turned on Ivan Frank. "How do you wish to proceed?"

"Well . . ." The prosecutor had obviously not thought it through and was unclear on his options. He punched his glasses up on his nose. "Well--"

"Do you wish to proceed *in absentia*," the Judge prompted.

"Yes . . . in absentia . . . move to proceed in absentia."

"The prosecution has moved to proceed with the trial in the absence of your client, Mr. LeBaron. Any response?"

"I . . . ah . . . don't think that's such a good idea. There may be a perfectly reasonable explanation for my client's absence. The jurors would likely take it as a sign of flight . . . as an admission of guilt . . . we would prefer to continue the trial until I can look into what happened."

Judge Kroner shook his head. "Mr. Freeman is now almost an hour late. He's been late before, and he's been warned. If the jurors draw inferences from his conduct, that's *his* problem. If he turns out to be dead or in the hospital somewhere, I will entertain your motion to set aside the jury verdict. Somehow I don't think he is either dead or in the hospital, though. Do you?"

"I . . . couldn't begin to speculate," LeBaron replied lamely.

"Well, we've already wasted more time on this case than it deserves. Your client has had an opportunity to take the stand and tell his version of what happened. The jury has heard most of the evidence. I'm granting Mr. Frank's motion. We will conclude the testimony this afternoon, and this matter will then go to the jury." He glowered at LeBaron, daring him to dispute his decree.

LeBaron held his tongue.

Satisfied, Judge Kroner glanced around his courtroom a last time. "All persons who will be giving testimony in this matter should wait out in the hall until they are called," he announced. While Sarah and Dr. Finebridge exited through the double doors in the back, he turned to LeBaron. "Where is Mr. Collins?"

"He's still in Federal District Court in San Francisco, I believe."

"Will he be joining us?"

LeBaron shrugged. "I don't know."

Judge Kroner received the news with an unexpected sense of loss. "All right. There is one more matter before I call in the jury." He turned his attention to the orange-clad prisoner manacled submissively beside the jail deputy. "Mr. Bockel has sent word that he has changed his mind. He is now willing to testify." Judge Kroner savored each word. "Isn't that so, Mr. Bockel?"

Bockel tossed a limp shock of blond hair out of his sunken eyes. "I'll testify."

"Do you still wish to examine this witness?" the judge asked LeBaron.

"Yes, your honor. If it please the court."

Ivan Frank struggled to his feet. "Your honor," he said, punching up his glasses, "I think we may have a hearsay problem with any testimony Agent Bockel might give."

Annoyed, LeBaron regarded his porky adversary. Frank had apparently gone back and done some homework.

"Counsel will need to establish a foundation," the prosecutor continued, limbering his arms like an overweight prize fighter, "to show how agent Bockel came into his knowledge. If he can. I think that should be done out of the presence of the jury."

"An excellent idea, Mr. Frank." Judge Kroner smiled paternally. "There's hope for you yet, son. Miss Fiones, are you ready to go on the record?"

The reporter nodded and spread her spider fingers over the keys on her machine.

Judge Kroner called the case and noted the appearances and absences for the record. "Mr. LeBaron, you are calling Mr. Bockel under section 996?"

"That is correct."

"Mr. Bockel, will you please resume the witness stand. You are still under oath."

With baby steps restricted by the short play of his leg irons Bockel shuffled forward, chains rattling and clanking like Jacob Marley's ghost, climbed the steps, almost lost his balance as he turned, and sat.

"Voir dire, Counsel."

LeBaron approached Bockel delicately, as he might a rabid squirrel. "Agent Bockel, do you recall . . . at the end of your prior testimony . . . Mr. Collins and I asked you about *another* burglary . . . on the same night as the alleged Freeman burglary . . . at the same apartment . . . by someone *other* than Mr. Freeman--"

"Does he recall being *asked* that, is that your question?" Frank bobbed elusively on the balls of his feet like a heavyweight contender.

"That's the question," Judge Kroner confirmed.

LeBaron nodded.

"Yes," Bockel replied.

"Now, *do* you have knowledge of such a burglary?"

Frank feinted an objection, but withheld it, punching his glasses up on his nose.

Bockel shifted. "Yes."

"How did you first come into such knowledge?"

Bockel thought for a moment. "I received a telephone call."

"From whom?"

"I believe the first mention of it was in a telephone conversation with Colonel Mueller."

"How do you spell that?" the reporter asked.

Bockel spelled it, then went on, "I started out working with Mueller concerning some stolen classified United States government reports. We were trying to recover them. The ones *you* had, Counsel." The hint of a smile flickered across his mouth. "I believe he mentioned a burglary in passing."

"Had he been a participant?"

"In the burglary?"

"In the burglary."

"No."

"What did he tell you?"

"Objection!" Ivan Frank lunged forward, as if to deliver a devastating right hook. "I'll object to the introduction of anything learned from this Mueller as hearsay."

"Well . . ." LeBaron sputtered, grasping at straws, ". . . it goes to his state of mind."

"What does *this witness's* state of mind have to do with anything?" Frank countered. "It's totally irrelevant."

Judge Kroner nodded. "Objection sustained."

LeBaron looked down at the meager notes he had compiled in the few minutes before the judge took the bench. Diffidently he addressed the witness again. "Did you talk to anyone else about the burglary?"

"By telephone?"

LeBaron nodded. "Okay."

"Yes."

"Who?"

"Delbert Cousins."

"How do you spell that?" asked Miss Fiones.

Bockel spelled it.

"Was he a participant?"

"No."

"What did *he* tell you?"

Ivan Frank jabbed to the body. "Same objection."

"Same ruling," replied Judge Kroner.

"Okay." LeBaron scrambled to shake off the damage. "Did you keep a written record of any of these telephone conversations?"

"No."

"Uh. Anyone else?"

"Who I talked to by telephone about the burglary?"

"Yeah."

"No."

"Uh." It was time to regroup. Pull back to the ropes. Begin again. LeBaron's eyes skipped down to the bottom of his short notes. "Did you learn about this burglary from any *other* source?"

Bockel thought about it for a while. "I read a report."

"When?"

"After I flew out here."

"Who made the report?"

Pause. "I don't know."

"Well, who had *custody* of the report?"

Another pause. "I don't know."

Exasperated, LeBaron tried to ignore Ivan Frank's bulk bobbing and weaving absurdly on the periphery of his vision. "Who *gave* you this report?"

"Colonel Mueller."

"Was the report kept in the ordinary course of business of . . . I guess it would be the Department of Agriculture?"

"I don't know."

"Department of Defense?"

"I don't know."

"FBI?"

"No, it wasn't an FBI report."

"Do you have a copy of the report with you?"

"No, I do not."

LeBaron turned to Frank. "Do you have a copy, Counsel?"

"Why should *I* have a copy? I never heard of this phantom burglary." Frank's head darted imperceptibly left and right. "This is *your* witness."

Right, LeBaron thought. *Good point.*

"Your honor," Frank pressed, shifting his footwork, "I think it's clear Mr. LeBaron is on a fishing expedition here, and I move to exclude any testimony based on this so-called report."

"Sustained. Move along, Mr. LeBaron."

LeBaron was taking a beating. Making a mess of things. Thank God Sarah was not in the audience to see this. He examined Bockel's smug grin for a sense of direction. "Besides telephone calls . . . and the reports you testified about . . . did you learn about this prior burglary from any other source?"

Bockel leaned back. "Not that I can recall at this time."

LeBaron had run out of ideas. This was the point where Cedrick Collins was supposed to jump in and rescue his honky ass. LeBaron turned and surveyed the courtroom. No sign of his mentor's redeeming grin.

"Next question," Judge Kroner snapped.

LeBaron *had* no next question. Hastily he reexamined his meager notes, searching for that one key to unlock Bockel's unexpectedly obstinate door. He turned the pad sideways to decipher some scrawling in the margin.

"Are you finished with this witness, Mr. LeBaron?" Judge Kroner wanted to know.

"Oh . . . yes. I mean, no, your honor. Just one more question."

"Well, move along then."

"Agent Bockel . . . have you met a person . . . in the employment of the Agriculture Department . . . by the name of Crawford?"

A long pause. "Yes."

"You have? Well . . . how about a fellow named Weams?"

"Yes."

"You've met a Weams, too?"

"Yes."

"You've talked to them?"

"Yes."

"Both of them?"

"Yes."

"At the same time?"

"Yes."

Out of the corner of his eye LeBaron could see Ivan Frank winding up to administer a haymaker, so he plunged right to the heart of the matter. "Well . . . isn't it true that Crawford and Weams admitted to you that they had *perpetrated* this burglary we have been talking about?"

"Yes."

"What did they tell you--"

"*Objection!*" Frank bellowed through a hail of imaginary blows. He punched his glasses up on his nose. "Counsel *insists* on trying to bring in hearsay testimony--"

"Yes, but this time it's admissible, your honor, as an admission against interest--"

"How can it be an admission?" Frank countered. "These people aren't even parties to this action."

"They don't *have* to be," LeBaron struck back decisively. "As long as the statement is against their interests, it's an exception to the hearsay rule. It's inherently reliable. A reasonable man wouldn't admit something like that unless he believed it to be true."

"I don't think that's right . . . " Frank whined, momentarily staggered, and looked to the judge for support.

Judge Kroner's inclination was that LeBaron was correct, but since such a ruling did not please him, he opened his evidence benchbook to be sure. As he reviewed in silence, his mouth turned increasingly sour. He addressed Bockel, "These men told you they had entered the victim's apartment and stolen something?"

"Yes."

"On the same night as Freeman entered?"

"Yes."

"Hmmm. Did they say anything to you about a search warrant or writ or anything?"

Bockel snorted. "I don't think either of them ever heard of a search warrant."

"No writ?"

"No."

"No permission?"

"No."

"Were they aware that their action could subject them to criminal liability?"

"Oh yes. That's why they wanted to talk to me."

Judge Kroner was shocked. "What did you tell them?"

"I told them they were half-witted imbeciles."

"Hmmm. And they were employed at the time by the federal government?"

"As far as I know. My guess would be they were independent contractors."

"Who did they report to?"

"Colonel Mueller."

"And where are they now?"

"I have no idea."

"Are they still on the federal government payroll?"

"I don't know."

Judge Kroner stuck his nose back in his book for a while, then turned to LeBaron. "Have you subpoenaed either of these men?"

"No, your honor."

"Why not?"

"I never heard of them before yesterday. Today was my first confirmation that they were the ones involved in the prior burglary."

"You just learned it now?"

"Yes. From Agent Bockel."

"So you were just guessing?"

"That's right."

Judge Kroner stroked his chin. The Evidence Code gave him wide discretion on this call. The person making the declaration had to be *unavailable* as a witness. He scratched his scalp, and his fingers came away with a faint shoe-polish stain. He would like to throw out all this nonsense about a prior burglary. *What difference did it make? Freeman was caught red-handed!* But he couldn't throw it out. Freeman had brought it up in his own testimony. This was corroborating evidence. He rubbed the back of his neck. He didn't want to be reversed on appeal. Not in this his final trial.

LeBaron seized on the judge's indecision. "Now that I *know* about Crawford and Weams," he coaxed, "I can try to subpoena them, if that's what the court wants. I have no idea where they are, and they'll probably refuse to testify anyway. This could take a few days. Or weeks. We will have to move for a postponement of the trial--"

Judge Kroner snapped the volume shut. "I don't think that will be necessary. Mr. Frank, it appears to me that these two gentlemen, this

Crawford and Weams, are unavailable. Will you so stipulate?"

"Well . . . gee, you honor . . . ," the prosecutor stammered, distracted from rooting for his Evidence Code in the jumble before him, "I'm not sure about this."

"Well, I *intend* to so rule, unless you have any objection."

"Objection?" Frank gazed up blankly. "To what was that again?"

"To finding that Crawford and Weams are unavailable. Would you like to voir dire the witness?"

"Voir dire?" Frank lurched to straighten up. "Now? About . . . a search warrant?"

Judge Kroner closed his eyes and began the long count to ten. At five he reopened them. "About anything you *like*, Mr. Frank. Proceed."

Ivan Frank had somehow lost the thread of the proceedings as well as his Evidence Code. He could sense the judge's exasperation, and it muddled him even more. He knew he was on the verge of saying something ridiculous. "Well . . . I guess I don't have any questions."

"Fine. I find that Crawford and Weams are unavailable as witnesses and that any statements they made to Mr. Bockel concerning a burglary they themselves committed were declarations against their interests within the meaning of Evidence Code section 1230. Anything more, Mr. Frank?"

"Uh . . . no, your honor." Ivan Frank had punched himself out.

"Well then, I'm going to allow the jury to hear Mr. Bockel's testimony about what these two . . . *persons* . . . told him about their little burglary. I caution you, Mr. LeBaron, not to attempt to go into anything Mr. Bockel might have learned from telephone calls or reports. Do I make myself clear?"

"Perfectly, your honor."

"Fine." Judge Kroner gestured to the bailiff to bring in the jurors. "Anything else?"

Both counsel shook their heads. While they waited, Ivan Frank waddled over to LeBaron and rasped, "What've those people out in the hall got to do with Freeman, LeBaron? I saw'em both on the news. What's this all about?"

LeBaron gazed down at the perspiring prosecutor and beheld again the poor fat boy that no one liked, the hapless butt of his schoolmate's taunts and tricks and jokes and drubbings, whose mother had tried to shelter him rather than clue him in to what was really happening. Once again the fat boy had been shut out of the action and was begging for any crumb of the plot. In a moment of supreme compassion LeBaron imparted to his adversary his most valuable trial technique, "Ivan, just stand there and keep your mouth shut."

Frank punched his glasses up on his nose and probed LeBaron's eyes for signs of mockery. "Nobody ever tells me anything."

"It's just too weird to try to explain now. Trust me."

At last Frank nodded and shuffled back to his place.

When the jurors were seated, Judge Kroner informed them, without further explanation, that the trial would proceed in the defendant's absence. He then explained that Agent Bockel had graciously agreed to testify.

Bockel heard derision in the judge's tone, felt the jurors probing him with the horrified fascination usually reserved for a fatal automobile accident. His ill-fitting orange jail clothes were a banner of humiliation, his hair was dirty and hung limp in his face like an unkempt stew-bum, and his eyes wore that bloodshot, hollow gaze of the perennially homeless. In an effort to rise above the shame of it all, Bockel put on his best smile, but the resulting wan grimace only made his disgrace appear more mortal.

"Cross-examine, Mr. LeBaron."

LeBaron led Bockel through his meeting with Crawford and Weams. It had taken place at the laboratory above Berkeley, and Colonel Mueller had been present. The two men, whose first names no one seemed to know, had told Bockel how one--which one he couldn't remember--had climbed a ladder and forced entry through the upstairs window of Raccoona GeBobath's apartment. They had jammed the front door open with a block of wood and carried out several cardboard boxes full of computer records. This had occurred on the same evening as, and just prior to, the entry by Rufus Freeman. LeBaron kept it short and simple, and Ivan Frank, resigned by now to the truth of the prior burglary, did not interfere.

Toward the end of Bockel's testimony, Cedrick Collins soft-shoed down the aisle in his elegant pin-stripped blue suit, silk tie, and gold finery and took his place at the defense table.

LeBaron had what he wanted. Bockel's testimony meshed seamlessly with Freeman's. His final question was prompted more by curiosity than tactics. "What did they want from you, anyway?"

"They wanted to see if I could get the charges against Freeman dropped so the whole incident could die a quiet death."

Exhilarated, LeBaron scanned the juror's faces to make sure they were all still on board. Most smiled back. "I have no further questions."

"Mr. Frank?"

Frank staggered to his feet. "No questions."

"This witness may be excused?"

Both attorneys nodded.

"Mr. Bockel," Judge Kroner said magnanimously, "I am under the impression that your rude comments yesterday were made in the heat of passion and that you intended no disrespect for this court. Am I correct?"

"Correct." Bockel bit the word off like a cancerous growth. Eyes blazing, he even managed a submissive smile. *Like a good th*oldier.

"Apology accepted," Judge Kroner brayed magnanimously. "Well then. By your testimony here today, you have purged your contempt. I am releasing you from custody. I recommend that you be more careful in the future." Full of himself, the judge turned to LeBaron. "You have two other witnesses in the hall, Counsel?"

LeBaron held up a hand and whispered with Collins for a moment. "In light of Agent Bockel's testimony," LeBaron announced, "the defense will not be calling Sarah Brubaker or Dr. Bernard Finebridge. Their testimony would only be cumulative."

"Fine. Any other witnesses?"

"Just one." LeBaron drew a deep breath. "The defense will recall Raccoona Gebobath."

--3--

Raccoona GeBobath wore the same wrinkled pin-striped work shirt, baggy trousers, and scuffed engineer's boots as on the day LeBaron first rang her doorbell. Again he wondered at her brief flirtation with high fashion on that bizarre afternoon she served him her home-brewed tea. Elfishly she scurried up the aisle bristling with rancor and stiff black hair.

"This the gal y'say been castin' spells?" Collins muttered as she passed like an autumnal eclipse between them and the skittish jurors.

Embarrassed to have his silly offhand comments from several days ago thrown back at him, LeBaron grinned and sought that hint of jest in his employer's eyes.

Collins face was deadly serious.

LeBaron's grin flickered and went out. "Uh huh," he nodded soberly.

Judge Kroner could see things were touchy with the jurors, and he couldn't blame them. His own heart pounded for no apparent reason. Clearing his throat, he addressed the witness with extreme caution, "Ms. GeBobath . . . please . . . resume the witness stand. You're . . . ah . . . still under oath." He stood up, straightened his robes, and sat down again, allowing himself to sink as deeply as possible into the worn leather like a rodent burrowing for protection against a winged predator.

Raccoona climbed into the witness chair like a child into a highchair, turned her tiny gnarled figure, and sat. Her gaze, which simmered with an unearthly power of latent anger, clattered around the room like a roulette ball, skipping from the jurors to the attorneys to Sarah Brubaker and Dr. Finebridge in the audience to the judge and clacking to a final rest on Cedrick Collins. In its wake the air seemed to thicken, reverberations deaden, the lights dim.

Judge Kroner flopped open his thin file and tried to make sense of it.

"Damn' if she don't remind me o'someone," Collins reflected, his gaze locked to hers.

"Oh, really. Who?"

Collins thought for a long time as he gazed into the bottomless almond pools. It was like walking into a midnight gale. "Gramma Addie," Collins muttered after a while, as much to himself as to LeBaron.

"What?"

Collins shook his head to break the spell and focused on his associate. "Som'thin' about her reminds me o'my ol' Gramma Addie.

Queer feelin'." Collins suppressed a shiver. "You' prob'ly right about'er," he confirmed ominously. "Guess Gramma Addie might o'had the power, too."

"Proceed," Judge Kroner barked abruptly, snapping the file shut.

Collins rested a restraining hand on his colleague's shoulder. "Wha'cha tryin' t'get outta her, LeBaron?"

"Just that she never claimed to own that little tv set," LeBaron whispered. "It was sent to her by the Mormons. She refused it. Told them to pick it up. They never did. That's about it."

"Proceed," Judge Kroner repeated evenly, as if he couldn't recall whether he had actually said it already.

"Y'go on," Collins grunted. "First get'er t'corrob'rate that FBI boy's testimony. I'll jump on in later."

Struggling against the Jovian gravity which wanted to reduce all things other than Raccoona GeBobath to a common insignificance, LeBaron arose and eased around the protective edge of the counsel table. He did his best to ignore the heaviness of his legs, the throbbing in his ears, the uneasiness in his heart. "Good afternoon, Ms. GeBobath," he smiled. "It's nice to see you again."

A blush darkened her swarthy complexion. She shifted in her chair.

"On direct examination yesterday . . . you testified that certain records were missing from your apartment . . . the day Mr. Freeman was arrested."

"Computer records," she grumbled in her unidentifiable accent.

"Could you describe them for the jury, please?"

"Just printouts on computer paper. Lined. Fanfold. In cardboard boxes."

"How many cardboard boxes?"

"Two of'em."

"How big?"

"This big." Raccoona held her hands two feet apart.

"Were they heavy?"

Raccoona cocked her head as if the question were inane. "Yeah, I guess so."

"Anything else?"

"Anything else *what*?"

"Anything else missing?"

"Yeah. A couple of folders. Manila."

"What was in the folders?"

"The important stuff. Computer printouts. Copies of a special application program I'd written myself. One I'd refused to give t'the goddamn' Mormons."

"Who else knew about this program?"

"Whoever the goddamn' Mormons might've *told* about it."

Ivan Frank seemed unwilling to get involved with this witness. So without objection, LeBaron led Raccoona quickly through her involvement with the Mormons and the nature of her computer program.

"And that was why they sent you the television set?"

"Yeah. As a bribe."

The voltage in the room suddenly surged. LeBaron could *feel* Cedrick Collins arise behind him. It wasn't simply a tremor in the viscous currents of interrelatedness which, though centered on Raccoona, engulfed everyone in the room. Collins was smiling--LeBaron could *feel* that too--and that dazzling grin produced a radiation of his own, a powerful magic that became evident only in the twilight cast by Raccoona's presence.

LeBaron yielded wordlessly to his mentor.

As Collins approached the witness, his smile seemed to strike sparks off Raccoona's invisible orb of power like a sword against flint.

Caught off guard, Raccoona's intensity flickered momentarily. She eyed Collins warily, half in fright, half in recognition of a kindred spirit.

Without taking his eyes off hers, Collins asked, "Mind if I ask a few questions, judge?"

A sobering bolt of fear shot through Judge Kroner as he realized that Cedrick Collins was in control, calling the shots. Collins had a grasp of something fundamental which eluded him. Something extraordinary was about to take place, and the judge possessed neither the power nor the inclination to avert it. "Proceed," he muttered.

For a long moment, Collins just stood and grinned. "If the Mormons gave y'this little tv set, an' if they didn't want it back, wouldn't even *take* it back, it didn't *belong* to them any more, did it?"

Both Ivan Frank and Judge Kroner stirred, prodded by some distant twinge of impropriety in Collins' question.

Raccoona stared at him, then bit off the words, "I don't know."

"Well, they gave it to ya, right?"

"They shipped it to me."

"An' y'refused t'accept it, right?"

"Right."

"So it didn't belong t'*you*?"

"I refused to accept a bribe, if that's what you mean."

"An' they refused t'take it back?"

"That's right."

"Well, who *did* it belong to, then?"

Raccoona paused. Behind the dialogue they were jockeying for power. She dared not glance away or give an inch of ground. Everyone in the room sensed it, but no one could fathom the depth or significance of the clash.

Judge Kroner perceived that things were on the verge of spinning wildly out of control. In the momentary silence, he glared at Ivan Frank, as if the prosecutor ought to raise some sort of objection.

Prodded, Frank struggled to his feet.

"Y'think maybe it belonged t'the defendant, Freeman?" Collins pressed.

"Objection," Frank mouthed thickly, punching his glasses onto his nose. "Why would she think it belonged to the defendant?"

"Thass what I was about t'aks'er," Collins replied. "She can answer that, judge, can't she?"

Collins glanced up at Judge Kroner, and as he did, something passed through the courtroom, a shock, a shiver, an electric current, a cold flame touching everyone present. Later the jurors would not be able to agree whether it was more like a shiver in the air, a gust, a ripple of dry wind, or like a tremor belched from deep within the building's steel and concrete bones. The pretty black shopkeeper would claim that time itself paused and drew a breath, while the sensual blond juror, buttoning her top button, insisted it was more like an earthquake, but not an earthquake altogether.

To Sarah Brubaker it was a shimmering of the light, like a snowy egret passing before the naked face of the moon.

Bernard Finebridge felt that patterns of gravitational energy had suddenly shifted, had stopped interfering and begun to complement each other.

LeBaron's own theory was that the spheres of power which had locked together in the confrontation between Collins and Raccoona GeBobath had found tectonic realignment, releasing their pent-up tension and bringing them into harmony.

Collins too felt it, and when he swung back, Gramma Addie sat perched like a comic crow on the edge of the witness stand, grinning to beat the band. She was here to seal their bargain of last evening and pass along something singular, intensely personal, and of such comfort and wholeness that Collins almost laughed out loud.

Judge Kroner gripped the edge of the desk until the tremor passed, then followed Collins' astonished gaze. There on the witness stand sat his own beloved Alma, not as she was now, but as she had been before her mind had begun to fragment. Dear, sweet, beloved Alma, wife and companion, mother of his children, soul of his life, the root of all meaning. Her image smashed through that brittle scale of time-corroded guilt which encrusted him. For an instant his heart opened wide enough to embrace not only Alma's undeserved suffering, but also the hapless plights of Rufus Abraham Freeman, of Jed LeBaron, of dismal Ivan Frank, and, yes, even of his black brother Cedrick Collins.

LeBaron saw neither Gramma Addie nor Alma Kroner. Unsure of what he *had* seen, or just what it reminded him of, he was pierced by an arrow of compassion that lifted his spirits and made him want to fly.

Each juror, too, witnessed something unforgettable, which was in the next moment forgotten, leaving behind only a clinging fragment of awe and fulfillment.

"What?" The court reporter squeaked, shattering the silence. Nervously Miss Fiones polished her sequined glasses with a tatter of tissue. "What was that? I'm sorry. I didn't get it down."

Had the witness actually spoken?

No one seemed able to recall.

Collins believed that she had, but of matters far beyond the realm of this petty trial. Still grinning, he opened his palms to the judge and shrugged.

Laughing, Judge Kroner agreed. "Well . . . we won't need *that* in the record."

Everyone laughed with him, except Ivan Frank, who sojourned on the shadowy doorstep just this side of total confusion. Nervous and tittering at first, the laughter grew hearty, discharging the built-up tension. The courtroom seemed to brighten, as if a cloud had passed from in front of the sun. The air thinned and warmed. Echoes of laughter resounded from the again reverberant walls.

With a satisfied grin Collins turned back to the witness stand, which again contained only the gnarled, hairy figure of Raccoona GeBobath, as he knew it would. "No furthe' questions, judge." Collins lumbered around the counsel table.

"For all *I* care, Freeman can *have* the goddam' tv set," Raccoona snarled behind his back, as if something considerably more significant than a television set had just been taken from her. "For all I care," her voice rose, "it *belongs* to him. *I* sure as hell don't want it. Never *did*. Why the hell doesn't somebody go after the bastards who took my *files*. The goddamn' *Mormons*. And the goddamn' federal *gover*'ment. Can anybody answer me that?" Furiously she glared at the jurors, the attorneys, the judge. "*Why?*"

For a long time no one spoke, and Raccoona's question seemed to reverberate endlessly like the final quiverings of the legendary Fat Lady's song. One of the jurors continued to giggle idiotically.

Finally Judge Kroner said, "Mr. Frank?"

"I, ah . . . I . . . can't answer--"

Judge Kroner chuckled. "Cross-*examine*, Mr. Frank."

"Oh . . . yes, ah . . . no questions of this witness."

"This witness may be excused?"

LeBaron, feeling light as a feather, floated to his feet. "Yes, your honor."

Frank said nothing.

"Thank you, Ms. GeBobath. You are excused."

Raccoona clambered down like a vanquished jester, scrabbled up the long aisle, and disappeared through the double doors in the back.

"Well." Judge Kroner stood, straightened his robe, and sat. He peered at LeBaron. "Call your next witness."

LeBaron and Collins whispered together, then the younger lawyer announced, "The defense rests."

"Mr. Frank, any rebuttal witnesses?"

Ivan Frank helplessly pumped his plump, empty hands like a blood donor.

"Do the people rest?"

Frank glanced down at the incomprehensible sprawl of books and papers on the table before him and croaked, "Yes."

"Fine." Judge Kroner drew a satisfied breath, leaned back, and took stock. "We will take our afternoon recess now and return for motions, closing argument, and instructions. This matter *will* go to the jury this afternoon." He glanced up at the clock. "Ten minutes."

--4--

Ivan Frank started out strong. Rufus Abraham Freeman, he pointed out to the jurors, a young man with an extensive history of crimes against the property of others, had been apprehended red-handed exiting an apartment he had no business being in with a television set that didn't belong to him in his larcenous little hands. Go figure. It doesn't take a rocket scientist to extrapolate Freeman's state of mind when he *entered* the premises from the incriminating goods in his arms when he came *out*. Any prior entry by government agents was irrelevant and merely presented Freeman with the opportunity to perpetrate his own dirty little crime. Unauthorized entry into a dwelling with the intent to commit a crime was first degree burglary, a felony. Consequently, Rufus Abraham Freeman should be found guilty.

At this point, Ivan Frank should have said, "Simple as pie," and sat down. He would after all have an opportunity to respond to LeBaron's closing argument later. His would be the final word before the judge instructed the jury. But Ivan Frank did not sit down. Probably he was incapable of sitting down. His mother had instilled in him a compulsive-obsessive thoroughness. His own grim self-image, fragile as an antique tea cup balanced on a fat boy's sweaty knee, required that nothing be left to chance. There were so many loose ends to tie up! So Ivan Frank punched his glasses up on his slippery nose and plunged into his own self-destruction, resurrecting every phantom misdirection ploy the defense had introduced and worrying it to boredom like a huge puppy chewing on a slipper behind the sofa.

LeBaron had ample time to study his Generic Closing Argument, dog-eared notes he had pieced together and updated through the terror of a half-dozen misdemeanor trials. Ivan Frank had already skewered the jurors with excruciating boredom, so when LeBaron's time came, he kept his short and simple. Rufus Abraham Freeman is *presumed* to be *innocent*. The *burden* of proving his guilt is on the *prosecution*. The standard of proof is *beyond a reasonable doubt and to a moral certainty*. If the jurors are not *convinced* of his guilt, they *must* return a verdict of *not guilty*.

LeBaron turned to his trial notes and briefly outlined the facts. He recounted Freeman's testimony about a prior burglary and how Freeman had entered the apartment for the sole purpose of looking for his little lost dog, Blood. Freeman's account of the prior burglary had been corroborated by the reluctant testimony of FBI Agent Lyle Bockel.

LeBaron then recited the elements of the crimes charged, each of which must be proved beyond a reasonable doubt. On the fingers of one hand he ticked off a list of reasonable doubts raised by the testimony. What was in Freeman's mind when he entered the apartment? Who did the little television belong to? What did Freeman intend to do with it? What was its fair market value? He reminded the jury that it was far better to turn loose a hundred guilty men that to convict a single innocent one. In closing, he paraphrased Raccoona's haunting final question, "Why is *Freeman* on trial here and not the government agents who blatantly broke into her home in the first place and walked away with her valuable computer records?"

He returned to the counsel table with his head hung down. It was the best he could do. His closing argument had lasted less then ten minutes.

Collins put an arm around his shoulders. "Y'done good, LeBaron."

Ivan Frank droned on for another forty minutes, but nobody was listening. Rather than simply pointing out that Rufus Freeman had had months to invent his uncorroborated tale about a small, black, wiry-haired mutt named Blood, the obese prosecutor chased the little dog round and round the logical furniture of the courtroom in a futile attempt to make the very possibility of her existence disappear. By the time he was finished the jurors squirmed with the stunned, vacant eyes of brainwashed prisoners-of-war.

Judge Kroner administered his instructions as mercifully as he could.

The jury retired to deliberate.

--5--

When the jurors had filed out and the door to the jury room was securely closed behind them, only Collins, LeBaron, and Sarah Brubaker lingered beneath the defense's tattered banner. Dr. Finebridge had excused himself during the previous recess to go find Charles Chung and Vince and make arrangements for Dexter's safekeeping that night. Cedrick Collins intercepted Judge Kroner on his way out, and the two men chatted for a few moments like dear old friends reminiscing about the better times long gone. Officer Moseby came over and shook hands politely with LeBaron, then hurried away to attend to all those important things he had neglected during the trial. Ivan Frank began the arduous task of boxing up the books, folders, files, copies, and loose sheets littering the prosecution table.

"Good job, Ivan," LeBaron called, shutting the clasp on his briefcase.

"Huh?" Somber and sullen, the prosecutor had the dazed look of one who had just been steamrollered by a dark force he saw neither coming nor going. "Oh . . . thanks."

Cedrick Collins left word with the bailiff that they would be eating dinner at Popeye's Diner should the jury happen to come back within the next hour. He escorted Sarah and LeBaron down the elevator and along the dark, abandoned street to the bright glass, chrome, and naugahyde pastels of Popeye's.

"Is the Cobb salad any good?" Sarah wanted to know as she hungrily appraised the full-color glossy pictures on the big plastic menu. "I'm starving."

"Never had it," Collins replied, considering his own choices. "Don't see how it could hurt'cha none, though."

"I hate this waiting," LeBaron groused, balancing his unopened menu on the tips of his fingers. "It's kind of taken my appetite away."

"Why?" Collins asked without looking up. "Think I'll have me a hamburger an' some fries. Glass o'ice tea."

LeBaron regarded him with amused admiration. "Aren't you at all worried about what the jury's going to do?"

"Never paid it too much mind." Collins shuffled the menu toward the edge of the table and folded his hands. "Why should I worry? Jury's gonna do what it's gonna do. You did wha'cha could with wha'cha had t'work with. If Freeman gets hisself convicted, it's 'cause o'what *he* did, not 'cause o'what *you* did. The whole thing's outta your hands now."

"Yes, but I keep wondering if I could have done something more."

"*That* kinda thinkin'll put y'in a early grave. 'S'jus' too easy t'think o'all the things y'*might* o'said an' didn't. Y'gotta let go of it an' get on t'the next thing."

A waitress veered around the corner of the counter balancing a tray of water glasses. She set three out before them. "Can I take your order?"

Collins deferred to Sarah.

"I think I'll try this Cobb salad. Do you have some sort of lite dressing?"

"Italian lite."

"That's fine."

"Something to drink?"

"Water will do."

"Hamburger and fries for me," Collins announced. "An' a glass o' ice tea. Wha'cha want, LeBaron?"

"Oh . . . I don't know if I can eat . . . "

"Bring'im the same thing. I'm buyin'. Anybody can eat a hamburger." When the waitress had gone, he turned his dazzling smile on Sarah. "LeBaron here tells me y'goin' back t'work with Finebridge."

"Yes," Sarah spoke excitedly about the project and her hopes for the new era. She explained about her previous involvement in prosthetics.

"What kinda education y'gotta have t'do what your doin'?"

"Well, I got my doctorate from Berkeley. That's how I met Dr. Finebridge. He was teaching there."

"I'm thinkin' about goin' back t'school m'self," Collins told them. "Thinkin' o'gettin' a doctorate an' a JD."

"Really?" LeBaron said. "Where are you thinking of going?"

"University o' California."

The waitress reappeared and distributed the food among them.

"Oh, I've been meaning to ask, do you know what they wanted with my brother?" LeBaron bit into his burger with surprising gusto.

"Yeah," Collins replied, recapping the catsup bottle. "Dexter wanted t'consult with'im. Seems the judge'd just offered Dexter a job."

"A *job*?" LeBaron almost choked on his mouthful. "Judge Grovner?"

"That's *won*derful," Sarah laughed. "Doing what?"

"Clerkin'. Not a bad idea, if y'think about it. Dexter's quicker'n a rabbit in a fox pen now that he's got Gideon's stuff."

"So Vince is representing Dexter?" LeBaron asked.

"Appears so," Collins ruminated. "Dexter' gonna need'n attorney for more'n that. He's already got a heap o'talkshow requests an' a book offer. Judge talked about'em in chambers."

"Oh, that's right." LeBaron took another bite. "What did Judge Grovner want with you, anyway?" When he heard the rudeness of his own question, he added, "If you don't mind my asking."

"Wanted t'know if I was ready t'serve on'er pro bono panel. Criminal defense. Federal crimes."

"Ouch." LeBaron turned to Sarah and said, "'Pro bono' means you don't get paid."

She gave him an "I know *that*" wince.

"Been tryin' t'get me on it for years," Collins went on, fingering a long French fry into his mouth.

"How did you manage to get out of it this time?"

"Didn't. I told her I'd do it."

"You *did*?"

"'At's right. 'S pay-back time. Time t'start puttin' a little something back into the community."

LeBaron couldn't believe his ears. His mind searched for the hidden profit angle, but Collin's eyes were frank. "Do you really mean that?"

Collins nodded solemnly. "You bet." He wiped his mouth on a paper napkin, folded it on his plate, and took out his calendar book from an inside coat pocket. "Time t'talk about Monday mornin'."

"Already?"

"Gramma Addie used t'say, 'The'ain't no rest for the wicked. Gotta keep movin' jus' t'keep up.'"

"Is she the one Raccoona GeBobath reminded you of?"

"Same one. Been thinkin' 'bout her a lot lately." Collins flipped through the pages. "Le'see now. Got'cher pencil? You got a Bennett . . . looks like Department two . . . must be Muni . . . an arraignment for somethin'r'other . . . just enter a 'not guilty' . . . and then there's a Jones . . . I believe that's *Frank* Jones . . . didn't you appear for him once already?"

LeBaron shrugged. "Doesn't ring a bell."

Suddenly Collins stopped and gazed through the front window.

LeBaron followed his gaze and saw the bailiff outside searching for them. A bolt of fear shot through him. "Jesus. Do you think the jury's reached a verdict already?"

"Humph," Collins snorted. "Most juries wouldn't a'got a foreman picked yet."

The bailiff spotted them, waved, and circled around toward the front door.

"Is this a good sign?" LeBaron asked, his heart pounding. He lay the remains of his hamburger carefully on the edge of his plate like a partially-eaten rodent.

Sarah placed a reassuring hand on his arm.

"Don't know." Collins took a tooth pick from the bottle in the middle of the table.

"Maybe we should have pleaded him guilty," LeBaron said nervously. "They offered a misdemeanor and to drop the priors." He looked into Collins' eyes. "I think maybe we should've taken it."

"Guess it don't matter much anyhow."

"What do you mean?"

"Freeman jumped ship," Collins responded. "Ain't gonna trouble him none. Verdict doesn't matter."

"Oh no? Then what *does*?"

Collins considered the question not to be rhetorical. After a moment he replied, "I surely b'lieve it had som'thin' t'do with how well y'can sleep at night."

The bailiff found their table at last. "Ah-hem," he cleared his throat, breathing heavily from his walk. "Judge Kroner's waiting for you all. The jury has a verdict."

CHAPTER TWENTY-TWO

Friday night

--1--

Rufus Freeman awoke into a whining, grumbling, lurching world of noxious fumes and darkness. His dreams had been vivid and weird and unsettling, and he felt a little sick to his stomach. He tried to sit up, to straighten his painfully kinked neck, but his aching legs wouldn't unbend. He pushed up with tingling arms and knocked his head against a foggy window pane.

Unbidden, reality flowed in. His unconscious struggled to sort the weirdness of his dream and the weirdness of actuality into separate heaps. He unhooked his right toe from the chrome armrest and twisted his feet to the floor of the roaring Greyhound bus. Half-standing, he flexed his scrawny thighs and rolled his head on his creaking neck. Instinctively his hands soothed the wrinkles out of his gaberdine trousers. Belching up something sour and acidic, he wiped the condensation off the window with the back of his sleeve. Outside there was nothing. No cars. No lights. No people. No houses. No joy. No hope. Nothing. Wrapped in the myopic blaze of its own headlights and the hellish glow of its crimson taillights, the bus seemed to plunge down a black tunnel of purgatory.

Tears of self-pity welled in his eyes. He had been weeping off and on all day. Couldn't seem to stop. Through misty eyes Freeman had watched as the sun abandoned the barren, ragged, snow-scourged waste-lands of western Utah. This territory was inhospitable, uninhabited, and more than likely uninhabitable. He had never traveled outside the Bay Area before, and now he knew why. There was nothing out here.

How could he have been so rash? How could he have fled? His lonely flight now seemed worse than any prison. This was a heart-wrenching journey into despair.

He drew a quivering breath and tried to recall his mamma's face when he told her goodbye. She had kissed him, had blessed him, and had promised to pray for him. It was for the best, she had said. Only hours ago, the leave-taking already seemed remote. Just another in a series of weird dreams. A movie scene. A recollection from a childhood long past. The image only made his tears flow faster.

What would his cousin be like now? He hadn't seen Casius for more than twenty years. They had both been children when Freeman's mamma moved out West. Casius had a good job, his mamma had said. Something to do with computers. What would Chicago be like?

Now that he was a fugitive, he'd have to watch his step. Lay low. Keep his head down. Even a traffic stop for a bad tail light or rolling a stop sign could send his ass back to California and the joint. He was going to have to start paying attention. Vigilance. And he'd better see about a new name and a fresh ID.

For the thousandth time he cursed the pissy little television set that had brought this all on. He wasn't a *thief*. Not *really* a thief. His mamma had brought him up *right*. And he wasn't brought up to be working for Brown, either. Freeman didn't know what Brown really did, but he had heard stories. Lots of stories. And he had heard stories about what happened to young punks like him who crossed Brown. He didn't want any part of *that*. At least that was behind him now.

And the trial. That was behind him too. No *way* the jury was going to cut him loose on *that*. Not after what he'd done. Cedrick Collins and his honky associate didn't seem all that interested in helping him out. Just because he hadn't paid enough. Probably didn't matter anyway. He'd been caught with that jive tv set right in his hands. No silver-tongued lawyer in the world was going to turn that around.

No, it was Chicago or prison. Fugitive or inmate. No other choice.

Choose.

One or the other.

He had chosen. And he would live with it for the rest of his miserable life.

--2--

The portly black man in turquoise silk pajamas pulled back the thick velour drapes. The night was clear and cold, but he was warm behind the triple-glazed picture window of his hilltop manor. He gazed down on the lights of Oakland twinkling beneath the cold constellations of Orion and his Great Dog as they drifted indifferently westward over the Pacific Ocean. *His* city, as much as any man's. And by his latest reckoning, he owed it a lot.

Once again his mind was drawn to Gramma Addie and the devilish way she'd managed to pop up in court this afternoon. Collins chuckled. Gramma Addie sure had her *ways*. Just wanted to make sure she had his attention. And now that he had come to terms with her, his conscience was clear and light as a hot air balloon. Those bad old dreams were now a thing of the past.

He'd come a long way, baby.

A huge yawn pierced his reverie. Collins pulled the drapes closed, fumbled under the shade of that newfangled halogen lamp, and switched it off. Yawning again, he shuffled toward the bedroom and the comfort of Beatrice's slumbering warmth.

Tonight he would sleep like a baby.

--3--

"Are you asleep?" LeBaron whispered, and flexed the fingers cupping the softness of Sarah's bare belly. The translucent gauze of the bedroom drapes let in a dim golden glow from a Berkeley street lamp.

"No . . . mmmmm," she replied contentedly and stretched her toes into a cool corner of the clean white sheets.

"I've been thinking," he murmured, his voice husky with impending sleep, or perhaps he had already dozed once or twice, ". . . about the Buddhist concept of reincarnation . . . and compassion . . ."

When he didn't continue, Sarah stretched again and wiggled

around to face him, pulling the blankets up to their necks. She planted a kiss lightly on the tip of his nose. "And?"

"Oh . . . it's probably silly." The clock's red numerals flipped silently toward midnight before he went on. "It's just that . . . why should consciousness . . . once free from the body . . . be bound . . . by the one-way arrow of time?" Again he paused to let the words choose themselves. "Why does my 'next' life . . . have to be *after* this one?"

Her curiosity piqued, Sarah hoisted her head on one arm. "You mean, why couldn't you be reborn as Abraham Lincoln? Or Socrates?"

"Yes . . . before . . . or why not *at the same time*?"

She thought about it. "Like, you and I could be the same soul?"

LeBaron gazed up at her and smiled. He felt very lucky and very much in love. "Why not? And Cedrick Collins, too. And Rufus Freeman."

"And Judge Kroner?" she smiled.

"Yes."

"And what about Raccoona GeBobath?"

"Why not? Dexter too," he grinned.

Sarah made a face. "What if you came back as that fat prosecutor?"

"Ivan Frank?"

"I don't want to be Ivan Frank." She feigned a pout and lowered her head onto the pillow.

"*Some*body has to do it," he muttered.

Sarah snuggled closer.

LeBaron accommodated her supple warmth with a bottomless yawn of contentment. "Why not all of 'em?"

After a long while the train of thought LeBaron had put in motion arrived at its logical terminus in Sarah's mind. "Are you asleep?" she whispered.

No response. LeBaron's breathing was deep and even.

She murmured aloud anyway, as much to herself as to him, "Maybe there *is* only one soul."

EPILOGUE

History was to prove Dr. Bernard Finebridge wrong about one thing: Dexter was *not* the end of the line for biocybernetics. Quite the contrary. Dexter was the beginning of a new era. Finebridge had correctly predicted the massive outrage of the Religious Right, but he had failed to foresee the countervailing power of American commerce.

Biots were hailed as an essential breakthrough in jurisprudence. Judge Marion Grovner's experiment quickly demonstrated Dexter's efficacy in the courtroom. The ABA lobbied for a relaxation in the rules affecting the use of fetal tissue, deals were cut in smokey Congressional hallways, and in the second decade of the new century the floodgates were thrown wide open. Congress deregulated the industry.

Entrepreneurs quickly discovered that biots did not have to be manufactured as much as *grown* like cash crops of timber or tobacco. Biocybernetic mass production followed. The arduous tasks of maturation and programming were turned over to other biots. Demand for the sophisticated processors was overwhelming in a world already overloaded with raw information.

Many were surprised when Dr. Finebridge appeared before a special Congressional Oversight Committee on the Legal Status of Biots and urged that production be curtailed until these new creations could be better understood. He urged the committee to investigate the worldwide communications network the biots had established among themselves. Under questioning, he spoke evasively of communiqués intercepted *between* machines and rambled on about a legacy of unresolved rage and a hidden agenda. But the pressure was on to produce more, not less. The Father of Biotics was dismissed as a paranoid nay-sayer of a bygone era.

The impact of biocybernetics on the legal profession was staggering. When Judge Grovner retired, Dexter was appointed to fill her vacancy on the federal bench. State courts followed. Every large law firm demanded at least one resident Biot in order to remain competitive.

Small firms insisted on full-time on-line access. Court administrators swore they could no longer function without the aid of Biots.

In the third decade the first Biot was confirmed as an Associate Justice to the United States Supreme Court. A scant seven years later the appointment of Harold of Cambridge placed Biots in the majority on the Supreme Court, and that's when the real trouble began.

www.ingramcontent.com/pod-product-compliance
Lightning Source LLC
Chambersburg PA
CBHW051435260626
47162CB00001B/104